# STARGATE
# ATLĄNTIS™

# THE INHERITORS

**Book six of the LEGACY series**

## JO GRAHAM • MELISSA SCOTT
## AMY GRISWOLD

# FANDEMONIUM BOOKS

An original publication of Fandemonium Ltd, produced under license from MGM Consumer Products.

Fandemonium Books
United Kingdom
Visit our website: www.stargatenovels.com

# S T A R G A T E
# A T L A N T I S ™

METRO-GOLDWYN-MAYER Presents
STARGATE ATLANTIS™
JOE FLANIGAN    RACHEL LUTTRELL    JASON MOMOA    JEWEL STAITE
ROBERT PICARDO and DAVID HEWLETT as Dr. McKay
Executive Producers BRAD WRIGHT & ROBERT C. COOPER
Created by BRAD WRIGHT & ROBERT C. COOPER

Print ISBN: 978-1-905586-62-2 Ebook ISBN: 978-1-80070-005-5

I who am dead a thousand years,
And wrote this sweet archaic song,
Send you my words for messengers
The way I shall not pass along.
I care not if you bridge the seas,
Or ride secure the cruel sky,
Or build consummate palaces
Of metal or of masonry.
But have you wine and music still,
And statues and a bright-eyed love,
And foolish thoughts of good and ill,
And prayers to them who sit above?

— *James Elroy Flecker*

# Previously, in Legacy...

THE WRAITH invasion of Earth has been defeated, and the city of Atlantis has settled to the surface of the Pacific just off San Francisco. The team assumes that this is a temporary respite before the city returns to Pegasus, but it becomes clear that the IOA and its member governments would like to keep the city on Earth. Woolsey recruits Teyla to be 'the face' for the people of Pegasus, and she and the rest of the team throw themselves into the unfamiliar political arena. Despite their best efforts, the IOA's decision goes against them: Atlantis is to remain on Earth, to be slowly dismantled for its technology.

This hits the team hard, but there seems to be nothing left that they can do about it. Rodney McKay resigns in a temper, and takes a job at Area 51; Jennifer Keller goes with him, and they begin to build their new life together. Colonel Carter, now in command of the George Hammond, begins siphoning off the cream of Atlantis's military personnel for her new ship; she also invites both Ronon and Teyla to join her team, as advisors. John Sheppard is left in limbo. There's no place for him on the Hammond, and neither Woolsey nor Jack O'Neill will accept his resignation. The only good thing about still being on the city is that he is able to thwart the IOA's attempt to take Guide, the captive Wraith known as Todd, for medical experimentation. Instead, John and Dr. Carson Beckett succeed in putting him into stasis, but that is only a temporary solution.

O'Neill, however, has one last card to play. As Atlantis has landed in US territorial waters, he claims the city for the United States, and in the ensuing uproar, the IOA agrees to send Atlantis back rather than see it fall into the sole possession of any one country. Woolsey resumes command, and the team reassembles to prepare the city for departure before the IOA can change its mind.

Atlantis lifts from Earth, and begins the long trip to Pegasus. Despite the shortened preparations, everything seems to be going well — until a hyperdrive emitter fails, throwing them out of hyperspace and using up nearly all of the power in their ZPM. There is a single planet close enough to reach at slower-than-light speeds. It's a cold world without a Stargate, but it's their only choice. After a difficult flight, John successfully lands the city, but there's not enough power left in the ZPM to move the city or gate back to Earth.

The crew reestablishes contact with their old allies in Pegasus, only to discover that things have not been going well in their absence. The Wraith have united under a new queen who calls herself Death, and they have destroyed a number of human worlds. As the team investigates the devastation on one such planet, Todd manages to escape, only to discover that he has lost control of his alliance and has only a single hive under his command. In a bid to weaken Queen Death and regain his former power, Todd informs Atlantis of the location of the queen's next great attack.

Trusting Todd is always a gamble, but John sees this as a chance to stop Queen Death in her tracks. The team travels to the planet Levanna, where they join with the local ruler and a detachment of Genii to wait for Queen Death's attack. The Wraith arrive in force, Darts and drone infantry backed by a hiveship in orbit. The battle is close and hard fought, but at last the Wraith retreat. For the first time, Queen Death has been defeated, and even it if it's only temporary, it's a boost for humans throughout Pegasus.

However, Queen Death's response is rapid and devastating. Atlantis receives a distress call from New Athos, warning of a Culling. John leads the team through, only to find — nothing. There has been no attack; everything is perfectly normal in the settlement. As they try to figure out what happened, the Wraith attack in truth — and the Darts target Rodney. Before the others realize what's going on, the attackers have snatched up Rodney and have vanished back through the gate.

Their first desperate searches turn up nothing, and the team splits up to pursue two sets of leads with two sets of reluctant allies.

John, Teyla and Carson Beckett meet with the Genii leader Ladon Radim, who promises them the aid of his spies all over the galaxy if they will help him with a project of his own. The Genii have found an Ancient warship that had crashed on a remote planet. Genii salvage teams have been repairing it but they need someone with the ATA gene to fly it back to the Genii homeworld. John agrees that they will accompany Radim's sister Dahlia and bring the warship back to the Genii in exchange for their help. Unfortunately, the Wraith ambush them, leaving them to a long hike across a hostile desert to reach the warship. An attack by carnivorous lizards leaves Teyla and Carson injured, and John questioning his own judgment about his rash decision to do this without consulting Atlantis or getting additional personnel — that this is like the mission in Afghanistan that cost the life of his friend Holland many years ago.

Meanwhile, Ronon and Jennifer have been sent to meet with Todd on a world controlled by Wraith Worshippers. Despite Todd's assurances that the Wraith consider this world neutral ground, all bets are off when Queen Death's people arrive and Ronon and Jennifer are forced to hide in a tomb. One of the Wraith Worshippers double crosses Todd and tries to kill them, thwarted only by Jennifer's quick thinking. Ronon blames Todd, but he assures them he is no fonder of Queen Death than they are, and says that he will let them know if he finds out anything about Rodney's fate. They must be satisfied with that, desperate as they are to save Rodney.

At the same time, Rodney is in a situation that's far more horrific than his friends have imagined. Queen Death's men have reverse engineered the retrovirus created by Dr. Beckett that turned a Wraith into the human the Atlantis expedition called Michael, and Rodney is now a Wraith! Known as Quicksilver, and believing himself to be fully part of Queen Death's court, he is now bending all his attention to helping the Wraith conquer Atlantis.

After a dangerous flight home, John returns to Atlantis with his team and the badly damaged Ancient warship. Shortly thereafter Sam Carter arrives in Atlantis with her new battlecruiser, the *George Hammond*. When Todd contacts Atlantis and tells them where Queen Death's ship will be powered down briefly for repairs, it seems like a good time to attack and retrieve Rodney. However, the mission goes wrong when Rodney, believing he's a Wraith, resists the attempts of the team to rescue him. He stuns John and as the hive ship powers up, Sam beams off John and the rest of the team before they can be captured. But Rodney is still in the hands of the Wraith, and now Atlantis faces a more dangerous foe than ever before — their own man turned against them!

Meanwhile, back in Atlantis, Dr. Zelenka discovers that Rodney
has left 'back doors' into the city's computer systems, and that some
of them are active. Now that Rodney is helping the Wraith, he will
be able to not only betray their location to the Wraith but let the
Wraith in. Zelenka and Sam Carter work on finding Rodney's
code, but it's taking too long and neither of them can put aside all
other work. Fortunately, it's possible to bring in an expert both on
the code and on Rodney: his sister, Jeannie Miller. Jeannie agrees
to come and help, and arrives in Atlantis aboard Daedalus. Also
aboard Daedalus is an old friend of John's, Lt. Col. Melissa (Mel)
Hocken, now in command of Caldwell's 302s, and the city's new
archaeologist, Dr. William Lynn.

Jeannie's arrival is timely, because Rodney, believing himself
to be the Wraith Quicksilver, has agreed to help Queen Death
invade Atlantis by remotely dropping the shield on the Stargate.
Once within the city, Rodney plans to steal the ZPM, thus crip-
pling Atlantis's defenses.

The Wraith attack, led by Rodney, who manages to get to the
ZPM room and take the ZPM. Though John and Ronon mount a
counter attack, Rodney escapes through the Stargate, badly wound-
ing Lorne in the process.

Without a ZPM, Atlantis is in serious trouble. They cannot dial
earth, and the only way to keep the Wraith from dialing in is to
keep dialing out, rendering the gate busy, but sooner or later they're
going to have to stop. Carter suggests building a mechanical iris
like the one at the SGC which isn't attached to Atlantis's computers, but doing so will require large titanium plates, something that
isn't easy to find in the Pegasus Galaxy. However, Ronon has an
idea where they might get them — the ruins of his home planet of
Sateda. The Satedans had the technology to make them, and it's
likely that some usable stores remain.

Ronon believes that Sateda is presently uninhabited, but when
the gate team arrives on Sateda it's clear that isn't true. A group
of Satedan refugees led by a man named Ushan Cai have returned
home and laid claim to parts of the old city. They greet Ronon with
enthusiasm and are willing to trade large titanium plates they've
salvaged for goods from Atlantis. Ronon also suggests that they

might want to have a look at the old city museum on Sateda, as there might be a ZPM. The team goes to check it out but finds bad news — the Genii are here, and they're also looking for something at the museum.

When Ronon confronts Cai, Cai says that the returned Satedans don't have the weapons or the numbers to stop the Genii from looting Sateda if they want to. If there is going to be an agreement about who owns the city and the salvage rights, it's going to have to be brokered by Atlantis. Backed by Colonel Caldwell, John and Ronon work out a deal with Ladon Radim to keep the Genii off Sateda in return for John not exposing Radim's plan to get rid of Sora, who has remained a thorn in his side. In return, the Satedans let the team keep the ZPM they have found, though it is almost drained and only has enough power left to fire a few drones and hold the shield for a few minutes.

Meanwhile, the IOA is unhappy with Woolsey's performance and recalls him to Earth to face a hearing. Despite Jack O'Neill's support, it looks like Woolsey may be relieved of command in Atlantis. However, since Atlantis is now out of communications with Earth, no one knows what is happening.

The worst looks like it may come to pass when a Wraith patrol finds Atlantis. In the ensuing battle, John uses the remaining power in the ZPM to hold off the Dart attack, while the *Hammond* and the *Daedalus* fight off the hive ships. In the process the *Hammond* is badly damaged. Carter and Caldwell decide that *Daedalus* will return to Earth to reestablish communications, leaving the 302 wing with Carter while the *Hammond* is under repair.

Meanwhile, Jeannie has found a message embedded in the code the Wraith transferred to the city during an attack — what appears to be a cry for help from Rodney. John goes to the gate address Rodney specified, only to be caught in a culling. A prisoner aboard the hive ship of a young queen named Waterlight, he realizes that Rodney has not betrayed him. These Wraith don't know who he is, but they will surely find out.

Guide, finding out that John is a prisoner, has no choice but to tell Carter where he is, fearing that otherwise John will disclose to Queen Death Guide's own duplicity. In Atlantis, the team tries to

figure out how to rescue him. However, at the moment they have
no spaceworthy ship and the hiveship is not near a Stargate. Teyla
has an idea. There is a Wraith cruiser that was wrecked in the battle. She can fly it. If she resumes the disguise she wore last year as
Guide's queen, perhaps she can persuade the Wraith to release John
to her custody. It's a dangerous plan, but it's the only one they have.
While Zelenka and Carter repair the Wraith ship, Jennifer once
again transforms Teyla into Queen Steelflower.

Arriving at the rendezvous, Teyla persuades Waterlight to give
her John, but at the cost of promising Waterlight the assistance of
Guide's alliance against Queen Death. Guide shows up and Teyla
suggests to him that they become allies in truth — Atlantis and
'Steelflower's' Wraith against Queen Death. Both Guide and John
are skeptical. Teyla talks both of them into considering the arrange-
ment. Guide reveals that his scientists have been working on a retrovirus of their own, entirely unlike Queen Death's. Theirs works
on humans to make the feeding process not be fatal, a potential
game changer. He wants Jennifer to come and assist him in per-
fecting the retrovirus. Though John is disturbed by the notion, he
agrees to take Guide's proposal under consideration.

Meanwhile, on Earth, Woolsey's hearing with the IOA is going
badly. Jack suggests that Daniel would make a good replacement
for Woolsey in Atlantis.

In Atlantis, Ronon goes to check out the site of an Ancient
installation on the planet where Atlantis has come to rest on the
theory that perhaps once it had a ZPM, taking Laura Cadman, Dr.
Robinson, and the new Dr. Lynn. They determine that it once did
but that the ZPM was removed long ago, and also that the installation was a prison that was abandoned thousands of years ago.
Unfortunately, they disturb some dangerous wildlife living there
and in the firefight Dr. Robinson breaks her leg. Also they bring
down the ice ceiling, leaving them trapped.

Fortunately, John and Teyla return and John rescues the overdue
gate team. Together, everyone considers the implications of Guide's
proposal. If they don't help, Guide may make the retrovirus work
by himself and then they will have no idea what he's doing. If they
do help him, they may be able to use it to prevent Atlantis person-

nel from being killed by the Wraith. Decisively, Jennifer volunteers to go and work with Guide while Teyla goes with her to resume the role of Steelflower and rally Guide's alliance against Queen Death. Jennifer and Guide work together and ultimately test a version on Jennifer, but it doesn't work.

Also, the IOA, afraid they're going to wind up with Daniel Jackson in charge in Atlantis, reinstates Richard Woolsey.

Meanwhile, everyone else prepares for a raid on Queen Death's ship in hopes that they will be able to recover Rodney who is still a prisoner. The team gets aboard her ship while Carter engages the Darts, but are separated. Ronon and Jennifer find Rodney and stun him. Cut off and with the hive ship about to explode, Guide beams out John, Teyla and their team, while Ronon puts Rodney and Jennifer, who is having some kind of seizure, into a lifepod.

Ronon ejects as the hive ship blows up and the *Hammond* goes to hyperspace, leaving them adrift and alone. Rodney recovers from being stunned, and together Ronon and Rodney land the lifepod on a nearby world. Unfortunately they land some distance from the Stargate and will have to travel across country to get there. Jennifer awakens and has no explanation for what happened — except perhaps it was a side effect of the retrovirus trial, which may have made her immune to the aging effects of being fed on by a Wraith. As they travel it becomes clear that Rodney is in serious trouble. He's starving, and the food that Ronon traps gives him no sustenance. The only way he can feed is as a Wraith. Faced with the possibility of Rodney's death, Jennifer tells him to feed on her. She thinks she will not age, and it's a gamble she's willing to take. Ronon doesn't like this plan, but when Rodney does feed Jennifer doesn't die. Still, tensions between the two are high when they reach the Stargate and dial Atlantis.

But once back in Atlantis Rodney isn't out of the woods. Queen Death's retrovirus is wearing off and his body is rejecting the Wraith implants. With Rodney's life in the balance, Carson and Jennifer operate to save him and hopefully restore him to himself.

Meanwhile, Dr. Lynn suspects that there's more to the installation Ronon found than meets the eye. John takes the team to look around. They find little, but their investigations spark long-buried memories of Teyla's, the memories of one of the First Mothers, Osprey who is her long ago Wraith ancestor. These memories reveal that the Ancients created the first Wraith as part of a medical experiment at the installation on the island, a retrovirus test that went badly wrong and that the Ancients then tried to kill their creation. However, some of the test subjects escaped, taking with them the installation's ZPM, which was nearly full.

Teyla goes to Dr. Robinson and asks for her help in retrieving more of these memories, specifically what Osprey did with the ZPM. She discovers that Osprey and her first hive hid the ZPM on a world with an orbital Stargate. There's a possibility it's still there, so the team with Rodney now restored to them take a puddlejumper to investigate.

The human inhabitants have been isolated since they have no way to get to the Stargate, but are helpful. However, when the team goes to the caves they were directed to, they come face to face with a Wraith queen and her young son. John prevents Ronon from shooting them and Teyla and Rodney discover that she has been stranded here for many years since her ship crashed, living among the humans and trading healing for feeding shallowly on willing subjects. Her name is Alabaster, and Teyla realizes that she is Guide's daughter who has been believed dead for many years. Now they have something of real worth to trade to him for his aid against Queen Death.

With Alabaster's assistance they find the ZPM and something else besides — the weapon built by the original creator of the Wraith to destroy his creation. It will kill all Wraith in the galaxy and anyone with Wraith DNA, including Teyla, Torren and the Athosians!

Returning to Atlantis, John puts the question of what to do with it in the hands of Woolsey and Jack O'Neill, who has arrived in Atlantis to help deal with the crisis.

Meanwhile, unbeknownst to them, Queen Death has ordered the final, all-out assault on Atlantis!

## CHAPTER ONE
# Hyperion's Weapon

THE SUN rose over the icy sea, pale and watery, but at least today wasn't overcast. John Sheppard and Sam Carter stood on the balcony off the gateroom, both of them nursing steaming cups of coffee as they watched the light touch the tips of the towers of Atlantis, gilding them with light that slid down them like liquid as the sun lifted clear of the horizon.

"So do we have a plan for destroying this thing yet?" John asked.

"I'm still going with 'let's drop it into a sun,'" Sam said. "It may not be elegant, but it'll get the job done."

"Maybe a little overkill."

"Or maybe not," Sam said. "If Hyperion's weapon has a naquadah casing, it's going to be very hard to destroy by any other means. A large enough nuclear explosion would do it, but it would have to be a really big nuclear explosion. Not very practical."

"Let's not nuke our own planet." It didn't sound to John like much of an option.

"I'm with you there. If we drop the thing into the sun in front of a Wraith observer, that should take care of the problem. It would be nice to have a chance to study it first, but I'm not sure we have that luxury right now."

"I'm pretty sure we don't," John said. "Todd and his people are understandably unhappy about our having a weapon that could destroy all the Wraith. If we want their help against Queen Death — and whether we want it or not, we need it — we can't play around."

"I'm with you there, too."

John looked at her sideways. "Is General O'Neill?" He figured she'd talked to O'Neill after the official briefing. O'Neill had been wearing his best poker face, but if anyone knew what his true feelings were, it was Sam.

"You mean does he agree that we have to act on this quickly?"

"I mean does he agree that destroying the weapon is the right thing to do?"

"Do you?"

"Yes," John said after only a momentary pause. "I do."

"Because it might kill humans with Wraith DNA as well as the Wraith themselves?"

"That's what Alabaster says it'll do," John said. "I'm not sure I trust Alabaster any farther than I can throw her. But, okay, say you looked at it and said you thought it would just kill Wraith, and we said we were all willing to take that chance. Press a button, and, bang, no more Wraith. We win, right?"

"By committing genocide," Sam said. She looked grim, and John wondered if she was thinking about the Asuran Replicators. They'd had no other choice, and Sam had clearly taken a fierce satisfaction at the time in wiping out the Replicator threat once and for all, but that probably didn't make it easier to live with late at night.

"Yeah, let's not go there today. But is O'Neill in our corner?"

"Always," Sam said seriously. "But if you mean does he agree with you, yes, he thinks that destroying the device is the right thing to do."

"You talked him around?"

"I didn't have to. Apparently Woolsey was pretty persuasive." She didn't quite say *go figure*, but she didn't have to.

"You know, he's not so bad," John said.

"He used to be. I'm glad he's changed."

"Atlantis does that to people." John started to say *Look at McKay*, and then remembered with a twinge just how much Rodney had changed in the hands of the Wraith. He seemed more or less his old self, despite being left with shockingly white hair and the telepathic abilities of a Wraith, but having lived as one of the Wraith, actually led a deadly attack on Atlantis… it couldn't be easy to come back from that.

"I've noticed," Sam said, a little teasingly. He smiled crookedly in response. He'd be the first one to say that Atlantis had changed him for the better. The people he'd met there, and the city itself.

"As long as O'Neill's on board."

"He's on board," Sam said. "And he's in the best position to see the other reason we have to destroy this thing fast. The IOA," she added when he raised his eyebrows. "If they find out we had a weapon that could have destroyed the Wraith and didn't use it, Woolsey will probably lose his job, and Jack might not be far behind. Of course, he's been saying for years that it would be a relief if they finally kicked him out of the Air Force, so that he could dump it all on someone else and go fishing." Sam smiled a little ruefully. "But he doesn't mean it."

"So let's get this done," John said.

"Well, I'll need the device before I can destroy it," Sam said. "If you'll go get it from wherever you hid it..."

"You may as well come with me," John said, after a moment's hesitation that he decided wasn't entirely rational. "I'd rather not handle the weird Ancient device we don't understand any more than I have to. You don't have the ATA gene, so you're less likely to destroy all the Wraith in the galaxy by accident."

"Assuming that the user has to have the gene," Sam said. "We have found some Ancient devices that will work for anyone as long as someone with the gene turns them on."

"I didn't turn it on," John said, but he knew that sometimes touching Ancient machinery was all it took to make it respond to him, waking up eagerly in his hands. "I hope I didn't turn it on."

"We'll see, right?"

Sam followed him up a transport chamber and several sets of stairs to the catwalks where he usually went running with Ronon. Above them, a tangled grid of struts and roof supports extended up into the shadows.

"I keep some stuff up here," John said. "Just in case." He wondered if she'd call him paranoid, but she only nodded.

"You should see all the stuff we had stashed around Cheyenne Mountain," Sam said. "In case of a foothold situation, or the government being taken over by aliens, or something. We had a list of worst-case scenarios. A lot of them happened, eventually."

"And the important thing is that you were prepared."

"That's right," Sam said. He wasn't sure if she was joking or not. For that matter, he wasn't sure if he was or not.

"It's up there," John said. He scrambled up onto the rail of the catwalk, and then hauled himself up the jungle gym of struts and poles until he could reach the ledge where he'd stashed the weapon in between a spare Wraith stunner and a box of C4.

The stunner and the C4 were both still there, still securely duct taped to the ledge. In between them, the web of duct tape had been slit neatly with a knife.

"Damn it!"

"What?" Sam called from the catwalk below.

"The weapon's gone," John said. "Somebody got here first."

Ember had buried himself deep in the clevermen's section of the hive *Just Fortune*, in a laboratory sufficiently inconvenient of access as to remain largely private. Guide had ordered him to continue work on the human's retrovirus, and he was starting to make new progress. It would have been easier had he been able to recover more of the twinned humans that were so common on Lymours; among the Tenassan refugees had been a single pair, twin males, and they had agreed to serve the experiment, but with mixed results. He had fed on both, the treated and the untreated, and given the Gift to the latter when it was clear he would die, but the one who had been infected with the retrovirus now lay unconscious, his brother at his side, bathing his forehead in a pointless attempt to comfort. Ember believed he would wake, in time — his life signs were good — but he had hoped to create more resilience in the human subject.

The door slid back and he turned, frowning, to see a young blade, his hair wound into the heavy cords affected by the current crop of Dart pilots.

*Your pardon,* he said, his mind a thread of warmth on a cold day, *but Bonewhite has returned. He wishes to speak to all the masters of the hive.*

*What, now?* Ember frowned at his own question, recognizing its folly, but the blade bowed politely.

*He did say it was urgent.*

Ember glanced over his shoulder at the humans, the one brother still unconscious, the other lost in tending him, and decided they could safely be left. None of the lab equipment would respond to anyone not Wraith, even if they had understood its use. If he had been a master of sciences physical, or a weapons-master, it might have been different — the humans of Tenassa had been trained to understand the rudiments of those sciences — but this was safe enough. *Very well,* he said. *Lead on.*

He followed Thread through the twisting corridors, the blades' direct paths rather than the clevermen's, sanctioned by Thread's escort and Bonewhite's orders, and came more quickly than he had expected to the Hivemaster's quarters. The others were there before him, no surprise, and a stone-game had been laid out on the central table, Precision and the First-Watch-Captain, Ease, idly tossing dice for first-move. Hasten, the shipmaster and master of sciences physical, gave him a nod of greeting, and Ember gave a quick half-bow in return.

*And the Commander?* he asked, shading his thought to reach Hasten alone.

*Still on Atlantis,* Hasten answered. *Still treating with their queen.* He glanced toward the inner door. *I have heard that indeed Snow's daughter is alive —*

*That is true,* Bonewhite said, the door sliding closed again behind him. *And that is only part of the news I bring.*

*Snow's daughter alive?* Precision said. He had been born to this hive, unlike many of the others; for him, this was memory, not rumor and story. *Alabaster?*

*Alabaster,* Bonewhite agreed, and shaped an image of a young queen, a few years older than their own Steelflower, perhaps, pale of skin and scarlet of hair. *And her first-born.*

A son, Ember saw, and felt the same whisper of relief from the others. Bad enough to have two queens demanding Guide's loyalty, but at least they were spared the struggle that a daughter would have made inevitable.

*Guide believes the Lanteans rescued her as an earnest of the alliance they propose against Queen Death,* Bonewhite continued, *and he orders us to bring Just Fortune to orbit Atlantis, pledge in turn of our willingness to keep this bargain.*

There was a moment of silence, no one wanting to be the first to question. To cooperate now and then with the humans of Atlantis was one thing, Ember thought. Hives had always played groups of worshippers against each other, or, more subtly, pitted one human world against another, supporting one in order to hold another back, or to prepare it for a greater Culling. Even if the Lanteans were indeed the heirs of the Ancients, they were not those all-powerful beings; it was no worse to work with them than with any other of their species. But a formal alliance, bound under the signs of truce — a formal alliance directed against another queen — it spoke of desperation. But then, they were desperate: Death was determined to bring all the Wraith together under her command, and she had proven herself willing to do anything, even destroy her enemies' feeding grounds, to bring them to heel. It was against everything every Wraith knew in the crèche, unnatural and dangerous and to be fought with all their strength. Ember lifted his gaze, saw the same reluctant conclusion on Precision's face, and Hasten's, but Ease shook his head.

*This cannot be,* he said. *Hivemaster, the Commander goes too far. Surely our Queen would not wish to a true alliance —*

*She spoke of it herself,* Hasten said. *We all heard her.*

*She said she would treat with any who came under her peace,* Ease retorted, *and that is not at all the same as an alliance.*

Precision cocked his head to one side. *That is so.* He fixed his eyes on Bonewhite, who gave an infinitesimal shrug.

Hasten's mental voice was carefully controlled. "The Commander has every reason to see Snow's daughter safely returned to her people."

That way lay danger. Ember didn't look at him, and schooled face and mind to equal impassivity. The implication was unthinkable — that Guide would betray Queen Steelflower to place his untried, unproven daughter in her place — and yet such things had happened before.

Ease said, cautiously, *Guide was many years the humans' prisoner..."* He let the thought die, and Precision let his handful of dice fall with a clatter. They fell all fours and threes, a House of Night, but Precision ignored them.

*For Alabaster's sake.*

There was another, deeper silence, and Ember said, *I do not know that story.*

*When we were attacked, and Queen Snow was killed, her daughter Alabaster had only just quickened with her first child.* Bonewhite's tone was scrupulously neutral. *At the queen's order, she took to a cruiser to escape, and disappeared. After the battle, we searched and found nothing, only the report of an enemy commander that her ship had exploded as it entered hyperspace. The Commander did not find this entirely convincing, and continued to search for any word of her or her ship and crew. A Worshipper brought wqrd of a young queen dead on a human world controlled by the Genii. Despite the dangers the Commander was determined to investigate, and — was taken. The Genii commander held him prisoner for many years before he was able to make his escape.*

With the help of Atlantis's Consort, Ember knew, and was careful to mask the thought. That was the beginning of this road, this peculiar alliance. And the implications — Bonewhite was suggesting, so carefully that it could easily be denied, that Guide was not entirely rational about his daughter, might betray his true Queen to save her. He didn't think it was true, but once raised, the question could not entirely be put aside. He glanced around the room, saw the same knowledge in the others' faces, and took a careful breath. He was Guide's man: Guide had welcomed him, a lone straggler, hiveless, let him earn his place as chief among the clevermen.

*And what is our course, Hivemaster?* The words were not — quite — a challenge, but Bonewhite showed teeth anyway.

*We will do as the Commander bids, cleverman. I will leave Farseer in command here, and we will set course for Atlantis.*

Ember ducked his head, joining in the murmured chorus of agreement. There was an undertone of unease, however, the same doubts he had felt, but he could not identify its source. *Oh, Guide,* he thought, *I hope you're not playing one game too many.*

Radek had been in the control room since the last hour of the night shift. Strictly speaking, he wasn't supposed to be on duty, but since he'd been taken off the gate team and appointed Head of Sciences, he no longer worked a regular shift. Most of the time, this was a good thing, as it meant sleeping and waking in a pattern that actually matched the planet's day/night cycle. Sometimes, though, he was the person you called when there was a problem, even when that problem turned out to be nothing after all. He looked at the screen again, the display now showing clear, and glanced up again at the young airman who'd been assigned to this console.

"It looks as though it is normal ice build-up," he said, and did his best to keep any annoyance out of his voice. "You see there, on the exterior camera? Watch when I trigger the cameras." He touched keys as he spoke, and light flashed out into the murky water, plankton swirling like heavy snow. The camera panned down and sideways, at the limit of its turn, to show a craggy beard of sea-ice growing down from the edge of the platform. "That explains the unusual mass."

"Yes, sir." The airman was very fair, pale as a Russian, eyebrows and eyelashes almost invisible. "I'm sorry, Dr. Zelenka."

"Don't be," Radek said briskly, and meant it. "It is better to be concerned and find out that it is nothing serious than to ignore something you can't identify. Do that, and it will certainly be the Wraith. Or worse."

The airman managed a smile at that, as Radek had intended. "Yes, sir."

"Now," Radek said. "Are you familiar with the de-icing procedures?"

"Yes, sir."

"Then let us see you apply them." Radek slid out of the chair, letting the airman take his place, and watched as the younger man called up the program. He entered the parameters quickly and correctly, frowning over his screen, and Radek stepped back. The people he'd like to yell at were Dr. Merritt, suspiciously busy at his screen, or possibly Sergeant Trin. Either one of them should have recognized the pattern of the readings, and realized what they were seeing — they'd both been on Atlantis long enough to know to check for ice before sounding an alert.

Before he could say anything, however, a door slid back on the main floor and Sheppard emerged, heading purposefully for the main stairs. That rarely meant anything good, not at this hour of the morning, and Radek wasn't surprised when Sheppard nodded to him.

"Morning, Doc. Got a minute?"

"Of course." Radek let himself be herded out of earshot of the others in the control room, along the railing where they might be talking about something innocuous. Through the long windows, the aurora was fading to pastel wisps against a lightening sky, thin veils of purple to herald the dawn.

"We have a potential problem," Sheppard said quietly. "Can you access the security cameras without everyone knowing about it?"

Radek paused. "Yes. Or at least they won't know immediately. But once I have looked, anyone who comes after me will see the search."

"That's probably all right," Sheppard said, though he didn't look as though he entirely believed it himself.

"It would be helpful if you had a place you wanted me to look," Radek said. "And a time? A range of times? Or maybe you could just tell me what is going on."

Sheppard gave a crooked grin. "Oh, come on, Doc, nobody ever tells anybody that." He sobered abruptly. "An object has gone missing — a package, about so big." He mimed a rectangle half a meter long and maybe a hand's-breadth wide. "It was in a secure location, or at least what I thought was secure, but someone's taken it. I need to find it before anyone knows it's gone. And that means —"

Radek nodded. "I will keep my mouth shut, of course. Where was this — package — taken from?"

Sheppard looked over his shoulder. "Maybe we could take this somewhere more private?"

"Okay." Radek beckoned to Dr. Merritt, who rose reluctantly from his place. "You're all right with the underwater sensors now?"

Merritt nodded.

"Then I am going to get some breakfast. Next time, it would be better to check the cameras first."

"Yeah," Merritt said. "I'm sorry, Dr. Zelenka, I just forgot."

"Yes, well," Radek said. "Not again, please?" He nodded to Sheppard. "And I am at your disposal, Colonel."

"After you," Sheppard said.

After a moment's thought, Radek took him to one of the smaller system labs, not often used except when they were running full-systems tests on the city. He entered his passcodes and brought the consoles to life, then typed more commands to let himself into the security system. A map of the city blossomed on the screen, slowly rotating, and he looked over his shoulder at Sheppard.

"Okay," he said again. "Tell me where this thing was so I can start to look."

"Here." Sheppard touched one of the smaller southwest towers, just below the top chamber. "I'm guessing you don't have cameras there, right?"

"Right," Radek answered, entering coordinates. "But we do have cameras in the stairwells and outside the transport chambers. When did this happen?"

"That's an excellent question," Sheppard said. "Start with overnight."

"Yes," Radek said, typing that in, and grimaced at the size of the datafeed. "It will take me some time to go through this, Colonel —"

"I was afraid of that," Sheppard answered. "Look, if you find anything — radio me right away, got it?"

"Yes, of course," Radek said, "but it would help if you told me more about what I might be looking for —"

He stopped, realizing that he was speaking to empty air. "Of course not," he said, and frowned at the screen.

Luckily, they had already developed algorithms that could do the preliminary analysis of the footage, but it was still almost an hour before he spotted the first anomaly, and even then it was sheer chance that alerted him. The camera in the ZPM room showed that he had entered the area at 9:19 the previous night for a routine check of the subsystems' direct readouts. Radek touched keys to reverse the image, and played it again, watching himself enter the ZPM room and walk purposefully to the console. The problem was, he hadn't been anywhere near the ZPM room yesterday. That footage — he slowed down the image, zoomed in to look at his own left hand. Yes, it had been taken the day before, there was no question about it. That was the bandage he had gotten in the infirmary after he'd cut his left forefinger reaching into one of the less accessible parts of the *Hammond's* engines. It was a small cut, and he'd only gotten the bandage so that he didn't bleed on the more sensitive equipment. He'd taken it off again at the end of the day, and the only sign it had ever been there was a tender spot on his finger. At 9:19 last night, he'd been in the shower, not in the ZPM room, and that meant someone had tampered with the security footage. Once he examined it more closely, it was easy to see what had happened. Someone had erased a section of the security record and replaced it with footage taken on an earlier occasion. It was easy enough to spot once you knew to look for it, and Radek quickly set up a search algorithm of his own to find the all-but-invisible anomalies. He wasn't surprised when the program found three more, and then another, but when it finished its search, he shook his head, swearing softly at the screen.

He touched his radio. "Colonel Sheppard."

There was a brief pause before Sheppard answered, and he sounded faintly breathless. "Yeah, Doc?"

Radek hesitated, not sure he wanted to make this announcement on an open channel. "Do you have a moment?"

"I'm kind of in the middle of something," Sheppard said slowly. "Can you give me the high points?"

"Yes," Radek said. "You asked me to let you know at once if I found anything. I have found gaps."

"Gaps," Sheppard repeated. "Crap."

"Just so."

"How many? And where?"

"More than twenty," Radek said, glancing at his screen. "I am not quite finished with the analysis, but — too many to blame on any normal malfunction. At least one of them occurred in your area of interest, and there are others throughout the city."

"Someone has edited themselves out of the security footage," Sheppard said.

"That is my conclusion," Radek said.

There was a moment of silence, and Radek guessed Sheppard was talking to someone off-channel. "Can you get me locations covered by these edits? Times, too, but the locations are the main thing."

"Yes," Radek said. "I'm already compiling that." He glanced at his screen, checking the progress bar. "Give me another ten, fifteen minutes, and I'll have it ready."

"Thanks," Sheppard said. "I'm sending Captain Cadman to collect it. Don't say anything to anybody else, all right?"

"Yes, I understand that," Radek said. "Though if you would tell me more, I might be able to help —"

He stopped, aware that he was speaking to empty air. He swore in Czech, glaring at the screen, and wondered what new disaster they'd stumbled into.

## CHAPTER TWO
# Broken Trust

"HERE'S where we need to concentrate our search," John said. It was a small briefing, with only Carter, Cadman, Ronon, and Lorne in attendance. "You all have assigned areas to search, and we need to move fast."

"While being discreet," Carter added. "We need to find the... object... without drawing attention to the fact that we're looking for it."

Cadman's eyebrows went up, but she didn't ask questions. Carter and Lorne didn't look like they had questions. Ronon figured he'd wait until everyone else left before getting the real story out of John.

"All right, move out," John said. The others headed out, Lorne still leaning on a cane but managing a brisk pace despite it.

"So what's this thing we're looking for?" Ronon said.

John's face went suddenly closed. "Just find it, okay? It's about so big, made of naquadah, looks like some kind of scepter or club."

"I heard that the first time," Ronon said. He waited a moment. "So what aren't you telling me?"

"Nothing you need to know."

"You sure?"

John's gaze slid sideways. "I'm sure. Let's just find this thing."

"Whatever you say," Ronon said, and went out into the hall. He waited until he was out of earshot, and then called Teyla on the radio.

"Yes, Ronon?"

"Are you up there with the Wraith?"

"Not at the moment."

"Sheppard knows something he doesn't want to tell me," Ronon said. "I thought you might know what that is."

There was a pause, and then Teyla said, "We should talk. But not over the radio."

He met her in the gym, their usual place to talk in private. Teyla was there when he arrived, standing with her hands folded as if in meditation, although he thought her calm didn't reach below the surface.

"The device that is missing is the Ancient weapon we found on Alabaster's world," she said.

"It's not her world." Alabaster might think of the place as hers, and of the humans there as her pets, but it had been the humans' world first.

"The world where she has lived for many years. She is not the first Wraith to make a home there, Ronon. Thousands of years ago, the first Wraith visited the same world."

"So?" His voice was harsh in his own ears, but Teyla went on undaunted.

"They had been human beings themselves, once. They were the product of a very unwise experiment by one of the Ancestors, a man named Hyperion. He may have been trying to find a way for the Ancients to live forever without Ascending."

"Becoming a Wraith? Not a good trade."

"That was not his intention. But the experiment went badly wrong. Instead of creating humans with the powers of Ascended Ancients, it created the Wraith. Hyperion imprisoned them to study them, trying to find out what had gone wrong. They were here on this planet. The island base we found beneath the ice was Hyperion's laboratory."

Ronon felt a chill run down his spine. He'd wondered who the prisoners were who'd been imprisoned in those cells on the island. He'd been glad to think that they escaped. But they'd been Wraith. The first Wraith, setting off to prey on the rest of the galaxy.

"They killed Hyperion, and escaped his laboratory," Teyla went on. "They could not return to their homes, so they scattered to many worlds. Eventually they created the hive ships, and made their homes in space."

"And made more Wraith."

"They had children."

"Same thing."

Teyla's mouth tightened, but she carried on. "Hyperion also created a failsafe, a weapon created to kill the Wraith. The first mothers of the Wraith took it with them when they escaped. They could not destroy it, so they hid it on Alabaster's world."

He let the question of whose world it was go that time. "A weapon that kills Wraith. Okay. What's the big secret?"

"It is not just a weapon to kill Wraith," Teyla said. "It is a weapon with the power to destroy every Wraith in the galaxy."

It took Ronon a moment to find words to reply. "That's impossible."

"Colonel Carter tells me that the Ancients once created a weapon that could destroy all life in an entire galaxy," Teyla said. "Such things were within their power. And Hyperion was a brilliant man."

"He made the Wraith."

"Brilliant and very arrogant. He believed his experiment would be a success. And he never imagined that the humans he thought of as laboratory animals could truly overpower the Ancients who created them."

"So why aren't we using the weapon?"

"Even if we wanted to, we could not," Teyla said. "It would kill all those with the genetic markers of the Wraith as well. Myself, Rodney, Torren, Kanaan, and every other human being with the Gift. Hundreds or thousands of innocent humans would die."

"How do we know this?"

"Alabaster warned us when we found the device."

"Oh, Alabaster says so."

"She does," Teyla said firmly. "I do not trust her unduly, but she is skilled in the sciences, and she knows more of the history of Hyperion's weapon than we do. And Rodney agrees with her. If you cannot trust Alabaster, surely you can trust Rodney."

"Unless he's working for the Wraith himself."

"He is not."

"It's happened before. And don't say they couldn't break McKay. They can break anybody. Who knows what it did to him, turning him into a Wraith, messing with his head—"

"Guide and Alabaster have no idea where Hyperion's weapon is," Teyla said. "Their anger that it is missing is real. And if Rodney had been compromised by the Wraith, that would be all the more reason for him to want the weapon destroyed."

"I'm not going to argue with that." Ronon shook his head. "Sheppard should have told me himself."

"I believe John felt you should not have to share the responsibility for destroying a weapon that could kill all the Wraith. He wanted to spare you that."

"I'd still be responsible even if I didn't know," Ronon said.

"I thought you would see it that way."

"I guess I'd better go look for the weapon. So that we can do the right thing."

He started to shoulder past her, but she caught his arm. "Please tell me that I have done the right thing by telling you about the weapon."

"Don't you trust me?" Ronon said, and shrugged her arm away as he went by.

The news reached Ladon Radim in the still hours before dawn: one of their most valuable agents, a man so well-placed that only the innermost circle of the government even knew of his existence, had stumbled through the Stargate on Taadin, and was demanding to see the Chief. Ladon dressed quickly, listening to the report, the sky outside the high window still glazed with stars, and gave his aide Ambros a thoughtful glance. This could not be good news, unless Varelon had lost his nerve, and that seemed unlikely. It was more likely that the Wraith had turned him, sent him back to wreak what havoc he could before he died. Ladon did not need to say that, however, and tugged on gloves against the cold.

"Who's with him?"

"Arrasid Bak and Colonel Hanan."

Ladon nodded. They were both good men, loyal and reliable; if this were a Wraith trick, he could trust them to defend him. Even so, he slipped a knife into the sheath hidden beneath the sleeve of his uniform jacket, and made sure his pistol was loose and ready in its holster. There was no need to take unreasonable chances.

They had brought Valeran to a secure site not too far from the Stargate, a low stone house distinguished from its neighbors only by the government truck pulled up inside the courtyard gate. There were soldiers as well, Hanan's men on discreet watch.

Ladon returned their salute, and was ushered into what had been the informal receiving room. The curtains were drawn tight, and a fire blazed on the hearth; all the lamps were lit, and Varelon sat huddled in the central armchair, his arms folded tight as though he were cold. He shot to his feet as the door opened, and Ladon saw the movement of his shoulders as he stopped himself from bowing as though to a Wraith Queen.

"Varelon," Ladon said, keeping his voice scrupulously neutral, and the spy ducked his head in awkward acknowledgement.

"Chief. You know I would not have left my post for anything but dire emergency—"

"I know," Ladon said. He eyed the other man, tall and whip-thin, his hair long and loose in the style affected by most Wraith worshippers, saw the tremors in his muscles that spoke of having been too long without the Wraith enzyme. "Sit, man, and speak plainly. I expect there's no time to waste."

"No." Varelon sank gratefully into his chair. "Chief, you know I have been placed in the household of a Wraith commander and that he has joined the alliance of Queen Death."

"Yes," Ladon said, when it seemed that some response was required.

"Death has summoned her commanders and their fleets," Varelon said. "She intends to attack and destroy Atlantis."

Ladon saw shock and fear on the others' faces, and let his breath out in a soundless sigh. "You're certain." It was not a question, but Varelon nodded anyway.

"Sure enough that I abandoned my post and came to warn you directly. Chief, their fleet will be underway even now."

And that was the next question answered: not merely a planned attack, but one already begun. That forced his hand. He could not allow Death to destroy Atlantis. "Ambros. Summon the inner council—tell them it's urgent, but don't give them any details. And make sure my sister attends, and the commander of the *Pride of the Genii*. Then contact Atlantis. Talk to them yourself, and get me a meeting with Mr. Woolsey as soon as possible." He looked back at Varelon. "I know you're in need, but can you accompany me to Atlantis? The Lanteans will want to hear the details from you directly."

Varelon shivered, but nodded. "Yes, Chief. I'll be fine."

I doubt it, Ladon thought, but clapped him on the shoulder as though he believed him. "Good man."

Ronon finished searching the third location on his list and pulled out his tablet to look at the city map. It could easily take them all day to search every inch of every location where the security footage had been tampered with. There had to be a better way.

Think like your prey, his grandfather had said, years ago on childhood hunting trips. That would be easier if he knew who the thief had been. It had to be a scientist or a specialist, someone who could alter the security footage. Someone who knew about Hyperion's weapon and knew or guessed where Sheppard had hidden it. Someone either reckless or driven enough to steal it. Or else someone compromised by the Wraith.

If it were the Wraith themselves, they'd keep it on their persons, figuring it would create a diplomatic incident to search them. So assume it's not the Wraith. Who else fit the picture? Teyla was sure that it wasn't Rodney.

Ronon wasn't so sure. Rodney knew about the weapon because he'd been there when they found it. And he'd been compromised by the Wraith. Ronon knew better than anyone how good they were at breaking people. Rodney might still be working for them, carrying out some plan for Queen Death while he smiled and promised all his friends that he was fine. He'd been acting strangely since he came back, a new twist in his smile and something slightly off-key about his conversation, especially when the Wraith were around.

If it were Rodney… Ronon glanced at the map. Suspicion hardened into certainty. Only one place on it mattered, a rarely-used tower room with skylights that let in the sun, some Ancient scientist's laboratory too far out of the way of the central tower and mess hall to be attractive as work space. He'd followed Rodney up there years ago, watched him stash things there and leave without ever noticing he'd been followed.

A lot of the longtime Atlantis personnel, veterans of too many invasions and alarms, kept emergency caches of food and equipment somewhere in the city. Ronon had made something of a game of looking for them, never disturbing what he found, but remembering where he'd found it.

He headed for Rodney's cache of supplies, despite the fact that it wasn't on his list of places to search. The transport chamber opened only three floors below the lab, and he took the stairs at a fast jog.

Of course the door was locked, and its control panel demanded a password. He started trying passwords he knew Rodney used, both ones he'd watched Rodney enter and the ones Jeannie Miller and Radek Zelenka had painstakingly worked out during Rodney's absence. Finally one of them worked, and the door slid open.

Most of the room was empty. A computer was set up in one corner, on a table cluttered with bags of snack food and bottles of soda, most unopened. Pieces of Ancient laboratory equipment sat in the opposite corner of the room, none looking like they'd been in frequent use. Overhead, thin gray light filtered in through the skylight, now glazed with ice.

Several crates were stacked under the table, and Ronon pulled them out cautiously. The first two crates he searched were full of various electronic parts, most of which Ronon couldn't identify, but none of which could possibly be Hyperion's weapon.

He was starting to think he was wrong when he opened the next crate. Resting on a tangle of circuit boards and wires was a simple rod with a sphere at one end, looking as if it had been carved from a single block of naquadah.

Hyperion's weapon.

It was warm in his hand when he picked it up, which Teyla hadn't mentioned. Ronon frowned. They'd all learned to treat Ancient devices that grew warm or glowed with caution. That was usually a sign that they'd been activated by someone who had the ATA gene, the Ancestors' legacy that let a lucky few of their descendants use their technology.

Ronon didn't have the ATA gene, and the gene therapy that sometimes activated it hadn't worked on him. But John and Rodney both had it, and they'd both handled the weapon. John might have left it in the box Teyla said they'd found it in, but Rodney obviously hadn't, because the box was gone.

And of course Rodney hadn't left it in the box. He would have taken it out and handled it, at least for a few minutes, trying to find some clue to how it worked. That might well have been enough to activate it, priming it so that anyone could use it.

Some devices didn't work that way, like the puddlejumpers; even after they were turned on, it took someone with the gene sitting in the pilot's seat to make them fly. But some did. It was entirely possible that he could use the weapon. It was entirely possible that he was holding in his hand a weapon that he could use to kill all the Wraith in the galaxy.

The weapon moved in his hand, shifting, and Ronon stiffened, wondering what he'd done, his heart racing. The globe was peeling apart, its pieces shifting, some sliding down the rod to form the familiar shape of a trigger, others now strongly resembling the muzzle of a gun. What he held in his hand now, its oddly slick material still unmarked, was unmistakably a weapon.

If it could do this, why didn't it do it for McKay? That was a question for the scientists to answer, but he thought he might have a guess. Most of the Ancient devices responded to thought — no, that wasn't right. To the will. The force shield they'd once found had been like that; Rodney hadn't been able to turn it off until he'd truly wanted it to turn off.

Rodney had been altered by his ordeal more than the others wanted to admit. Even if he wasn't compromised, he was still acting like he thought the Wraith were people. And maybe he was compromised. Either way, he wouldn't have held Hyperion's weapon in his hand and thought about how much he wanted to wipe out every last Wraith in the galaxy.

Ronon's hand opened convulsively, the weapon dropping with a clatter back into the open crate. Every last Wraith, and all the humans who were victims of Wraith experiments, or descended from their victims. That's what Teyla had said would happen. That using the weapon would kill Teyla and Rodney and everyone else with the Gift along with all the Wraith.

And could he say it wouldn't be worth the price?

Of course it wouldn't be worth it, he told himself firmly. Teyla and Rodney were his friends, his family, and he would have willingly died to protect them. But there had been a time when they would have just as gladly laid down their own lives to save humans from the Wraith. At least, Teyla would have done it gladly; Rodney would have done it in frightened, furious resentment, his racing complaints about the unfairness of their imminent deaths somehow adding up to his own kind of courage.

But they weren't going to do that now. They were going to find a way to destroy the weapon, despite the fact that destroying it meant letting the Wraith go on killing and killing and killing. Letting it go on when he could stop it right now by pulling a trigger.

He picked up the weapon again and let it lie in the palm of his hand. It was heavy for its size, a warm weight that invited his hand to curl around it. He held it for a long moment, and then put it away in his coat.

No one knew he'd found it. The Wraith might be kicking up a fuss about the weapon being missing, but they'd probably get over it. It wouldn't hurt to hold onto the weapon just for a little while, until they had a better idea how their forces stacked up to Queen Death's. What if they destroyed the weapon and then realized it had been the last hope of ever freeing humans from the Wraith?

He could always hand it over to Carter to destroy. But once it was destroyed, they couldn't get it back. John might be willing to hand over their last card that way, but Ronon wasn't. At least not yet.

He closed the storage crate and stacked them the way he'd found them, heading back out of the room toward the stairs. Hyperion's weapon nestled in his pocket, warm and heavy; his fingers caressed it, just for a moment, before he forced himself to let it go.

# CHAPTER THREE
## Face to Face

JACK O'Neill balanced his paper plate containing one slightly mis-shapen doughnut on top of his cup of coffee and hugged his tablet more tightly under his elbow. There were days when he missed the old-fashioned briefing folder, and this was one of them: the consequences of dropping a folder or spilling coffee on it were a lot less dire than they were even with the supposedly hardened tablets. He had yet to meet a computer that could stand up to the usual day-to-day work of the SGC, never mind battle conditions. And he was, he admitted, doing his best not to think too hard about the upcoming negotiation. It was all too clear to him that there was no way Atlantis was going to be able to stand up to Queen Death without Todd's help, and that meant allying with people who had, over the past six years, done their level best to eat the Atlantis crew. On balance, that shouldn't feel worse than what the Goa'uld had wanted, but somehow this felt... personal.

Woolsey was there ahead of him, of course, a tall travel mug his only concession to the hour. It was filled, Jack knew, with half-caf sweetened with a single packet of artificial sweetener and topped with a splash of skim milk, and for a moment he really missed Daniel's extra sugar habit. Todd was there, too, smiling toothily at Woolsey, and as Jack took his place at the table, the young queen Alabaster arrived, trailed by Marines and one of her human escorts. He was big and blond and carried a plate piled with doughnuts, which he seemed to be urging on Alabaster. Jack couldn't hear what she said, but she accepted a small piece of the pastry, her smile almost human. One of the Marine escorts opened the door, and she came to take her place beside her father, sniffing curiously at the doughnut. The big blond leaned against the wall across from the Marines and began to eat, his honor apparently satisfied."Colonel Carter is not here?" Todd — Guide — asked. Beside him, Alabaster took a careful bite of the doughnut, cocking her head as if considering the taste.

"Colonel Carter has been delayed," Woolsey said. There was an edge of annoyance in his voice. "She will be here as soon as possible."

"I do not see the point in beginning without her," Guide said.

"I am sure Colonel Carter will find a way to destroy Hyperion's device," Woolsey began, and Guide showed teeth.

"But if she cannot, then our discussion is moot."

Jack took a sip of his own coffee. It felt really weird to be eating in front of the Wraith, considering, but he shoved that feeling down. "I have every confidence in Carter."

"I'm sure you do," Guide answered. "And I have no doubt of her technical ability, either."

He let the rest of his thought hang unspoken — he doubted their willingness to destroy the device — and Alabaster said, "As you have said yourself, the Lanteans have much to lose themselves by using the device. Let us at least discuss what shape some alliance between us might take."

Guide glanced at her, then shrugged one shoulder. "As long as it is understood that the destruction of this device is not negotiable. Until it is destroyed — until we see it destroyed — we have no incentive to help you."

"Except that Queen Death wants you dead, too," Jack pointed out.

Guide gave him a sidelong glance. "It is possible that we will treat with her, attain some terms. We are all Wraith, after all. Surely you do not wish to give us a common threat."

"I can't see Queen Death letting you, or Alabaster here, live," Jack said bluntly. Woolsey looked pained, but didn't intervene. "Alabaster's a rival, and you keep finding ways not to help her. All Queen Death is going to do is get rid of you."

"But if the choice is between the death of all my kind, and my own demise?" Guide let his voice trail off. "Ask Colonel Sheppard what I would do to save my people."

That I don't doubt, Jack thought. And I don't want to push him too far.

Woolsey gave them both a reproachful look. "As we have said before, we don't even know if this so-called device will function, or if it will do what it is claimed it will do without having unforeseen side effects. Even if it only does what it was apparently designed to do, that still places some of our own people at grave risk. I do not believe that this is a choice any of us wish to make."

"If Carter destroys the weapon," Jack said, "what are you willing to do to help?"

"To stand with you against Queen Death," Guide answered. Was he smiling? Jack wasn't sure how to interpret the twist of his mouth. "Which you need as much as we do. Alone, neither of us can withstand her fleet. Together…"

"That depends on what you have to offer," Jack said.

Guide did smile this time. "Teyla Emmagan will have given you Steelflower's strength in detail."

"Absolutely," Jack said. "Except for whatever's changed since she left."

"It has happened before that certain specifics have been — elided," Woolsey said, his eyes on his tablet.

"That has been a fault on both sides," Guide said. Alabaster laid her hand on his wrist, and whether it was a simple warning or silent conversation, he seemed to relax slightly. "As you know, there are two hives at the core of our alliance, mine — Steelflower's — and that of a young Queen who has allied with her as a sister. Since Queen Steelflower left us, we were joined by a third hive, who fled Queen Death when she demanded they despoil their own territory. Sadly, their ship was badly damaged, and I do not believe they will be of much use in battle. However, they have Darts in plenty, which will be placed at our disposal. The former consort of Queen Iceheart, who was killed by Queen Death, has brought three cruisers to join us as well — Teyla Emmagan is well aware of him. And there are others, a considerable number of others, who will hold off from any combat for as long as possible. They do not love Queen Death, but they cannot see their way clear to oppose her."

Jack nodded. All of that dovetailed nicely with the reports on his tablet, though it meant that, at best guess, Queen Death's fleet still outnumbered them. On the other hand, they had the *Hammond*, and *Daedalus*, when it returned from Earth, and those tough, Asgard-designed ships had proven themselves more than a match for Death's cruisers.

"Of course," Guide said smoothly, "it would be far better to wait until your missing ship returns before we confront Queen Death."

"Can't argue with you there," Jack began, and Woolsey put a hand to his ear.

"What? No, I —" He broke off, his frown deepening. "Very well. I'll come at once." He took a deep breath, pushing back his chair. "Gentlemen, I'm sorry, but I've just received an urgent message. General O'Neill, I'll be back as soon as I can."

"Right," Jack said, but Woolsey was already gone. He glanced at his tablet, but there was neither text nor email: Atlantis business, then, and he just hoped it wasn't a new disaster. Guide smiled at him, showing teeth, and Jack did his best to match him.

The usual Marine escort was waiting when Ladon Radim came through the Stargate. Ladon submitted to seeing his men escorted away, but did not volunteer to hand over his sidearm. The young captain didn't ask for it, either, and Ladon couldn't tell if it was an error or if the Lanteans were worried enough by what he'd told them that they weren't going to draw out the preliminaries. They followed the captain up the stairs and across a corridor — not to the usual meeting room, Ladon noted, but a place more private. He lifted an eyebrow at that, but it was too soon to guess what it might mean. He settled himself at one end of the narrow table next to Varelon, accepted an offer of coffee — Varelon needed it, even if Ladon himself disliked it — and composed himself to wait.

Woolsey did not delay long, arriving on the heels of the coffee. He looked vaguely unkempt, as though he hadn't slept, and Ladon's attention sharpened. Either the Lanteans had already heard his news, or there was some other trouble afoot.

"Mr. Radim," Woolsey said, extending his hand, and Ladon took it with a slight bow.

"Mr. Woolsey. I apologize for my insistence, but the matter is urgent."

"So you said." Woolsey seated himself on the opposite side of the table. For once he didn't have any of his subordinates with him, and Ladon wondered again what was going on. "And — forgive me — if it is that urgent, I hope we can speak plainly."

"Certainly," Ladon said. The simple shock of it should work in his favor. "We have received information that Queen Death has launched an all-out attack on Atlantis. This is Varelon, who has been our primary agent among the Wraith. He left his post to warn us, so that we could warn you."

Woolsey's expression didn't change, though Ladon thought his hands tightened on the edges of his tablet. "Can you give me more details, Mr. Varelon?"

Ladon nodded, and Varelon took a shuddering breath.

"I have been in place as a Wraith worshipper for four years," he said. "In the household of the Wraith his people call Terror. He is commander of a larger cruiser, one that carries a full Dart contingent, and he allied himself with Queen Death seven months ago. Three days ago, Death summoned all her people, committed commanders and distant allies alike, and announced that her fleet would move at once to attack Atlantis. Those summoned were given the choice to join her or die. Two other hives and six cruisers had answered the call before I was able to steal a Dart; there may be more still. But I made it to one of our hidden bases, and from there I came straight to Chief Ladon with the news."

"How long did it take you?" Woolsey asked.

"The fleet should have embarked by now," Varelon answered. "They were forty-three hours out when I left."

Woolsey's eyes flickered, doing the math, and Ladon said, "I make it thirty-six hours left, Mr. Woolsey."

"Yes." Woolsey's mouth was a thin line. "If you'll excuse me a moment, Mr. Radim?" He rose without waiting for an answer, and went to the door. He spoke to the Marine guard, and then into his radio, and Ladon caught snatches of the words, orders for an expanded sweep at the limit of Atlantis's sensor range. "And now — you're certain of this? We've known for some time that we were eventually going to have to face Queen Death's fleet."

"Varelon wouldn't abandon his post for anything less dire," Ladon said. "I hope that your second warship has returned from Earth."

Woolsey's lips were almost white. "Regrettably, it has not."

"I have the agreement of the ruling council to offer you the assistance of our own *Pride of the Genii*," Ladon said. "In exchange for tissue or DNA samples that would allow one of my people to pilot it properly."

"I don't know if that will be possible," Woolsey said.

"You wouldn't want to burden one of your men with the task," Ladon said. "There will be enough to do merely to fly your own machines."

"And do you really think that two cruisers will be enough to provide an effective defense against Queen Death?" Woolsey glared across the table. "Particularly if she has the kind of fleet your man describes."

"We can buy time for you to move the city," Ladon said. "You would, of course, be welcome on any of our worlds."

"I'm sure —" Woolsey broke off, touching his radio. "I see. Thank you, Dr. Zelenka." He looked back at Ladon. "Our long-range sensors are picking up no sign of a Wraith fleet."

"Perhaps your sensors are not quite as effective as you believed," Ladon said.

"If there is a Wraith fleet thirty-six hours from orbit, we should be able to see them," Woolsey said. "I'm sure you understand that I cannot take such drastic action without more proof than this."

"I know our peoples have had their differences," Ladon said carefully. This was not going precisely as he'd planned. "But you know as well as I do that neither one of us can stand alone against the Wraith."

"It is true," Varelon said. "I swear it." His hands were shaking badly. He snatched them out of sight, but Woolsey frowned.

"What's wrong with your agent?"

Ladon said, "He has spent the last four years as a Wraith worshipper."

For a moment, Woolsey looked blank, and Ladon wondered if he would have to explain. He'd do it, of course, but he'd rather spare Varelon's feelings, particularly since he was already in the throes of withdrawal. Then Woolsey's face changed, and Ladon allowed himself a sigh of relief.

"In that case," Woolsey said. "I have a — proposition for you, Mr. Radim. If you and Mr. Varelon would come with me?"

"Of course." Ladon rose, hiding his uncertainty. What was Woolsey up to now?

He and Varelon followed Woolsey down a short stretch of corridor, the Marine guard tagging along at their heels. Woolsey lifted his hand, opening the door, and gestured for Ladon to precede him. "Er — Guide, Alabaster, may I introduce Mr. Ladon Radim, Chief of the Genii?"

Ladon checked abruptly, seeing what waited. Wraith, warrior and queen, both with teeth bared in shock, the warrior starting to his feet, his body already half in front of the queen's.

"You cannot be serious —"

"Mr. Radim's man, here, has come at great personal risk to inform us that Queen Death's fleet is already on the way to attack Atlantis," Woolsey said, his tone utterly emotionless. "I propose that we have no choice but to join forces."

"You've allied with the Wraith?" Ladon heard his own voice scale up, and didn't care. "Are you mad?"

"Guide is commander of an alliance that is opposed to Queen Death," Woolsey said. "We have a common and deadly enemy."

"And I," the Wraith warrior said, "have no desire to ally myself with the Genii."

Ladon looked at him again, and swore. "Kolya's Wraith."

"Yes, I was Kolya's prisoner," the Wraith said. "And from him I learned never to trust a Genii."

"No more than we can trust a Wraith," Ladon snapped.

"Gentlemen," Woolsey said. "If we do not work together, Queen Death will surely destroy us all."

Ladon took a slow breath, then another, willing his heartbeat to subside. Woolsey was right, that was the damnable thing: with only the Lantean's *Hammond* and the *Pride of the Genii*, they had no hope of holding off Queen Death's fleet, and relocating Atlantis only postponed the inevitable. "I'll listen," he said, and the Wraith dipped his head slowly.

"As will I. Go on, Mr. Woolsey."

"Your man is unwell."

Jack looked up sharply at Alabaster's remark. Radim and Guide had been sniping at each other for the better part of an hour, and the Wraith was no closer to accepting the spy's information as accurate. Woolsey looked startled, too, and Radim frowned.

"He is," Radim said. "The condition is common enough among Wraith worshippers."

"I am aware of that." For the first time, Alabaster's voice held a hint of steel. "But in it I believe we have the opportunity to resolve several difficulties. You, Commander, wish confirmation of this news, and you, Chief Ladon, surely you do not wish your man to suffer?"

The silence was heavy, Wraith and human staring at her with suspicion. Jack couldn't see where she was going either, and said nothing.

"I can eliminate both problems," Alabaster went on. "I can — with your consent, Varelon — confirm this tale and provide some relief. And then we can return to truly pressing issues."

Provide relief? Jack thought, and Radim shook his head. "I cannot allow one of my men to be fed upon —"

"Chief." The spy gave Radim a shamefaced look, and the Genii leader closed his mouth unhappily. "I am willing. If you please, Lady."

"Wait just a minute," Jack began.

"It is not the same as feeding," Alabaster said, indignantly, "as Mr. Radim well knows."

Woolsey didn't look any happier, and Jack wasn't feeling all that good himself. But the Genii spy was on his feet, moving quickly around the table. Alabaster stood to meet him, her feeding hand flexing, and Jack flinched as she caught Varelon just below the throat. His head snapped back, eyes closing; Jack's hand twitched, but he managed to keep himself from reaching for his pistol. Woolsey looked distinctly green, and Radim wasn't looking at all. Alabaster bared teeth, but did not snarl, and Varelon did not wither under her touch. He swayed, staggered, and then she released him, letting him slump down into the nearest chair. He was pale, but the tremors that had racked him earlier had stopped.

Alabaster looked at Guide. "He speaks the truth, Commander."

Guide did snarl then, but Alabaster ignored him, and returned to her place, arranging her skirts neatly about her.

"I believe that we must accept this temporary alliance."

"Perhaps," Guide said.

Woolsey cleared his throat. "Mr. Radim, you came here to warn us of grave danger, and I assure you we are grateful for that."

Just not too grateful, Jack thought. We don't want to go overboard.

"And I agree that an at least temporary alliance against Queen Death is the only option that offers a reasonable chance for all our people to survive." Woolsey folded his hands on the tabletop.

"And when the alliance comes to its inevitable end?" Radim asked.

"All bets are off," Guide said, with something like a laugh.

Radim smiled fiercely. "Yes, indeed."

All right, Jack thought. We've got them to agree to work together, so now the trick is to get Radim out of here before anyone says anything about Hyperion's goddamn weapon. We do not need him to find out there's a weapon that destroys Wraith, particularly when we're going to destroy it…

Radim looked at Woolsey. "So now the question is what must be done in the extremely limited time left to us."

"We have —" Woolsey looked at his tablet. " — a little more than thirty-five hours. But I agree, there is a great deal to do."

## CHAPTER FOUR
# The Pride of the Genii

WOOLSEY and Radim returned to the original conference room, leaving O'Neill behind to continue talking with the Wraith. Woolsey was in two minds about that, but he told himself firmly that O'Neill was a competent and experienced negotiator. The Wraith seemed to respond better to military personnel, anyway — Todd had always seemed far happier to talk to Carter or Sheppard, and now O'Neill had stepped easily into those shoes. That just left him Ladon Radim to deal with.

They went through the motions of settling in, Woolsey offering refreshment, Radim accepting, exchanging barbed chitchat while they waited for the mess hall staff to arrive with a tray. The main thing now, Woolsey thought, as he poured a careful measure of skim milk into his mug, was to get Radim and his people to agree to join the attack, and — perhaps more important — get them out of Atlantis before they got any inkling of the existence of Hyperion's weapon. The Genii would have no compunction about using it, and Woolsey could understand their position.

"Under the current circumstances," he began, "it seems that it would benefit both our peoples to join forces."

A fleeting smile crossed Radim's face: as an opening, that was weak, and they both knew it. "And we would, of course, be willing to honor our agreements."

"Then we can expect the *Pride of the Genii* to join us." Personally, Woolsey agreed with Sheppard, the Ancient cruiser should have retained its previous name, but he wasn't about to offend Radim over something that small.

"Of course we'd be glad to," Radim said. "But we're somewhat hamstrung at the moment."

"Oh?"

"As you know, none of my people have the Ancient blood, the ATA gene." Radim smiled sweetly. "Without it, our ability to crew the ship is limited."

"We would, of course, we willing to loan you appropriate personnel," Woolsey said. "In fact, it might be helpful in any case, as we have had somewhat more experience in interstellar warfare."

Radim inclined his head. "A very generous offer, Mr. Woolsey, and one I would like to accept. But it doesn't change the fact that at some point we will need to handle the *Pride* ourselves. And for that, we do need this gene. Or the genetic therapy that your people have developed."

Woolsey spread his hands. "My understanding of that therapy is that it allows a recessive gene to emerge, to be expressed. It only works on people who have a copy of the gene. On anyone else, it's useless. And I am told that the ATA gene is very rare in the Pegasus Galaxy."

"So it seems," Radim said. "However, our scientists have been pursuing a different possibility, a therapy that would allow a functioning ATA gene to be inserted into an individual's DNA. Your technique would allow us to shorten the process considerably."

"Indeed," Woolsey said, in a tone calculated to express polite disbelief.

Radim gave a thin smile, acknowledging the unspoken skepticism. "You would be surprised, Mr. Woolsey, at how quickly biology has advanced on our worlds once we realized the key to our problem."

And, of course, they could steal from the Wraith, Woolsey thought. He knew better than to say that, however, and merely nodded.

"We believe we have isolated at least a variant of the ATA gene itself," Radim said, "If it can be activated — well, we would be more than happy to exchange the use of our warship for a sample."

"As you know, we on Atlantis," Woolsey began. The request startled him, and for a moment he was afraid he let it show. "We are an exploratory mission. It's something we simply didn't bring with us. Our people were treated before they left the Milky Way."

We must have it, though, he thought. They wouldn't have come to Pegasus without it, but– He couldn't see the IOA being willing to give the Genii the key to Ancient technology. And saying they didn't have any — well, it might buy him as much time as it took

Radim to point out that they could use the Stargate to send for it.

"And certainly we're in a difficult position at the moment," Radim said.

"Which we need each other's help if we're to survive," Woolsey pointed out. There was nothing to be lost in making that explicit.

"Precisely. However, it would certainly make things easier on my people if we were able to start with your therapy." Radim smiled. "Surely that can be arranged, even on short notice."

Over my dead body. Woolsey swallowed the words, managed a thin smile of his own. "My government frowns on using unwilling subjects for medical experimentation, Mr. Radim."

"My volunteers are all willing," Radim answered. "Nor would I call it 'experimentation.' After all, you know perfectly well that the gene therapy works."

"It's against the policy of my government," Woolsey said. He put his hand to his ear as though he had received a radio signal. "Yes?" He paused, letting imaginary words roll through his mind — excuse me, we need to talk to you — and turned back to Radim with the best smile he could manage. "I'm sorry, Mr. Radim. I'm needed urgently. Perhaps we could return to this discussion a bit later?"

"Of course." Radim rose politely. "But I do want to make our position clear, Mr. Woolsey. Unless we get access to the ATA gene, the *Pride of the Genii* remains where she is."

"Commendably clear," Woolsey said, and let the door close behind him.

Rodney McKay bent over his laptop in the new quarters he'd picked out as temporary housing. It wasn't as nice as the rooms he'd given up, but it did have an actual bathtub, and the outer room had a tiny balcony, which was less important, given the weather, than the fact that the balcony came with a clear glass door that gave onto a view of ocean between two of the towers. On the negative side, the bedroom was small and dark, but then, he wasn't doing much except sleeping in it these days. He hadn't really unpacked yet — there was bound to be something better once he had time to explore a little further — but it would do for now, and it kept Sheppard happy, in that everyone knew where to find him when he was off duty. That wasn't something Rodney actually wanted to think about in any detail, and he bent closer over the screen, studying the model he'd created. The order was to destroy Hyperion's weapon, and he could guess what Carter's solution would be. Surely there was something more elegant than just dropping it into the nearest sun.

The trouble was, there might not be a more efficient method. He'd pulled up all the files on "destroying things in naquadah casings" — of which there were rather more than he'd expected — and most of the successful results seemed to come from large nuclear devices or dropping it into a sun. Of the two, the sun was probably preferable.

A part of him wished there was a chance to examine it more closely. He'd like to know how it was supposed to work, as well as what it actually did, but Alabaster's warning had been enough to sober him. "Burn out the brain of everyone with Wraith DNA": it wasn't just that the category now included him, but there were too many innocent, non-Wraithy people who carried some trace of the Wraith. Teyla and Torren, for two, and he wasn't about to risk them. Not when she and John finally seemed to have gotten themselves together. It was nothing to do with worrying about his own fate.

Besides, he was feeling less Wraith-like with every passing day. Yes, there was still that weird residual telepathy, though he was getting better at tuning it out, and his hair was still stark white, but other than that he was unmistakably himself. It was a pity some people didn't seem to recognize it. He grimaced at the thought, ducked his head closer to the screen. They'd get over it. Eventually.

"Rodney."

Zelenka's voice sounded in his ear, as close as telepathy, and Rodney straightened, scowling even though he couldn't be seen. "Yes, what? I'm busy."

"Sorry." Zelenka didn't sound particularly regretful. 'You're needed in the control room. Immediately."

"Would you like to tell me why?" Rodney was working as he talking, putting his laptop to sleep and shrugging into his jacket. "Or at least whether we're being invaded?"

"If we were being invaded, I would not be calling just you," Zelenka said. "It is — urgent, but not dire? We are searching for something that should be there, but we have the sensor field at maximum, and we cannot pick it up."

"I'm on my way," Rodney said, and slung the laptop over his shoulder.

The control room was busier than he'd expected, and when he glanced over the railing into the gateroom, there was a trio of Genii soldiers standing to one side under the watchful eye of an equal number of Marines.

"What are they doing here?" he asked, and Zelenka looked up from his console.

"Oh, good, you are here."

"Yes, obviously. Why do we have Genii in the gateroom?"

"Ladon Radim is here," Zelenka said.

"Ok, yes, but why is he here? What does he want from us this time?"

Zelenka finished typing in a series of commands, and pushed himself back from the keyboard. "He says that Queen Death has launched an all-out attack and that her fleet will be here within thirty-six hours."

He kept his voice low, but Rodney flinched in spite of himself. That explained the tension he could see in people's faces, the way they kept querying their screens, erasing the results, and querying again. "We should be able to see her if that's the case —"

"Yes, yes," Zelenka said. "Except that we can't. The ships would be at the limits of our sensors, yes, but we ought to be seeing something. And we're not."

"Then Radim is lying," Rodney said. "It wouldn't be the first time. And that's Woolsey's problem, not mine."

"Woolsey wants us to find the Wraith fleet," Zelenka said. "Or prove it isn't there. At the moment, I am unable to do either."

"Let me see." Rodney took his place in front of the main sensor array, frowning at the screen. "OK, that's — look, all you need to do it extend the bandwidth, here, and channel more power through the phased array—"

"No, wait—"

Sparks flew under Rodney's fingers, and he snatched his hands back. "Ow!"

Zelenka reached past him, swearing in Czech, and hit another switch. The sparks died.

"What the hell did you do that for?" Rodney demanded. Now that he looked again, he could see that the settings were different, the power routed through new pathways.

"Why do you think?" Zelenka retorted. "We had to make certain changes while you were — away."

They both stopped, Rodney for once speechless, all too aware of what Zelenka wasn't saying, and after a moment, Radek gave an awkward shrug.

"Well. You see what we did."

"Yeah." Rodney looked at the screen again. He was not going to pursue the issue. There was nothing he could say that would make them trust him any sooner — though, really, of all people Zelenka ought to know him better than that. Except that there was that moment in the ZPM room, when he'd come too close to killing Zelenka, and he doubted either of them had forgotten. He made himself concentrate. "Well, that's why you're not getting the readings you want. With the power fed that way, you're losing efficiency in the long-range band."

"Yes, I know," Zelenka said, "but it meant —"

He stopped abruptly, but Rodney could fill in the rest. It meant that he didn't know how the sensors were routed, meant he couldn't control them even if he had managed to gain access to Atlantis's systems, and it meant that anyone left in Death's fleet who knew what he'd done would have the same problems.

"Yes, right. But right now it means you're not actually reaching the scanners' full range." Rodney frowned at the screen again, considering the new parameters. There wasn't any way to boost the power, not without rerouting everything, and that would take — well, hours, and presumably Woolsey and O'Neill wanted an answer sooner than that. All right, that was the obvious solution. What was less obvious, and more effective? A Wraith fleet was hiveships and —

"Wait," he said. "Just give me a minute here." Zelenka was looking dubious, but Rodney plowed on, his fingers busy on the keys. Just a little adjustment there, the search frequencies narrowed to one low band — yes, the available power would reach maybe even a little further than the sensors' original limits. "Yes. There."

Zelenka peered over his shoulder. "And this is searching for what, specifically?"

"Hiveships." Rodney took a last look at the settings, and hit the button that made it live. "See, hiveships tend to give off a low-frequency electronic field, not in a range that's particularly useful for anything, but it's a lot harder to get rid of than it is to just live with it, so if we concentrate on just looking for that…"

His voice trailed off as the results appeared on the screen, dull purple spots against the black. Two, three — four large spots, and half a dozen smaller purple flecks: four hives and at least six large cruisers. A fleet, definitely, and — his hands danced over the keys. Yes, the signal was increasing, slowly but steadily. Queen Death's fleet was on its way to Atlantis. "Crap."

Zelenka said something much stronger in Czech. "We must inform Mr. Woolsey right away."

"Yeah." Rodney stared at the screen. He knew those ships, knew how strong they were — knew just how determined Queen Death was, her and her zenana. *Daedalus* was still on Earth, the *Hammond* was still undergoing repairs — even if the Genii threw in their Ancient warship, there was no way they'd learned how to fly it in — what? — a couple of months. And an alliance with Guide was only good as long as it benefited Guide… "We are so screwed," he said, and only then realized he'd spoken aloud.

Woolsey paused in the corridor, put his hand to the radio at his ear, ignoring the Marines who waited outside the doors of both conference rooms. "Dr. Keller."

There was a moment of silence, long enough that he was already reaching to switch channels, and then Jennifer answered. "Mr. Woolsey?"

She sounded wary, Woolsey thought, and well she might. "I need five minutes of your time, Dr. Keller — perhaps ten — and it's urgent. Right away, if possible."

"I — yes. Yes, if it's really urgent, sure, I can make time." She paused. "Do you want Dr. Beckett as well?"

"Yes," Woolsey said. "I'll be down right away."

It didn't take long to reach the infirmary. For a wonder, it

wasn't very busy, just a technician working on one of the diagnostic machines, and a Marine corporal having her ankle brace
replaced. Both Keller and Beckett were waiting, and Keller waved
a hand toward her office.

"Is that okay—?"

"Fine, thank you," Woolsey said. He let her take her place behind
her desk, for all that every nerve screamed for him to blurt out his
questions, waited until Beckett had found a place to perch as well.
"Dr. Keller, Dr. Beckett, I need your assessment of Genii medical
technology."

Jennifer blinked, started to say something, but Woolsey ignored
her, laid out Radim's proposal as baldly as it had been made.

"So my question is, can Radim's people actually use our gene
therapy to insert an artificial ATA gene?"

Beckett pursed his lips, tilting his head to one side. "Aye, that's
a question."

"I don't—I wouldn't think they could," Jennifer said, frowning.
"I mean, nothing we've seen so far is that advanced. But I'm pretty
sure we haven't seen everything."

"That's for certain," Beckett said. "They couldn't do it three
years ago, or they wouldn't have taken Lorne prisoner. And what
we saw then—I'm not at all sure they were as advanced as Hoff..."

"I think they were at least that far along," Jennifer said.

"The Hoffans concentrated everything, all their development,
on their drug," Beckett said. "They were well in advance, I believe.
At least in that regard."

"All right, but that only puts them—well, I don't think they have
anything more advanced than we had in the 1950s. Maybe the early
1960s." Jennifer shook her head. "I'm not sure they'd even be able to
isolate DNA, much less create their own version of the ATA gene."

"They'll have stolen the technology for that from us," Beckett
said. "And they know what they want to do."

"But do they have the technology?" Jennifer asked.

"Doctors," Woolsey said. "I need an answer." It was suddenly
important that they understand, and he kept on, laying the words
out like counters in a game. "We can't let the Genii get full access
to Ancient technology. With that—I don't believe Ladon Radim

has any compunction about trying to become the dominant power in the Pegasus Galaxy and, with Ancient technology, I believe they can do it. On the other hand, we cannot stand against Queen Death without the *Pride of the Genii*. And Mr. Radim has made his position clear: unless we give him the gene therapy, their ship stays safely grounded."

Beckett shook his head slowly. "I don't believe they can do it, Mr. Woolsey. They just don't have the technology. Not to create a working ATA gene."

"But they believe it can be done," Jennifer said. "And the Genii — they're not stupid. In fact, they're pretty sophisticated, and they're desperate. They may not have the equipment now, and I'll even grant they probably can't make a working version of the gene even if we give them the therapy. But that just means they'll steal it. They've already tried it once."

"Eventually, yes, they'll get hold of the gene," Beckett began, and Zelenka's voice crackled in Woolsey's ear.

"Mr. Woolsey. You're needed in the control room right away."

Woolsey put his hand to the earpiece. "I'm in the middle of something, Dr. Zelenka —"

"It's urgent," Zelenka said. "We've sighted the Wraith fleet."

Only long training kept Woolsey from swearing, and he felt his face freeze into his most unrevealing mask. "I see."

"They are perhaps thirty, thirty-two hours away." Zelenka's accent was thicker than Woolsey could remember, the first indication of nerves he'd seen in the man. "And there is no mistaking their course. There are four hives, plus cruisers, and they are coming here."

Woolsey made himself take a breath, denying the fear that coiled at the base of his spine. This had been coming since they'd first encountered Queen Death, and there was no use wishing for a better time because there never would be one. "Dr. Keller, Dr. Beckett. I'd like the two of you to put your heads together and give me an answer to my question. Within the hour, if possible."

"But —"

He ignored Jennifer's automatic protest. "You will also need to begin preparing for a Wraith attack on Atlantis. Queen Death's fleet is on its way."

Jennifer said nothing, stricken to silence, and Beckett nodded, his expression grim. "We'll do that," he said, and Jennifer shook herself. "Yes. We'll be ready."

"I never doubted it," Woolsey said, and turned away.

## CHAPTER FIVE
# Compromises

"SO I EXPECT you'll want to start moving your fleet into position," Jack said.

"Yes," Guide said, pacing behind the chair where Alabaster sat. "As soon as we see that you have destroyed Hyperion's weapon."

"That could take a little time."

Guide showed his teeth. "How long would you like us all to wait?"

Jack thumbed on his radio headset. "Carter, are you almost ready to drop that weapon into the sun?"

"We've hit a snag, sir," Sam said over the radio.

"We don't have time to hit a snag. Figure it out and let's get this done."

"For that we would need the weapon, and right now we can't find it."

Jack looked at Guide and Alabaster. "Excuse me just one moment." Alabaster tilted her head to one side in a gesture that might have meant permission to leave. Jack stepped out into the hall, ignoring the questioning look from the Marine guard.

"What do you mean, you lost it?"

"I didn't lose it," Sam said firmly. "*I* never had it. Sheppard hid it for safekeeping, and when he went back to get it, he discovered it was gone. Someone stole it and tampered with the security footage to cover their tracks. We're combing the city for it now."

"Queen Death's fleet will be here in thirty-six hours," Jack said. "I need this thing destroyed about ten minutes ago."

"We're working on it," Sam said. "You're going to have to stall the Wraith until we find it."

"Stalling them isn't the problem," Jack said. "Getting their fleet moving is the problem."

"I don't know, be diplomatic. As soon as we find the thing, we'll take it out and dump it. The Wraith can ride along if they want to watch. But I can't destroy it when I don't know where it is."

"So find out where it is."

"Yes, sir."

Jack stepped back into the conference room. "We've hit a little snag," he said.

"Of course you have," Guide said. "As time is growing short, perhaps you should turn the weapon over to us. I expect we can think of some solution to your insoluble problem."

"Have you considered dropping it into the sun?" Alabaster said.

"I'm afraid I can't do that."

"Because you have no intention of destroying the weapon at all," Guide snapped.

"No, because it's missing," Jack said flatly. "You wouldn't know anything about that, would you?"

Guide and Alabaster exchanged a brief glance. "Why would we want to prevent this grotesque weapon from being destroyed?"

"You wouldn't," Jack said. "Unless you were looking for an excuse to back out of our deal."

"You are the one who is trying to deceive us," Guide said. He circled the conference table, teeth bared in a snarl. Jack stood his ground. Guide stopped a few paces away from him, flexing one hand as if considering how Jack would taste. "A dangerous gamble."

"I try not to gamble," Jack said. "I prefer to bet on sure things. Like the fact that Carter is going to destroy that weapon just as soon as we get it back in our hands."

"Not good enough," Guide said, raising his hand, claws outstretched toward Jack's chest. He had to force himself not to move. The worst thing you could do when you were trying to stare down a predator was to run.

Alabaster made a tsking noise. "I don't think eating him will help matters."

Guide didn't look as certain of that, but he did back off, his eyes still on Jack's face. He bowed to Alabaster in what looked to Jack like a slightly overdone show of obedience, turning up his palms and then deliberately lowering his hands to his sides.

"You know, we have this game on Earth," Jack said. "We call it 'good cop, bad cop.'"

Alabaster tilted her head to one side. "What is a *cop*?"

"We waste time," Guide snapped. "We must return to our fleet. With or without an alliance. Decide which you would prefer."

"I'd prefer with," Jack said. "We'll find the weapon." He nodded blandly to both Wraith and stepped back out into the hallway, try- ing not to feel like he was retreating under fire. "Carter?"

"Yes, sir?"

"Tell me you can find this weapon."

"We're doing our best," she said. "I've got Zelenka going over the altered security footage to see if there's any way of retrieving the original data."

"I am beginning to doubt it," Zelenka said as he came onto the radio. "Whoever did this was very good."

"And who do we think that is?"

"A good question," Zelenka said. "I suspect someone with legit- imate access to the security system. And very good at covering their tracks."

"And they would have to have known about Hyperion's weapon," Sam said. "I hate to say it, but…"

"You do not think…" Zelenka said.

"What?" Jack demanded.

"Well, sir," Sam said, "it's beginning to look like it must have been McKay."

"Then it's time we had a little talk with McKay," Jack said. "Tell Sheppard to find McKay and put him under arrest."

"Finally," Rodney snapped as John and Woolsey came in from the corridor outside the detention area. "Will you get me out of this ridiculous cell?"

"I'm afraid we can't do that until you answer some questions," Woolsey said.

Rodney threw up his hands. "How many more questions do you want me to answer? I've been debriefed a million times since I got back to Atlantis. Yesterday, you were fine with my going on mis- sions. Today, you're locking me up. How does that even make sense?"

"Hyperion's weapon is missing," John said. "We know you took it."

"Oh, is that all?" Rodney felt a rush of mingled guilt and relief, swiftly turning to indignation. "You could have just asked me. It's perfectly safe."

"What happened to it?"

"I moved it," Rodney said.

Woolsey frowned. "You don't deny you're responsible?"

"Why would I deny that? I mean, yes, I know technically I should have told you, but as the head of the Sciences department, it is my responsibility. And since Sheppard here was thinking about where he put it so loudly that the Wraith would have to have their hands over their ears not to hear him —"

"Were you in my head?" John said, with a look of distaste.

"Oh, like it's the first time you've had a Wraith poking around in there."

"You're not a Wraith. And I thought the Gift didn't work on humans."

"Teyla's Gift doesn't. But I wasn't a human with some Wraith DNA, I was actually a Wraith, and some parts of my brain are apparently still Wraith-shaped. And when someone is standing there very loudly thinking 'I really hope none of the Wraith can figure out my secret hiding place, because *that* would really suck'..."

"You read my mind."

"It's not like I did it on purpose."

"And that explains why you stole the weapon?" Woolsey asked.

"I didn't steal it, I moved it," Rodney insisted. "It seemed to me that it would be safer in a secure location that Sheppard didn't know about."

John scowled at him. "And what if they read *your* mind?"

"Well, we can't very well put it somewhere that none of us knows about, unless you're planning for us all to get that amnesia virus again."

"We've all had that already," John said.

"I haven't," Woolsey said, looking a bit worried.

John looked at him sideways. "Lucky you."

"I can keep the..." Rodney stumbled on his next words, with an abrupt and confusing sense of seeing the world through two competing perspectives. '*The other Wraith*', Quicksilver would have said, but Quicksilver had never really existed. "I can keep the Wraith from hearing what I'm thinking."

"Are you sure?" John asked.

"Pretty sure?"

"How sure?"

"Pretty sure! Which is better than any of the rest of us can say, except maybe Teyla."

"You could have given it to Teyla."

"So could you, Mr. Lone Cowboy."

"Let me get this straight," Woolsey broke in. He put his fingers to his temple as if he were getting a headache. "You found the device by extracting the location of its hiding place from his mind using Wraith telepathy."

"We have got to have regulations against doing that," John said.

"We'll come back to that," Woolsey said. "You took the device from its hiding place and moved it to another location. Did you at any time communicate that location to any of the Wraith?"

"No," Rodney said, staring at him. "Why would I do that?"

"If you were compromised, McKay," John said, as if he were a slow student. "Are you sure they didn't make you take it?"

"Of course they didn't make me take it," Rodney said. "I took it because I don't trust the United States military with genocide-in-a-box."

"We work for the United States military," John said.

"You work for the United States military," Rodney said. "I work for the IOA. Has anyone asked them what we ought to do with the device?"

"Does that sound like a remotely good idea to you?" John demanded.

"All right, no," Rodney admitted. "I don't trust them with this. I don't trust us with this. I'm not sure I'd trust anybody with this." He drew himself up to his full height. "I think it ought to be destroyed."

"Which is what we are currently planning to do," Woolsey said. Rodney blinked at him. "We are?"

"O'Neill decided that last night," John said. "Carter and I went to get the device to destroy it, only, hey, it's gone. As you can imagine, Todd and Alabaster are pretty pissed off with us, or at least that's what they tell us. So if you're not brainwashed, where's the goddamn weapon?"

Rodney hesitated. He hated to lose the security of his private retreat. Of course, there were other unused tower rooms, but he'd always liked the view there. "I could go get it," he said.

"Not a chance," John said. His hand rested pointedly on his stunner.

"What, like stunning me is going to make me tell you where it is? Which I'm about to do," he said, to cut off any further accusations. "North pier, tower 11, the west side of the top floor. The password is 23181401012218. It's on a box under the desk."

John tapped his radio. "Carter, this is Sheppard," he said. "McKay says he moved it to keep it safe." He sounded extremely dubious, but repeated the details Rodney had given him. "She's going to go see if it's there."

"I should go up there too," Rodney said. "This is a delicate piece of machinery we barely know anything about, and no offense to Colonel Carter, but—"

"She'll be fine," John said. "And you're not going anywhere."

"You've got to be kidding," Rodney said indignantly. "Queen Death's fleet is on its way. Every second I spend in here is time I'm wasting not preparing the city for a major Wraith attack."

Woolsey cleared his throat. "Under the circumstances, Dr. McKay, you'll understand why I think it's better if you don't help."

"So, what, you're just going to keep me in here?"

"Just sit tight, McKay," John said. "As soon as this is over—"

"Once this is over, what? I mean, assuming that we're not all eaten by the Wraith. Is there any way that I can ever actually prove that I haven't been compromised? Because I can't even begin to do my job if you don't trust me. I need to be back on regular duty, and I need full access to the computer system back."

"Which is exactly what you'd be saying if you had been compromised," Woolsey said.

"And exactly what I'd be saying if I hadn't been compromised, so that doesn't tell you anything. It's like the man who always lies and the one who always tells the truth."

John frowned. "What are you talking about, McKay?"

"You know, the logic problem. Where there's one man who always lies, and one who always tells the truth, and if you ask them if they're lying, they're both always going to say no."

"Have you been compromised by the Wraith?" John asked, but Rodney could hear the black humor in his voice.

"No," Rodney said, with the same bleak smile.

John shrugged. "Good enough for me."

"Does that mean I can go now? I still need to help Sam figure out how to actually destroy this thing."

"She says she's going to drop it into a sun."

"Oh, yes, that's elegant."

"We're not going for elegant, here, McKay, just gone. And you're not going anywhere until we hear from Carter."

"Fine," Rodney said, and crossed his arms. "We'll just wait."

After a few very tense minutes, John looked up, his hand on his radio earpiece. "What do you mean?" He listened again for a moment, his whole body tense. "No, I copy that."

"What's going on?" Rodney demanded.

"You tell me," John said in a dangerous tone. "Carter found your secret clubhouse. The weapon isn't there."

"That's where I left it," Rodney said. "Someone must have found it." John and Woolsey exchanged looks. "You have to believe me."

"Believe me, I wish we could," Woolsey said.

"But we can't," John said flatly. "Not unless we can get someone to tell us what's really going on in your head."

Woolsey looked skeptical. "I know Alabaster has the ability to read human minds, but I don't see how we could possibly trust her."

"I'm not talking about Alabaster," John said. "I'm talking about Teyla."

Another break from another interminable meeting, this time ostensibly for lunch, though Teyla doubted anyone would actually eat. Certainly the Wraith would not, and she had no appetite, too tense from four hours at the conference table. Instead, Teyla walked out on the balcony. She would stand for a moment in the wind and sun and hope to find balance.

The bright sun caught the white caps of the waves breaking against the piers below, glittered off windows scrubbed by rain.

The wind was cold, but she could feel the warmth of the sun on her skin, turning her face toward it like a dayflower.

The door opened again behind her and she knew without turning that it was Alabaster, and knew just as clearly that two Marines stood behind just inside the door, technically guarding the door, not the young queen. The thought lay on the surface of Alabaster's mind, a sardonic aside — as though what? She might suddenly leap from a forty story building? Why?

*It is their job to guard,* Teyla said, mind to mind. *You would not rebuke any blade for doing his duty.*

*To guard you?*

*I do not need guarding,* Teyla said, but there was no heat in it. Alabaster knew it well enough.

Instead she rested her elbows on the railing, looking out over city and sea. Her red hair caught the sun brighter than any hue natural to humans, and she stretched out her hands, palms downwards, as though the warmth felt good to her too. For a long moment she stood thus, watching the shadows of clouds on the sea and across the City of the Ancients.

*It is beautiful,* Alabaster said contemplatively. *I have never seen anything like it, and Osprey had no memories of Atlantis.*

*No,* Teyla agreed. *Osprey was never in Atlantis.* The only memories of the City of the Ancients were her own — her own life, her own path, her own choices — not those of a woman dead ten thousand years.

*It is beautiful,* Alabaster said again. *One of many beautiful things they wrought. So much that was wrong, and yet so many things that are beautiful.* She turned to Teyla, her hands at her sides and she smiled in a way that no doubt disconcerted the Marines just within. *And can you say that we are not beautiful, you and I?*

Odd and strange, yes, but beautiful still, the turnings of the hive, the light on the towers of Atlantis. *All of the daughters of the Ancients are beautiful,* Teyla said, and a strange peace opened in her heart. *All of the daughters, whether the daughters of Amytas in Pegasus, or the daughters of the women of Earth, or Osprey and her kind. We are all the heirs of the Ancients.* Towers reflected sun and sea or each other, dazzling brightness. *This belongs to all of us. We are all their children.*

*Yes,* Alabaster said. She looked away, toward the sea again, and her face seemed very young, a girl of eighteen or so, which perhaps she was in Wraith years, a woman young for her service. *I do not believe you would use this weapon. I do not think it is in your heart to do so. But that is not true of everyone here, and you know it.*

*I do,* Teyla said. *But we will prevail. I have known all these people for years, and I put my trust in Mr. Woolsey and General O'Neill.*

*Then why is it not done?*

*I do not know,* Teyla said. *But it shall be. I give you my word.*

Alabaster's eyes searched her face, as though looking for some sign there which it would be improper to seek mind to mind. *And then what? Once we have defeated Queen Death, then what will we do? Shall I try to kill you, or you me?*

*I hope that the retrovirus Dr. Keller and Guide have made will give us another option,* Teyla said.

*My men are eager to try it,* Alabaster agreed. *Each of them has pledged already to give of their lives to save others who are gravely injured or ill, a heroes' pledge among their people, just as they pledge to give their lives as warriors or rescuers for those lost at sea. It is an honor among them. Do you understand this?*

*Yes,* Teyla said.

*If they must die for others they shall, or be gravely injured or lose years of their lives. They know this. But if it is possible to save others and not die, it is better. If they may save others without the sacrifice of their lives or health, they would prefer it. Are not your people the same?*

*Yes,* Teyla said again, and an ache stirred in her. *It would be better if they did not have to die, even though they are pledged to the sacrifice.*

*That is what I think too,* Alabaster said. *Life must come from somewhere. We must eat if we aren't to starve. But if we could feed without causing death, and if those who have promised to pay the price did not have to pay with their lives, but only with pain that lasts a few days, perhaps...*

*...perhaps in time there might be peace,* Teyla said. *I do not know if this can be. But I know what lies in the other direction.*

The pictures were there in her mind, the ruined city of Emege, the drawings of the Athosians on the walls of their refuge, Osprey burning with the pain of starvation.

*So do I,* Alabaster said.

Teyla's radio clicked. "Teyla?" John's voice was sharp. "I need you in the brig now."

"What has happened?" she asked, putting her hand to the headset.

"I'll tell you when you get down here."

Alabaster did not seem alarmed. "I shall wait for your Mr. Woolsey to open the session again. It seems your Consort needs you greatly."

"It seems so," Teyla said. She opened the channel again. "I am on my way," she said.

## CHAPTER SIX
# Mind to Mind

JOHN was waiting for her just outside, four Marines on guard at the entrance to the brig, two looking outward and two inward. Through the door she could see Rodney pacing the cell, an expression of intense irritation on his face.

"Why is Rodney in the brig?" she demanded.

John looked harried. "Rodney stole Hyperion's weapon," he said shortly. "He said he wanted to keep it safe. He says he told us where he put it, but when we looked it wasn't there. So either somebody found it and stole it, or…"

"Or Rodney is lying," Teyla said. "And he is Queen Death's agent." It was clear in an instant how that might be. And why.

John nodded grimly. "I need you to find out which it is. Can you get in his head?"

"Yes." She looked past him at Rodney, who had stopped pacing and was watching them. "I can take that from his mind. I do not think he will be able to resist me." No blade or cleverman could. Not even when what she ordered was for them to fall on their own knife, though John had not seen that, only Guide. She didn't know what he would think of that. Probably that it was necessary.

"I'm sorry to ask you to do this," John said. In the chaos this morning he hadn't shaved, and the stubble on his jaw made him look older somehow.

"You do not need to apologize," she said, and lifting her chin went in. "Turn off the force field."

Rodney put his hands in his pockets as the door slid open, bars parting as she stepped through. "What, you're going to interrogate me now?"

"Yes," Teyla said. She stopped a few feet from him, aware that if he were Death's agent this would be the point of no return, the moment at which the deception would be done and he would have nothing to lose. "Rodney, we must know if you are telling the truth or not. If you are, you have nothing to fear. And if you are not…"

He gave her a lopsided smile that was very Rodney. "If I'm not, then you're going to kill me?"

"If you are not, you will remain in custody until this is over," Teyla said firmly. "And then we will find a way to return you fully to yourself." She took a step closer, aware of John just behind her, of the way his hand moved involuntarily to his pistol. Would he shoot Rodney if he resisted? He should not have to.

She raised her right hand, the palm crossed with the healing scar from the handmouth, the gesture of a Wraith queen who expected obedience, and she bent her will to him. *Rodney,* she said with her mind voice, *there is no choice. You will do as I ask.*

She saw the set of his shoulders change, his expression relax infinitesimally. There was enough of Quicksilver in him still. He could not resist a queen, not face to face and mind to mind. And in that case how much more of Quicksilver remained, Queen Death's cleverman? Teyla took another step forward, her hand rising toward his cheek. He shivered as she touched him, her palm flat against his face, the scar of the handmouth against his skin.

*Rodney,* she said. "Open your mind to me.*

Fear. The surface of his mind was riddled with fear. What if he were turned? What if he had stolen the device because of some deeply hidden order? What if he were truly not to be trusted, broken in ways beneath the surface that even he didn't know about? That was the thing that terrified him most — the memory of those days when he had acted as Quicksilver, serving the Wraith, attacking Atlantis —

*Radek, lying crumpled on the floor of the ZPM room, a Wraith bending over to feed…*

He had not known him, had nearly let Ember kill his friend.

*But you did not,* Teyla said. *Enough of you remained.*

*Jennifer, her face changing in pain and terror as he drew life from her, her fear and anguish a spur to his hunger, life flowing into him sweet and bright even as her muscles clenched in pain…*

She had felt it before, through Guide as he fed, the same dark wonder but tempered by control. Rodney had fed starving, in desperation, while Guide had sipped as a man will at an unfamiliar drink he is offered in a strange village, staving off intoxication with will.

*You could not help it,* she said. *A starving man will eat, no matter what the cost.*

And that was memory again, hers rather than his, Osprey's memory long buried within her, and she lifted it up like a gem from a case to give to him, the horror of those first days when they fled world to world, the first Wraith pursued by all. They had learned to feed because they must. Those who did not, those who would not, died.

*It is that simple,* Teyla said. *You are too strong to die, Rodney. So you do what you must.*

She felt his assent, as though she had given him some blessing, a thing that had never been hers to give.

*Show me,* she said. *Show me who you serve.*

Death was there, yes, but it was skin deep, an allegiance shed with the scraps of the drugs they had given him, as illusory as their control of Michael. And beyond that, no one. At the heart, at the core, there was no one in that place where true allegiance lies, no parent or friend, no lover, no child. No Jennifer. In the end, Rodney followed his own heart. He had taken the weapon because he thought it best, because he thought he was most able to guard it, most qualified to decide its fate. And beyond that he truly did not know its fate.

Relief, his and hers, washed over Teyla. He truly did not know. And he did not belong to Death.

She opened her eyes. "Rodney is telling the truth," she said. Teyla dropped her hand, turning to John, certainty in her voice. "He does not obey Queen Death, and he has no idea where Hyperion's weapon is."

John nodded gravely. "Ok. That's what we needed to know."

"I thought you needed to know where the weapon was," Rodney said sharply. "Which I told you I didn't know."

"That too," John said. "But at least now we've got one possibility off the table."

"So I can go?" Rodney asked.

John shook his head. "As soon as Mr. Woolsey says it's okay."

"Oh come on!" Rodney exclaimed. "I'm not Queen Death's secret agent. Teyla says so. Let me out of here!"

"As soon as Woolsey says it's okay," John stepped back, letting Teyla proceed him out of the cell. "Just hang in there a few more minutes, Rodney."

The door closed behind them, and she walked ahead of him out of the brig and around the corner before he stopped, dropping his voice. "You're sure?"

"I am sure he does not know where the weapon is," Teyla said. "And I do not think he consciously obeys Queen Death."

"Consciously?"

"Yes," she said. "He does not know of any loyalty or allegiance to her."

"But?" John met her eyes directly.

Teyla shook her head. "I cannot say whether there is something at work that even Rodney is not aware of. I do not know enough about what is possible, John! Rodney knows of no such imperative, and as far as he is aware he is in control of himself and his actions. But I cannot promise that there is no hidden imperative left below the surface."

"Okay." He nodded. "Then it's better if Rodney just stays where he is until we deal with this. If we're all still here tomorrow, then we can sort Rodney out."

"I think that is best," Teyla said.

*Proud Journey's* clevermen had done their best and more, but Farseer's hive was not yet ready to stand the stress of combat. Ember examined the temporary lattice of steel and skin that spanned the gap in the hull, glowing at the edge of sight with the forcefields that braced the repair and encouraged healing. Blackiron, Farseer's Master of Sciences Biological, gave him a wary look.

*We've done all we can for now,* he said.

Ember nodded his agreement, feeling the other's relief wash through him. *I am amazed you have coaxed it as far as you have. But, no, you cannot fight. I will tell the Commander so.*

*We will do whatever we can in support,* Blackiron said. *Our cells are full, and we have worshippers as well who would be glad to serve in any way — from Tenassa, remember, trained and willing.*

Tenassa was one of the few depot worlds, supposedly neutral and served by tame humans taught to serve the Wraith, and Queen Death had destroyed it, breaking the covenants of generations. Ember's lips curled back at the thought. It would be another century before they could repair the damage, and hive and cruiser alike would suffer for it. He realized that Blackiron was watching him uneasily, and made himself relax.

*We are grateful for the offer. My thought was to leave them here in safety until after we have faced Queen Death's fleet. We will need their skills then, their hands alongside ours — if you have supplies enough to maintain them.*

*They brought foodstuffs aboard,* Blackiron said. *Their Lady is managing it.*

*She's competent?*

*Entirely.*

Ember nodded. *Then that is what I will recommend to Guide on his return.*

Blackiron paused. *He has not returned?*

*No.* Ember made his tone deliberately discouraging. Exactly what Guide was doing on Atlantis, what bargain he would make in the Queen's name to gain allies against Queen Death — that was a matter for commanders and blades to deal with, not clevermen. And especially not clevermen of Farseer's hive, Farseer who had been Death's loyal ally until very recently.

Blackiron hesitated again, his thoughts close-held, unreadable. Ember watched him, a thread of fear winding through him.

*What is it?*

*Nothing, I think.* Blackiron's tone was less certain even than the wavering words, and Ember frowned.

*Even so, if it disturbs you — a burden shared is a burden eased.*

*So they say.* Blackiron turned abruptly. *I will show you something, but — I'll deny it came from me.*

Ember suppressed a shudder. *I'll follow.*

Blackiron waved his hand at the door controls, and the lattice slid back. Ember followed him down the healing corridors, out of their soft light into the normal paths of the ship. Corridors and compartments alike were crowded, and here and there a human moved freely among the Wraith, each badged with the mark of Tenassa's storeyards. They came at last to a smaller laboratory, set off from the main sections of the ship, the sort of space the masters of sciences tended to claim for themselves. Certainly Ember had his own space on *Just Fortune*, workspace and sleeping niche and hiding place all in one. Blackiron let the door close behind them both, and the lights brightened and warmed around them, puffs of mist rising from the floor. There were two workstations against the far bulkhead, but the majority of space was given over to pleasant-looking seats and an elaborately inlaid game table stood at the center of their rough circle. Ember gave the nearest chair a regretful glance — they were the comfortable sort that let you curl into their padding as though you were held in a giant hand — but followed Blackiron to the nearest console. Blackiron touched controls, not bothering to hide his access codes: a cheap gesture of good faith, since those codes could and would be changed, but worth noting.

The central screen lit, a familiar image coalescing: *Just Fortune*, hanging still against the starscape, the curve of the planet the fleet orbited a thread of blue at the bottom of the screen. Ember cocked his head to one side, waiting, and Blackiron adjusted the controls, moving the image into another part of the electromagnetic spectrum.

*I wished a comparison,* Blackiron said. *A healthy hive, one similar in age to *Proud Journey*, that had suffered damage, but was healed. Steelflower's hive seemed an obvious choice.*

Ember nodded. It was reasonable enough, though some commanders were more wary of such analysis than others. *And?*

*There is this.* Blackiron touched the controls again, calling up a cascade of data. Ember frowned as the data whirled to form a schematic, thin lines of gold tracing communications patterns over *Just Fortune*'s skin. Familiar, normal — and then not, a brighter node where none should have been. It brightened, flared white, and then was gone.

*Were you able to capture it?* he asked, and Blackiron shook his head.

*It was very narrowly directional, and, as you saw, short. It was luck I saw it at all. I assumed it was a communication with the Commander.*

Ember glanced at the automatic timestamp, and his mouth tightened. No, not Guide, not unless there had been a message to which he himself was not privy — and in any case it had been an outgoing transmission. Possibly it was Bonewhite replying to some message, but he doubted it. He studied the schematic, fixing the particular node in memory: the seventh dorsal node, linked to *Just Fortune*'s communications web in ways that would make the transmission almost impossible to trace.

*I don't know what that was,* he said quietly. *But I'm grateful that you told me.*

Blackiron bowed, accepting the acknowledgement of debt between them.

*Keep this evidence safe for the Commander,* Ember said. *And I —* Will what? If this wasn't Bonewhite, wasn't the Commander, it was evidence of a possible spy on board. And if there was one spy, how was he to know who could be trusted? *I will deal with it,* he said, firmly, and hoped he could make it true.

Richard Woolsey let the door of his office close behind him, cutting off the murmur and hurry of the gateroom. He'd been meeting with Ladon Radim off and on since that morning, and he was beginning to feel the need for a moment's quiet thought. Radim was still politely adamant that he would not send for the *Pride of the Genii* without a sample of the ATA gene therapy, and now Hyperion's weapon was missing. The Wraith weren't happy about that, and Woolsey couldn't really blame them. If he were in Guide's place, he wouldn't believe them either.

But that was O'Neill's problem for the moment. Right now, he needed to get Radim off Atlantis and headed home to collect the *Pride of the Genii* before he heard anything about a missing weapon and figured out what that weapon did. In fact — Woolsey stopped abruptly. Surely it was impossible for the Genii to have had anything to do with the missing weapon. Radim himself had been in the conference room since he came through the Stargate, and the Marines had been watching his guards and the spy. Or at least they were supposed to have been. He glanced quickly at his watch, and touched his radio.

"Major Lorne."

"Sir?" Lorne's voice was wary, as well it might be.

"I need you to confirm for me that the rest of the Genii — Mr. Radim's escort and the messenger — have been under observation since they came through the gate."

"Yes, sir," Lorne said. "I'm still trying to coordinate the search of the city —"

"This needs to take priority," Woolsey said firmly, and could almost hear the snick of teeth as Lorne closed his mouth over further protest.

"Yes, sir," he said again. "I'll let you know as soon as possible."

"Thank you," Woolsey said. Unfortunately, it didn't entirely solve the problem. If the Genii had an agent in the city — it was admittedly unlikely, but couldn't entirely be ruled out — then someone could have gotten them the weapon, or be waiting to give it to them before they left. And that had to be prevented. He glanced again at the shelf of books he'd brought with him from Earth, the books that he had carried with him through hundreds of postings, stories of heroes to remind him that, while he himself was not a hero and never would be, nonetheless actions mattered. As did decisions. He needed Radim's cooperation, and he couldn't afford to let him get access to any Ancient technology, never mind Hyperion's weapon: how to arrange both?

The radio clicked, and he touched his earpiece. "Woolsey."

"Lorne here, sir. My men confirm that the Genii escort has been under direct observation the entire time they've been in the city. No one has seen anything out of the ordinary."

"Thank you, Major," Woolsey said, and Lorne cut the connection without further comment. Heading back to the search, Woolsey knew, but he would not feel guilty for distracting him. There was more to deal with here than just finding Hyperion's weapon.

He looked out into the control room again. If Radim and the Genii were somehow involved in the weapon's disappearance, they hadn't gotten it in hand yet. And that meant they probably weren't involved and had no idea the thing existed, and his job should be to get them out of Atlantis before they found out anything more. But he needed to be sure before they left that they weren't carrying the thing…

Naquadah. The weapon's casing was naquadah, and there was such a thing as a naquadah detector. The Genii party could be scanned in the gateroom before they went through — for that matter, they could be scanned now, in the conference room, and no one would be the wiser. He waved his hand at the door and walked back into the control room.

"Dr. Zelenka."

Zelenka looked up sharply, and came out from behind his console. "More troubles?"

"Not exactly." Woolsey tipped his head toward the redundant stations at the end of the row of consoles, empty now while the scientists concentrated on the sensor suite, and Zelenka followed, his frown deepening. "I need a word with you."

"And I am here."

"I need you to scan the Genii party for traces of naquadah," Woolsey said. "I understand the limitations on the process, but surely that room doesn't contain undue amounts? And I need to be certain that — however unlikely it seems — Ladon Radim has not gotten his hands on the missing item."

Zelenka pursed his lips. "Yes. Yes, I think I can do that. There is always naquadah, of course, that's been our problem, but I believe I can discount that, at least in that volume." He paused. "And before you ask, that is why we cannot find this object by scanning the city. If we knew where to look, that would be different, but not knowing —"

"I understand," Woolsey said, and Zelenka adjusted his glasses.

"Yes, sorry. Give me moment." He turned back to the bank of screens, said something quiet to one of the airmen, who promptly gave up his seat. Woolsey moved quietly to look over his shoulder, though the images that flashed across the screen were mostly unfamiliar. He recognized a tower schematic, and then something that seemed to be the plan of the conference rooms, but most of the code was in Ancient. The schematic reappeared, a green dot swelling until it seemed to fill an entire section or corridor. A chime sounded, and the light vanished.

"Well," Zelenka said, swinging away from the console. "That is your answer. There is no more than a normal trace of naquadah in those rooms."

"Thank you, Dr. Zelenka," Woolsey said, and took a deep breath. This was the hard part, the judgment call, and regardless of advice, the decision was his alone. "General O'Neill, it's Woolsey. I need a quick word with you. In person."

There was a moment of silence, and then O'Neill said, "We were just about to take a break — not for snacks. I'll meet you."

Woolsey straightened his jacket, not for the first time wishing for the armor of a proper suit and tie, and made his way toward the main conference room. O'Neill was there ahead of him, of course, leaning one shoulder against the wall, head cocked to one side as he listened to Major Lorne. He looked up alertly at Woolsey's approach, and Lorne broke off.

"Any news?" Woolsey asked.

Lorne shook his head. "Sorry, sir." He looked back to O'Neill. "If you'll excuse me, sir?"

"Actually," Woolsey said, "this is something that concerns you, Major. If you don't mind."

"That doesn't sound good," O'Neill said. Lorne looked as though he wanted to agree, but regulations kept him silent.

"We are very nearly at an impasse with Mr. Radim," Woolsey said, "as well as with the Wraith. And I believe we need to remove the Genii from Atlantis as quickly as possible for — well, reasons that I know you both understand. Mr. Radim is demanding a sample of the gene therapy that activates a recessive copy of the ATA gene before he will order the *Pride of the Genii* to join our fight. And, although the ATA gene seems to be vanishingly rare in the Pegasus Galaxy, it does exist. Also — Mr. Radim has obtained a sample of the ATA gene in the past, though we don't know if his technicians have been able to isolate it well enough to use in the gene therapy."

"He's bluffing," O'Neill said.

"Maybe," Woolsey said. "But we don't have the time to find out."

O'Neill grimaced. "You're not seriously proposing that we give them the therapy —"

"Neither Dr. Keller nor Dr. Beckett think the Genii will be able to rework our technique to allow them to insert an artificial ATA gene," Woolsey said. "Nor do they think the recessive is significantly more common than the expressed gene. I think it's more important to get them out of here and bringing a warship to our aid than to stonewall on this. I would like to offer them access to the therapy and a volunteer who could pilot the ship for them."

"That's a lot to ask," O'Neill said.

"I know." Woolsey met his gimlet stare squarely. "I don't believe we have another choice."

The silence stretched between them, and at last Lorne's cane scraped on the floor as he straightened further.

"General O'Neill. I volunteer, sir."

"That's not required, Major," O'Neill said. "I'm aware you have a history with the Genii —"

"Yes, sir." Lorne stood very straight. "But that's not going to matter at all if we can't get their ship to join us. And — I have flown an Ancient warship before. The *Orion*."

"All right," O'Neill said. "But you're not going alone. Pick a team, technicians, Marines in support, and I'll agree."

"Yes, sir," Lorne said again.

O'Neill glared at Woolsey. "And you can explain the situation to Mr. Radim."

"Yes," Woolsey said, his voice dry. "That would be my job."

## CHAPTER SEVEN
# Homeward Bound

THEY came through the gate into a cool and sunny afternoon, the sort of chill that Lorne associated with mid-spring or the middle of the autumn. The trees around the Stargate were tall and deep green, probably coniferous, unfamiliar and of no use in guessing the season. Not that it mattered, Lorne thought, but it would have been nice to know.

Radim had a heavy transport waiting, and they all climbed aboard, Cadman and her Marine contingent unobtrusively taking the controlling positions. Not that he really expected trouble, since he was fairly sure that the Genii weren't going to sacrifice the few scientists and military personnel who had trained to fly their warship, but it made him feel a little more secure. From the rigid lack of expression on Cadman's face, it made her feel better, too.

It took them just over an hour to reach the valley where the Ancient warship was waiting. It looked as though Radim's people had done a good job with the repairs, Lorne thought, surveying the solid mass of the hull. Yes, you could see where patches had been made, and probably the actual control elements were more jury-rigged than not, but at least it looked as though it would stand up to vacuum. He glanced at Dr. Campbell, and Campbell met his eyes with a smile and a tiny shrug. You didn't have to be a mind reader to know what that meant — we'll see once we get aboard — and Lorne concentrated on getting himself up the steep gangway to the ship's control room. His leg was better than it had been, but steep angles still caused the healing muscles to twinge painfully.

Radim's sister Dahlia was waiting in the control room, supervising a team of scientists who seemed to be activating the last of the ship's systems. She turned at their entrance, and Radim nodded a greeting.

"Dahlia. May I present Major Lorne, Captain Cadman, and Dr. Campbell? Mr. Woolsey has sent them to assist us with the *Pride of the Genii.*"

"A pleasure, Major," Dahlia said. She was taller than her brother, and fair-haired, with deep shadows under her eyes. "I do not believe we met before—"

She stopped then, color flooding her face, and Lorne fought to keep his face impassive. No, they most certainly hadn't met, because she'd been sent to Atlantis as a hostage when her brother had kidnapped Lorne and the rest of his team—but there was no point in mentioning that. "I don't think so, ma'am," he said, in his most neutral voice, and Dr. Campbell cleared her throat.

"With all respect, ma'am, gentlemen, we don't have much time here."

"No," Dahlia said, and sounded faintly relieved. "We do not."

"Major Lorne is the one with the Ancient gene," Radim said, and she nodded.

"Then I will leave you here to accustom yourself to the controls, and I will take Dr. Campbell to the engine room so she can see what we have had to do to make the repairs."

"Excellent," Campbell answered.

"Sergeant Garces," Cadman said. "Go with Dr. Campbell."

Lorne nodded. "Sergeant Garces is a technical specialist," he said, to Radim.

The Genii leader nodded in turn, though Lorne doubted he was believed. "And in the meantime—I believe Dahlia is right, it would be well if you were to familiarize yourself with the controls."

"Yes, sir," Lorne said, wooden-faced, and settled himself in the control chair. Someone had already initialized the systems—Sheppard, presumably, when he retrieved the ship for them in the first place—and only a couple of boards remained dark. Lorne frowned, and a Genii technician looked over his shoulder.

"Those systems were damaged beyond our ability to repair them," he said. "If we had more time, or more of the proper equipment—"

"But we don't," Radim said. His voice was brisk, but not hostile, and the technician spread his hands in silent acceptance.

"What do those systems do?" Lorne asked.

"One is the monitoring system for the cargo space," the technician answered. "It seems to be redundant — we can get the same information on the general interior scan. That one is the manual override for the environmental system."

That didn't sound good. Only long service with the SGC kept Lorne from saying that aloud. Besides, as Radim had already pointed out, there wasn't much they could do about it anyway. He nodded instead, and turned his attention to the controls.

He had had basic training on several different types of Ancient ship, and the *Avenger* — *Pride of the Genii*, he reminded himself, though the ship itself was slow to answer to its new name — fell into familiar categories. By the time Campbell returned, talking a mile a minute while Dahlia nodded, Lorne was confident he could handle her under battle conditions. He said as much to Radim, who nodded.

"I'm glad to hear it, Major. How soon can you be ready to launch?"

Lorne glanced at the boards. All the essential systems were either green or dead, and he shrugged slightly. "Whenever you're ready, Mr. Radim."

Radim looked at his sister. "If you'd clear the noncombatants off the ship —"

"Yes." Dahlia moved to a device hanging from the nearest bulkhead and began speaking into it, ordering the technical staff to finish any last minute work and clear the ship.

Lorne tuned her out, concentrating on the controls. *Avenger* was coming to life under his hands, systems waking, power beginning to flow. Everything seemed normal, and he was aware suddenly of the two Radims standing close behind his chair.

"You'll go with them," Radim said quietly.

"And will you?" Dahlia asked.

"I'm staying with the ship."

"That's folly."

"I have no choice," Radim said. "But there's no need for you to be here. I had in mind to leave you in charge if anything happens."

"If we lose this fight," Dahlia said, "it's unlikely the Genii state will survive. And if it did, they will not follow a woman. I'm more use to you here. But you don't have to be here. Chief Cowan —"

"I'm not Cowan," Radim said. "Or Kolya. Or any of the other leaders we've seen in our lifetimes. But none of them were afraid to fight. I have to be here. You know that."

"Yes," Dahlia said, after a moment. "Well, it's simpler that way."

"That, too," Radim said, and turned away.

Well, Lorne thought, and kept his eyes firmly fixed on the controls. That — wasn't entirely encouraging, really. But he'd known the score when he volunteered. "Mr. Radim?"

"Yes, Major?" The Genii leader stood ramrod straight, fighting for every inch of height.

"We're ready to lift."

"Ground reports all nonessential personnel are off the ship and accounted for," another technician reported, one hand to his heavy earpiece.

"Very well." Radim drew a deep breath. "Raise ship, Major Lorne."

"Yes, sir." Lorne rested his hands on the controls, feeling the ship respond to the touch, sensing the genetic makeup of the Ancients. He could feel the ship's presence at the back of his mind, as though a sleeper woke, and he urged it on, rewarding each new evidence of awareness with as much attention as he could give. The engines rumbled, a sound too deep to be heard, felt through the floorplates and deep in the marrow of his bones; he felt the inertial dampeners establish their fields before the boards lit, pressed both hands gently into the yielding control surface. The *Pride of the Genii* groaned deep in her core, and rose.

"We have launch," a technician reported, somewhere in the distance, and the screens with the live feed from the hull-mounted cameras darkened rapidly from blue to black.

Lorne felt the moment they reached orbit, velocity and mass settling into a pressure he could feel tingling in the palms of his hands, and he made himself focus enough to look at Radim. "We're in orbit, Mr. Radim."

"Thank you, Major," Radim said. "Take us to Atlantis."

*Atlantis.* The ship knew that name, secondary and tertiary systems coming to singing life. *Atlantis,* Lorne agreed, watching the grid form and reform around him, hyperspace calculations streaming past as though blown by wind. He could feel the ship's memory banks calling up images of the towers, matched them with his own memories, tropical sky and snow, but always the towers shining against the sea: Atlantis. Home. They leaped into the dark.

Guide paced the length of the conference room, careful still to keep more than an arm's length from any of the humans. There was nothing to be gained by baiting them, though he was beginning to think that there was also nothing to be gained by remaining here. He couldn't blame Carter's consort for trying to keep Hyperion's weapon — Guide could make the calculations himself, and could see just how O'Neill would think it was worth the risk, because none of them could stand alone against Queen Death. But neither could he leave his people still facing the risk of the weapon, no matter how reluctant the Lanteans might be to use it now. They were short-lived, and their children and grandchildren might well see the problem in a different light.

He glanced at Alabaster, now curiously examining one of the small cakes with pink tops that the Lanteans had brought several hours ago. She sniffed it, then took a wary taste, her nose wrinkling as though she were trying to decide if she actually liked it. He remembered that expression from her childhood, when she had been fond of the sweetest fruits, and for a moment the memory threatened to overwhelm him, the favorites of the zenana at ease in the chamber behind the formal gathering place, leaning against Snow's chair while she and the Hivemaster played at tables, while her two favorite clevermen vied to offer treats to Alabaster. She'd just been walking then, so small that she ricocheted from chair to knee and back, giggling and tugging at sleeves and skirts of coats until blade or cleverman lifted her. Spark had brought a stalk of *melos* from the world where they had last Culled, and Alabaster crowed with delight as she sucked on them, her thoughts filled with the honey-sweet taste of the fruit. Seeker had brought snap-rose, and she stuck the blossoms solemnly in his beard, where they nipped at his chin and drove Snow to snorting undignified laughter... Dead, all dead, except for himself and Alabaster, and Darling was older now than she had been then.

He closed his mind over that memory as though he closed his fist, looked up as the door slid back to admit O'Neill again. "General O'Neill. It is time that I spoke to my alliance."

"So it is." O'Neill contrived to look surprised. "I really hope you're ready to tell them to come join the party."

Guide smiled in spite of himself. "Sadly, this — party — is not yet ready to begin. Unless you bear good news?"

He saw with satisfaction that the shot had gone home. "No," O'Neill said shortly. "We don't have it yet."

Guide spread his hands. "Then you cannot expect us to join you. However, I will speak with my ships."

Properly speaking, it was not Ember's place to wait in the control room with the other lords of the council. Clevermen belonged in the bowels of the ship, in the laboratories and secret spaces, unless and until they were invited; this was for blades and commanders. Guide had never enforced that rule, and Bonewhite seemed disinclined to concern himself with it either, so Ember hovered by the environmental monitoring station, deeming it a plausible enough excuse should his presence draw comment. Guide was due to contact them, to confirm that they should continue to Atlantis, and Ember couldn't bear to wait for that news to filter through the ship, not after what Blackiron had shown him.

He kept his thoughts closed tight, his head bent over the perfectly ordinary readings. If Blackiron was right, someone among the men assembled here was a traitor, served Queen Death — he couldn't imagine it, except out of fear. And fear was reasonable enough, given everything she had done, but even if it was a hopeless cause, he could not bear to think of serving her. He remembered the feeling of her hand on his chest, the sting of her claws and the pain as she fed. If it had been Steelflower who demanded that service, that taste of his life, he would gladly have given it, and more than a taste... But that was not to the point: queens rarely admitted clevermen to more than momentary favor. But if they were to survive — if they defeated Death, well, he'd had as much of a hand in that as any blade, and she was extraordinary, wise beyond her years, and no stickler for convention.

He curbed that thought as well, shaking his head at his own folly. The old proverb whispered through his mind: first find your humans... First survive this war.

The main screen lit abruptly, and Bonewhite bared teeth as the cleverman on duty adjusted the system to receive the signal. Ember could feel the tension in the chamber, each one of the waiting blades eager to find out their fate. How soon would they reach Atlantis, how soon would they face Death? He let his gaze slide from one man to the next, trying to read their loyalty in the set of their shoulders, the way they held their hands and head, but he could see nothing more than the general wariness.

"Commander," Bonewhite said, and Guide's face appeared in the screen. Behind him was a fuzzy image of Atlantis's control room, a double handful of humans vague shapes in the background. Hairy stood at his shoulder, looking less than happy, and another gray-haired human stood behind him, frowning slightly, his eyes narrowed as though he looked into a bright light or a great distance. Ember had never seen him before, but didn't dare draw attention to himself by asking.

"Is all well?"

That was the prearranged signal, and Ember felt the tension ease a little. Guide was unharmed, and the Lanteans were negotiating: the rest was details.

"All is well," Bonewhite agreed. "We await your next orders."

"There will be a delay," Guide said.

Ember looked up sharply, felt his own surprise echoed around the control room.

"Hold the ships at your present position," Guide continued. "I will be in contact shortly with further orders."

"Very good, Commander," Bonewhite said. "Is there some — difficulty?"

Guide's smile showed too many teeth for true humor. "Let's say we've hit a sticking point. And if I were not confident in General O'Neill's — intentions — this deal would already be off."

"Understood," Bonewhite said, bowing.

"I will contact you again in three hours," Guide said. "If not sooner."

"Three—" Bonewhite broke off. "Very well, Commander."

"Until then," Guide said, and the screen went abruptly blank.

*Three hours!* That was Precision, the leader of the Darts. *Bonewhite, if we're not underway by then—we won't make Atlantis in time.*

*We're closer than that,* Hasten said, with some reluctance. Ember hadn't seen him there—another cleverman keeping out of sight until his word was needed. *We'll have to make our best speed, yes, but we can be there.*

*We should be there in good time to prepare,* Ease said. *And if the Lanteans go back on their word—well, there will be time to deal with them, and then with Queen Death.*

*Enough!* Bonewhite's mental voice was outraged, stunning them all into silence. *I put it to you, this is no place to discuss such matters. I will meet with any who wish to discuss the matter in one hour, and you may have your say. But for now—the Commander's word is clear.*

Ember bowed along with the others, and kept his head down as Bonewhite stalked from the control room. In an hour, he could ask for audience, and no one would think twice—no one would suspect that he knew something he shouldn't. But if Bonewhite didn't believe him—and Ember was well aware of how flimsy his evidence was—or, worse, if it were Bonewhite who was the traitor... Ember slipped from the control room, once again aware that he was a stranger here, without kin. He didn't know if he dared take the risk, or if he dared avoid it.

"I believe we have little else to discuss." Guide did not move from his place at the table, but his tone of voice was underlaid by his mental dismissal. Teyla frowned. In the last two days she'd begun to wonder if anyone would ever get out of this conference room for more than an hour at a time. Certainly they had discussed everything there was to say. The only thing that signified now was action—an action they couldn't take—the destruction of Hyperion's weapon.

"Surely," Mr. Woolsey began, but Guide cut him off.

"My fleet was warned of possible treachery before I came here," Guide said sharply. "I assure you that my commanders will not move without my order."

"Or Steelflower's," Teyla said quietly.

He rounded on her, coming to his feet. "The medical procedures to transform you take many hours. Hours which you do not have. And no one will follow your orders as you are now." He rested his hands on the table before him, looking at Woolsey. "I came here in good faith, and you assured me that you would destroy this weapon. Now you either cannot or will not. My fleet will not move until it is destroyed. Is that clear?"

What was clear to Teyla was that Mr. Woolsey had also exhausted everything he might say. He had delayed and delayed and delayed, but they did not have the weapon and there was nothing that would convince Guide of their good faith.

"We are leaving," Guide said with a quick glance to the side at Alabaster. "Unless of course we are your prisoners. In which case you should consider that our fleet will never move."

Teyla made herself stay very still. Too much moving and pacing was a sign of weakness in a queen. She had learned that well. "If your fleet does not move soon, it will not get here in time no matter what your intentions or ours are."

Alabaster put her head to the side as though this were no more than a matter of scientific interest. "We are prepared to move as soon as the weapon is destroyed. I do accept that you are unable to do so at this time, but you must see our position. What is to stop you from using it as soon as you find it? If we are not your prisoners, then we shall return to our fleet and you will contact us when the weapon is found."

Our fleet, Teyla thought. Oh yes. Steelflower has become superfluous. Alabaster is queen, and so she will be.

"And if we do that," Woolsey said, "what guarantee do we have that you will come at all?"

"None," Guide said sharply. "Just as we have no guarantee that you will not use the weapon."

The alliance was unraveling before her eyes, collapsing under the weight of history. In a moment too many things would be said.

"I have a counterproposal," Teyla said, her eyes on Alabaster. Guide might think he ruled, as he had these many years, but Alabaster was more amenable to compromise, and ultimately he must learn once again what it was to serve a queen. She was not a child, and he would not rule her. "Let Guide remain here and oversee the destruction of the weapon when we find it, while you and Darling return to the fleet and await his word." He would be hostage for his daughter's behavior, but she and the child would be free, which was no doubt what he wished most.

Woolsey frowned. "I suppose that's possible." He looked at her as though he wished for a moment that he had Wraith telepathy.

"I am to be the hostage," Guide said. "And who is to be the hostage that Alabaster bears away? Who will guarantee your part of the bargain?"

"I will," Teyla said evenly. "I will go with Alabaster if she wishes it, not as Steelflower but as Teyla Emmagan, hostage for Atlantis' word."

Woolsey's frown deepened. "I don't think we can allow one of our people to be a hostage."

Teyla fixed a smile on her face. "You may call me a liaison then. I shall be Atlantis' liaison to the Wraith."

She saw him consider, saw the possibilities cross his face, and Woolsey nodded. "Our ambassador."

"Just so," Teyla said. She looked at Alabaster. "If that is agreeable to you?"

"It is," Alabaster said serenely, and if Guide disagreed he did not publicly rebuke his queen.

## CHAPTER EIGHT
# Ultimatums

"THANK you for seeing me on such short notice," Jennifer Keller said.

"I had the hour free," Eva said. Her own part in the preparations for the imminent Wraith attack had consisted of lending a hand to move things people asked her to help move and trying not to get in people's way.

Jennifer shrugged, her mouth twisting. "I was guessing that Rodney's usual appointment time might be free, since he's still locked in a cell."

"Is that what you want to talk about?" Eva asked.

"I hardly know where to start," Jennifer said. "Last night Rodney and I broke up. I think. He asked me to marry him, and I said not right now, and he said then we shouldn't be dating seriously anymore. And this morning he took his cat and 'moved out,' only half of his stuff is still all over my quarters. And then this afternoon, I found out that he may still be under the control of the Wraith. I don't know what to think."

"Let's leave the question of any Wraith influence on this aside for a moment," Eva said. She was getting plenty of practice at saying things like that. "How did you feel when he said he was leaving?"

"Well, upset, obviously," Jennifer said. Eva waited. "And relieved," Jennifer said after a long pause. "And I know exactly how horrible that sounds."

"I think that's very understandable," Eva said. "You're under a lot of pressure at work, and at the same time you're trying to care for a partner who's been through a traumatic experience."

"And I'm not sure I want to get married. But I thought we could work things out. I wanted to work things out. I didn't expect him to just say, well, if you don't want to get married, I'm leaving. And now I don't even know whether he really means it, or whether he's just acting strangely because he's being controlled by the Wraith."

Eva sipped her cooling coffee and took a moment to think about her answer. She figured she'd have to add that one to her mental list of questions that most psychiatrists in private practice never got asked, right up there with "is there any point in talking about my childhood issues if I'm a clone of the person who actually had the childhood?"

"So what you're asking is whether being controlled by the Wraith would mean that he might change his mind?" she said finally.

"Something like that."

"Do you want him to change his mind?"

Jennifer let out a long breath. "I really don't know." She shook her head. "I love Rodney. I really do. But it seems like he wants to spend the rest of his life in Atlantis. And I don't... really think I like my job here." She looked guilty, but went on clear-eyed. "You know, when I got my medical degree, I wanted to do field-work. Disaster relief and public health. When I go to New Athos, or help people who've lost their homes to the Wraith, it feels like I'm doing what I always wanted to do. But that's maybe a few days out of every month. The rest of the time, I'm a general practitioner for a military base where we do a lot of questionably ethical things. And that's not something I ever wanted to do. It's not even something I like."

"You've done a lot of good work here," Eva said.

"I know. That's part of the problem. They need me here."

"Just because you've done a good job here doesn't mean you have to stay forever. There are other doctors who would also do good work here. Just because you stop doing something, it doesn't mean you've failed. Sometimes, it just means you've finished."

"I guess I've been waiting for Rodney to be finished," Jennifer said. "But I don't know if that's ever going to happen. And I know I shouldn't even be worrying about this now, because we're about to be under attack by the Wraith, and my relationship problems aren't a priority."

Eva shrugged. "What would you be doing if you weren't sitting here talking to me?"

"I don't know. Maybe taking a shower. We're pretty much set

for tomorrow. I've triaged the patients to be transferred back to Earth, and we've packed up nonessentials in case they decide on a total evacuation. And we're pretty much always stocked for an apocalyptic disaster."

"Would you rather talk, or take that shower?"

"I think talk," Jennifer said. "I'll risk having to face the Wraith without my hair washed."

"All right, then," Eva said. "What do you want? Never mind what Rodney wants for a minute. What do you want?"

"I want a different kind of job," Jennifer said. "And I want to be able to figure out what that should be without making someone miserable. And when I do get married, someday, I want it to be when I'm ready to settle down and have kids somewhere that's not a war zone. Maybe that could even be Colorado Springs. Or Area 51. Both of them get invaded by aliens a lot less often."

"True enough."

"And when I thought that was what Rodney wanted, I figured, okay, we'll go ahead and move on to the part where we live in Nevada and have a cat and a baby and neighbors who probably aren't going to all die. If that's not on the table, then I don't think I'm ready to go home yet. I'm still okay with working in a war zone. It's just my actual job here that's driving me crazy."

"Then maybe you should think about how you could change that," Eva said.

"In all my copious spare time?"

"Try to make some time," Eva said. "I'll grant you tomorrow is probably all booked up."

"Yeah, I think the Wraith have penciled themselves in. My life crises will have to wait."

"Once we're through this, you can talk to Rodney about what you both want in the future. And that includes whether you want a future together or apart."

"You mean if he's not still brainwashed and carrying out a secret plot to kill us."

"If that's the case, then obviously we'll want to address that problem first," Eva said dryly.

Jennifer breathed a laugh. "Good plan," she said. "I think I'm going to see if I can take that shower."

"Good luck," Eva said, and hoped they'd all have it in the day to come.

The blade's face was smooth and old, but his voice was sharp. "The time has come," he said, the transmission crackling faintly on the screens of the hiveship *Promised Return*, "to make a choice. Will you stand with Queen Death against the Lanteans?"

Waterlight took a deep breath. At her side she felt Thorn stir, her Father who stood in the place of a consort until she was grown.

"We are in no condition to engage in battle," Thorn temporized. "Our ship is in poor condition, and we are far shorthanded since the war with the Replicators. We would be of little assistance to so great an alliance."

The blade snarled. "That may be. But it is your loyalty in question, and your courage. Are you too much of a coward to face the Lanteans? Is that true, Thorn?"

She felt his humiliation, the slow burn of disgrace that accompanied him, a consort who had not died for his queen and lived yet, branded coward and with nothing to do about it. "It is not Thorn's decision," she said clearly, lifting her head, and the blade's eyes fell upon her though he had previously held her of little account. "I am the Queen, and I choose." Thorn moved, but she spoke on, her eyes on the Old One. "I reject alliance with Queen Death," Waterlight said. "I stand instead with my sister, Queen Steelflower."

At that he did hiss, his face contorting. "You will regret that, little queen. Death will drink your overlady's life, and she will not spare you in your turn. I name you renegade! None shall succor you or treat with you."

"Except my sister and her alliance," Waterlight said. Anger welled up in her, fierce and proud. "I do not fear you or that harridan you serve!"

Her father's voice was sharp in her mind. *Waterlight, mind what you do.* He feared. But she did not. His fears were for her safety, but if one cannot spend one's own life in pursuit of what is right, what can one spend?

*What manner of queen would I be,* she said to Thorn, *were

I to yield to this?*

The Old One sneered. "What else could I expect of a hive such as yours? Criminals, who trespassed upon the oldest rules, creating monsters as that madman Michael did! It will be well when your line is snuffed out."

"Not while I live," Waterlight said, and with a mind touch she instructed the ship to cut the transmission. The last sight was his snarl, but his retort was lost. She dismissed him as though he were lowly indeed.

Thorn took a deep breath. *Daughter,* he said, and his mind was filled with warring fear and pride.

*Death would not have spared us anyway,* Waterlight said. *Better to defy her openly and perhaps we will draw some to us who hate her. It could not make it worse.*

*It could,* Thorn said. *The Old One will not let this be forgotten.*

*It would not be anyway,* Waterlight said. She paced to the other side of the chamber, kicking her skirts before her, too long and too confining. *What did he mean about Lastlight, who he called Michael? About criminals?*

Thorn sighed. *A long story, and worth little. It is simply one of those things that any hive does not wish to speak of.*

*It is my hive, and I wish to know. I have the right to know.*

He sighed again. *Before the last hibernation, before you were born, your mother had a brother.* Thorn went to the screens, bending over the control boards. *He was a cleverman, brilliant but headstrong. Had he but tempered his genius with sense he might have been Master of Sciences Biological. But instead he decided to conduct an experiment, one that has been forbidden to us since the earliest days of our people.*

*He created monsters?*

*He mingled his own genetic material with that of humans. Not sharing the Gift of Life as one may with ardent worshippers, but giving them a part of ourselves, partially transforming them. And that is forbidden.* Thorn did not look at her. *That is the thing that is forbidden — to change human into Wraith, the greatest crime we can name, at least by the old ways. He gave them our genes, our gifts, and then he released them to breed.*

Waterlight caught her breath. *What happened?*

*Your mother had to stop him. She closed his testing facility and destroyed his notes so that no other could follow him, but it was too late. His specimens had spread to a dozen worlds, and there was no way to seek them out or identify them. They did not look Wraith, you see. And yet he defied her. He tried it again, and that time she had to kill him.* Thorn bent over the board more closely. *He was her brother and she loved him. And so it fell to her to kill him for his crimes. The sorrow never left her.*

*Oh* Waterlight closed her mind so that he would not see her horror and think her weak. No doubt her mother would have told her in time, a disgrace in their line, even if it had been attended to. *What happened to the humans?* she asked.

Thorn looked up, surprised. *No one knows. Presumably as they spread world to world they mingled with the human populations they encountered. They live such short lives and breed so quickly, in the five or six generations of humans since then our blood would have become dilute. It would become an interesting recessive, but one never expressed. So it is a matter of no concern.*

*Ah,* Waterlight said. Her brow furrowed, a question forming. *And why is that forbidden? Why should we forbid something that is of no use?*

Thorn glanced away. *I do not know,* he said.

Perhaps that was not the right question, but now she found the right one, the one at the center surely as one may find the keystone at towers. *Lastlight — Michael — what did he hope to create?* Thorn did not answer, but she could find it herself, putting the pieces into place. *One who appeared human," Waterlight said slowly, "yet who spoke mind to mind and had our abilities. A human blade. Not a half-witted drone or a worshipper who could not use our technology or a mindless thrall. A human blade to be a knife to the heart of the Lanteans.*

*It may be so,* Thorn said grudgingly.

*And did he ever find such?*

*I do not think such has ever existed,* Thorn said. *But we have far greater worries now. Queen Death…*

Waterlight's chin rose. *We shall take our ship to join Queen

Steelflower. Find her ships and we shall meet them at their next destination. We will stand with her against Queen Death.* She saw the expression in his eyes, and said softly for his mind alone, *Father, it is better to stand together than wait for her to come upon us alone.*

He knew that it was so.

A mess hall was a mess hall no matter where it was or what variety of human was in it. Laura Cadman glanced around the compartment the Genii had designated as the place to serve meals — very possibly it had served the same purpose on the Ancient ship, given the long counter along the far wall, though she had always somehow imagined that the Ancients were above mundane things like meals. They'd been people, though, or so she understood. They'd Ascended, yes, and left all that behind, but they'd been people once, and had needed starships and mess halls and ordinary things. And cities. Like Atlantis.

She couldn't help smiling a little at that thought, in spite of everything. She'd done her tour there, and never thought she'd get to come back, and now here she was again, off on another crazy stunt. She glanced over her shoulder at her team, seated around one of the unsteady square tables, a mix of MREs and local food spread out in front of them. Yeah, it looked like Hernandez had traded all of his for a bowl of the Genii stew — which looked like the posole she'd had when she was stationed at Area 51, though the smell was sweet rather than spicy — and, also typically, Johnson was eating only the mac-and-cheese and the dessert. He was pickier than McKay on a bad day, and that was saying something. They looked good, relaxed and ready, and she turned her attention back to the row of urns.

The Genii didn't use paper or plastic, but thin unglazed pottery that the new archeologist said could be re-worked as soon as it was broken. She picked up a cup and held it under the spigot that seemed to produce something that would pass for tea. It was hot, at least, and smelled a lot like her grandmother's Russian Caravan Tea in the shiny red-and-gold tin, and for just an instant she was overwhelmed by the image, the family at Thanksgiving all hanging out by the television for the big games, and Grandma making mug after mug of smoky tea because Uncle Bill wasn't drinking beer any more...

She shook the thought away and went back to join her team, once again aware of the Genii watching her with something that wasn't quite hostility. It was a little bit like being in Afghanistan, where the local friendlies dithered between treating you like an honorary man and loudly not noticing you were a woman, but at least the Genii didn't seem to think there was anything actually wrong with women, just that they weren't suitable for the military. Still, she was glad it was Major Lorne who was doing most of the talking.

"Hey, Captain," Hernandez said. If anyone was going to ask an awkward question, she'd bet on Hernandez to be first.

"Yeah?"

For a wonder, Hernandez kept his voice down, so that the handful of Genii at the far tables were unlikely to hear. "Is it true that these guys are taking blood samples from the Major? Going to clone him or something?"

Well, she couldn't really expect that would have gone unnoticed. "Major Lorne is just here as a pilot," she said carefully. "We also agreed to let them try our gene therapy, the one that activates the recessive ATA gene. But it's not about the Major, and it's got nothing to do with cloning."

"Outta sight," Hernandez said.

Johnson started to say something, then stopped.

"Spit it out," Cadman said. Whatever it was, it was better out in the open.

"Sorry, ma'am. It's just — is that a good idea?"

No, actually it sucks, she thought, and lifted an eyebrow. "That's not our problem, now, is it?"

Which was answer enough, really, and Johnson shook his head. "Guess not, ma'am."

Cadman looked around the table again. Peebles, the only other woman on the team, hastily lowered her head, but not before Cadman had seen the swollen lip.

"Lance Corporal Peebles."

"Ma'am!"

"What the hell?"

"Ma'am." Peebles straightened her back. "It was a demonstration, ma'am. Just got a little out of hand."

"How out of hand?" Cadman demanded.

"Not really out of hand, just — I thought I should show them what a Marine could do." Peebles fixed her eyes on the far wall. She was a judoka, Cadman remembered, black belt or probably higher — had a judo scholarship before she joined the Marines, and still worked out regularly. In fact, she taught a couple of unarmed combat classes back in Atlantis. And Peebles was maybe 5'3" on a good day, a petite 120 pounds of deceptively solid muscle. For a moment, Cadman was sorry she hadn't seen the "demonstration."

"I'd prefer you didn't teach them judo, Peebles," she said, and Peebles relaxed.

"Yes, ma'am."

"Tell me what you need right now," Jack said. He'd managed to catch both Sheppard and Sam in the mess hall as they stopped in to fill their mugs with coffee.

Sam and Sheppard looked at each other. "*Daedalus*," Sam said.

"What you need that'll fit through the Stargate, Carter."

Sam made a face. "In that case, I could use some more repair technicians for *Hammond*. We're still trying to get her back to a hundred percent. I know there's no way we can repair the Asgard weapons until we get back to Earth, but we can do everything else if we have enough people. And I'm down three 302 pilots."

"I can do that. Sheppard?"

"Hyperion's weapon," Sheppard said grimly.

"Do I look like Santa Claus to you?"

Sam's lips twitched. "A little, sir."

"Knock it off," he said without heat.

"More Marine teams if you have them to spare," Sheppard said. "Whatever the tactical situation shapes up to be in the morning, it can't hurt to step up our ground forces."

"If we can't keep the hive ships off and we lose the city's shield, we're already pretty much screwed," Jack pointed out.

"At that point, additional Marine teams would help cover a retreat," Sheppard said. "If we reach that point, I'd like to try to get some of my people out before we have to blow up the city." His people, not him. Those words were unspoken, but Jack didn't think for a second that Sheppard planned to leave Atlantis.

"The databurst goes at 2200 hours," Jack said. "I'll see what I can order up for you."

"In the mean time, I'll see if we can get Zelenka and Kusinagi out there to help you with *Hammond*," Sheppard said.

Sam nodded. "Thanks." She met Jack's eyes for a moment, and he was struck suddenly by how long he'd known her, and how proud he was to see her in her element like this. He hoped some part of that came through in the moment before he looked away.

"And I'm going to keep looking for Hyperion's damn weapon," Sheppard said.

"We've tried scanning for naquadah," Sam said, before Jack could open his mouth. "The problem is, there's too much of it in the city. We've got entire storerooms full of small artifacts that are made of naquadah or naquadah-powered."

"Check the storerooms," Jack said. "Maybe somebody decided to hide a piece of hay in a haystack."

"Yes, sir," Sheppard said. If he'd already thought of that, he didn't feel the need to point it out. He'd mellowed over the years, settled into the fine officer Jack had hoped he could be without losing his flashes of reckless brilliance. They needed that as much as they needed more steady men like Hank Landry, even if Sheppard drove Jack nuts sometimes.

"We'll keep working on refining our scanners," Sam said. "Zelenka thinks one of the geologists with a background in mineral exploration may be able to help. But I can't make any promises."

"Morning briefing is at 0600 hours," Jack said. "Be there or miss out on the doughnuts."

Sheppard looked like he wasn't sure whether he was supposed to smile.

"Wouldn't want to miss that," Sam said.

Jack made his way up to the gate room at a brisk pace and arrived in time to catch Woolsey preparing to send the databurst.

"I've prepared a report for the IOA on our situation," Woolsey said.

Jack let out a breath. "Do we have to?" Woolsey gave him a look, and Jack relented. "Better you than me."

"I haven't mentioned anything about an Ancient device that might hypothetically kill Wraith," Woolsey said. He shook his head. "I used to feel more guilty about this kind of thing."

"It's hypothetical," Jack said. "If you told them every time we found a device that might turn out to be interesting, it wouldn't be good for their blood pressure.

"I said that we were hitting some snags in negotiating with the Wraith," Woolsey said.

"You could say that again."

"I have every confidence that Sheppard and his teams will find the missing device."

"When?" Jack said shortly.

"Soon."

"If it's too late for Guide to move his ships into position, it won't help."

"That depends," Woolsey said. "I expect Teyla is working right now on persuading Alabaster to start moving her ships into position tonight."

"That's not what Guide thinks she's supposed to do."

Woolsey looked at him shrewdly over his glasses. "Then the question is whether Guide or Alabaster is really in charge. At least, that's how I expect Teyla is putting it to Alabaster at the moment."

Jack snorted. "That should be interesting. You think Teyla can pull it off?"

"If anyone can handle the Wraith, she can," Woolsey said.

"In other words, you don't know."

"I don't know," Woolsey admitted.

"Understood. Let's dial up Earth."

The wormhole opened brilliant blue, and Jack stepped up to use the radio. "This is General O'Neill," he said.

"Landry here," Hank Landry replied after a pause just long enough for him to push his way forward to the mike. "What goes on in Atlantis?"

"The databurst explains, but I'll sum up," Jack said. "A massive Wraith fleet is bearing down on Atlantis. Our Genii and Wraith allies are not playing nicely with us at the moment. We're still hoping we can get them on board, but we may have to work with what we have."

"What do you need?"

"Dr. Lee and a repair team would help. Also some Marine backup. SG-3, if you've got them."

"They're offworld," Landry said. "I can send you SG-5 and SG-18."

"That works. And we could use some doughnuts for the morning briefing."

"I'll see what I can do about that," Landry said dryly.

"More news when we have more news. O'Neill out."

"Databurst transmission complete," Salawi said, her eyes on her computer screen.

"Shut the gate down," Jack said when Woolsey didn't say it first. "We're in no position to waste power."

Woolsey glanced sideways at Jack. "I thought you might want to return to the SGC, under the circumstances."

"What, and miss the doughnuts?" Jack clapped Woolsey on the shoulder. "I'm going to try and get a few hours sleep. Call me if anything interesting happens."

"I'll be sure to do that," Woolsey said, and moved to look over Salawi's shoulder at the long-range tracking signal. The cluster of lights it showed had brightened, a dozen ships still closing in slowly but relentlessly on Atlantis.

# CHAPTER NINE
# Night Watch

TORREN was already asleep when John got to Teyla's quarters. Jeannie Miller was curled up on the couch, her tablet propped on her knees. She looked up as he came in, and put a finger to her lips with the tired ghost of a smile.

"He sleeps like a rock," John said quietly. "Thanks for watching him."

"It was no trouble," Jeannie said. "He went down about an hour ago. If you're good for a while, I want to go see Meredith. If that's okay?"

"Sure. Don't worry about McKay, though. He's fine, just kind of cranky."

"Well, he is in a cell." She frowned. "You don't really think he's still... brainwashed, or whatever?"

"I don't know if he was ever brainwashed, or if he just couldn't remember who he was and believed what they told him. But I've seen them turn our own people against us before. They did it to Ronon, and he hates the Wraith more than just about anybody."

"My brother." She raised her chin bravely. "He does get into the weirdest kinds of trouble."

"That would be McKay for you."

"I wish he'd come to see me when we were on Earth. The rest of you are always welcome, too, you know. Torren ought to meet Madison, since they're kind of related in a weird kind of way."

"Not exactly related."

Jeannie looked at him, her head to one side. "Close enough. I think whatever happens with Jennifer Keller..." There was a question in her voice, and John shrugged. He had no idea how that one was going to turn out, and at the moment just hoped they'd live long enough for it to matter. "Whatever happens with that, he's found sort of a weird surrogate family out here, and... I'm glad. I want him to be happy. I just want to see him sometimes."

"Next time I'll twist his arm and make him go to Canada," John said. He should have done that last time they were on Earth, he thought, but he'd been busy feeling sorry for himself. He'd thought there was no point in trying to stay in touch with his team, because they weren't going to be his team anymore. Now he was only sorry that he'd wasted time. "If there is a next time," he added quietly.

Jeannie bit her lip. "Is it that bad?"

"It's not good," John said. "I'm going to take Torren to his father on New Athos."

"They tell me they're evacuating non-essential personnel in the morning," Jeannie said, unfolding herself from the couch and tucking her tablet under her arm as she stood and came over to him. "So I want to see Meredith before I go. Not because I think you won't be fine, but I can't pass up the chance to have him as a literally captive audience."

"Go on," John said.

She managed to smile. "Good luck, John."

"Thanks," he said.

"Take care of my stupid brother." Jeannie leaned up to kiss him lightly on the cheek. Before he could figure out what he was supposed to do about that, she was already gone.

John tossed Torren's clothes and favorite toys into a bag, wondering when that had started to feel like familiar routine, and then scooped up Torren, who made a sleepy noise of protest.

"Going to go see Papa," John said, and Torren curled heavily against his shoulder, accepting.

Torren woke up more in the gate room, his eyes lighting at the sight of the bright blue wormhole. John curled his hand around the back of Torren's head for a moment, feeling the soft warmth of his hair, and then stepped through.

On the other side Kanaan was waiting in a soft circle of torchlight. Jinto held the torch, and reached out willingly to shoulder the bag of Torren's belongings. John handed Torren to Kanaan, who settled him in one arm.

"Thanks for meeting me at the gate," John said.

"I know you are a busy man," Kanaan said, not entirely graciously.

John glanced down at Torren. "Jinto, could you take Torren for a minute? Torren, go with Jinto, buddy."

Jinto shrugged and traded torch for child. "Did you have fun in Atlantis, Torren?"

John drew Kanaan aside, far enough away that Jinto and Torren were dark shadows at the edge of the circle of torchlight. "Queen Death's fleet is going to reach Atlantis in less than twelve hours," he said. "We're going to put up a hell of a fight, I can promise you that."

"But not that you will be victorious."

"I wish I could promise me that."

Kanaan nodded. "And Teyla?"

"She's on a mission," John said. "Trying to get us some allies."

"That is what she does best," Kanaan says. "And then I expect she will join you in fighting the Wraith."

"She does a pretty good job of that, too," John said. "When she has to."

"If you see her, tell her not to worry about Torren."

"I will."

Kanaan's eyes searched John's face. "Don't worry about Torren," he said.

John nodded wordlessly. He extended a hand, and Kanaan clasped his arm and then, after a moment's hesitation, drew him into the Athosian bowed-head gesture of farewell. It felt awkward — for both of them, he thought — but John didn't flinch away.

"All right, Torren," Kanaan said, raising his voice as he straightened. "It is long past time you were in bed."

"Not sleepy," Torren protested, but his voice was already blurred by sleep.

"Goodbye, kiddo," John said. "I'll see you back in Atlantis." Teyla had told him once that it always sent a shiver down her spine to say that, that *I will see you in the City of the Ancestors* were the words of a man who sees his own death coming.

He let himself linger just long enough to see Kanaan and Jinto round the trees out of sight with Torren, and then dialed the gate for Atlantis.

In the dark middle of the night, Ronon sat alone in his quarters, Hyperion's weapon resting on his knees, his fingers tracing its curves. He ought to turn it over to Sheppard, one part of his mind said. He ought to pull the trigger, another part said. Wipe out the Wraith in one blow, like a legendary hero.

Of course, there would be a price. In that kind of story, there always was.

Sheppard would kill him, afterwards. At least, he'd have every reason to try, and Ronon wouldn't have much reason to run. He'd have done what he meant to do, and he'd have nowhere to go. Sateda, maybe, but he couldn't actually imagine going to Sateda and trying to make a life there after he pulled that trigger.

Not any more than he could imagine the rest of his life as the coward who let the Wraith live.

He looked up at Tyre's sword where it hung on the wall. The choice had been simple for Tyre in the end, to trade his life to regain his broken honor. If firing that weapon and killing the Wraith would have meant Ronon's death, he would have done it in a heartbeat.

Instead all he had to do to defeat the Wraith was pull the trigger and kill his friends.

It felt like a choice out of a fable for children, one of the stories his grandfather had told him as a child that started with "Time was..."

*Time was, there was a man who lost everything to the Wraith. They killed his friends and his family and the girl he loved; they destroyed his home; they made him a hunted animal instead of a man. And one day he came to the City of the Ancestors, and there he learned that he was still alive.*

*And then...*

He didn't know the ending. He only knew there had to be one, some reason he was still alive. And maybe this was the meaning staring him in the face. He had suffered and thousands of Satedans had died, but no one else would have to die at the hands of the Wraith, or crawl to them as their minions. The Wraith had trained him to kill more ruthlessly than his instructors ever had, and now he would be the one to end them.

All he had to do was kill his friends. But he would have killed Tyre, if he had to, to free him from the Wraith. Tyre would have wanted him to do it, for the sake of his own honor. If McKay were still a Wraith queen's worshipper, her trained animal, and if Teyla were too changed to know it, or maybe too changed to care —

His fingers tightened on the weapon. If he closed his hand, it would all be over.

His hand opened.

They still might defeat Queen Death without either using or destroying the weapon. Todd would have to face facts eventually. He couldn't afford to hold his forces back from the alliance when it was his best chance to get Queen Death out of the way.

If they defeated Queen Death, there would be time to decide what to do with the weapon. Maybe one of the scientists could even find a way to modify the weapon so that it would destroy the Wraith without killing humans who shared Wraith genes. Or a way to cleanse the blood of humans with the Gift so that they were no longer any kin to the Wraith.

And if Todd didn't join the battle, and the only other choice was to let the Wraith take the City of the Ancestors...

Ronon tucked the weapon into his belt under his shirt, feeling it hard and cool against his skin. If it came to that, then at least that would answer the question of how the story ended.

*And in time, he made the Wraith pay for what they had done.*

He stretched out on his bed, eyes open, and waited for dawn.

The quarters aboard *Just Fortune* were the same as the last time Steelflower had been aboard, but the queen was not. Now, like Perssen and Thessen, Teyla was merely part of Alabaster's entourage. To be sure, she was taken for a body servant rather than a guardsman, a human handmaiden who tended her queen's clothing and person, but it was very strange to Teyla to see the same blades and clevermen who had fallen at her feet when she was Steelflower completely ignore her. Their eyes passed over her, and her mental voice remained silent.

Only when she was alone with Alabaster in the rooms that had so recently been hers did she dare speak. That, at least, they could not fail to recognize.

Alabaster caught her thought and held it, turning to Teyla with a quizzical expression on her face. *Do you wish you were Steelflower in truth?* she asked.

Teyla looked around the queen's chambers, lush with soft lighting and fine fabrics, cool mist rising from the floor to ease breathing and soothe the skin, each screen and fret designed to give delight, all while *Just Fortune* moved through the coldness of space, an oasis amid a desert of stars. *No,* she said. *I would not want Osprey's choice. To kill or to starve.*

Alabaster nodded slowly. *So it must seem to you, a choice. But it is not a choice to those who have never known anything else. We are not the First Mothers, and we were born this way.*

*If I were Osprey,* Teyla began. But who knew what she would do if she were Osprey? How could anyone who had not lived her life know?

Alabaster sat down on the edge of a soft chair and held out a hand to her. *Let me show you,* she said. *Let me show you what I remember.*

*The transport ship* Cormorant *had carried a cargo of raw wool, bale upon bale of it stacked up in the hold. They had captured it grounded on Nemors, a swift rush and a sudden departure.*

*"We might as well throw all this out the airlock," Ashes said with disgust. "What's it good for?"*

*On the other side of the hold examining pallets of whole sheepskins, Wind shrugged. "Might be something. Trade, maybe."*

*"It's good for quite a lot," Osprey said indignantly, prying open a plastic shipping case by the door. "In case you haven't noticed, our clothes are in tatters." It contained what she had hoped, spun yarn fine drawn, one full dye lot done in near-black.*

*"There's the crew," Wind said, climbing up on one bale of sheepskins to look behind it. "They won't need theirs anymore."*

*"I should like some clothes of my own that fit," Osprey said decisively. "Not something you've pillaged from a crewman you killed." The next plastic container was marked differently. She thought those symbols meant that the wool was dyed dark blue.*

*"I don't see what this gets us," Ashes replied. He came back toward the door, the dim lights shining off his pale hair pulled back in a short tail, still stocky and solid as he always had been.*

Osprey looked at him with astonishment. "And you think I can't weave? You, born in the same village?"

"I don't see a loom, do you?" Ashes said. "And building a freestanding loom is a lot of work.*

"Knit, then."

Ashes put his head to the side. "A fine lot of deadly pirates we'll look, kitted out in little knit overalls like Athosian babies!"

"Nothing wrong with knitting," Wind said mildly from behind a bunch of pallets. Only the silver top of his head was visible. "We used to do it on shipboard to pass the time."

"And we can do it on this ship as well," Osprey said firmly. "Everybody can learn to knit. All of you. We'll have a class and everyone can learn together."

"No needles," Ashes said stubbornly.

"I can make those," Wind said. "Metal's hard, but I could do them from wood or bone."

"We've plenty of spare bones just now," Osprey said.

"Do you ever hear yourselves?" Ashes demanded suddenly. He was leaning on the door and his greenish face looked pale. "Do you ever hear what you're saying?"

Osprey looked up at him from a case of moss green yarn, dyed to just the color of late summer leaves. "We can't afford to," she said gently. "Not if we're going to live. It's the same as cattle at home. When the time comes you have to make a neat job of it and not waste anything."

"Kine," Ashes said flatly.

"There are some whole tanned hides back here," Wind called from across the hold. "That's handy."

The lights brightened and then dimmed again, everyone looking up.

"Bellwether playing with the ship's environmental systems," Osprey said.

"You hope," Wind replied.

"Does he actually know how to fly this thing?" Ashes asked.

"He'd better," Wind said darkly.

"He says he does." Osprey straightened up. The next box was gold-yellow. She'd teach them simple stitches first, but there was no reason she couldn't knit patterns. "He says he thinks he's flown ones like this before. Bellwether thinks he was the mate on a cargo ship before he owed gambling debts he couldn't pay."

"He thinks." Ashes shook his head.

"He got us off the ground and into hyperspace while they were shooting at us," Wind said sensibly. "That's something."

Osprey stood up, shaking the dust of the floor off her hands and tattered baggy pants, a revenant indeed, gray and torn and filthy. "Do you realize what this means?" she asked. "Hyperspace, I mean?"

Wind looked at her over the pallets, waiting. "What?"

"We're safe. Truly safe for the first time in...forever!" She turned about, white hair following her, long and untidy like a beldame. "No one can find us in hyperspace! No one can track us or know where we are! No one can come upon us unexpectedly! For days and days and days we'll be really, truly safe!"

Wind's face changed, sharp lines relaxing as he realized it was true. An end to watchfulness, to the constant wariness... He was always on guard, day upon day, dozing fitfully a few hours here and there.

"We can wash and sleep and sew and rest and no one can attack us! No one can find us. We can stop and think for a change."

"I'm not sure that's a good idea," Ashes said. He put his hand to the doorplate and went out into the corridor, the hold doors sliding shut behind him.

Osprey frowned, looking after him.

Wind climbed back over the pallets. "He's been like that since Fable killed himself."

"I know." Fable refused to feed, and yet could not stop himself when starvation riddled him. And so instead he had taken his own life, wordlessly and without warning. Those who would not feed died one way or another.

She waited as Wind came up to her, his crossed belts holding long knife and stunning truncheon on opposite sides. She looked up into his face, willing him to understand. "But if we are going to live, then we have to live. We have to build some sort of life, not just survive. Not just stay one step ahead until we step wrong. If we're going to live we have to be more than that." She looked at him and saw his face change. "I am not done, Wind. I want beauty and rest and joy and love. I want to live."

Wind nodded slowly. "And because you do, we all will. I'll protect *you. I'll protect them all. As long as I can."*

*"I know you will," she said, and put her feeding hand against his chest as he inclined his head to hers.*

Teyla opened her eyes. Alabaster's hand was smooth and oily in hers. It should have been frightening, a Wraith queen's hand, but it wasn't. Not given their shared memories. *Ashes didn't want to feed,* she said.

Alabaster nodded. *And yet he did. And Wind... I think there is something of my father in him.*

*There is something of John.* The thought escaped her before she could stop it. Yes, that was John. Even in the most desperate straits, he found purpose in protecting others, in being the shepherd always.

*They lived,* Alabaster said. *And in the centuries to come, Osprey bore three daughters and fourteen sons, and they spread across the spaceways in ships made of bone and shell, living in the spaces beyond the heliopause where the Lanteans did not go. And why should they? They controlled the Stargates, and with them they might go anywhere they wished in the blink of an eye. The long routes between stars were for lesser folk, for subject peoples who traded through the great void. And in those places we lived. We sewed our clothes and raised our children and built our weapons and our scanners, made our plays and our rites and joined our bodies in ecstasy.* Her voice quieted. *And there too we killed our enemies and became strong, until at last Death fed on the children of Athos. The prey became the hunter, and we destroyed the Lanteans and their works.*

Teyla bent her head. *That vengeance was achieved long ago,* she said. *Who seeks it now, and why? It is not needful, sister. Queen Death slays for joy, not for food, and they spoil what they cannot take. This is revenge, not necessity.*

*I don't know,* Alabaster said. *But at least if we could abjure that, it would be a beginning.*

## CHAPTER TEN
# Dawn

THE BLADE who stood on duty at the entrance to the queen's chambers was a relative stranger, and Ember didn't know if that was a good sign or a bad one. At least, he told himself, he has no cause to suspect me. The thought was not as much comfort as he had hoped.

The outer room was just as it had been when Steelflower was in residence, and Ember could not help approving. Alabaster was Guide's daughter, yes, but she was not the queen. She was here at Steelflower's pleasure, and would do well to remember it. He buried that thought — it would not help him, not when he needed Alabaster's favor — and bowed deeply.

*Lady.*

*You are the Chief Cleverman,* Alabaster said, and Ember straightened.

*I am.* He thought she was older than Steelflower, though not by much, or perhaps it was merely that she had already chosen a mate and born her first child. Her looks were very different, too, her skin milky, her hair scarlet, and he hid as well the knowledge that Steelflower was by far the more beautiful.

*My father's man.*

*And Steelflower's.* He did not want to cross swords, not yet — not ever, if he could avoid it — but that needed to be made clear. Behind Alabaster, the human handmaid shifted uneasily and then disappeared behind the screen that hid the entrance to the queen's inner chamber.

Alabaster smiled, and the expression seemed genuinely pleased. *So I see. My sister is fortunate in her men.*

Ember bowed. There was no sensible answer to that, and he did not try to make one, just waited for her to go on.

*But you would not be here if there were not some grave matter to consider,* she said. *Sit, and tell me more.*

Ember settled himself on the stool she indicated with a wave of her hand, and in spite of himself arranged the skirts of his coat neatly about him before he continued. *Lady, I come to you because you are Guide's daughter, and you have come to us so recently that you, at least, cannot be involved. I have reason to believe that someone within this hive has been sending transmissions, and, while I do not know the destination, I can only fear the worst.* He laid out the evidence he had, knowing as he spoke just how meager it really was. *I fear that someone aboard wishes to see Queen Death defeat us.*

Alabaster was still for a long moment, her hands quiet in her lap. *Who else have you spoken to about this?*

*None other.*

She cocked her head to one side in silent question.

*Only one of the Commander's confidants could access that node,* Ember said. *And I could not tell which one.* He paused. *I am new-come to this hive, Lady, a refugee. Guide made me chief among the clevermen, yes, but I have no faction, and no close allies among the blades. I had hoped you, Guide's daughter, might have some way of warning him.*

*I see.* Alabaster shook her head. *This is ill news, cleverman.*

Ember dipped his head, aware that she had not denied his suggestion. *I am sorry, Lady.*

*Leave this to me.* She rose, her movements graceful, not martial as Steelflower's had been. *And if you find out more —*

Ember rose in turn. *I will inform you at once, Lady,* he said, bowing, and retreated to the corridor. He should not feel lightened — but she was Guide's daughter, he reminded himself. That would count for something.

Teyla heard the door slide shut behind Ember, but did not move from the queen's inner chamber until Alabaster appeared in the doorway.

*You followed that,* she said. It was not a question, and Teyla nodded.

*Yes.*

Alabaster paced the length of the chamber and back, her pale gown hissing at her ankles. *You had no suspicions, I take it.*

*None.* Teyla perched on the padded stool that Ember had vacated, drawing her knees up under her. She was desperately tired, but there was no time to sleep. *I knew that not everyone approved of Steelflower's policy, but I didn't think there was anyone who was bold enough to take action against her.*

*Or against my father,* Alabaster said thoughtfully. *A man might find it easier to justify thus.*

*Possibly.* Teyla watched her move. It reminded her of Rodney's cat, stalking back and forth between its humans, though at least Alabaster did not wail her discontents aloud as Newton did. *It changes things.*

*It does.* Alabaster bared teeth. *It forces my hand, and his.*

*It should not need saying, but this is not — cannot be — our doing.* Teyla spoke with a calm she did not entirely feel.

There was a flash of surprise and then wry amusement. *That is so. Though it is undeniably to your advantage.* Alabaster collapsed abruptly into the queen's chair of bone, sprawling at her long-limbed ease where Steelflower had always been determinedly erect. *Tell me, what do you know of this cleverman?*

*Ember.* Teyla pictured the banked strength of his mind. *Not as much as I might wish. As he said, he was not born to this hive, but came here after his own was destroyed. Guide recognized talent and promoted him.*

*Is he reliable, I wonder?* Alabaster asked. *Or is he so clever that he finds shadows to worry him?*

*That transmission is real enough,* Teyla answered. *And Guide trusts him.*

*True.* Alabaster wound a strand of scarlet hair around her fingers, released it frowning. *If he is right, I believe we must move the fleet now — we should be underway before Death can send an attack against us here, and before her man can sabotage the hive and prevent us from reaching Atlantis in time. Yet my father has forbidden it, and for good reason.*

She was careful not to let more than the ghost of a whisper of Hyperion's weapon to color her thoughts, and Teyla did the same. *That reason may be gone already, though I agree Guide would surely have contacted us were it so.*

*I believe you do not wish to use it,* Alabaster answered. *Nor those who love you and wish you to live. But can you say as much for all the Lanteans?*

Teyla sighed. *No. I cannot. But I can say that all of them will abide by our word once given.*

*Or so they have always done in the past,* Alabaster murmured. *But. We will wait for that moment. And the fleet must move, and yet I do not have the authority to move it*You are queen,* Teyla said.

*I am *a* queen,* Alabaster corrected. *This is Steelflower's hive, and Guide is her consort.*

*Does not the judgment of a queen prevail?*

*Do not teach me my duty,* Alabaster said, but without heat. *I know better than you who and where I may push. But the fact remains, Steelflower rules here, not I.*

*And if Steelflower had greeted you with honor,* Teyla said slowly. A plan was taking shape in her mind, though it would depend on Alabaster's ability to sustain an imagined memory —

*I am a daughter of Osprey, too,* Alabaster said, catching the edge of the thought. *I can do that much. Yes, if Steelflower had acknowledged me as sister, as she has done other younger queens — we could do something with that. Bonewhite knew me when I was a child, knows I am who I say I am, and if I say Steelflower has named me sister and ally — yes, I believe he will move the fleet, even against Guide's order.*

Teyla held out her hand. *You have seen me in others' minds, but take what you need from me.*

Alabaster took it in her off hand. *Thank you.* She gave a wry smile. *We may make this work after all, in spite of my father's scheming.*

*Guide has done his best by his people,* Teyla said, and was surprised to find she meant it. *And that best has been very good indeed.*

Radek stepped carefully through the hatch that led to the *Hammond's* port weapons control system, three large cups of coffee in his hands. The front panel of the main console had been removed, and rested against the far bulkhead; cables snaked across the floor, the thick ones that carried temporary power and the multi-colored cables that connected laptops and Asgard devices to the internal systems. Miko Kusanagi backed out of the console, holding her finger to her lips. Radek stopped, tipping his head to one side, and she nodded to her right. Radek looked where she was pointing, and saw the young German plasma beam expert asleep on the floorplates, tucked into the corner between the larger display panel and the console itself. Miko had covered him with her jacket — a bit ridiculous, considering that Sommer had to be 185 centimeters, and the outspread jacket barely reached from his shoulder to his waist, but that was Miko for you. Radek set Sommer's coffee carefully on the console, and Miko stood to take hers.

"He was falling asleep on his feet," she said softly. "So I told him to lie down for a bit, until we finish this diagnostic. We don't need him for that."

"No," Radek agreed, and took a sip of his own coffee. He'd put in extra sugar and cream, as much for the energy as to cut the taste of the *Hammond's* very American brew, and tried to tell himself he could feel new energy coursing through him. What he really felt was exhausted, but he wouldn't let himself acknowledge that. "How are we coming?"

"I had to reconnect the secondary cable," Miko said. "Unfortunately, the original port was damaged, and has not yet been replaced, and I don't believe we have time to do that now."

"Indeed not," Radek said, and she nodded, smiling.

"So unfortunately I haven't yet started the diagnostic. But now that you are here, perhaps you —?"

"No, go ahead," Radek said. He glanced at the young man asleep in the corner. He looked like a teenaged boy, with his too-long brown hair straggling over his collar, too young to have much stubble even now. "And we can let Dr. Sommer sleep a little longer."

"Yes," Miko said, approvingly. She leaned over her laptop, calling up the program. "And the diagnostic is running."

It would take at least twenty minutes, and more likely half an hour, and Radek leaned against the bulkhead on the opposite side of the room. After a moment, Miko came to perch on the edge of the console opposite him.

"Perhaps you should also take some sleep?"

"I'll sleep later," Radek said. "The Wraith can wake me up if they need to kill me."

Miko blinked, and then put her hand over her mouth to hide a silent laugh. "Of course we who are older need less sleep."

"That may be true," Radek said. "Though I never thought I would get used to the idea of sleeping through an impending invasion."

"Nor did I," Miko said. She smiled again, but her eyes were sad. "Do you remember the first time, when they said we could send a message to our families?"

"Yes." Radek gave her a careful look. "Do you wish Mr. Woolsey had done it this time?"

"No." She shook her head. "The situation is different, those who wish to can send emails and the like — there will be databursts going out until the last possible moment, I'm sure. It's not necessary, not the way it was then."

"No." Radek wrapped both hands around his cup of coffee, and let himself slide down until he was sitting on the floorplates. He hadn't realized until he was down just how much his legs had been hurting, and he put his cup aside to massage the muscles of his calves.

Miko made a small sound, almost of disapproval. "You should let me do that, Dr. Zelenka."

Radek looked up at her, small and pale with exhaustion, her hair finally fraying from its tight bun, her glasses smudged. "I think I can take care of myself, Dr. Kusanagi." He smiled to take any hint of rejection from the words. "And anyway, I suspect you are in no better shape."

She hesitated, and then sighed. "I am very tired."

"It's very late."

Miko nodded. "I only — I hope we can finish. There is still so much to be done."

"We'll do everything we can," Radek said. "That's all we can do."

"Yes."

She was silent then, staring at her coffee, and Radek tipped his head back against the wall. His eyes ached, but he knew that if he closed them he would fall asleep where he sat, and unlike Sommer he wasn't young enough to wake fast and refreshed.

"I have been thinking," Miko said, and Radek looked up grate-fully. "If I were to send such a message again, I think I would speak more of what I had seen, and not so much about my work."

Radek nodded. He had tried that, though he suspected that young Lieutenant Ford had erased the message as soon as it was made — even knowing better, he had had to try, to say something about the miracle that was this city, Atlantis rising from the waves to save them all. "We have seen marvels," he said, and Miko nodded.

"I do not regret this."

"No more do I." And it was true, Radek thought, whatever happens.

The laptop chimed softly, and Miko looked over alertly. "Ah. The program is finished."

Radek hauled himself to his feet, seeing half a dozen flashing notices — worse than he'd hoped, better than he'd feared — and crossed the compartment to shake Sommer's shoulder. "Wake up, please, Dr. Sommer."

"Ja, ja." The boy sat up, shaking himself like a large damp dog, and came to join them.

"So," Radek said. "Let us get to work."

There were doughnuts in the conference room, four enormous trays tented in plastic wrap and obviously brought straight through from the SGC mess hall. And not just plain doughnuts, but the full assortment, frosted ones with sprinkles, chocolate, coconut-cov-ered, and even jelly-filled. John grabbed two of the ones that oozed dark red jelly, then succumbed to temptation and took a third. If he was going to suffer through another meeting, he was at least going to have his share of the treats. Further down the table, Carter was already halfway through her first doughnut, one hand cupped to catch falling sprinkles, and the new Marine major from SG-5 was polishing off the first of four chocolate. Only Woolsey seemed not to be taking advantage of the unexpected bounty. John slid into a seat next to Zelenka — who had just finished something cream-filled, by the marks on his plate — and tried to deal with the jelly discreetly.

Zelenka gave him a wry look. "I hope this is not a bad sign, this breakfast."

"I try not to think too much about it," John answered, and wiped a blob of jelly off his chin. Zelenka looked like hell, red-eyed and disheveled, but he seemed more cheerful than John would have expected. The engineer smiled.

"I have left Dr. Lee's team to get on with the *Hammond*. I think we will be in good shape there—"

He broke off as Woolsey cleared his throat, and John stuffed the last of the second doughnut in his mouth and tried to look attentive.

"As most of you know," Woolsey began, "we started evacuating the infirmary last night, and are on schedule to begin the evacuation of non-essential personnel. Thanks to Dr. Gupta and Dr. Miller, we have completed the first download of key data to the SGC, and will be following that with three more transmissions timed to make use of the Stargate when it is already open for personnel transfers. We have also received further support from the SGC, and I would like to acknowledge both Dr. Lee and his team, and Major Holmes and SG-5 and SG-18."

He nodded to the Marine major, who managed to respond with dignity despite the mouthful of doughnut.

"Dr. Keller, if you could provide an update on the status of the infirmary transfers, please?"

John glanced down the table. Keller was looking better than he expected, in her Atlantis jacket instead of scrubs, her hair damp from the shower, and her voice was firm when she answered.

"The most serious cases were transferred to the SGC last night, and the last of the minor cases as well as personnel with conditions that would endanger them should they remain on the city will be going through the Stargate with the 7 AM group. Dr. Beckett and I are still looking at seven cases where we believe the individuals should be evacuated, but the person in question doesn't agree, and we'll have final decisions before the 9 AM transfer."

Zelenka leaned forward. "I know we have spoken about this, Dr. Keller, but there are key personnel on that list."

"Yes, Dr. Zelenka, but I can't let them stay if they are likely to do themselves harm." Keller looked down the table at General O'Neill. "Or if they're not going to be able to fight."

"It's your call, Doctor," O'Neill said, mildly enough, and Zelenka shrugged agreement.

"Very good," Woolsey said, but Keller kept talking, folding her hands tightly on the tabletop.

"There's one other thing I wanted to bring up, and that's the retrovirus. The one that we've been working on that keeps the Wraith from killing people when they feed. Dr. Beckett and I have an experimental version which has worked, in the one trial we've made of it." She took a deep breath. "It's not hard to make, now that we know how, and Dr. Beckett and I — we thought it might be worth offering people the option of taking it."

There was a confused murmur of response around the table, and John sat up straighter. He'd known about the retrovirus, of course — Rodney had only survived his transformation back to a human being because he'd been able to feed on Keller without killing her, and he knew that Alabaster had brought some of the humans from her planet to test the serum — but he'd thought the side effects were too severe to risk in any kind of larger trial. "I thought —"

He stopped, realizing that everyone was looking at him, and O'Neill said, "Go on, Colonel."

John chose his words with care. "It was my understanding that the side effects were — at best — pretty serious."

Keller nodded. "That's possible. Dr. Beckett and I think we've modified the retrovirus in such a way that it won't cause as severe a reaction as it did when I took it — and that included convulsions and a ten-hour coma — but it hasn't been tested as anything except a computer simulation."

"But it works?" That was the Marine Major, Holmes, his eyes narrowed.

"It worked on me," Keller said. "And the simulations say it should work on everyone. But that's the problem, Major. It hasn't been tested on a wider sample, and right now there isn't time."

"What do you think the side effects are likely to be?" Carter asked.

"We think —" Keller emphasized the second word. "We think that it's likely to be headache and nausea and maybe dizziness, plus pain at the injection site. Possibly fever."

"Which sounds debilitating enough," Carter said.

"And that's why I'm bringing it up now," Keller said. "The Wraith are still some eighteen hours away — there's just barely time to take the retrovirus and let it take hold before they get here."

"If you're right about the symptoms and their duration," O'Neill said. He shook his head. "Carter?"

The colonel looked at her hands. "I don't know, sir. Yes, it's protection, but — I don't like the risks."

"Holmes?"

The Marine didn't answer for a long moment, rubbing his impeccably shaved chin. "If we had more time — I'm with the Colonel, General. I don't think it's worth it."

"I agree," O'Neill said. "Sorry, Dr. Keller. It's too late to try it now."

"At least let me make it available to civilian personnel," Keller said. "The side effects don't matter so much there."

"Except for critical personnel," O'Neill answered. "But that's Mr. Woolsey's call."

Woolsey shot him a look that should have melted steel. "I'm afraid I have to agree with General O'Neill. I don't think we can risk losing key personnel to side effects at this point. I am certainly willing to let you make the shot available to others, but I will personally recommend against taking it."

"All right, then," Keller said. She pressed her lips together, but said nothing more. A year ago, she would have argued, John thought. Two years ago, she wouldn't have tried to push it through at all.

Woolsey glanced at his notes. "Next — Dr. Zelenka, if you'd give us an update on Queen Death's fleet."

"Yes, of course," Zelenka answered.

John tuned him out and reached for his last donut. He'd looked at the scanners before he'd come to the briefing, and he didn't need to hear the details again. Queen Death was on her way, the fleet getting closer every hour. They'd be within range in a little more than eighteen hours, with half a dozen hives and an equal number of cruisers and support craft: no matter how you sliced it, it wasn't good.

Maybe they did need the retrovirus to give them the advantage — except that if it went wrong, they'd have put their own side out of action, worse than shooting yourself in the foot. Once this was all over, well, with a bit of luck there'd be a chance to test it properly, and then... Would he want to take it? He didn't know.

On the one hand, to know that he wasn't going to die like so many of his men — that he was never going to end up like Sumner, withered to a skeleton. He remembered all too clearly what it had felt like when Todd stole his life, left him gasping like a stranded fish. The shock of life returned was almost as bad, a tangle of fear and anger and gratitude, and a rush of strength and vitality that left him almost weeping with relief. Yeah, maybe he'd do it, so he never had to feel that again. Though if the Wraith could never kill you... He suppressed a shudder, the picture all too clear. You could hang in a feeding cell forever, death an unattainable mercy.

Zelenka had stopped speaking, and John looked up quickly, hoping he hadn't missed anything important.

"Ok," O'Neill said. "There are a lot more of them than I'd like, and they're closer than I wish. So what else is new?"

It was probably a joke, John thought, but not many people were smiling.

"There is some good news on that front," Woolsey said. "As of 0400 this morning, Major Lorne reported the *Pride of the Genii* on course with an anticipated arrival time of 1800 hours. That puts them here several hours ahead of the Wraith."

Yeah, assuming they really were going to cooperate, John thought. Though Radim wasn't stupid enough to think that he could stand up against Queen Death without Atlantis's help.

"Any word from Todd's fleet?" Carter asked.

"Unfortunately, no." Woolsey's mouth thinned. "And as — I assume — we are still unable to meet his conditions..." His voice trailed off.

"Sheppard?" O'Neill asked.

John spread his hands. "No luck so far. We're still working on it."

"Keep me posted."

"Yes, sir." John refrained from adding that he'd be getting more done if he wasn't in this meeting, particularly since half the people here were the ones who'd been looking for the weapon. Ronon will find it, he told himself. If anyone can come up with that needle in this haystack, it's Ronon.

"Colonel Carter," O'Neill said. "What's the *Hammond's* status?"

"Thanks to Dr. Zelenka's team overnight and Dr. Lee this morning, we're in pretty good shape," Carter answered. "We're at ninety percent of optimum right now, and Dr. Lee tells me he can get us to ninety-five percent by tonight."

"Nice," O'Neill said, and there was an appreciative murmur around the table. "Colonel Sheppard, what about the city itself?"

John collected himself. "With the evacuations proceeding, we'll be down to essential personnel, plus Major Holmes's teams. We'll have enough people to defend the central spire, though we'll want to evacuate the outlying areas once the shooting starts." He could see the look in O'Neill's eye, and forestalled the question. "We'd need a couple hundred men to defend that perimeter. But we can hold the center."

"Okay," O'Neill said. "Which brings us to the big question. What are our options as far as Atlantis goes?"

There was a long silence, no one wanting to be the first to speak. Woolsey cleared his throat at last. "General, the IOA has a long-standing recommendation that, if attacked in force by the Wraith, the expedition should evacuate all remaining personnel and destroy the city behind them."

"Or we could fight," John said, in spite of himself. O'Neill was looking at him, and he shrugged one shoulder. "We've held off the Wraith before, and we've got a fully-charged ZPM. We can sit here and take pot-shots while they try to break through the shield."

"The shield will hold for quite a while," Zelenka said. "And — we have tried to work out a way to destroy the city before this, and could not do it. I am not confident we could do it now."

"If we overloaded the ZPM," Carter began, and the engineer shook his head.

"We thought of that. Even a ZPM at full power is not enough to do the kind of damage we need."

"Or we could fight," John said again, not quite as softly as he'd meant.

"We could," Carter said. "But if it's just the *Hammond* and the *Pride of the Genii* and the city's puddle-jumpers against the fleet that Queen Death's bringing in — much as I hate to say it, we need Todd's fleet if we're going to have a chance."

"Todd's going to cave," John said. "He can't afford not to. If we don't fight Queen Death together, he's going to be her next snack."

"We can't count on that," Woolsey said. "He has made his position very clear."

"And yet we simply cannot destroy the city," Zelenka said. "Not we must not or we may not, but we cannot. And the Wraith must not take it."

"If we destroy most of it," O'Neill said, though he didn't sound particularly enthusiastic about the idea. "The Wraith don't have the ATA gene, how much use can they make of the wreckage?"

"They're not the Replicators," Carter said.

"But they are very, very clever technicians," Zelenka said. "We have seen that time and time again, they match what we have found to stop them. And if they capture the ZPM even partially intact — they could reach Earth."

John bit his lip. There had to be another way, something that didn't mean destroying the city, or sitting down to the same long siege that had nearly destroyed the Ancients… "General," he said. "We launch the city."

There was another moment of silence, everyone staring at him, and finally O'Neill said, "Go on."

"Look." John took a breath, trying to order his tumbling thoughts. "Atlantis was designed to fly, designed to go into hyperspace, and it's a hell of a weapons platform. We've got enough drones to make this work. When Queen Death's fleet gets here, we lift the city and use it as our mothership. If Todd joins us, great, we can kick Death's ass. If he doesn't — well, we've got the option of taking the city into hyperspace and getting the hell out of here, so we can fight another day."

"We will not be able to use the Stargate once we are flying," Zelenka said, but he didn't exactly sound displeased.

Both Carter and Holmes were nodding, and even Keller looked impressed. John looked down the length of the table, waiting for O'Neill's decision. For some reason, the Antarctic base loomed in his mind, the city barely a hint of domes hidden under snow and ice. He could barely remember the man he'd been then, the one who'd said he liked the quiet, liked having nothing more demanding to do than to ferry visiting brass around. And then a rogue drone nearly knocked him out of the sky, and O'Neill had told him he was crazy not to want to walk through the gate into another galaxy, a potentially one-way trip to the lost city of the Ancients. Six years ago, and O'Neill looked older and more tired, but surely he was still the man to take the chance.

"Is there enough power in the ZPM for this?" O'Neill asked.

"We have two now," Zelenka answered. "Yes, I think there is."

"All right," O'Neill said. "We'll make that our main plain."

"The IOA," Woolsey began, and O'Neill lifted an eyebrow.

"I don't think there's any need to let them know what we're planning until we're sure we can do it, do you?"

Woolsey gave a thin smile. "Perhaps not."

"Colonel Sheppard," O'Neill said. "She's your baby. Get her ready to fly."

"Yes, sir," John said, the relief washing over him. "Thank you."

## CHAPTER ELEVEN
# Preparing for the Worst

WILLIAM Lynn closed the last of the storage cases and looked around the long narrow room he'd called his lab for the few months he'd been on Atlantis. It was stripped nearly bare, only a few cables and the spare laptop to remind him of what the room had become; now that it was returned to its Ancient form, he wondered again what it had originally been intended for. Beyond the long window, the sea was gray in the city's shadow, the sun sparking from the waves beyond its edges.

The word had come through at twenty-two hundred hours the night before: non-essential personnel were to prepare for evacuation starting at oh-eight-hundred, and archeology fell firmly into the non-essential category. Fortunately, fieldwork for the SGC taught one to be ready to run at a moment's notice, and none of his staff had lost the habit. They'd been ready by oh-one hundred hours, and now it was only the final boxes that had to be hauled to the gateroom, along with the last of the backup drives. They were all perched now on a little cart, not heavy and not even very awkward, just waiting to be taken away.

He turned again, surveying the empty room, and Miranda James looked up from the laptop.

"That's everything transferred, Doc."

"Thank you." He forced a smile. "You can shut it down, then."

"Right." She frowned as the screen went dark, then closed the lid with a final-sounding snick. "When are you scheduled to go through?"

"I don't have a time yet," William answered. "You?"

She glanced at her watch. "Eleven-fifty. Time for coffee, anyway. What are you doing about your stuff?"

"Leaving it, I suppose," William said. "I'd settled in, rather, and there's quite a lot to try to move."

"Yeah, me, too." She shook her head. "I don't know, it's not that I want to stay — I've done a Wraith invasion twice now, thank you very much! But I feel kind of guilty leaving."

"There's not much either of us can do that would be useful," William said. Sensible though he knew they were, the words left a bitter taste in his mouth. He didn't want to leave, he realized, and shoved the thought aside. He reached for his tablet and checked the screen. "The next step is to check in with Sergeant Pollard so he can put it into the transfer queue." So that everything moves through the Stargate as efficiently as possible, he thought, and every scrap of power is conserved for the coming battle.

"Want me to take care of that?" Miranda asked. "It looks like you've got plenty still to do."

"That'd be brilliant, thanks." William helped her push the cart through the door, and glanced back at the window as the door closed behind her. No, he didn't want to leave — somehow, in the middle of work and all the ordinary tasks of an SGC social scientist, he'd fallen for Pegasus, and for Atlantis. He stared blindly at the sun-lit towers, seeing instead the ruins of Sateda, half rebuilt, smelling of wood smoke and mint-and-lemon tea. Even on this world, icy and barren, there were things still to be explored. He remembered Radek taking him down to the city's lowest levels, where unexpectedly the sea's black depths teemed with light, with life, a squid's tentacle mimicking a flashlight waved behind thick glass.

And yet, practically speaking, he was of no use to anyone. He wasn't a soldier and he wasn't a technician, and those were the skills needed now. And quite possibly he'd merely be in the way, a nuisance, though if he stayed in his quarters and did nothing, surely no one could object. It was only his own life he was risking…

He shook his head, and turned his back on the window. He would do what he had to do.

Radek found Dr. Keller briskly stacking boxes in cabinets in the infirmary and waited for a moment until she noticed him.

"Sorry, just trying to get the fragile stuff squared away in case we get shaken up in here," she said, wedging boxes into the back corner of a shelf tightly enough that they seemed unlikely to shift.

"What can I do for you?"

"I would like you to give me the retrovirus," Radek said.

Jennifer put down the box in her hand and turned to face him. "You know that Mr. Woolsey recommended against distributing the retrovirus."

"He said it was optional for civilian personnel."

"It's really early in the testing process," Jennifer said. "Carson and I have made a couple of changes that we hope will eliminate the side effects I had, or at least make them much less serious. But we haven't had time to see if that works. I want to be very clear about the risks. You could go into convulsions. It's possible that you could die."

"I am willing to take the risk."

"Do you mind if I ask why?"

Radek shrugged. "I have been in Atlantis since the first year we were here. That was a very bad year." Faces rose unbidden in memory, friends withered into corpses. He had seen death before, but not like that, shocking and obscene and terrifying. He had thought, briefly, about returning to Earth once that was possible, where he would never have to watch that kind of death again.

He had decided that Atlantis was worth it, and never regretted it. But it was always a shadow underneath everything they did, the knowledge that one bad mission could mean returning to Atlantis in a bag, a shrunken thing to be buried in a closed coffin so his family would not see what he had become.

"The Wraith have killed so many of us," he went on, shaking off the memories. "I do not want to die that way. If there is fighting in the city, or God forbid if I am ever captured, I want to have every chance."

"You know that if you are captured, having the retrovirus could mean being trapped in the feeding cells... pretty much indefinitely."

"From which there is a chance of escape. From death, not so much so."

"I'm not arguing with that," Jennifer said. "I just want to make sure you know what you're getting into."

"I am sure."

"All right. If you're absolutely sure." She crossed to a different refrigerated cabinet and withdrew a small bottle, which she set on a tray as she began unwrapping a syringe. Her white coat was crisp, her hair drawn back in her usual tight ponytail, but there were dark circles under her eyes.

"How are you doing?" he asked.

She looked up. "What do you mean?"

"I heard about you and Rodney. I am sorry."

"Yes, well," Jennifer said. "I guess we just... aren't working out."

"He is a difficult man," Radek said. "I say this as his friend."

"He's not so bad," Jennifer said. "We just want different things, I guess. Eventually, I'd like to go home, and I don't think he does. Which is a problem."

"I am starting to settle down here, myself," Radek said. "I am not sure I will ever go back to Prague. But life in Atlantis is very much an acquired taste."

"I wish I could acquire it. Everyone else seems to have the knack."

"It is not heaven," Radek said. "It is just another small town. Not everyone wants to live in the same small town, no matter how many wonders it holds."

"I suppose not," Jennifer said. She picked up the syringe, and he could see her drawing her professional dignity back around her. "Roll up your sleeve."

The needle stung, and afterwards his arm burned. He flexed it gingerly.

"If you have any unusual symptoms, any nausea or light-headedness, come back right away," Jennifer said.

"I will."

"If all goes well, in twelve hours we can test your immunity with a willing Wraith," Jennifer said. "Assuming there are any of those around at that point, and that you're even up for that."

Radek shifted uncomfortably. "Is that actually required?"

"It would be helpful to me in figuring out whether the formula actually works," Jennifer said. "But, again, there's an element of risk. I'm not going to ask you to do it, and certainly nobody's going to order you to do it."

He let out a breath. "I will do it," he said, although his skin crawled at the idea.

"Thank you." She glanced down at her hands and cleared her throat awkwardly. "And, umm, thank you for not deciding I'm the bad guy in this whole mess with Rodney. I know he's probably talked about it to you."

"Because when we work I am a captive audience," Radek said, and then relented. "He is my friend, and I would like him to be happy, but not at your expense."

She smiled at him, a more genuine smile that lit her face. She was only very young and a bit shy, he thought, not his romantic type, but someone who might make a good friend in time. "Thanks," she said.

"I should be thanking you," Radek said, rolling his sleeve back down. "You may have just saved me from the Wraith."

"Thank me when we know it works."

"If you believe it will work, then I trust you."

"Try not to test it by being attacked by a Wraith today, okay?"

Radek breathed a laugh. "I promise you, I will try."

John stopped in the mess hall for yet another cup of coffee, though by now his teeth were starting to feel as though they were coated with a thin film. After the real doughnuts at the briefing — O'Neill hadn't been kidding — the long-packaged pastries still on the counter were less than appealing, and he settled for just coffee. He still wasn't entirely sure this was going to work, but all in all he thought they had a better chance flying than staying on the planet. Of course, it would be better if Todd would just cooperate…

"Colonel Sheppard?"

He looked up, startled, to see a couple of the civilian scientists hovering uncertainly. He recognized the city's new archeologist — well, not new, exactly, but newer than some — but not the freckled woman with him. "Yes?"

"Might we have a quick word?" That was the woman, and she seemed to realize in the same instant that he didn't recognize her. "Claire Greensmith. I'm one of the geologists."

John nodded. "As long as you really mean quick — yeah, go ahead."

"Very quick, I promise." That was Lynn, with a fleeting smile. "Colonel, how would we go about becoming essential?"

John blinked once, and then the meaning hit him. "You'd be a lot better off leaving. Both of you."

"Yes, well." Lynn spread his hands. "All my things are still here, and it's just such a bother to pack —"

"We know the risk, I assure you," Greensmith said. "It's just — I don't want to leave the city. Not now."

Not ever, John thought, reading the determination in her face, and wondered if Lynn felt that same passion. "How good a shot are you?"

"Not bad, actually." Greensmith smiled, and Lynn shrugged. "As good as any social scientist who's been with the SGC."

"Passable," John said.

Lynn nodded. "About that, yes."

John sighed. He ought to tell them to leave, to protect themselves, but he understood loving the city, this astonishing place, alien and familiar all at once. "Exploration geologist?" he said.

Greensmith nodded.

"That sounds essential to me," John said. He looked at Lynn. "And I'm sure you've memorized a lot of useful gate addresses and could help people get along on those worlds if our people have to go to ground somewhere."

Lynn smiled. "Yes, I believe I have."

"I'll put you both on the list," John said.

"Thank you, Colonel," Greensmith said, and Lynn echoed her.

"Yeah," John said. "Thank me later."

Radek had managed to snatch a three-hour nap since the briefing, and that and the shower and clean clothes had given him a shot of energy. And if he needed more incentive, he thought, all he had to do was check the screens that showed the oncoming Wraith fleet. They were now well within range of the normal sensors, without resorting to Rodney's jury-rigged adjustments, and it wasn't looking good. Half a dozen hives was a lot of ships at the best of times, and at least some of them would be equipped with the new shield technology. Thanks to Rodney, Radek thought, shoving his glasses up on his nose, and couldn't manage to feel guilty. At least Colonel Carter had gotten a description of how the new shields worked, and thought she could use that to wear down the enemy.

He glanced back at his consoles, seeing displays he hadn't seen since they arrived on this unnamed world. Atlantis was stabilizing her towers, readying her systems for flight. Capacitors were charging, drawing from the thin sun and the motion of the waves, extra bursts of power to spare the ZPM. It was all going according to plan.

Except it wasn't going fast enough. He frowned at the graphs that showed the city's progress, system and structural readiness and the time needed to complete all the essential tasks. At the current rate, it would be done just after the Wraith reached attack range. Presumably the Hammond and the Genii ship would engage before then, but that was cutting it too close. He glared at the systems, and then began typing, moving the least essential items off the list entirely, telling the city and his teams to skip steps within other processes. The computers considered, and displayed a new result: he'd gained an hour.

Radek swore under his breath. There had to be another way — something he wasn't seeing, some shortcut he was missing...

"Problems, Doc?" That was Sheppard, coming up behind him so quietly that Radek jumped and swore again.

"Yes and no," he said. "This takes time, this process, and that is not something we have an infinite amount of."

"Preflight for something this big has to be a bitch," Carter said. She came to join Sheppard, peering at the displays. "What's the estimate look like?"

"Not what I would like," Radek answered, and leaned back to let her see more clearly. "Right now, we will launch about an hour before the Wraith fleet comes within shooting range. That is not counting on the Hammond and the Genii, of course —"

"That's not good enough," Sheppard said flatly. "We need to be in orbit when they enter the system, preferably before."

"I am trying," Radek answered. "There are things that can be cut, but — you know how complex the systems are."

Carter nodded slowly. "And I'm going to have to pull my people out to get the Hammond ready to launch."

"Could you give me another couple of hours?" Radek asked. "The more people we have, the more likely we can get this done. Or perhaps Dr. Lee's team?"

"We're still locking things down," Carter answered. "I'll send Dr. Lee as soon as we're ready for takeoff. They've already said they'll be the last team through the gate, that should help."

"It will help some," Radek said. You had to admire Bill Lee, he thought. The man had no real desire to travel to distant worlds, to put his life on the line, and yet here he was, doing exactly that, and not for the first time, either. He shook the thought away, tapping his fingers on the console. "Perhaps — no, damn it, that has to be cleared before the shield generators can be tested."

"I hate to say it," Carter said, "but we may need to put McKay on this."

"Rodney," Sheppard said.

Is there another McKay here? Radek swallowed the words. "I don't think that's necessarily a good idea —"

"You don't seriously think he's compromised," Sheppard said.

"The — this device is still missing," Radek said. "I do not like the risk."

Sheppard looked over his shoulder as though he expected to find the weapon lying under a console. "We'll find the damn thing. And if we don't, it's even more important to get the city ready to fly."

"And we will waste as much time double checking Rodney's work as we will save having him help us," Radek said. "I — no, I don't believe he is compromised, or certainly not consciously, but nonetheless we will all worry."

"It's your call, Dr. Zelenka," Carter said, in a tone that meant precisely the opposite, "but I think it would be helpful."

"What would be helpful?" And that was General O'Neill, drawn inevitably toward any cluster of senior people. Radek blinked up at him.

"We are looking for ways to speed up the preparations," he said. "Colonel Carter has suggested we get Rodney to help."

"And you don't like it," O'Neill said.

Radek shoved his glasses back up on his nose. Did he really think Rodney would betray them again? Not consciously, not knowingly or willingly, no: Teyla had said he was not Queen Death's man, and Radek trusted her implicitly. It was just — there were so many variables to juggle, so many things that all had to be gotten exactly right, and the truth of the matter was that no one else in Sciences could tell for sure if something was one of Rodney's brilliant ideas or a clever attempt at sabotage. And yet, it was Rodney. They had to trust him some time. "I do not, particularly," he said. "But Colonel Carter is right. We don't have a better choice."

"I could assign Ronon to keep an eye on him," Sheppard said. "If that would make people feel better."

"I like it," O'Neill said. "Go get McKay."

*Just Fortune* dropped out of hyperspace, the transitions shivering through its massive length. In the queen's quarters, Teyla looked up sharply, and Alabaster lifted her head.

"Surely we are too early," Teyla said aloud.

Alabaster rose from her couch and crossed to the nearest console, brushing aside a screen of metal vines. *By several hours. I wonder...* Her mental voice faded as she reached for the intercom. "Hivemaster. What has gone wrong?"

There was a little silence before Bonewhite answered, and when he spoke, he sounded faintly breathless, as though he had only just come to the bridge. "I don't yet know, Lady. We have dropped out of hyperspace — apparently a failsafe tripped. I'll inform you as soon as I know more."

"Do that," Alabaster answered, and closed the connection.

*I do not like the sound of that,* Teyla said.

*No more do I.* Alabaster was pacing again, as unable to wait in stillness as her father.

*It is pointless to speculate,* Teyla said, as much to herself as to the queen, and Alabaster showed teeth in genuine amusement.

*No, but one cannot help it. Failsafes can fire when they're not needed, that happens. Much depends on how cautious the Hivemaster is, though Bonewhite was never known for that.*

*He is Guide's right hand,* Teyla said her tone dry, and Alabaster laughed.

*It is true that my father was always called reckless. Even when I was a child, I remember —* The words stopped, but the image continued, Guide bowing deep to another scarlet-haired queen, her mind caught between amusement and exasperation. Alabaster's mother, Teyla realized, Guide's lost queen, her mind as cool and bright as the unmelting snow on the highest peaks of Athos.

Alabaster nodded, following her thoughts with ease. *Yes, that is Snow, my mother. The Seed had been planted for my own hive when she was killed, and I — was trapped in exile.*

Teyla repressed a shudder at that. She'd seen what happened when Dr. Keller had accidentally been infected, and she doubted the process was any more pleasant for the human just because the Wraith were controlling it. She did her best to conceal that thought, but some trace of it must have escaped, and Alabaster gave her a thin smile, daring her to comment.

"Lady." Bonewhite's voice spoke from the console, and Alabaster turned to answer. "Yes."

"We've found the problem. A failsafe was tripped, and Hasten is working to be sure it will not happen again."

"Surely we can get underway without it?" Alabaster said.

"Hasten believes it will merely fire again if it isn't replaced," Bonewhite answered. "Give us an hour, no more than two, and it will be done."

*We don't have that time.* Teyla swallowed the words, and saw Alabaster's back straighten. "An hour, Hivemaster. No more. We must reach Atlantis before Death's fleet."

"Yes, Lady," Bonewhite said, and the screen went blank.

*I would also very much like to know exactly how that component came to fail,* Teyla said.

Alabaster nodded. *As would I. If Ember is right…*

*Then this may not be the last failure,* Teyla said, her voice grim. And if they did not reach Atlantis in time — no, she wouldn't allow herself to think that, any more than she would believe that Guide would fail them in the end.

## CHAPTER TWELVE
# Saboteur

THE HYPERDRIVE window opened and *Just Fortune* passed through. Ember felt the shiver as he bent over the failsafe dissected on his workbench, and Salt glanced quickly at the displays on the far wall.

*We should still be in time to the rendezvous.*

*Good.* Ember lifted a slender probe, touched the damaged fibers that served as nerves to carry signals to the cut-off mechanism. A spark flared, brighter and bluer than it should have been, and he frowned. *Here, take a look at this.*

*All right.* Salt stooped over the bench, shoving the heavy cords of his hair impatiently over his shoulder. He glanced at the tool Ember held, and chose a more sensitive instrument before touching the damaged ends. The same spark showed, and he looked up sharply.

*Just so,* Ember said.

*It couldn't have been damaged when it was removed from the hull,* Salt began, and shook his head.

*I wouldn't expect heightened sensitivity,* Ember answered.

*No.* Salt glanced sidelong at him, the thought hovering in the back of his mind, and Ember articulated it for him.

*Yes, sabotage.*

*But why —?* Salt shook his head again. *I suppose there are men who do not wish to ally with the Lanteans.*

Ember paused, wondering if he cared trust the other cleverman. But Salt had been a stranger to the hive, too, and had come with him to Death's hive to work with Quicksilver. He knew what Salt thought of Queen Death's ways. *Or those who would prefer to see Queen Death our overlady.*

Salt hissed softly. *That is madness.*

*Can you say for certain that there are none who'd follow her?*

*I cannot.*

*Then.* Ember swept up the pieces of the mechanism, slid them into a storage cell. *Let them stay there until they're needed.*

*You're an optimist,* Salt said.

Ember bared teeth at him. *I wish to see whoever's done this punished.*

*You are the chief cleverman,* Salt said, *but you are still a cleverman. Do not bare your chest for feeding before you must.*

Sadly, he was right. Ember took a deep breath. *There will be proof.*

*But must you be the one to find it?* Salt touched his shoulder cautiously, off hand carefully brushing leather rather than hair or bared skin. *Whoever has done this — he will have status in the hive, you know that.*

*Yes,* Ember said. Certainly it had to have been a man of status, to penetrate the depths of the hive unquestioned. Or perhaps a cleverman of middling rank, but certainly any blade would have been noticed: the failsafes were deep in clevermen's territory, and, while the devices were of necessity accessible, still it would take time to damage the triggering fibers.

*Anyone could have done this,* Salt said, his thoughts running on the same lines. *In terms of technical skill, I mean.*

*Yes,* Ember said again, *but why would they? Queen Death might promise favor, but most clevermen, I think, favor Queen Steelflower.*

*She has treated us with honor equal to her blades,* Salt agreed. *Which might provoke a blade to favor Queen Death — but such a one would be noticed, wandering about in our territory, and I've heard of none such.*

*Nor I.* Ember stifled the thought that crept to the front of his mind. The only blades — the only people — who could move freely throughout the hive were the lords of the commander's council. The Hivemaster himself, the Chief Engineer, the master of the Darts, the First-Watch Captain: they were the most likely suspects, and he dared question none of them. At least not directly, he amended. He was certainly within his rights to seek answers among the blades, and if in the process he very carefully made inquiries about the council... He would have to be very careful indeed, and there was very little time. *We'll do what we can,* he said, and hoped it would be enough.

Rodney's head snapped up as the door to the corridor outside opened. "What, are we interrogating me again?"

"Probably should," Ronon said, coming in with Radek at his side. "But they're letting you out."

"We need your help to prepare the city for launch," Radek said.

Rodney stared at him for a moment. "Launch? What are we doing, retreating? I mean, not that it might not be a good idea under the circumstances, but... really?"

"We're not running away," Ronon said.

"Colonel Sheppard believes it will give us more tactical options to be in orbit when we engage the Wraith fleet," Radek said. "He is the military commander, so who am I to argue? But it means we have a lot to do and very little time." He glanced at Ronon, who reached out with obvious reluctance to lower the force field on the cell.

Rodney forced himself to step out casually, as if he were merely deciding that now would be a good time for a stroll. "Does this mean you've decided I'm not secretly working for the Wraith?"

"No," Ronon said flatly. "Sheppard sent me to guard you."

"Guard me, right, like you're going to know exactly what I'm doing. If I were in league with the Wraith, there are a thousand ways I could sabotage our systems without you knowing it. Not that I am in league with the Wraith," Rodney added hurriedly. "I'm just saying."

Radek shrugged. "I know," he said. "For what it is worth, I recommended against your being released."

Rodney frowned, unreasonably stung. "Really loyal friend you are."

Radek threw up his hands in frustration. "Rodney, you were held captive by the Wraith!" He added a fervent oath in Czech. "You broke into our computers, let the Wraith into the city, and have caused as much trouble as it is humanly possible for one man to cause. We lost the ZPM. Good people died."

"It wasn't my fault."

"That is not really the point."

"I'm much better now," Rodney said, but he was aware of how weak the words sounded.

Radek rubbed his forehead. "Yes, well, I hope so. Because we will need your skills to prepare the city for launch in the time we have left, and Colonel Carter believes that at this point it is worth taking the risk."

Rodney brightened a bit. "She said that?"

"She does not believe you will sabotage the city," Radek said. "Please do not take it as a sign of romantic interest. No one has time for that."

"I'm just pleased that she has faith in me."

"Yes, well. I want you to go over the checklist for launch preparation with me, make sure we are leaving nothing out. Then you can help me try to optimize power for this. That way I will see what you are doing."

Rodney looked up at Ronon. "In that case, do you have to loom that way?"

Ronon shrugged. "I'm not leaving Zelenka alone with you."

Rodney huffed in frustration. "What do you think I'm going to do, stun him and…" He trailed off, remembering abruptly that he'd stunned John, and probably would have killed him if he could, in his fury that this strange human had killed Quicksilver's brother.

He shook off the flush of anger that came with the memory. He remembered who he was, now, and that he'd never really been Quicksilver. Dust had been his captor, not his brother. The twist of uncomfortable feelings lingered, along with the memory of what it had felt like to desperately want to please Queen Death, to make himself worthy in her eyes…

"Something like that," Ronon said.

"Let us not go there," Radek said. "No one is going to stun anyone. We will just optimize the power, and then you can supervise our preparations and leave me free to fix any problems we find that might kill us." He hesitated. "You know I cannot give you unsupervised access to the computer system."

"Yes, that's what I told you," Rodney said. "At least you're listening now."

Radek looked at him searchingly. "Are you working for the Wraith?"

"I already told Sheppard no."

"Humor me and tell me as well."

"No, I'm not working for the Wraith."

Radek shook his head. "Which of course tells me nothing."

"You asked," Rodney said. "I'll meet you in the control room." He began striding down the corridor, but Ronon stepped out to block his path.

"That's not the way to the control room," Ronon said.

"It's the way to my quarters," Rodney said. "I'd like a shower and to put on clean clothes. If we're going to have an epic battle with the Wraith, I'll think better if I don't smell. All right?'

"I'm coming with you."

"I figured that, yes." They walked down the corridor, unspeaking, Rodney having to race to keep up with Ronon's strides. "You know, it's not my fault."

"I never said it was," Ronon said.

"No, but you're acting like it."

Ronon turned on him, backing him up against the corridor wall. "I think you're still working for the Wraith," he said flatly. "I was there when you fed on Jennifer, remember?"

"I was *dying*. And she wanted me to."

"You're lucky she's alive."

"What do you want me to say? What do you think would have happened if they'd used the same process on you? You'd have been the one who wanted to suck the life out of people."

Ronon stood and looked at him, his jaw set hard. "I know that," he said after a while. "I know they can break me. They've done it. I can't blame you for whatever they've done to you. Not the real you."

"But you still think I'm working for the Wraith."

A flicker of dark humor passed across Ronon's face. "Yep."

"Fine, come keep me under guard while I take a shower." He strove to make his voice light. "I warn you, Newton's loose in my quarters."

Ronon shrugged. "I've got a stunner."

"You are not stunning my cat," Rodney said indignantly.

"Whatever it takes," Ronon said, and his voice was grim.

John was finishing briefing the two Marine teams that the

SGC had sent through — good guys, all of them, but new to
Atlantis — when Ronon came in with Rodney. They'd obviously
taken time for Rodney to go back to his quarters and shower and
shave because he was wearing fresh clothes and his hair was still
wet. Ronon took the steps two at a time, going up to the control
level like he was relieved to be away from Rodney for a minute. "We
have a problem," Rodney said. "A big problem."

John acknowledged him with a nod. "Hang on a second. Think
you've got it, Captain?"

"Yes, sir," Captain Ryan said. "We'll cover the infirmary level,
stairs and transport area both."

"We won't lock down that transport unless we've gone to code
red on an infiltration," John said. "It's the main way we're getting
the wounded to the infirmary. So keep a close eye on it."

"Yes, sir." He gave John a sharp nod and peeled off with his team.

John turned around. "What's the problem, McKay?"

"He's gone."

"Who's gone?"

"Newton," Rodney said. "I went back to my quarters, and Ok,
they're not the quarters Newton is used to because Jennifer... But
anyway, Newton's not there. And I radioed Jennifer and he's not in
her quarters either. Which means he got out. He could be anywhere.
Someone could shoot him. Someone could steal him..."

"Maybe he's wherever the weapon is," John said.

"Very funny. Just because you don't care what happens to pets
doesn't mean I don't take my responsibility as a pet owner very
seriously. A little kitten, lost and alone in the middle of a battle..."

"If we have a battle in the city we have a lot worse problems than
a lost cat," John said. He was having trouble taking this one seriously. "Look, he's a cat. He's probably hiding in an air vent somewhere or under a sofa, and he'll come out in a couple of hours when
he gets hungry. Why don't you just chill out about it and do the
thing you're supposed to do, which is get the city ready for lift off?"

"Incredibly callous..."

"Rodney!"

"What?"

"Get the city ready to fly," John said very distinctly. "We'll find your cat later. I'm sure he's fine. Now go up there and get on a console.

He followed Rodney up the steps to the control center. Sam and Radek were at the station at the far end, looking over the shoulder of one of the other scientists, a geologist John thought was named Greensmith. "I don't think that's got it," Sam said.

"We need a finer setting," Radek said.

"I think this is the finest setting there is," Greensmith said. She shook her head, her long braid swaying, and tried a different sensor setting. "That's a little better, but — I'm afraid it's just not going to work."

"What's not going to work?" John kept his voice low so that the rest of the watch wouldn't hear, still keeping an eye on Rodney out of the corner of his eye. Ronon was casually standing just a few feet away from Rodney's usual terminal.

"We're still trying to scan for naquadah," Sam said.

"We can detect naquadah just fine," Greensmith said. She looked up over her glasses, as if wondering if she'd spoken out of turn, but Radek motioned for her to go on. "But below a certain point, the city's internal sensors won't give us a precise mass, just that they're detecting 'trace amounts.' And we're finding trace amounts of naquadah in almost every room of the city."

"The item is very small," Radek added, "and this city is full of things that are made of naquadah. We have not been able to distinguish finely enough — what is the thing we are looking for and what is a power relay, for example? It is just too small and the scanners will not do such fine work. They are not meant for this."

John scrubbed his chin with his hand. "So what does that mean?"

Radek looked down at Greensmith, and she shook her head regretfully.

"It means we're out of technical solutions to find it," Sam said, straightening up. "I think we need to consider what happens if we don't find it in time."

"We've got to figure out who took it," John said.

Radek looked exasperated. "And how do we do that? I am an engineer, not a detective!"

"Jim," Sam added.

It took a second before John got it. Greensmith looked like she was trying not to smile. "Yeah, and I'm a pilot not a doctor, Bones, but we've still got to find this thing."

"We may not," Sam said. "I don't think we're any closer than we were yesterday. Whoever has it is keeping mum. We're sure it's not the Wraith and it's not the Genii and we don't think it's Rodney." She glanced down the boards at Rodney, complaining full tilt as his fingers flew over the symbols on the control panel. "Where does that leave us?"

"Screwed," John said. But at least Torren was on New Athos. At least he'd taken care of that. Which was a lot more important than Rodney's cat.

"There's nothing more I can do until we find it," Sam said. "My time is better spent on the *Hammond's* repairs."

"I know." John took a deep breath. "Thanks, Sam."

"Call me as soon as you find it," she said, and strode off toward the transport chamber.

"I will," John said.

"I really thought we could find it this way," Greensmith said.

"We do our best," Radek said, resting a reassuring hand on her shoulder for a moment. "But now we must use logic. It must be one of two things. Either someone took it because they do not want it destroyed, in which case they may use it, or someone took it who does not know what it is."

"If they use it…" John's heart sank.

"Most likely they do not know what it is," Radek said. "Perhaps it is time to announce that something is missing. I can say it is some vital part of the city's systems. That way if it is someone who has simply picked up an interesting device that they do not know what it does, perhaps they will return it."

"It's worth a try," John said. "I'll ask Woolsey."

John paused in the mess hall to draw himself yet another mug of coffee. He was still in pretty good shape, despite the early morning and the rush of preparations. With any luck, he'd be able to grab a few hours sleep sometime early in the evening, and be ready to lift the city once O'Neill and Woolsey made the final decision. Not that he had any real doubts about what that would be. If Atlantis

was going to have any chance at all, she had to be in orbit, with
the choice to fight or flee. That didn't mean that the IOA wouldn't
try to make them destroy the city, but he was pretty sure neither
O'Neill nor Woolsey would go along with it, if only because they
both believed Zelenka when he said he couldn't truly destroy the
City of the Ancients. And O'Neill, at least, was in a position to
make it stick.

He moved to a sunny corner where he could look out over the
city, the sea glinting under the sun, the ice melted to damp patches
on the terrace below. Zelenka said the city was fit for hyperspace,
and that they had enough power to make the jump; they could run
if they had to. They might even end up on a more pleasant world,
maybe another tropical ocean like their first two homes. But running wouldn't work forever. They'd have to face Queen Death someday. Better to do it now, if they could.

Of course, the problem with that was Todd. No weapon, to be
ceremoniously destroyed in front of him, no Wraith fleet to fight
against Queen Death. John couldn't entirely blame him: if the
Wraith had something like that, he'd want to have it in hand, see
it smashed into little pieces, before he lifted one finger to help. But
they were running out of time.

He moved a little closer to the window, out of earshot of any of
the tables, and touched his radio. "Dr. Zelenka."

"Yes, Colonel?" The little engineer sounded almost cheerful, and
John couldn't help raising his eyebrows.

"Any luck with our hide-and-seek project?"

"That. No, no luck. Nor has anyone reported finding anything
that might be it."

"Damn."

"On the other hand, we are making good progress with Rodney's
help." There was a pause, as though Zelenka was consulting a screen.
"And the *Hammond* is within four hours of readiness, with only
minor work left to do."

Which is great, John thought, except that the *Hammond* and the
*Pride of the Genii* aren't going to be enough to hold off Queen Death,
not even with the city to back them up. And we can't risk losing
the city. "Good work," he said aloud. "And thanks. Sheppard out."

He glanced at his watch, a vague idea taking shape in his brain. He had almost two hours before his next scheduled meeting; in that time, maybe it was worth having another word with Todd. Todd had to know that he didn't stand a chance if Queen Death won — she'd feed on him and take his withered carcass up on a wall somewhere to remind people that opposing her was a bad idea. And he also had to know that there was no percentage for Atlantis in using a weapon that would kill some of their best people, never mind every random human who happened to have Wraith DNA. It was worth a try.

Todd — Guide, John reminded himself — had been taken to a suite of rooms several levels below the gateroom. There were Marines on guard who came to attention at John's approach, and one of them reached across to open the door. Guide spun to face him as the door opened, and John nodded a greeting.

"You can close up," he said, to the nearest Marine. The man visibly swallowed his protest, and did as he was told. The door hissed shut behind him. "I hope you're comfortable."

"Oh, entirely." Guide waved a hand at the furnishings, but John couldn't tell if the gesture was ironic or not. "Dare I hope you've brought good news?"

"'Fraid not. But I did want to discuss that with you." "There is nothing to discuss." Guide turned his back, the black coat flaring, crossed the room to peer out the single narrow window. "If Hyperion's weapon is not destroyed — I cannot help you, Sheppard."

"You need Death destroyed just as much as we do," John said.

"Yes, but I have some chance of doing it on my own."

"If you really thought that, you wouldn't be here."

Guide showed teeth at that, and John pressed his advantage.

"You have to know we can't risk using it. We'd kill our own people."

"It has happened before," Guide said.

"Look," John said. "We didn't kill you. Back on Earth, we could have turned you over to the IOA, and we didn't. Why would we risk killing people as valuable as McKay and Teyla?"

Guide sighed deeply. "First of all, I believe you are keeping the weapon until McKay and Colonel Carter can figure out how to modify it so that it only kills us — you see, I am being frank with you. "

"We wouldn't do that," John said, but his voice wasn't as confident as he would like. That was what Ronon had wanted, certainly what the IOA would argue for if they knew about the weapon — if they didn't order Woolsey to use it regardless, and accept the collateral damage. They'd seen Teyla and Torren once or twice, for ten or fifteen minutes at a reception. The face of the Pegasus Galaxy, yes, one woman and her child, but acceptable losses compared to losing more of their own people. The unknown, incalculable number of others who possessed the Gift, any trace of Wraith DNA, wouldn't weigh any more in the scales.

"Second, even if I were to believe you," Guide said, "you are no longer the authority here. Nor is Mr. Woolsey. It is General O'Neill who gives the orders in Colonel Carter's absence, and I do not know him. I cannot risk trusting him."

John bit his lip, but there wasn't anything he could say to that. Oh, yeah, he could get into a distracting argument about rank and precedence, try to explain that humans weren't always ruled by the equivalent of Wraith queens and that O'Neill really was in charge, not Carter, but that wasn't going to change the essential facts.

Guide nodded as though he'd followed the thought. "In my shoes, John Sheppard — what would you do?"

## CHAPTER THIRTEEN
# The Final Countdown

RODNEY bent over his console, the sun streaming in through the long windows of the gateroom. So far, everything was going perfectly, just a shortcut here, a minor tweak there, all to bring the city into perfect readiness. When he had last paused long enough to listen, it had sounded as though the *Hammond* was ready, too, and apparently the Genii were on their way. That actually surprised him a little, though, really, Ladon Radim ought to have figured out which side his bread was buttered on...

He frowned at his screen, watching the last of the secondary systems nudge firmly into the green, and then leaned back with a sigh. "Where's that coffee I asked for —?"

"Next to your left hand," Zelenka said precisely.

"Ah." Rodney picked it up, slurping at it before he registered that the cup wasn't burning his fingers. "It's cold!"

"Where it has been for the last twenty minutes," Zelenka went on. He had a cup of hot coffee, Rodney noticed, but he wasn't offering to share.

Dr. Kusanagi looked up from her console, smiling. "Here, you can have this one," she said, and held out a cup.

"Oh, I couldn't," Rodney said, but reached for it anyway. It was just the way he liked it, and he couldn't repress a blissful smile. "Ah, that's better."

"Rodney, you are impossible," Zelenka said.

"Airman Salawi brought him a fresh cup on her way back from her break," Kusanagi said, to Zelenka. "It was very kind of her."

"Yes. Yes, it was," Zelenka said. "But Rodney can get his own coffee."

"Can I?" Rodney pointed to Ronon, who leaned against the end of the console. "At the moment, I can't go anywhere with Chewbacca there keeping me company."

"I'm fine with you getting coffee," Ronon said.

"You see?" Zelenka said. He looked at his own screens, touched keys to compare two sets of readings. "Oh, yes. Yes, that is going very well."

Rodney looked over his shoulder. "If you'd cross-connected the secondary conduits here and here, you'd have gotten a faster power-up—"

"Possibly," Zelenka answered. "Or equally possibly we would have blown that entire bank of circuits."

Rodney opened his mouth to protest, and Zelenka rode over him.

"And in any case, we've already started the process. There's no point in interrupting it now."

"No." Rodney stopped, blinking.

"And I could not have consulted you," Zelenka continued, "because what you were doing there was the priority."

"Well, yes," Rodney said. "Yes, it was." And that left him with nothing to say, so he took a deep swallow of his coffee. "Ow!"

"And if now you complain that it's too hot—" Zelenka broke off, muttering to himself in Czech.

"Some people let being Head of Science go to their heads," Rodney said, but not so loudly that Zelenka couldn't ignore him. He looked back at his own screen, saw that there was nothing to do until the next diagnostic finished running. That was a little weird — he felt as though he'd been working at top speed ever since he got back to Atlantis — but there was nothing he could do about it, and he took a more careful sip of his coffee, wincing at the heat on his sore tongue.

Okay, there was nothing he could do here. That left his other problem, proving that he hadn't been tampered with by the Wraith, and that — well, surely all his work getting the city ready to fly had to count for something? But, no, probably some minor component would blow out, and they'd all blame him for something like unconscious sabotage. He was pretty sure that wasn't really possible, and if only he had the time, he'd get Dr. Robinson to tell them as much.

And what the hell had happened to the weapon? He knew where he'd hidden it, he knew nobody knew about that little private stash — was it possible Sheppard had been looking in the wrong place? Maybe that was it. Maybe Sheppard had gone to the wrong lab. There were at least a dozen of them up there in the towers, all identical — that was part of why he'd chosen one to hide his emergency supplies. That was probably it. His directions hadn't been clear enough, and Sheppard had gotten it wrong. He turned to Ronon.

"We have to go back up the tower."

"What?"

"To where I hid — you know, the thing. Sheppard went to the wrong place."

Ronon was shaking his head. "No. He went to the right place."

"You can't be sure," Rodney said. "All those little labs, all the towers, they all look alike. He must have gone to the wrong one."

"McKay." Ronon sounded as though he were trying very hard to be patient and not succeeding. "He went to the right room. All your other stuff was there."

"How do you know that? You weren't there!"

"Sheppard said so." Ronon folded his arms as though that settled the matter.

Which Rodney supposed it did. Sheppard was good at his job, he wasn't going to confuse Rodney's gear with, say, Kusanagi's or that German kid's. He picked up his coffee again, frowning. And that meant the weapon was still lost, and he was still a suspect. Still potentially Wraith. The heat of the cup traced the line that had been his handmouth, as prickly and uncomfortable as all his other memories. And the worst of it was, there was nothing he could think of that would fix the problem.

Deep in Cheyenne Mountain there was trouble brewing at the SGC.

"Tell me it's not true."

Cameron Mitchell looked up from his computer with his best long-suffering expression to see Daniel Jackson glaring down at him.

"And don't give me that lost-puppy look. Is the IOA serious?"

"That was supposed to be classified information," Cam observed. "And, you know, people do sometimes knock. On doors. Before bursting in."

Jackson waved that away. "Oh, come on, nothing that important stays secret around here." He paused. "Well, not from us."

"No." That was inarguable: Cam himself wasn't supposed to know about the decision, either, but Landry had thought that the opinion of the leader of the SGC's most experienced gate team would be relevant. Or at least help him make a counterargument.

"It's insane."

"I can't argue with you there," Mitchell said, "but, yes, the IOA just ordered Woolsey to evacuate the city and destroy it rather than see it fall to the Wraith."

"We've got to stop them!"

Cam just looked at him, and Jackson waved his hands.

"All right, yes, I have no idea how we're going to do it, but we can't let them blow up the city. Particularly since I doubt they *can* blow it up, given that it's Ancient technology, and we all know how hard it is to destroy that when we need to get rid of it, not to mention that the Ancients already tried this —"

Cam wondered for a moment if he should just let him run down, but decided that could take too long. "Jackson. General Landry's already made those arguments."

Jackson stopped, took a deep breath. "Okay," he said, more moderately. "Is it doing any good?"

"I haven't heard."

"Jack won't let them do it," Jackson said. "Sam won't, either, and Sheppard — he'll never go along with it."

Cam nodded in agreement. That had become painfully obvious during the weeks Atlantis was on Earth. John Sheppard took a definitely proprietary interest in the city, and if the IOA had succeeded in getting control of it, Cam wouldn't have bet against Sheppard trying something stupid like stealing it. And it had become equally clear that an awful lot of the Atlantis team, civilian and military, would have been happy to help out. "And you're right, it probably wouldn't work — didn't they try to blow it up once before, only they couldn't figure out how? Not to mention that fleeing through the gate didn't work all that well the last time."

Jackson paused. "Well, technically, I suppose it did sort of work, only not as a long-term solution, and there are a lot more Wraith to deal with now anyway."

Cam stared. "Do you always have to play devil's advocate? No, sorry, dumb question."

Before Jackson could say anything, the door crashed open behind him. "Cameron! Oh, and you're here, too, darling." Vala Mal Doran gave Jackson a blinding smile, and leaned hard on Cam's desk. "Did you know that they're starting to evacuate people from Atlantis?"

"What?" Jackson straightened sharply. "They can't—"

"Hang on," Cam said. He frowned at his computer screen, checking back through his message queue. "Ok, calm down, both of you. They're evacuating non-essential personnel from a combat zone, not abandoning the city."

"So they say," Jackson said darkly.

"Abandoning the city?" Vala's eyes were wide.

"Don't tell me you didn't figure that out," Jackson said.

"That's all classified, darling."

"Which hasn't ever stopped you," Jackson said.

"Could we skip this part?" Cam asked. "And, while we're at it, could I remind people to knock—"

His door swung open again, and Teal'c blinked at him.

"There you are, Colonel Mitchell. I have been looking for you."

"Knocking," Cam said. "It's an Earth custom."

"The IOA wants to evacuate Atlantis," Jackson said.

"So I have heard." Teal'c fixed his eyes on Cam. "Is that in fact confirmed?"

Cam rubbed his forehead. "The IOA has issued an order, yes. There hasn't been an answer from Atlantis, though they are evacuating noncombatants."

Teal'c clasped his hands behind his back. "In that case, Colonel Mitchell, I respectfully tender my resignation from SG-1."

"Whoa!" Jackson said, not quite under his breath, and Cam felt his eyebrows rise.

"Now, hang on," he said. "I'm not sure that's strictly necessary—"

"I do not intend to remain here while Atlantis is under siege," Teal'c said. "And while Colonel Carter and General O'Neill remain in jeopardy."

"You don't think they're going to destroy it," Jackson interrupted.

"I do not believe that they can," Teal'c answered. "And it cannot be allowed to fall into the hands of the Wraith."

"Wait a minute!" Cam pushed himself up from his chair. "Teal'c, there's no need to resign from SG-1—"

"Because we're all going!" Vala exclaimed. "Cameron, you're a genius."

Jackson looked like he wanted to disagree, possibly violently, but Cam decided he was going to put that down to it having been Vala who said it. "Could we all slow down here just for a minute?" he asked. "As a matter of fact, it had occurred to me that it might make sense for the SGC to send its top gate team through to Atlantis in a support role."

Jackson's eyebrows rose toward his hairline. "And what exactly do you think we can do there? Not that I'm opposed to the idea, but we'll have to convince Landry."

"You're our biggest expert on Ancient everything," Cam said. Flattery never hurt, with Jackson. "You can advise on what we absolutely have to either destroy or rescue. And the rest of us—if any of our people get stuck in the Pegasus Galaxy, have to hide out until *Daedalus* can get there to pick them up, well, who better to arrange that than SG-1?"

Teal'c said, slowly, "I do not believe General Landry will accept that argument."

"Well, no," Cam said. "But I bet you it'll be good enough to get us through the gate."

There was a moment of silence, Jackson nodding slowly, Teal'c with his head cocked to one side as he considered, and then Vala smiled brightly. "Right! So what are we waiting for? We have a general to talk to."

Aboard the *Pride of the Genii*, Evan Lorne stood behind the pilot's chair, one hand resting lightly on the back, the other curled loosely at his side. He hoped nobody else could tell how much of an effort it took to hold himself like that, faking relaxation, but then he glanced at Ladon Radim. The Genii leader had both hands clasped behind his back, his expression gravely attentive, and Lorne guessed Ladon was just as nervous.

It was a Genii in the chair, after all, a young captain with a head of unruly red curls and no trace of the ATA gene. His hands were on the secondary controls, his eyes darting between his own screen and the twin navigation consoles, and there were tiny beads of sweat on the back of his neck between his hairline and his collar. Lorne wasn't at all sure he wasn't sweating himself.

"Ladon." That was Dahlia, arriving so silently that Lorne started at her voice. "Perhaps it would be better if Major Lorne handled the transition."

She kept her voice low, but Lorne saw the captain grimace. His hands were steady on the controls, though, watching the *Pride* approach the red line that marked the transition to regular space, and Lorne looked over his shoulder.

"Captain Nanion is doing fine," he said. "And I think it's important that as many of the crew as possible practice handling the ship without help from someone with the ATA gene." *In case something happens to me*: he didn't have to say that, and Dahlia dipped her head in acknowledgement.

"Yes, of course."

Ladon gave a crooked smile. "I suspect we'll all earn our stripes this trip."

Nanion did grin at that, and leaned forward again over the controls.

"Not yet," Lorne said. The *Pride*'s image had reached the edge of the red line, but he could feel that it wasn't time, and he dredged his memory for the visual sign that marked that moment. "The line will brighten — just like that."

Nanion shoved the drive lever forward, and light flared in the forward screens. The window formed and then they were through, hanging in blackness spangled with stars.

"Chief, I have Atlantis on the screen," one of the navigators reported, and beyond him, at the environmental stations on the lower boards, there was a steady murmur of voices as the technicians gave their status reports. If he were flying, Lorne thought, none of that would be necessary. It would all be instantly available, a lovely overlay conjured up as soon as he desired it, and gone again the moment he no longer needed it. The Genii could fly their ship, but they needed a crew of dozens to take the place of a single person with the ATA gene. No wonder Radim was so desperate to get his hands on it.

"Nice job, Captain," he said, and Nanion glanced up at him.

"Thank you, sir. Set a course for Atlantis?"

Lorne looked at Ladon, who shook his head. "Let's let them know we're here first. Not that I think they haven't seen, but it would be only polite."

Out of the corner of his eye, Lorne could see the communications officer frowning over his controls, and his fingers itched to do it himself. He could do it with a thought, the spark of a wish sending the information flying, the towers of Atlantis lighting to welcome them home…

"And while you're at it," Ladon said, "any sign of the Wraith fleet?"

Another technician began adjusting his controls. "Not yet — wait, there they are."

The image on the central screen shifted, stars replaced by a schematic of the solar system, planets and orbits picked out in shades of purple. There was the *Pride*, a blue-white star, maybe an hour away from Atlantis's orbit. There was Atlantis, her towers replacing the planet itself. And there, on the edges of the system, an arc made of a dozen orange wedges: Queen Death's fleet.

Ladon lifted an eyebrow. "How far out is that?"

His voice was impressively steady. Lorne looked at Nanion. "Captain —"

"Yes, sir."

Nanion scrambled hastily out of the chair, and Lorne took his place, sinking his fingers into the conductive gel with a sigh of relief. The sense of the ship washed over him, half a hundred individual status reports merging into a general sense of well-being, and he turned his attention to the long-range sensors. It didn't look good: four hiveships, six cruisers, a pair of smaller ships with an odd power signature that suggested they might be full of Darts… Assuming constant course and speed, they were four hours out of fighting distance; they were too close to try a hyperspace jump, so that was about what you had to expect. He was suddenly very glad he'd yielded to Ladon's suggestion and gotten a decent night's sleep.

"I'd say we have just under four hours before we can expect to engage," Lorne said. "Unless Atlantis has something else planned."

Ladon eyed the screen. "What if they made another jump through hyperspace? They'd be here much sooner then."

"They're too close," Lorne answered. "The way they have to drop out of hyperspace, Wraith ships don't seem to have a lot of fine control over their hyperdrives. We could make a microjump and engage them now if we wanted to —" The *Pride*'s controls pulsed confirmation in the palms of his hands. "But there's no way the Wraith could make the kind of jump."

There was another flicker of sensation at the tips of his fingers, and the communications officer said, "I have Atlantis, Chief."

The *Pride* passed him the image before it reached the main screen, and Lorne managed not to respond, though every fiber of his being wanted to. This was how the ship was supposed to be flown, by a pilot who was one with it, not at third hand, every sensation negated by the clumsiness of consoles and buttons and levers, relays so much slower than synapses. I'm sorry, Lorne said, in the back of his mind where only the ship could hear him. They have to do it this way — they found you, they repaired you, you can work with them. And we'll all face the Wraith together.

"Mr. Woolsey," Ladon said. "I see that we're in time. Though I don't see any sign of your — other — ally."

"We anticipate their arrival shortly," Woolsey said. His face was prim, and Lorne wondered just what had gone wrong. "In the meantime, may I suggest you join us in orbit? The *Hammond* will be lifting off within the hour, and we plan to raise Atlantis shortly after that."

"Raise Atlantis," Ladon said. "You plan to fly the city — to fight from her?"

"Yes." In the screen, Woolsey's face was bland, as though they did that every day. "Can you be here before we take off?"

Ladon glanced at Lorne, who felt the confirmation pulse through him almost before he formed the question. "We can be there in 51 minutes," he said.

"We'll be there," Ladon said, and nodded to his technician to cut the transmission. A sudden smile lightened his face. "That will be something to see, Atlantis in flight. Whatever else happens, at least we'll have seen that.

Lorne nodded, feeling the ship's acceptance wash through him, seeing the same wonder on the faces of the technicians and soldiers at their places. It was worth it to be there.

Sam pushed her hair out of her eyes and glanced at her watch. Six-thirty, time and past for Bill Lee's team to be out of the ship, out of the city, and on their way back to Earth. But no, there he was, on his hands and knees peering into the guts of a fire-control console, a younger uniformed technician crouching at his side.

"Okay, yeah, I see what you mean," he was saying, "but if you'll hand me that bridging bar —"

The technician did as he was told, inching forward a little as he did so.

"I wouldn't do that," Lee said, and both men jumped back as sparks flew. "Ok, see, that's the only problem with this particular technique, but if it holds…" He wormed his way back into the depths of the console, ignoring the wisp of smoke that curled out past him. "It's really solid."

"Yes, sir," the technician said, sounding genuinely impressed, and Sam tried not to flinch. Yes, the bridging bars would do the job, but if they blew in a firefight, they'd generally take the entire section with them. They were supposed to be ridiculously sturdy, but if anything was likely to override them, it was a pitched battle with a larger Wraith fleet. She shoved the thought aside as too late to worry about, and gently kicked Lee's back foot.

"Dr. Lee."

"Colonel?" Lee scrambled back out again, and peered up at her from the floor plates. "I'm just about done here, but there are a couple more things I want to go over —"

"It's time to leave," Sam said. "Your team is the last out."

"Yeah, about that." Lee came to his feet, adjusting his glasses. His jacket was peppered with tiny burn marks, and his hands were filthy. He seemed to realize the latter, and wiped his hands awkwardly on his pants. "If I were to stick around — I could get a few of the last little things taken care of, and, you know, then I'd be here to help with repairs and stuff."

For a second, Sam was tempted. The *Hammond* was so close to optimum status that even an hour or two of Lee's expertise might make all the difference. She curbed herself sternly. Bill wasn't a field operative, no matter how good he was when he was forced into it; it wasn't fair to let him risk his life for the difference between ninety-eight percent ready and one hundred. All the more so because both she and McKay were at risk, and after them, Bill was the biggest expert they had on Ancient technology. She shook her head. "Sorry, Bill. They're going to need you back at the SGC."

"But —" Lee stopped abruptly, obviously coming to the same conclusion she had made. "Oh. Right. Uh, yeah. I suppose so."

Sam grinned. She was suddenly very fond of him, this rumpled little man, never quite properly shaven, with his perpetually harried look and his fount of ideas. She wanted to hug him, to kiss his forehead, but she knew this was just the exhilaration that came with impending battle. "Not that I wouldn't rather keep you," she said, "but those are the orders."

"Thanks," Lee said, with a preoccupied smile, his attention back on the console. "Just one more quick thing —"

"Sorry," Sam said. "It's time to go."

Lee grimaced, but moved away from the console. She followed him down the corridor, feeling like a sheepdog as they collected the rest of his team, and walked with them across the landing pad back toward the towers. It was just sunset, the western horizon aflame behind them, while ahead the sky between the towers was dark blue velvet, spangled with the earliest stars. Warm light spilled from the doors to the city, and as they crossed into the tower, Lee glanced over his shoulder.

"You know, I never did see the aurora everybody talks about. Did you ever figure out what makes it so spectacular?"

"Something to do with the magnetic field," Sam answered. "Though I think the composition of the core probably plays a part."

Lee stopped dead. "Now that's very interesting. On M7K-991 —"

"Dr. Lee," one of the technicians said, and gave Sam an apologetic glance. "We really need to be getting to the gateroom now."

"Oh. Right." Lee picked up the pace uncomplainingly, and glanced over his shoulder with a shrugging smile. "It'll make for an interesting paper anyway."

"Yeah," Sam said. She wanted to follow them up to the gateroom, see them safely through the Stargate, but she wasn't in command of Atlantis any more. That was Woolsey's job, and she was needed on the *Hammond* to deal with the myriad last minute questions that inevitably arose. She retraced her steps, and the doors slid open to allow her out, but no wave of cold came in to meet her. Some sort of deflection field, she guessed, and filed a mental note to look into exactly how it worked. There were plenty of uses for such a thing. Assuming she survived — but that was a familiar gamble. The important thing was to win the battle.

On the pad, the *Hammond* stood waiting under the lights, a last technical crew busy on scaffolding around the engines. They were finishing up, by the look of it, taking down the platform even as Sam watched: one more thing to take off her mental list. The sunset glowed red-bronze along the horizon, the light caught between the distant towers at the end of the pier, the *Hammond* somehow more solid against that furnace glow. And now, too late for Bill Lee, a strand of the aurora coiled past the zenith, a pale blue thread against the black. He would be gone now, the last of the civilians and the technical personnel, the injured and the nonessential crew, the ones who didn't have to risk their lives. And it was her job to be sure that they had a city to return to: the bottom line, the thing she'd signed up for all those years ago, following in her father's footsteps. She lengthened her stride, her breath a plume in the cold air, heading for her command.

## CHAPTER FOURTEEN
# Battle Stations

DICK Woolsey looked at the typed memorandum with neither shock nor disbelief. It was precisely what he had expected. And so he left it uppermost on his laptop and walked out of his office to the upper bank of the control room, where General O'Neill was bending over a young airman's terminal. "General?"

O'Neill had traded service dress for BDUs and a T-shirt. Presumably either someone at the SGC had sent through his luggage or he'd borrowed a change from stores. He looked much more comfortable than he had earlier, much more like the hard headed colonel who had made Woolsey's life hell six years ago. It was rather comforting, actually. Colonel O'Neill might occasionally be certifiably insane, but he did get things done. Wordlessly, Dick handed him the laptop.

O'Neill read it and then walked him back in his office, shutting the door behind him. "So?"

"What do you mean, so?" Dick demanded.

"Pity you were so busy you didn't read that before we locked down the gate," O'Neill said.

"You mean the part where the IOA says to on no account lift the city and instead to evacuate completely and set the self-destruct?" Dick said. "The part where it's an absolute, clear direct order to destroy Atlantis rather than risk it falling into the hands of the Wraith? That part?"

O'Neill gave him a perky, irritating smile. "That part," he said. "The part you didn't read. Until after it was all over, of course. And then why would you do it after the Wraith are defeated?"

"And what if they aren't?"

The smile disappeared. "If they aren't, you won't be alive to face the music."

"Is that usually how you handle these things?"

"More or less," O'Neill said.

Below on the floor the gate to Earth was open, things coming through for the last time from the SGC. Landry obviously hadn't gotten the IOA's orders. Or perhaps, like O'Neill, he was ignoring them for the moment.

"I expect to be alive to face the music," Dick snapped. "And there is no way in hell that they're going to believe that I didn't disobey a direct order. If I do this and we're not all killed, it's the end of my career. They'll have me out of Atlantis by the end of the week. This will be the last thing I ever do."

"Then you'd better make it good," O'Neill said.

Dick took a deep breath. That was the bottom line. Win or lose, he'd pay the price, and that's what it meant to be in charge. He took another breath, looking out over the gateroom floor, at the stained glass windows darkening as night overtook this corner of this icy world in the middle of nowhere. Atlantis, the City of the Ancients. For a little while this had been his home. Maybe he would die defending it and maybe not, but either way he would lose Atlantis. For a moment he thought he heard Elizabeth Weir's voice behind him, but surely that was memory. "That's how it works, Richard."

He blinked. O'Neill was watching him, and surely he'd heard nothing. He cleared his throat. "Well," he said. "It's a shame I didn't get this before we shut the gate down."

"Then let's shut it down," O'Neill said.

Together they went out into the control room. Dick stood beside Airman Salawi's console. "Airman," Dick said, "it's time to close the gate down." The longer they waited, the more chance someone at the SGC would get the IOA's orders and feel like they had to heed them.

Salawi looked up. "I can't at the moment. We have inbound travelers."

"Well, as soon as they get here, tell the SGC not to send anybody else, and then shut it down," Dick said.

"Crap," O'Neill said, and Dick looked up from Salawi's screen.

The rippling surface of the wormhole parted, three figures stepping through, a fourth slighter figure coming behind the others, incongruous with a P90 and double pony tails like a four-year-old.

O'Neill came around the console, bellowing. "Daniel! What in the hell? What part of SG-1 is not coming to Atlantis did you not understand?"

Dick refrained from mentioning that it seemed to be about the same part as the IOA's order to evacuate and destroy the city. Apparently complete insubordination was one of the venerable traditions of the SGC. He followed the sputtering O'Neill down the steps to the gateroom floor as the wormhole died behind them.

"I told you no," O'Neill shouted. "I told Landry I needed Marines, not you!"

Dr. Daniel Jackson looked cheerful under the onslaught. "Sam had some questions about a problem she was having with an Ancient artifact, and as the foremost expert on Ancient artifacts on Earth, it seemed like I could help."

O'Neill's voice dropped to a low conversational tone. "The problem we're having with the Ancient artifact right now is that somebody's stolen it and we don't know where it is." He gave Colonel Cameron Mitchell a glare, who at least had the good grace to look solemn and attentive. "The last thing I need is SG-1 cluttering up the place."

Teal'c cleared his throat. "General Landry said that Colonel Carter required three additional 302 pilots. Colonel Mitchell and I were present and volunteered."

It was an unassailable fact that Carter had indeed asked for 302 pilots. O'Neill swore, rounding on Vala Mal Doran. "And you! What's your excuse?"

She shrugged perkily. "I'm decorative?"

O'Neill provided several more words not appropriate to the gateroom floor. "Do you realize that there is a giant Wraith fleet about to arrive, plus our allies aren't going to help unless we destroy an Ancient artifact that we can't destroy because first of all we don't know how, and second of all we can't find it?"

Mitchell turned to Vala Mal Doran. "It's an incredibly valuable Ancient artifact worth millions on the black market. Go find it!"

"And that's what I'm here for!" She gave Woolsey a brilliant and patently insincere smile and trotted off in the direction of the infirmary.

O'Neill shook his head, looking back at Teal'c and Mitchell. "Okay, you two report to Carter. And Daniel?"

"Yes?" Jackson looked smug.

"Go help Carter do whatever she needs to do to figure out how to get rid of this thing once we find it. Let's just assume we do before the Wraith arrive." He waited until Jackson had gone, then glanced up at the control center above, crew bending over their work again now that the excitement was over. "I've got no idea how we're getting out of this one," he said.

"All in a day's work," said Dick Woolsey.

The problem, Sam reflected, was that the *Hammond*'s crawl spaces sometimes required crawling. Apparently that crawling was best done by someone five foot two with shoulders no more than twenty four inches wide. How many actual people in the Air Force fit those specifications was a very good question. One would think, she considered as she leaned forward over a strut and attempted to work on something eighteen inches beneath her while dangling, that the average service member was a tiny little woman or a preteen child. Teyla would have trouble getting in here, and for Sam it was right out of the question. If she inched forward just a little more…

…she would fall on her nose into a pile of circuits and steel beams six feet down. This became apparent an instant past the point of no return.

Fortunately at that moment a very strong hand seized the back of her pants at the waistband, hauling her abruptly backwards with her middle over the strut and her feet on firm deck. Sam twisted around.

Teal'c let go with a broad grin. "Good afternoon, Colonel Carter."

"Teal'c!" Sam bounced up with something like her old buoyancy. Behind him Cameron Mitchell and Daniel were both beaming as she threw her arms around Teal'c. "What are you doing here?"

"We happened to be in the neighborhood," Daniel said, his hands in his pockets.

"And Landry said something about you needing 302 pilots," Cam said.

"It seemed that we could make ourselves useful," Teal'c said as she let go of him and hugged Daniel.

"Besides," Daniel said. "Do you think we'd let you and Jack get yourselves killed by a million Wraith while we sat in Colorado?"

"Hopefully we won't be killed by a million Wraith," Sam said. "Do you guys have any idea how glad I am to see you?"

"Yeah," Daniel said. "We kind of do. Now what's this about a missing Ancient artifact?"

Cam and Teal'c went to go suit up while Sam explained her missing artifact problem to Daniel; that wasn't Cam's problem, and he let it go, trusting that the people still in Atlantis would handle that. His job was to fly. He'd been one of the best, although he was all too aware of how long it had been since he'd climbed into the cockpit of a 302.

He stepped out onto the flight deck of *Hammond* with an insistent feeling of déjà vu. He'd borrowed a flight suit, and, helmet in hand, he half expected to find himself back on the good old *Prometheus*, with his own Blue Squadron waiting for him. Instead, Teal'c fell into place beside him, a steadying presence.

Across the deck, Sam and Lt. Colonel Hocken had their heads together, going over some last minute point of strategy. They looked up as he and Teal'c approached.

Hocken grinned at him. "If it isn't Shaft."

Sam's mouth twitched, but she refrained from comment.

"Hi, Mel," he said. "I thought I'd come lend a hand."

Hocken cocked her head. "You still remember how to fly these things?"

"Remember, sure," Cam said. "But it's been a while."

"We'll be sure to start you off nice and easy."

"I believe I remember how to pilot these craft as well," Teal'c said, looking amused.

"Teal'c," Hocken said more seriously. "It's an honor."

"The honor is mine," Teal'c said, inclining his head.

"This isn't social hour," Sam said. "Be honored later. Let's get this show on the road."

"Yes, ma'am," Hocken said.

"Yes, ma'am," Cam echoed.

"I'll show you your 302s," Hocken said. "They both took a beating, but we've glued them back together for you."

"As long as you used quality glue."

"Only the best on this ship." She sobered. "If you've never mixed it up with Wraith Darts before, they're faster than death gliders, but not as sturdy. A solid hit will take them out. It's getting the solid hit."

"Copy that."

"Not that I need to tell you your business."

"You're the expert here," Cam said. "I'm just visiting."

"You can drop in any time. We'll try to have a huge nasty battle waiting for you."

"Makes it feel just like home."

"I thought it might." Hocken stopped by a 302, putting her hand on the wing with easy familiarity. "Up you go." Her eyes swept the flight deck as he clambered up, confident in her people but scanning for any sign of anything out of place.

For a moment he felt a twinge of jealousy. He'd been senior to her in the old days, in overall command of the *Prometheus*'s 302s before the crash that had left him out of it for a year, wondering if he'd ever walk again. He'd gotten it back together, come a lot further than anyone had said he would in those first months. But he'd never have a fighter command again. His next step up was one of the big ships like *Hammond* where he could command from a chair.

But he'd had SG-1 for five years, and he'd never regret that.

He started running through the pre-flight checklist, still right there in his head as if he'd never stopped living and breathing flying, and stopped worrying about anything but the job at hand.

John glanced uneasily around the conference room. He was feeling distinctly outnumbered — Teyla with Alabaster's people, Ronon stuck watching McKay, McKay not to be trusted, even Lorne off flying the Genii ship — and the wary courtesy with which Woolsey was treating O'Neill didn't exactly make him feel any better. Not that he didn't trust O'Neill; he did, mostly. O'Neill had managed to get them sent back to Pegasus, after all. It was just... He glanced sideways down the length of the table, where Daniel Jackson was still typing furiously on a laptop. It was just he really wished he knew what O'Neill was up to.

"Colonel Sheppard," O'Neill said, and John hastily collected his thoughts.

"Sir."

"How close is Atlantis to being ready to lift?"

John suppressed a shrug as being more insubordinate than he actually wanted to be. "Dr. Zelenka says they're tweaking the last few systems now. We could lift if it was an emergency, but they're getting things optimized."

"Did he say how long?"

"By nine."

"That's good," Woolsey observed.

O'Neill nodded. "The Genii should be here by then, and the *Hammond*'s just about ready to go, too."

"I don't think we should factor out Guide's fleet," Woolsey said. "I believe Teyla will persuade Alabaster to at least make the jump here."

"We can't count on that," O'Neill said.

"I wouldn't underestimate Teyla," John said.

"I'm not," O'Neill said. "But do you think Guide is going to cave on this?"

*No.* John bit his lip. He didn't really want to get into the details of his conversation with Guide — was it only a few hours ago? "We may still find the damn weapon before then."

"I'm really kind of worried about that thing," O'Neill said. "I don't like weird Ancient devices running around loose, especially when nobody really knows what the damn thing does."

Woolsey looked as though he wanted to agree, but was too diplomatic to say so.

"And I really don't like that we don't know what's going on with McKay," O'Neill went on.

"McKay," Jackson said, not looking up from his laptop. "Jack, Queen Death's going to be in range in three, maybe four hours."

"In range?" O'Neill asked.

"As best I can figure out, anyway," Jackson said.

John glanced at his own tablet, touched the cool surface to bring up the ever-present sensor display. "It looks to me as though it'll be at least five hours before they get into Dart range," he said. "More than that before the hives can open fire. Assuming we meet them in orbit, of course."

"And the 302s can hit them sooner than that anyway," Jackson said. O'Neill turned to stare at him, and Jackson spread his hands. "Because they have greater range than the Darts. Mitchell was saying, before we came through the gate. I do pay attention, sometimes — and anyway, that wasn't my point."

"What is your point?" O'Neill said.

"I've been looking over what information we have about the Wraith," Jackson said.

He sounded uncomfortable, John thought, and his attention sharpened.

"It looks to me as though the Wraith can exert mental influence for quite some distance," Jackson said. "From a hive in orbit to the surface of a planet, even from a planet to a hiveship or cruiser in the same solar system, though I'm not entirely clear on whether that's achieved by using an external communications system to supplement their normal telepathy or not."

"Go on," O'Neill said. He didn't sound any more enthusiastic than John felt, which wasn't a good sign.

"Yeah. Um. Well, putting all those reports together, including the various times that Teyla was able to influence the Wraith long distance —" Jackson paused, then plunged on. "Presumably the Wraith themselves can do the same thing, in reverse, which is to say, their queens could theoretically influence someone on Atlantis itself."

"You're talking McKay," John said. His voice was flat, and he clenched his fists out of sight under the tabletop.

Jackson made an awkward, shrugging motion, spreading his hands. "We have to consider it, Colonel."

"They've never done it before," John said.

"Possibly they've never had cause," Jackson answered. "I mean, they haven't had anyone in the city before — or, actually, they could have been in contact with the various Wraith who've been dropped into the city, only you wouldn't have any way of knowing if they had."

"There have been single Wraith in the city who were killed before they could get word back to their hives," Woolsey said.

"Presumably the hive was out of range?" Jackson shook his head. "I don't like it either, but —"

"Look, Dr. Jackson," John interrupted. "I may be out of line here—" And I don't much care if I am. "—but you and McKay have a bit of a history. Are you sure that's not affecting your recommendation here?"

"Rodney and I—" Jackson began, and O'Neill gave an almost soundless laugh.

"Daniel doesn't hold nearly getting electrocuted against anybody. It's not like he was dead. Again."

"Thanks," Jackson muttered.

"Don't mention it." O'Neill's expression hardened. "So what are you suggesting?"

"I don't think McKay should be part of the team flying the city," Jackson said.

And that was it, John thought. That was where they ended up, not able to trust Rodney just when they needed him most. "You're talking McKay," he said. "The best scientist we have, the guy who knows more about the city than just about anybody. We can't afford not to have him."

"Dr. Zelenka can handle repairs," Woolsey said. "He's been a great success as head of sciences."

"McKay stole Hyperion's weapon," O'Neill said. "And it's not where he said he put it." He shook his head. "If Queen Death still has some hold on him, he could do more damage than anybody else on the city. We can't risk it, Sheppard."

John bit his lip, knowing O'Neill was right, and hating it. Right as far as it went, he amended, because it was Rodney, for God's sake, and Rodney would never—except he could remember all too well a Wraith with Rodney's face, yelling about revenge for his brother, all the drones turning at once to point their weapons, ready for a killing shot.

"It's my decision," O'Neill said. "I'll tell him myself."

"No," John said, and added, "sir." O'Neill lifted an eyebrow, and John plowed on. "I'd rather talk to him, General. If you don't mind."

"I figured you might," O'Neill said. "You don't have to, John."

"I know." John made himself meet the other man's gaze, pleased that his voice was still steady. "But I kind of owe him that much."

"Okay," O'Neill said. "It's your team."

John nodded, remembering tardily that O'Neill had been SG-1. He understood about gate teams. "Thank you, sir."

## CHAPTER FIFTEEN
# Alabaster's Gamble

ALMOST done. Rodney looked around the ZPM room with satisfaction, trying to ignore Ronon leaning against the nearest pillar.
Even though he hadn't been allowed to touch anything, he'd managed to make his ideas clear to Zelenka and the lanky German who
was currently working with him, and he thought the systems were
about as solid as they could be.

"One more thing. You should set up a phased fallback for if we
lose a ZPM, or if there's a massive drain on the shields. Which
there's likely to be, considering there's a Wraith fleet waiting out
there. The city's already programmed to narrow the shield and
abandon the city perimeter —"

"Yes, I do know that," Zelenka said.

"But if you set up a phased pullback —" Rodney stopped, the
words registering. "Oh. Right, yes, you were there. Anyway, I think
if you manage the powerdown so that no one sector has a decrease
of more than 18.8 percent, you could avoid triggering that proto-
col. And that means you can shape the shield to protect more than
just the tower."

Zelenka was nodding. "Yes. Yes, I see what you mean, and perhaps —" He reached for his laptop and began typing in numbers.
"Yes, you're right, and I think with some finessing of the system
we could maybe even stand a decrease at around twenty percent."

"Twenty? I don't think so."

"See for yourself." Zelenka swung the laptop so that he could see
the screen, and Rodney frowned at the numbers.

"Oh. Okay, yeah, that would work, but it's risky."

"If we have to do this, that will be the smallest risk we take,"
Zelenka said.

"True."

Zelenka spun the laptop away again, and typed a few final commands. "And that, I think, is all we can do now."

"Then McKay should probably go back to — whoever needs him next," Ronon said.

"I am not some kind of weird tool," Rodney began, and realized as Dr. Sommer smirked that he could have chosen his words more carefully.

"There you are," Sheppard said, from the door. He looked at Zelenka. "I thought you weren't going to have him work on the ZPM."

"He is the expert," Zelenka said, rather shortly. "And we are very nearly out of time."

"Yeah." Sheppard bit his lip. "How are you doing, anyway? How close to being done?"

Zelenka shrugged. "Almost there. We are ready to lift the city, at least, and the power is optimized."

"Yeah." Sheppard took a deep breath. "In that case — Rodney, I'm going to have to ask you to come with me."

"Come with you where?" Rodney glared at him. "Is this one of those stupid euphemisms like 'helping the police with their inquiries,' because if it is, I'm not going to be nice about it."

"For God's sake, McKay!" Sheppard swallowed whatever else he was going to say, and when he did speak, his voice was careful and cold. "Yes, it is like that. General O'Neill wants you locked up for the duration. For your own protection as much as anything."

"No, it's not for my protection," Rodney said. "It's because you think I'm still working for the Wraith, and you can't trust me. You're going to lock me up while Atlantis goes into battle, and you're not going to have me when you need me."

"Is that a threat?" Ronon said.

"No! No, it's a statement of fact!" Rodney glared at him. "I'm the person who knows more about this city, more about Ancient technology and more about the kind of physics that sustains this place than anybody else here, and for once I say this without ego, you're going to need me. We're up against six hiveships, and unless Todd's decided to join us — and he hasn't, has he? Then you're going to take damage, and you're going to need *me*."

Sheppard shook his head. "The reason Todd hasn't joined us is that you stole the damned weapon and put it somewhere—"

"I told you where I put it!" Rodney snapped. "It's not my fault it's not there."

"You shouldn't have taken it in the first place!"

"If I'd left it there, every Wraith in the city would have known the location the minute they looked at you." Rodney stopped, abruptly aware that his calculations might have been at fault.

"McKay." Sheppard was glaring at him now. "You took the weapon. The weapon is now missing. No, we—I am not going to let you run around loose during the battle. You said it yourself, most of us wouldn't be able to tell if you were sabotaging something, and the people who could be sure are going to be too damn busy to watch you."

"This isn't O'Neill's call," Rodney said. "Woolsey's in charge here."

"And he agreed," Sheppard said. "I agreed. So unless you want me to have Ronon stun you and carry you back to the detention area, you'll come with me right now."

"You wouldn't dare." Rodney was breathing hard, short indignant breaths that made him wonder if he was going to have some kind of attack. That was all he'd need, and they'd probably find some way to blame that on the Wraith, too.

"Ronon." Sheppard's face was set. Ronon heaved a sigh, and drew his blaster.

"Wait! Just—just wait a minute." Rodney looked from one to the other. They really meant it, he thought, they really were prepared to shoot him. "All right, fine, I'll go with you. You can lock me up if that's what you want, but you know it's not going to solve the problem."

"It just might," Sheppard said.

Rodney threw up his hands, and started toward the door. "Not likely."

"Look, it protects you, too," Sheppard said.

"Oh, that's really feeble." Rodney glared at Ronon. "Walking carpet!"

"Just don't start," Sheppard said, wearily, and Rodney fell silent. There was nothing left to say, not if nobody was actually going to listen to him, but when they reached the cells he stopped in the open doorway.

"If you lock me up for the battle and nothing happens, then what? You haven't proved anything. I'm still a suspect, and you won't have me when you need me."

"And if something happens and you're locked up tight, then we have proved it's not you," Sheppard said. "And — damn it, Rodney, you took Hyperion's weapon. What in hell were you thinking?"

Rodney stepped back, suddenly too tired to fight any more. "That I didn't want the Wraith to get it," he said, quietly. "But I swear to you, John, I left it exactly where I told you."

Sheppard bit his lip again. "Can you tell me for sure that Queen Death hasn't put some other hold on you? Something deeper?"

Rodney hesitated. Of course there was no knowing, he wanted to say. It was a stupid question — how could he know whether or not the queen had implanted a subconscious command? That was why it was called 'subconscious.' But — no, he couldn't be sure. None of them could be sure.

Sheppard nodded as though he'd read the thought. "Yeah. I didn't think so."

Rodney took another step back, allowing the door to slide closed. "You know, Sheppard, if the city blows apart —"

"We'll try to remember to come get you," Sheppard answered, but Rodney had seen him flinch. It didn't feel like much of a victory, though.

John stalked out of the detention area, trying not to look as guilty as he felt. That was Rodney after all, Rodney who'd been part of the team for five years, and no matter what the Wraith did to him, Rodney wasn't going to betray them when the chips were down.

Except that wasn't true. He remembered all too clearly the Wraith with Rodney's face ordering the drones to destroy him. But that wasn't really Rodney, or rather, Rodney hadn't known himself, had believed he was a Wraith. Now that he knew who he was, he was too tough, too downright contrary, to give in to Queen Death no matter what she'd done to him.

Except that wasn't true either. The Wraith had broken Ronon once, and if Ronon could break, anyone could. He glanced at the big Satedan, who looked away. "I don't know, I think we're making a big mistake."

"O'Neill doesn't think so," Ronon said.

"Yeah, but he doesn't know Rodney."

Ronon looked at him.

"Doesn't know Rodney now," John amended. "I mean, yeah, Rodney can be difficult —

"They turned him into a Wraith, Sheppard."

John looked away. That was the crux of the matter, and there still wasn't any good answer. "Teyla says —" And he stopped, because he knew what Ronon thought of that, too. But there Ronon was wrong. Teyla was Teyla, Athosian — human — to the core, and if she thought she saw a better way to deal with the Wraith, well John would back her, just like he'd back her when she said Rodney wasn't under Queen Death's control.

As far as he knew. As far as she could tell. She wasn't certain either, not entirely.

*But it's Rodney, damn it!* he thought. Rodney might bitch and moan, worry about allergies and weird crap like that, but he was part of the team, he understood what that meant. He wouldn't let them down. And that meant — if there was a problem, if there was some disaster in the city, Rodney had to be let loose, because he was still the best man to deal with it. Someone had to let him out, because John himself would be in the chair flying the city.

"Ronon —"

The corridor was empty. He hadn't even heard him go. He took a step back toward the cells, as though the Satedan might be lurking, but stopped himself. He hadn't felt this alone in years.

Aboard *Just Fortune*, Teyla paced the width of the queen's quarters and back again, able to indulge herself with no one watching. Perssen and Thessen were in the inner room with Darling, the three of them playing at a three-handed board game that had been popular among Steelflower's blades. Teyla had no patience for games at the best of times, but she was grateful that it kept them busy. The third human, Erach, seemed to be sleeping, to judge from the faint snores that blended with the sound of the ventilators.

She wanted to lay her hand on the bulkhead, to feel the ship's progress. They were due to drop out of hyperspace any time now, and that should bring them to the edge of Atlantis's system. Queen Death's fleet would be closer, too, moving inexorably toward Atlantis, and she hoped again that John had found Hyperion's weapon. What had Rodney been thinking, to take it in the first place? Had he been compelled by Queen Death?

It was not the first time she had worried at that problem, and she shook her head yet again. If there was a bond, Rodney did not know it: she was still confident in her word. But if there was a compulsion of which he was not aware... She could see how it could be done, could do it herself, and if she could, so could a true Wraith Queen. Had she been able to question herself, when she faced Coldamber, she might not have seen the subtle bonds...

But that was not to the point. She started to lay her hand on the bulkhead again, and again stopped herself. The ship would know her, and might unwittingly betray her presence — Steelflower's presence — and she could not risk that; she would have to wait until Alabaster returned to know what was going on. Being queen had spoiled her: she still half expected to be able to bend the blades and clevermen to her will.

The deck shuddered underfoot and she looked up sharply. Had the lights flickered as well? It was hard to tell. She trailed a finger along the nearest bulkhead, the heavy hide warm to the touch. She kept her own mind tightly closed, thoughts hidden, ready to pull away the moment the ship seemed aware of her presence. Instead, there was a rush of confusion, discomfort, anger — as though the exit from hyperspace had not gone well? She took her hand away, unwilling to probe more, and went back to pacing.

*Just Fortune* had left hyperspace too soon, the numbers botched; they hung at the outer fringes of the target system, ten hours or more from their planned rendezvous, too far to reach the city before Queen Death's fleet could engage. Ember frowned over his console, ducking his head as the Hivemaster's anger filled the control room.

*What incompetent programmed this jump?"

*I did.* Ease matched him glare for glare. *And my calculations were correct.*

*Manifestly not!* Bonewhite snapped.

*I say they were,* Ease answered. *Ask the Engineer what happened, not me.*

*There was no flaw in the engines,* Hasten said, coldly calm as always. *I have run a second diagnostic, and my systems are unaffected.*

*Nor was there anything wrong with my navigation,* Ease snarled.

Ember ignored them both, fixing his attention on the screen. There was something wrong, something he couldn't quite see yet, an irregularity — yes, there, a flaw in the smooth code, the beautiful and perfect codes that had been shared among all the ships of the fleet… *Hivemaster,* he said, sharply enough to cut through the swelling quarrel. *Someone has tampered with the navigation programming itself. An extra calculation was added, just here. It subtracts a set amount from our final calculation, and drops us out of hyperspace early, without damaging the ship.*

*Let me see that.* Bonewhite leaned over the console, and Ember ducked out of the way, making himself small and quiet while the Hivemaster scrolled down the waterfall of code. *By all the Mothers, this is madness!* He swung away, heavy coat swirling. *Sabotage again —*

*Indeed, sabotage again,* Alabaster said, and her words silenced the confusion of conversation as though she had flipped a switch. She stood in the hatchway, her scarlet hair loose on her shoulders, her expression mildly curious. That was frightening enough on Guide, but terrifying on a queen, and Ember was not the only one to bow in instinctive answer.

Bonewhite did not bow, but his tone was respectful. *Lady.*

Alabaster came forward, laid one hand on his sleeve. *This must be rooted out.*

*Lady, that I know!*

Alabaster showed teeth. *I say this as She Who Speaks for Steelflower. There is a promise to be kept, and we are close to failing her.*

*I know that, too,* Bonewhite said, through clenched teeth. *Hasten! You say the engines are solid? Well, here's your chance to prove it. Open a hyperspace window for me, and I'll bring us through to Atlantis.*

*Madness!* Ease said. *We cannot jump so close to a sun, the fields won't stand it.*

Bonewhite looked at Hasten. *Well?*

*It's a risk,* the engineer answered. *The deeper one falls into a gravity well, the greater the chance that the ship will break apart. But I believe we can stand it.*

*And I will lay the course myself,* Bonewhite said. His tone dared anyone to object. *Now.*

The duty pilot ducked hastily away from this state, and after a moment Ease backed away as well.

*On your head be it, to kill the daughter of the Commander.*

Bonewhite bared teeth in a sudden grin. *And if I fail, what does it matter? We'll all be dead.*

Alabaster smiled. *You are confident, Hivemaster.*

*I am, Lady.* This time he did bow.

*Then begin.* Alabaster leaned against the commander's station, tall and lithe and vital. Ember allowed himself one long look, drinking in her courage, and turned his attention back to his console, attending with half his mind while Bonewhite and Ease and Hasten contacted the rest of the fleet, Ease raising his voice to shout down any opposition. Ember couldn't blame the other commanders, but — there was no other choice, and so they all eventually agreed. Bonewhite studied his calculations a final time, and raised his face to the communications web.

"Take the course from me, or lay your own, but follow me now!"

A jumble of voices answered, affirming their readiness, and Ember braced himself against his console.

*Open the hyperspace window,* Bonewhite ordered, and *Just Fortune* surged through.

Zelenka said something rude in Czech, staring at his screen, and then shook his head. "Sergeant Ling!"

"I saw it, Doc," the technician on the sensors answered. "It looks like Todd's hive, but they're way out on the fringe of the system."

"Well, what are they doing there?" John demanded. He'd only planned to stop in the control room long enough to touch base with

Zelenka, and it looked as though all hell was breaking loose. I've got to stop coming up here, he thought, and came to stand behind Ling.

"How far out?" Zelenka asked, and Ling typed a quick query.

"Seven, maybe ten hours? I don't get it."

"Are you telling me Todd's ships aren't going to get here for seven hours?" John's voice started to rise, and he controlled it hastily. "Crap! What's he playing at?"

"Perhaps there was some kind of problem," Zelenka said. "They are not powering down to normal — maybe they didn't solve their navigation problem correctly" "They're opening another hyperspace window," Ling said. "Holy crap —"

The hiveships vanished from the screen, and reappeared a moment later further into the system. Much closer, John thought, maybe an hour or maybe less, almost in orbit. Zelenka swore again.

"I would not like to try that, and I'd rather they didn't do it anywhere near my planet, thank you."

The communications screen chimed at that moment, and a picture formed: another long-haired Wraith male. This one looked vaguely familiar, and John dredged his memory: Kenny, Todd's second-in-command on the ill-fated mission where Teyla had first masqueraded as Steelflower. And now Teyla was on his ship. John didn't know whether that was likely to be good or bad.

"Atlantis." Kenny's voice hissed from the speakers. "We are here as our Queen and Commander have ordered."

"Nice to see you, too," John said. "You may have noticed we have company."

"I see Queen Death's fleet," Kenny answered. "But I do not take my orders from you. We will engage when and if our Commander orders, and not before."

John bit his lip. "Fair enough. And I'm guessing you want to talk to him, too."

Kenny made a sound that might have been laughter. "Indeed we do."

"Absolutely," John said. "Look, just kick back, have a beer or something, and I'll go get him." He made a slashing gesture, and Banks cut the connection. "Get Woolsey and O'Neill on the double."

Guide had been waiting for some time, though he had lost

precise track of the time. Not long by Wraith standards, but an unreasonable amount of time by human reckoning, and he filed that knowledge as possibly of use. The Lanteans did not know what to do in the way of courtesy if they could not offer food and drink; there was no place in their ritual for the play of dice or tiles, or the sharp exchange across the stone game. They had left him a carafe and glass as though they could not quite believe he did not require it, and someone had had the wit to dim the lights a fraction, but that was all.

The room had chairs and a long low daybed as well as the table, and Ancient writing coiled across the wall. It was the form of his youth, familiar shapes though he could only read one word in ten — invocations, blessings, perhaps, on the city's peoples? He could not tell. He turned to the long window instead, peered out into the fading evening. A chill radiated from the glass, and he hunched his shoulders inside his heavy coat, careful to keep his feeding hand well away from the cold metal of the frame. An aurora bloomed in the sky, tendrils of light rising like pale flame from the horizon, as thin as smoke, coiling silently behind the towers. He had seen auroras before, on other worlds, but nothing quite like this. He had not seen it when he had been here before — Sheppard had brought him from stasis to the Stargate in haste, there had been no time for gawking. Presumably no one else had seen it either, at least not before the Lanteans were forced to land here, but he could not shake the sense of unease.

The lights brightened, the colors stronger, whips and veils of green and blue scourging the skies. *Once before we slept...* The words of a children's story, long forgotten, flashed through his mind. *Once before we slept there was a world where the skies streamed with fire, and the First Mothers turned their back on it and fled.* He couldn't remember the rest of it, or even why the Mothers had abandoned it — the story had been old and tangled even when he was in the crèche, which made it old indeed. It would be a bad sky to fly in, he thought, reaching deliberately for rationality, hard on the instruments and tricky on the eye. He turned his back on the window, reaching into his pocket for a set of pyramids, and set himself a game, off hand against feeding hand.

It was full dark when they came for him, Sheppard and Woolsey and the consort O'Neill, and his feeding hand was winning at an improbable rate. Guide palmed the pyramids as the door slid back, and turned easily to face them.

"So my fleet is here?" It was an easy guess: Teyla would have exerted all her influence to bring them regardless of his orders, and Alabaster unquestionably had a mind of her own.

"That's right," Sheppard said, and Woolsey cleared his throat.

"Yes, and they'd like a word with you."

"I'm sure they would."

"But we'd like a word with you first," O'Neill said. "Specifically, are you going to fight beside us, or not?"

Guide studied him carefully, wishing it were Sheppard he had to deal with. Or even Woolsey; he'd come to understand a bit of Hairy's mind since they'd begun the game of diplomacy. But O'Neill he did not know at all. "You know my conditions," he said, playing for time, and saw Sheppard bite his lip.

"We don't have it," O'Neill said. "And believe me, that doesn't make us any happier than it does you."

"Forgive me if I doubt that," Guide snapped.

"It is not to our advantage to lose two of our best people," Woolsey said. "Not to mention an unknown number of others. Nor is it the policy of my government to wantonly murder its allies."

Guide's eyes slid to Sheppard at that, saw the hint of doubt in the younger man's eyes. "Perhaps you do not generally kill your allies," he said, "but our alliance is… tenuous at best."

"And not made any stronger by you not siding with us against Death," O'Neill said.

"And if you were in my place, would you throw your fleet into battle alongside 'allies' who hold a knife to your throat?" Guide shook his head. "Hyperion's weapon must be destroyed. That is not a matter for negotiation."

"But we don't have it," Sheppard said. His frustration was palpable, and for a moment Guide felt a shiver of doubt. If in fact the Lanteans weren't bluffing, if they'd somehow lost the weapon — but, no, they could not be that careless. This was just another attempt to get something for nothing.

"I'll be honest with you," O'Neill said. "Without your fleet, we don't stand much of a chance against Queen Death. I think we can get the city away safely, and maybe without getting the *Hammond* and the *Genii* shot up too badly, but we'll just have to do it again someplace else. And maybe you're thinking about that, thinking that maybe we'll soften up Queen Death enough that you can take her out by yourself. But I think if you thought you could get away with it, you wouldn't have bothered making a deal with us in the first place, weapon or no weapon. Which says to me that you're running one hell of a risk not helping us out here. And I really get the impression that the lady doesn't like you."

Guide grinned. "She does not, no. But I say again, Hyperion's weapon negates all other considerations. You say we cannot risk fighting Death alone. I say that it would be worse, far worse, to leave Hyperion's weapon intact and in your hands."

"If we were going to use it," Sheppard said, "we wouldn't be planning to fight Queen Death ourselves."

Guide rounded on him, deliberately moving at his full speed. "But you have lost the weapon, have you not? You have no choice but to fight."

To his credit, Sheppard didn't flinch. "Yes, we have lost it, and no, we don't have any choice. And, no, we're not going to use the damn thing!"

He believed it, Guide thought, his eyes flickering back to Woolsey and O'Neill. But the others... They were bluffing, hoping to force his hand. But for the sake of his people — of all the Wraith — he could not give in. "I would do the same if I were you," he said, "and I will speak to my fleet. But I will not order them to move until I see Hyperion's weapon destroyed."

## CHAPTER SIXTEEN
# Atlantis Rising

THERE was a moment of quiet as they came up into the control room, a heartbeat's silence like an intake of breath. John knew exactly where it came from, the moment of panic they all still felt when an unfettered Wraith walked into range, even when that Wraith was technically an ally. The talk resumed, determinedly, technicians and airmen alike trying to pretend Guide wasn't there, half a hand's-breadth taller than either of the escorting Marines, and Guide bared teeth in something that might have been amusement.

"Well, John Sheppard," he said. "We come round the circle again."

"We've been here before, all right," John said, and Woolsey drew himself up to his full height.

"Er — Guide."

You could see it almost killed him not to have an honorific to tack onto the name, John thought.

"Your fleet has arrived, and their commander wishes to speak to you."

"I'm sure he does." Guide looked at him and then at O'Neill. "I ask you again, are you prepared to meet my terms?"

"Yes," Woolsey said. "It's to our advantage to do so. We just can't do it right now."

Guide shook his head, the long strands of his hair hissing against the leather of his coat. "Then there is no bargain. I would like to speak to my commander now."

"Be my guest," O'Neill said. The frustration in his voice was very clear.

"Banks," Woolsey said, and the dark-haired woman nodded.

"I have them on the screen, sir."

She nodded toward the larger of the communications displays, and John turned toward it as it lit, revealing Kenny's straggling hair and high forehead. The tattoo on his right cheek seemed very dark against his marbled skin.

"Commander. What are your orders?"

"To do nothing, for now." Guide looked back at O'Neill as if waiting for him to change his mind. "We will not engage just now."

"Very good, Commander."

Did Kenny look a little confused? John wondered. He hoped so — anything that would disrupt Guide's plans had to be good for them. Maybe.

"And now…" Guide looked down at Woolsey, clearly relishing the difference in their heights. "If we can come to no agreement, Mr. Woolsey, then I must return to my ship."

To his credit, Woolsey didn't step back, just lifted his chin a little to meet the Wraith's slit-eyed stare. "If you wish, of course —"

"But we're a little busy to be running a taxi service," O'Neill said.

"Now that," Guide said, "begins to sound like a threat. And that, surely, would be unwise."

"No threats," Woolsey said, with a minatory look at O'Neill. "And I'm sure we can arrange transport, as Ms. Emmagan will surely want to return to Atlantis. Her presence with your fleet is no longer required."

"Of course," Guide said. He looked back at the screen. "I will be returning to the hive, and Teyla Emmagan will be coming back to Atlantis. Inform the Young Queen."

"At once, Commander." Kenny bowed, and the picture disappeared.

John glanced at the sensor display, calculating times and distances. Half an hour out and back, a quick switch-over on the hive — yeah, the city could spare him that long. "With your permission, General, I'll take Guide across to the hive in a jumper, and bring Teyla back."

O'Neill lifted an eyebrow, but didn't say anything. Woolsey nodded. "Thank you, Colonel."

John touched his radio. "Lieutenant Clark. I'd like a Marine escort in the jumper bay immediately."

"Yes, sir," the lieutenant answered, and John looked at Guide. "I just don't want you getting any ideas."

Guide showed teeth. "It is not I who needs help, John Sheppard."

It was not a long flight to the hive. Kenny had the Dart bay open for them, and John brought the puddlejumper neatly into the open space. In the viewscreen, he could see Teyla waiting, flanked by Alabaster and a handful of drones, and he pushed himself up out of the pilot's chair as the Marines lowered the tailgate.

"Guide."

The Wraith looked over his shoulder.

"You know neither one of us can beat Death alone."

Guide paused. "I know. And you know my price, John Sheppard."

He turned, coat swirling at his heels, and stalked down the ramp to join his daughter. Teyla moved at the same moment, and they passed without speaking. Teyla climbed into the jumper, and the nearest Marine hit the switch that closed the tail.

"We're clear, sir."

John was already back in the pilot's chair, the board lighting blue at his touch, and a moment later Teyla settled into the copilot's place. "Good to have you back," he said, without looking up, but he could almost feel her smile.

"It is good to be back," she said. "Though I think it would be well if we did not linger."

The Dart bay door was still open, and John brought the puddlejumper up and around in a single smooth curve. He braced himself for collision alarms, for closing doors and the crash of energy weapons, but nothing happened. They slid smoothly out into the night, and nothing pursued.

He set a course for Atlantis, sliding from day into night, the towers' lights a tiny point in the distance, and finally glanced at Teyla. She looked completely composed, as usual, her hands resting lightly on the arms of the chair, but there was a faint line between her brows. "Any luck with Alabaster?"

She gave a rueful smile. "Indeed, I do not know. She has a solid claim to have spoken with Steelflower, and to be doing her bidding, but — I do not know if the men will follow her in preference to Guide." She shook her head. "I've done what I can, John."

*If only we could find the damn weapon — if only McKay hadn't screwed around with it in the first place.* If only they'd never

found the thing. If only. John swallowed those thoughts as pointless, letting the puddlejumper slide deeper into the atmosphere.
"Yeah. So have we all."

"What can I do for you?" Jennifer said as Daniel Jackson stuck
his head diffidently into her office.

"Actually, I just figured I might not be in the way down here,"
Daniel said. "Everyone's pretty busy, and I always find it hard to
nap when we're about to have a space battle."

"Me, too," Jennifer said. "I probably ought to get some sleep,
because I expect we'll have casualties coming in later, but…" She
shook her head. "Want some coffee?"

"Please," Daniel said. He took the cup she handed him and hovered politely behind the visitors' chair.

"You're welcome to have a seat," Jennifer said. "There's nothing
else for me to do until the shooting starts. When it does, I'll have
to kick you out."

"Of course," Daniel said. He shook his head. "I always used to
wonder how Jack could sleep when we were waiting for a battle. I
used to think it was a trick I'd pick up eventually. Apparently not."

"If you were going to, I think you would have by now."

"Yep. I've been doing this for… too long." Daniel shook his head.
"I'm hoping to have the chance to see more of Atlantis when this is
over, but this doesn't seem like the moment for sight-seeing."

"It's not the best circumstances."

"It never seems to be."

"At least you haven't been nearly electrocuted this time."

"Not yet. Don't jinx it."

"Sorry."

"I'm sorry to have missed the Wraith," Daniel said.

Jennifer looked at him in bemusement. "You know, most people don't say that."

"We still know so little about them," he said. "I mean, looking at
the recent reports, this is the first confirmation we have that the
Wraith even have personal names. And we've learned something
about the status of Wraith queens within the hive, and about divi-
sion of labor, and a tiny bit about family relationships. But that's

pretty close to the sum total of what we know about the Wraith after six years, aside from the obvious and admittedly distracting fact that they eat people."

"We've studied their written language."

"We've started studying their written language, but, again, we've mostly been focused on basic translation, so we haven't gotten much farther than establishing that it's based on Ancient, which of course follows. But I'd like to actually look at how the two languages diverged, given that now we have some idea of when the Wraith were created. And get some idea of how the language works in practice in a telepathic society — we know that Wraith names have a telepathic component, and that what they're giving us are rough equivalents, so I think looking at their non-verbal communication would be fascinating." He trailed off, with a wry expression. "That may just be me."

"No, it is interesting," Jennifer said. "It's been really hard to find out anything about Wraith culture. Basically most of our interactions have been with prisoners, and they haven't wanted to talk to us very much. Like you said, this is the first time they've even been willing to tell us their names."

"And I see that the part where they eat people makes ethnographic study tricky."

"We haven't really been in a position to send somebody to observe them, no. They think of us basically as livestock."

"That was always fun with the Goa'uld," Daniel said. "Except they thought of us as slaves and potential hosts, which was a little better, but... not really that much. But at least when we were dealing with the Goa'uld we had the Jaffa to explain them to us."

"I suppose we could talk to the Wraith worshippers," Jennifer said. "But I think a lot of them don't ever see the Wraith at close quarters. It would have to be someone who'd lived on a Wraith hive ship, and we've never heard of anyone who did that and then left the ship alive."

"Believe me, I see your problem."

"At least the Wraith — Guide's Wraith — are talking to us right now. I don't know how long that's going to last after we defeat Queen Death. Assuming we defeat Queen Death. And then there's the question of the retrovirus."

"The one that makes humans able to survive being fed on by the Wraith?"

Jennifer nodded. "We don't really have any idea what that's going to mean for Wraith society, assuming it's even used on a wide scale. Whether they can ever start thinking about humans as people."

"What do you think?" Daniel asked.

She sipped her cooling coffee and considered that. "I think it's possible, once they don't have to eat us," she said. "I think some of them — Guide, for instance — are aware on some level that we're people, but they have to be able to feed to live, so they tell themselves that most humans are no better than cattle at the same time that they're willing to work with us."

"Do you think they'll accept the retrovirus?"

"It's not entirely up to them," Jennifer said. "Humans in Pegasus are going to use it whether the Wraith want them to or not. I think it's a strategic advantage in some ways — they have a population problem, and being able to feed on humans more than once would help them avoid having to go into hibernation because there's not enough for them to eat. Guide was certainly interested in our previous retrovirus, which would have made it unnecessary for them to feed at all, although I'm getting the impression that would have been harder for them to accept."

"A bigger cultural change," Daniel said. "If humans didn't have to eat or drink, that would be great, right? Only think how disruptive it would be to have all of our cultural rituals around eating and drinking suddenly become unnecessary, and maybe impossible."

"And people do like eating and drinking," Jennifer said, raising her coffee cup. Beyond its effect as a stimulant, she had to admit that the coffee was comforting to have in her hand.

"They do. It's pleasurable and psychologically rewarding, and it's a major part of social rituals. A dietary shift is easier to accept."

The intense light of interest on his face was hard to resist. "If we win the battle, I'll see if I can introduce you to the Wraith, all right?"

"I'd like that," Daniel said.

Sam scrolled to the last page of the reports, her eyes skimming past the details to the final summary: ninety-eight percent ready.

Ninety-eight percent of optimum, and forty-eight hours ago she'd have laughed if you'd said she could get the *Hammond* ready for battle in that amount of time. But her crew had worked miracles, her people and Zelenka's team from Atlantis and Bill Lee and his crew from the SGC. She hoped they got the respect they deserved for it, especially Bill. He'd been in her shadow, and Daniel's, and even McKay's, and if he'd been anywhere else he'd have been the top man, not the guy who was always second best. She'd said as much in the report she'd just finished, and now she touched the keys to add it to the queue for the next databurst, but she wasn't under too many illusions about the likelihood of it reaching Earth any time soon. Yes, they'd been in impossible situations before and somehow survived, but there were four hiveships bearing down on the planet, and still no sign that Todd was going to help them.

She touched keys, bringing the current tactical plot to the foreground. Not that Todd's fleet was all that impressive. He had three hives, yes, but one of them was smaller than the others, its mass and power signature both less, and he certainly lacked the support vessels. Queen Death had eight cruisers of varying sizes and who knew how many Darts; Todd had only a pair of cruisers and a smaller ship that she suspected was supposed to be some kind of support vessel. Sensors said it was armed, but not heavily enough for the coming battle.

Of course, they also had the *Hammond*, and the *Pride of the Genii* — with Lorne flying the Ancient warship, she felt reasonably sure it would stay on their side and not vanish into hyperspace as soon as things got difficult — and Atlantis itself, which was still kind of amazing to contemplate. But all in all, she suspected that their best result was going to be to do significant damage to Queen Death's fleet and get Atlantis into hyperspace before her Wraith could press the attack. And that wasn't going to be as easy as she'd like.

She glanced at the time display and straightened her shoulders. T-minus twenty, and it was time she took her place on the bridge. Her eyes strayed to the pictures above her bunk, held to the bulkheads with plain black magnets. They were all here, all her old team, Jack and Teal'c and Daniel and Cam and Vala, and though she knew she should wish them safe on Earth, she couldn't help being glad of their presence. God knew she needed 302 pilots, and Cam and Teal'c were two of the best.

The bridge crew was ready, even though wires hung untidily from a few of the consoles. Sam took her seat, and nodded to Major Franklin. "Status, Major?"

"We're ready to go, Colonel," he answered.

Sam nodded. She'd never yet managed to have that conversation with him, though she thought she knew what she was going to say when she had a minute, but at least there was no question about his abilities as a tactical officer. "Get me Atlantis," she said, and the pony-tailed airman on the communications board jumped to obey.

"Atlantis here, *Hammond.*" That was Jack's voice, faintly ironic as always.

"We're at ninety-eight percent of optimum, General," Sam said. "We're ready to lift."

"Good job," Jack said. His voice chanced slightly, became more formal. "Colonel, the city will launch after you. Proceed to a low parking orbit and wait for us to join you. Then you and *Pride of the Genii* can go hunt Wraith."

"Yes, sir," Sam said. "Permission to lift?"

"Lift when ready." Jack paused. "Give 'em hell, Carter."

Sam grinned. "Will do, sir. Captain Chandler. Take us into orbit."

"Yes, ma'am." Chandler's hands moved on the controls, and Sam felt the *Hammond* shudder as the inertial dampeners took hold. Engines rumbled, steadied, and the *Hammond* rose from the pad. Chandler spun her horizontally, facing away from the towers, and pointed her at the sky. Sam couldn't suppress her grin as the sky went from blue to black, the *Hammond* sliding from atmosphere to vacuum, stars filling the screens. Steering engines fired, and she caught a glimpse of the Genii ship hanging further out, a graceful shape bright against the black. A secondary screen showed the night side of the planet, haloed in white, the pinpoint of light that was Atlantis the only mark on the perfect circle.

"We've achieved stable orbit, ma'am," Chandler said.

"Nice job, Captain." Sam looked at the technician. "Comm, let Atlantis know we're here."

"Yes, ma'am." The airman's hands flew across her board, and

she looked over her shoulder. "Atlantis acknowledges — and the Genii ship is signaling."

"Put them through," Sam said.

"Colonel Carter." It was Ladon Radim in the screen, polite and unreadable as ever. "It's good to see you again."

"And you, Chief Ladon." Sam repressed the urge to cross her fingers.

"Major Lorne has suggested that after Atlantis is established in orbit we make a microjump to just within range of Queen Death's fleet, strike, and jump back out of range."

"Hit and run," Sam said. She could see how it would work, a quick strike to damage the cruisers, and then jump away again. "Major Franklin?"

"We can do it, ma'am."

Sam nodded. "I concur, Chief Ladon. Assuming Atlantis agrees."

"We'll await their approval," Ladon answered, and cut the connection.

"Colonel," the airman at the communications board said. "Atlantis is ready to lift."

Sam looked at the side screen, the black disk of the planet with the tiny glint of light. So tiny, to carry so many lives — but it was the Ancients' Lost City, Teyla's City of the Ancestors, unimaginably old and unimaginably powerful. She might be rising now to her last battle, but she had Sheppard in the chair and Jack in command and that had to mean something. "Confirmed," she said, and turned her attention to the tactical displays.

John settled into the chair, stretching his hands along the arms. It felt cool, waiting. He took a deep breath.

In his headset, Radek spoke from the control room, "Colonel Sheppard, we are all systems green."

"Okay," John said. "Let's do this." He closed his eyes and leaned back, the pads of his fingers sinking in the soft silicone gel that allowed the chair to connect to his own nervous system. There was the usual momentary disorientation as connections formed, the universe broadening until his own body was only a tiny part. John Sheppard sat in the chair in Atlantis.

And John Sheppard was Atlantis. He was the city, thousands of years old, home of millions of people throughout time, lost beneath the waves and found again, a wandering relic, a caravan, an ark, a place of safety that traveled through the stars as surely as a Wraith hive ship.

It's the same, John thought. It's the same idea, the same heart of it — a place that can be anyplace, a ship to sail the wide seas of night and carry people in it safe from the hazards of any shore. My home.

Yours, the city whispered, each circuit reaching for each synapse like a child reaching for its mother, like lover speaking to lover. For a moment he knew them all as the city had known them, pilot upon pilot who sat in this chair through the long centuries, chosen by luck or by skill, in honor and in hardship, a boy barely into his teens sinking into the city's systems to speak through it, its voice now his, an old woman who had died in the chair's embrace, gratefully breathing her last as a hyperspace window opened. They were the ones who had come before him, guardians all.

For a moment he saw himself, black uniform and graying hair. The chair tilted back to welcome him. This was where he belonged. This was what it needed. His mind, his touch, his strength to yield. And long after John Sheppard was dead, Atlantis would remember.

*We need to go,* he said.

Lines of force appeared, the city calculating the best trajectory. Far beneath, there was a rumble, mighty engines coming online, ports closing beneath the water.

That was Radek's voice on the headset, distant and near at once. "We are showing optimal power from the ZPM."

He knew that. The city knew it. It was ready.

*Then go,* John said.

The city trembled, engines firing, sliding upward almost impossibly slowly at first and then gaining speed, water streaming away, steaming in vast clouds superheated in the cold air, billowing out over the surface of the sea. Atlantis rose.

"God, that's beautiful." Carter's voice on the line, hushed, as though she hadn't realized she was transmitting.

The sky above darkened, a hemisphere of stars. The *Hammond* was below, a small bright shape against flowing clouds.

"We have achieved a stable orbit," Radek said.

Yes, the city said. All is well. Lines of force flowed about the world, easy to direct, easy to choose a path that looped the city around the world in a high equatorial orbit. There.

John opened his eyes. "Okay," he said into the headset. "I think we're good."

## CHAPTER SEVENTEEN
# Ronon's Decision

THE *PRIDE of the Genii* had no trouble maintaining the link to Atlantis; it had a bit more trouble collecting the *Hammond's* transmission, and Lorne suspected it might be taking the feed from the city rather than from the *Hammond* directly. He and Radim had retreated to what had probably been intended as a secondary control room, but which Radim had co-opted as his personal suite. One wall was covered in display screens, the feeds from the *Hammond* and Atlantis surrounded by the ever-changing status of *Pride of the Genii* herself. In the corner, Radim's cot, half-hidden by a tent-like drape for at least the illusion of privacy, looked entirely incongruous. One of Cadman's Marines had managed to make coffee, and Lorne clutched his travel mug in both hands.

In the main screen, General O'Neill was frowning down at something, presumably the tactical screen, while Woolsey had his eyes fixed on the camera. Sheppard appeared a moment later, looking predictably rumpled, and O'Neill looked up with a silent question.

"Sorry, sir," Sheppard said. "I had to get Beckett settled in the chair."

Lorne filed that for reference — they wouldn't want to ask the city to do anything complicated if Beckett was flying her, and they probably wouldn't want to try launching drones, either. In the second screen, Colonel Carter was talking to her exec, but turned back to face her camera.

"We're good to go, sir."

Lorne looked at Radim, who nodded for him to go ahead. "We're ready, too, General."

"And is there any further word from your potential ally?" Radim asked.

"Unfortunately, nothing new," Woolsey answered. "Todd — Guide — still intends to sit this one out."

Radim made a face, but said nothing.

"Do we know yet if the hives are using their new shields?" Carter asked.

"Zelenka says we're not seeing the new power signature," Sheppard answered. "But you know how much that means."

"Well, maybe they decided it didn't work the way they wanted," O'Neill said.

"More likely they couldn't make it work without the ZPM McKay stole for them," Carter answered. "That would be nice."

Sheppard grinned. Lorne repressed the childish urge to cross his fingers. Yes, it would help if the hives weren't shielded, but they were still outnumbered and outgunned.

"Gentlemen," Radim said. "Major Lorne has come up with an idea that I think will be effective."

"Go ahead, Major," O'Neill said.

"Sir." Lorne straightened his shoulders. "If we and the *Hammond* were to make a short jump, to bring us into range of Queen Death's fleet, we could do a quick hit and run, do some solid damage and get back out again before they come in range of Atlantis."

"Carter?" O'Neill asked.

"Sir, I agree. The microjump is a little dicey, but I think it's worth it. Their weapons have always been shorter-range than ours. We'll jump in, hit them before they can close, and jump back out again."

Sheppard was nodding. "I like the sound of anything that takes some pressure off the city. We're pretty maneuverable for something this size, but we're not going to be dodging any of their fire."

O'Neill looked at Woolsey. "What about the remaining civilians?"

"We've assigned anyone who doesn't have an immediate duty post to one of several interior rooms that Dr. Zelenka identified as the most protected," Woolsey answered. "They're to proceed there as soon as the fighting starts — or sooner, if so ordered."

"That seems to cover it," O'Neill said. "Carter. You're sure this microjump thing is going to work?"

"Yes, sir," Carter answered. "You saw the Wraith do it, and we have finer control over our hyperdrive."

"All right. When can you do it?"

Carter looked slightly guilty, and Lorne cleared his throat. "Uh, we've already made the calculations, General."

O'Neill shook his head. "Of course you did. All right, Colonel, Major, you have a go."

"Thank you, sir," Carter said, with a quick grin, and Lorne glanced at Radim. The Genii leader nodded, and Lorne cut the connection.

"So," he said. "Do you really think this is going to work, Major?"

"Yes, sir," Lorne said. He picked up his P90, slung it over his shoulder. Not that he actually needed it, or he certainly hoped he didn't, but given that all the Genii went armed, he felt more comfortable with the weapon slung around his neck.

"It's fairly common knowledge that it's dangerous to open a hyperspace window too deep into a sun's gravity well," Radim said. "And I've figured out enough about the workings of this ship to know that it's not exempt from that limit."

Lorne hesitated. "That's true. It's tricky, and we could end up shredded. Or blow out the hyperdrive and end up trapped in the system. But — it's the best idea we've got."

"Sadly." Radim smiled. "All right, Major, let's do this thing."

Sam sat down in her big chair. "Ok," she said. "Ready for the microjump. Ikram?"

"Just another moment, ma'am," Ikram said, bent over his forward console.

"Fine," Sam said. The last thing she wanted to do was rush the navigations. An in system microjump had to be extremely precise. "Let me know when you're green." She opened internal communications. "Everyone secure for the microjump, please."

"Bay doors are secured," came the swift reply. The *Hammond*'s landing bays were the most vulnerable part of the ship, and for hyperspace entry it was best to physically close the doors in addition to the energy shield.

"Okay, boys," Mel Hocken's voice carried easily on the line. "The garage is zipped up. Everybody take a minute to make one more run through. There's not going to be time when we revert. I'm in the A lane. Jimbo, you're right behind me."

"Right behind you, boss," confirmed Lt. Pulaski. "I've got Ellis and Mitchell in the B lane behind me."

"Confirmed," Hocken said.

Sam tried not to smile, listening to the familiar litany of the launch order confirming. Cam wouldn't like being fourth, with Teal'c behind him fifth, but it wasn't his show. The first two 302s at the front of the bay, side by side, were the A lane, the B lane the two behind them, the C lane the two behind them and so on. Needless to say, everybody had to wait their turn or there would be a big problem.

"I have the calculations," Ikram said.

Sam nodded. "Let's do it. Everybody, prepare for microjump. On my mark."

The *Hammond* leapt forward, starfield blurring for a moment, almost a blink rather than the usual elongation of stars, and then before she could draw a breath they were out again, almost on top of the enemy.

"Rail guns online," Davies announced.

"Fire as you bear," Sam said into the comm.

The rail guns opened up at the same time that the bay doors opened, the first pair of 302s hitting full turbos and launching into the night.

Hit and disengage — that was the name of the game. Mel Hocken spun her 302 into a hard left bank, shots telling in a long furrow along the hive ship's hull. The *Hammond* and the *Pride of the Genii* provided covering fire, the white angel streaks of Ancient drones slashing one at a time through the dark. The first time she'd seen them had been over Antarctica, General O'Neill launching them from the chair against Anubis' fleet. They'd been outnumbered and outclassed, twenty 302s against seventy or eighty death gliders — all the 302s there were, every one that had ever been built. It was the first time they'd engaged, and it stung. They'd lost nine out of twenty, including Colonel Mitchell, but Mel had been lucky. Well, lucky and good. She never discounted that.

"Take out weapons emplacements if you can," Mel said, flipping over to make a second pass on the same line. And that was pay dirt, an atmosphere plume from a hull breach beneath her, a tumble of debris.

"What the…?" Pulaski's exclamation came just as her heads up display changed, three cruisers appearing almost on top of the *Hammond*, Queen Death's fleet playing the microjump card too.

"Crap."

The *Hammond* heeled, caught in a sudden barrage of fire.

"Fall back to protect the *Hammond*," Mel said.

"Copy that." That was Mitchell's voice on the line. He probably wasn't actually checked out in a 302 anymore. The kind of crack up he'd had in Antarctica wasn't one you walked away from. But if Carter wasn't going to ask that question, neither was she. It wasn't like 302 pilots grew on trees.

The *Hammond's* shields flared, almost opaque under the volume of fire, and Mel pushed her ship harder. "Come on. Let's keep them busy."

"Cruiser's launching Darts."

"I see them, Jimbo."

This whole scene was getting dirty real fast.

Alabaster had taken the queen's station as though by right, and Guide was startled to feel something that might almost have been resentment. This was his fleet, built from the wreckage of his plans, the disaster of his capture by the Lanteans; Alabaster was not Steelflower, for all she had managed to convince Bonewhite and the others that she spoke for her. And yet… She was his daughter, after all. He took his place at her left hand, his gaze sweeping across the displays.

The *Hammond* and the Genii ship were underway, and even as he focused his attention on their course, they opened hyperspace windows and vanished. Surely Atlantis was not going to run, not so quickly — but no, there they were, blinking back into normal space at what he guessed was the limit of their weapons' range. Bonewhite hissed at the sight, and in the same moment three of Queen Death's cruisers opened windows. They reappeared within range of the Lantean ships, ready to open fire, and Guide bared teeth. Not so clever after all, he thought, watching blue fire bloom along the distant hulls.

Alabaster made a small sound, not quite a hiss of distress, and her hand reached out to touch his wrist in private communication. *We should stand with them.*

*You know we cannot. And why.*

*We cannot face Death's fleet alone.*

*They will 'find' the weapon soon enough,* Guide answered. *You'll see.*

*You have spoken with Ember.*

Guide snarled in spite of himself. The cleverman had begged an audience as soon as Guide came aboard, spilled a confused story about sabotage and mysterious transmissions. If it had been anyone but Ember, he would have discounted the matter, but Ember did not make that sort of mistake. *I have. And I will find the traitor. But — not now.*

*Commander,* Bonewhite said. *What are your orders?*

*We do nothing yet,* Guide answered.

Ease looked up from his console. *Is it wise for us to remain here, then, if we don't intend to fight?*

*We cannot run,* Alabaster said. *Even if we will not fight with them, to run would be to declare our position unequivocally. Queen Death will attack with all her strength, knowing she needs to keep nothing in reserve to face us with.*

That was certainly true. Guide caught Bonewhite's eye, saw agreement on his strong-boned face. Hasten turned from his console.

*And if Death's fleet attacks us, Commander?*

*Then we will fight back,* Guide said. *But she will not.* Let Death worry, he thought. She knew she couldn't handle both fleets, not easily; she wouldn't attack until Atlantis was defeated, and by then he could be long gone.

*We cannot be sure of that,* Ease said. *We should join her, or flee.*

Several of the other officers snarled at the bald verb, the hint of cowardice, and Alabaster raised her head. *I do not believe your queen would wish to hear such words.*

*Our queen listens to advice,* Ease snapped. "Nor does she punish a man for speaking his mind.*

*Enough,* Guide said. *We will stand off and observe.* He would give Sheppard that much, and hope that would force the Lanteans' hand.

Time to get out of here, Sam thought. With Todd's fleet sitting it out, the *Hammond* and the *Pride of the Genii* were seriously outnumbered. They'd hit. Now it was time to run. She opened the comm again. "302s, this is your recall order. Return to the *Hammond*."

"Forward shield at 30 per cent," Franklin said. "There's a crew on it."

But that would take time. Repairs weren't instant, even when possible. "Repeat, this is your recall," Sam said.

"That is not possible, Colonel Carter." Teal'c's voice was measured, and no one but she would have noticed the stress in it. "We are tightly pressed."

It meant something if Teal'c was tightly pressed, but he had five Darts on him, zigzagging and rolling as if to scrape them off along the *Pride of the Genii*'s shields. He'd better not hit the shields either. It would be the same as if he'd hit a solid surface at Mach 4.

"Hocken?"

"*Hammond*'s hit the recall," Hocken said. The stress in her voice was evident, ducking under the *Pride* to try to get on the tail of Teal'c's pursuers. "Break off if you can."

Which she wasn't doing, as that would mean abandoning Teal'c. You don't do that.

Mitchell dropped in on her wing, so close their silhouettes overlapped on the heads up display, both firing at once. One Dart exploded and the other four broke the formation, scattering to evade.

"Colonel?" Lorne asked on the comm.

"We can't jump," Sam said. "Our 302s are stuck."

No more time, then, Ronon thought, watching the specks of light on the sensor screens cluster together in increasingly heated battle. Out there good men and women were fighting what could only be a losing battle. It was time to end this, and he was the only one who could end it all for good.

He muttered some excuse and left the control room, walking out on the balcony. No one was paying much attention to him anyway. Outside, the shield arched against the stars, their planet hanging blue and bright overhead.

He drew Hyperion's weapon out of his coat. He held it for a moment, feeling its weight in his hand, and took a deep breath of the chill air. His finger rested on the trigger.

Behind him, he heard the doors to the balcony open, and heard John's familiar step. There was enough time to act, a long few heartbeats to either pull the trigger or put the weapon away out of sight. Instead, he drew his pistol left-handed, turning with both weapons trained on John.

"Give it to me, Ronon," John said.

Ronon shook his head slowly. John's hand inched toward his sidearm and Ronon shook his head more sharply, his hand tightening on the trigger of his pistol. He could stun John before John could draw, and John knew it.

"You don't want to do this," John said.

"Yeah, I do."

"It's not worth it."

"No more Wraith," Ronon said. "I'd happily die for that."

"I know you want people to be safe."

"I want the Wraith dead," Ronon said.

John's eyes seemed to look into him. "Do you want that more?"

"This'll do both."

"It'll kill Teyla and Rodney."

"I'm sorry," Ronon said flatly. "I wish there was time to figure out a way to save them, but there's not. That fleet out there is going to bury us, and if we don't use the weapon we're going to lose our only chance."

"You're going to be the one to kill them, Ronon, just like putting a bullet through their heads," John said. "Rodney, and Teyla, and every other person in the Pegasus galaxy whose only crime is that one of their ancestors was experimented on by the Wraith. Could you do it if you had to look them in the eye and shoot them? Say that all those people are acceptable collateral damage and shoot them one by one?"

"If I had to," Ronon said. His hand was sweating despite the cold, and he tightened his grip on Hyperion's weapon. "If it was the only way, I'd do it."

"Even Torren?" John's voice was even and unrelenting. "If it were Torren standing here in front of you, I want to know if you could get down on one knee, and put your gun against his little head, and look into his eyes, and pull that trigger."

He wanted to say yes. He had to say yes. He'd sworn that he was

willing to make any sacrifice, to do anything to destroy the Wraith.
If what it took was killing a little kid he'd seen born, a little kid he'd
played with and watched tucked into bed at night —

"Give me the weapon, Ronon."

He was holding onto the weapon so hard that his hand was shaking. "I ought to do it," he said from between gritted teeth. "Why
can't I do it?"

"Because you're human," John said softly. "And you love Torren,
and you love Teyla and even Rodney, and if the Wraith turn you
into someone who's ready to kill the people he loves, then they win,
Ronon. They win. Because they've made you worse than they are."

For a long moment, his finger trembled on the trigger. The
Wraith had made him into a runner, a hunted animal, and then a
hunter who killed them ruthlessly and without mercy. In Atlantis
he'd remembered what it was to be a soldier and a man. And now
he had people who trusted him to protect them. People like Torren.

"I'm nothing like them," Ronon said. In one swift move, he held
Hyperion's weapon out to John, and John took it from him.

"You're a good man, Ronon."

He shook his head. "Tell that to the people who are going to get
eaten by the Wraith because I couldn't pull the trigger."

"We'll see about that," John said. "There's still time to destroy
this thing. If we can get Guide's fleet in on our side, we've got a
fighting chance."

"And after that?"

"Let's worry about 'after that' after that, okay?" John turned on
his heel and headed inside, Ronon trailing after him. He felt drained
and strangely weightless, as if he'd been carrying something heavy
at arm's length for days and had finally put it down.

John jogged into the control room and skidded to a stop. "We
found Hyperion's weapon," he said. "Radio the *Hammond* and tell
them to come get it."

"The *Hammond* is out of range," Woolsey said.

"So get it back in range."

Woolsey shook his head, his face pale. "Colonel Carter reports
that she is heavily pressed by Wraith ships. The *Hammond* can't
come back for Hyperion's weapon."

## CHAPTER EIGHTEEN
# The Willing Sacrifice

THE MARINE guards were gone at last. Presumably with Atlantis under attack by the Wraith they had better things to do than watch Rodney McKay sit in a cell. He'd felt the city lift, a low rumble of subsonics in his bones. They'd done it without him. Presumably Zelenka had handled the technical end and Sheppard had been in the chair.

And he was still here in the cage, unable to give vital help because they wouldn't trust him even though they needed him.

But the Marines were gone now. Everyone was busy. So it was time.

Rodney sauntered casually over to the corner pillar that had the control box on the outside, out of reach of course, and on the other side of the force field. After that time with the Replicators, did they seriously think he'd ever again put himself in a position where he couldn't get the cell open in two seconds flat?

The brig control boxes weren't part of the city's systems, a security feature intended to prevent someone from seizing a control terminal somewhere and being able to release prisoners remotely. No, you had to go to each cell and use the self-contained unit. Definitely safer, and also highly unlikely that Zelenka and Jeannie had checked them when they cleared all his code out of the system.

Rodney leaned over, speaking clearly and distinctly. Sometimes simple was best. "Two, three, five, thirteen, eighty-nine." The force field died and the door bars slid open.

Rodney McKay was back in business.

They finally had the weapon, just a little too late. John Sheppard leaned over Zelenka's shoulder in the control room. Data streamed in from Atlantis' sensors, much more simplistic than the data feeds to the chair but clear enough. Those distant points of light were the

302s engaging Queen Death's Darts, while the *Hammond* and the *Pride of the Genii* evaded the hive ships' fire, trying to take shots and back off. But it wasn't going to work. They were outnumbered, and the cruisers were herding them, closing in in three dimensions, boxing them in a translucent cube of fields of fire from which there would be no escape.

Meanwhile, at the edge of the system, Guide's fleet waited. And they would wait until the weapon was destroyed. Or they would wait until it was too late.

Sam had thought she could dump it in the sun, but Sam was engaged, her life and her ship on the line with no margin for error. Sam wasn't going to be able to do anything about the weapon, not now and maybe not ever.

Okay. Dumping it in the sun would destroy it. And the only way to do that was with a puddle jumper. Yeah, that would mean taking a puddle jumper through the edges of the battle zone, but it could be cloaked. He could do that.

He could. And nobody else. John looked around the control room. O'Neill bent over a console on the lower tier, no doubt giving Airman Salawi hives by rubbernecking over her shoulder. He could fly the city in a pinch. Or Carson. But neither of them could take a puddle jumper smoothly through incidental fire, and besides it was his job, not the general's, not the doctor's.

John straightened up, walking purposefully toward the stairs. Woolsey was in his office but didn't look up, his head bent over data screens. Dump it in the sun. He'd have to get in pretty close to make sure the weapon was destroyed quickly, but the jumper's shields could handle it. The cloak couldn't. Once he got into the coronasphere the level of radiation would render the cloak useless. Anybody could see him. Including Queen Death's Darts. Not that they could dip into the coronasphere, but they could sure as hell shoot at him. And he couldn't exactly dodge.

He stopped on the stairs, turning back to look, Atlantis in her hubbub, the gateroom filled with everyone about their work. No one looked up, not even Radek, pushing his glasses back up on his nose as he toggled power around, talking in his headset at the same time. He thought he'd seen a flash of red by the console, the place where Elizabeth had stood before, the first time he'd taken out a puddle jumper to stop a Wraith fleet, but of course there was no one there. It was memory.

He turned and bounded up the stairs to the jumper bay.

John Sheppard's hands were quick and confident on the controls of the puddle jumper, putting it through the preflight warmup. They didn't hesitate at all. After all, he'd done this hundreds of times. It wasn't any different because it was the last time.

This time it was truly the last.

How many times had he done this before expecting to die, even courting death? Each time he'd figured it was fair. Someone had to do it and it ought to be him, the marked man. Borrowed time ran out.

The first time had been with the Genii's improvised nuke, a desperate Hail Mary pass, the last chance to take out a hive ship. He'd figured he'd had two years, more than Holland or Mitch or Dex got — two years when he'd sometimes felt like it would have been better if he'd gone with them, paid the price in full. He hadn't resented it. He'd looked Elizabeth full in the face and run up the stairs to the jumper bay and she hadn't called him back. She knew. And she knew it had to be.

The last time he'd had more time to think, waiting for his target over Earth sleeping below, cities stretching like chains of light across continents. He'd drifted in low orbit, his 302 inert, watching oceans and continents beneath him, watching a last sunrise over the Pacific Rim, swift and sudden and so beautiful that a lump came in his throat. And it was still fair. Him, not Ronon. Him, not Rodney who had Jennifer now and a whole life ahead of him. Him, not Teyla, who had Torren who needed her… It was his job, his life for his team's, his life for everyone on Earth. He was the marked man, and it was fair. It had to be, and he was at peace with that.

And now. John's eyes flickered shut for one moment, feeling the jumper's engines warming beneath him.

This time it was hard. He couldn't help but imagine all the mornings he might wake up beside someone who loved him, all the days that might be spent in the city of his dreams, all the years of watching Torren grow from baby to boy to man. John Sheppard didn't want to die.

And maybe that was how it worked, he thought. Maybe that was part of the price. You had to want to live to die. You had to want to live for it to be worth something.

But it still had to be done.

John checked the power indicators one last time. Show time. He heard a faint noise behind him as his hand slid to the button to close the tailgate...

...a blue flash enveloped Sheppard and he sprawled sideways, dropping out of the chair half in the middle of his turn, hand open against the deck plates unmoving.

"Sorry, John," Rodney said, stepping over him. He grabbed him by both wrists and dragged, hauling him through the back and out the tailgate, his white hair gleaming blue in the jumper's running lights.

He left him lying on the deck just behind the tailgate and went forward, the back gate rising obediently. The jumper was already warmed up, the controls ready under his hands. Rodney eased the jumper forward, lifting up as the ceiling above opened to the starry sky.

Jack glared at the tactical display as though he could somehow change what he was seeing. Three of Queen Death's cruisers had made their own microjump to engage the *Hammond* and the *Pride of the Genii*, and now his ships were fully engaged. A light flashed, became a swarm of tiny dots, and he swore: the biggest of the cruisers had just launched Darts. *Hammond* launched 302s to counter, but that was going to delay them even further. He pushed himself away from the display.

"Colonel Sheppard!"

There was no answer, and he looked around the control room. "Where's Sheppard?"

"He was here," Woolsey began, and a new light began to flash on the console in front of the young airman — Salawi, her name badge read.

"What's that?" Jack demanded.

"Someone's launching a puddlejumper, sir," Salawi answered, her hands busy on the board. "I can't shut it down."

Jack swore again, loudly and with greater feeling. "Sheppard."

"What?" Woolsey looked up sharply, shock replaced with comprehension as he made the same calculation. "No, that would be suicide—"

"Yeah." Jack glared at the screen. "Salawi, open a channel."

"Sorry, sir," she answered. "They're not answering."

"Damn it, Sheppard," Jack said. He could do the same math, though: take the jumper, drop the weapon into the sun so Todd could see it, and just maybe save the day for everyone. He might even, if he was very lucky, actually survive, though the odds against were astronomical. All of which paled when weighed against the lives he might save. Trust Sheppard to see it first, and to act. I ought to bust him back to airman for that—except if he survives, he'll have saved us all, and if he doesn't... Well, he may still have saved us all, but even if he hasn't, even if Atlantis has to cut and run, it won't matter in the slightest. And maybe I'm just jealous because I didn't think of it first.

But that wasn't a general's job—wasn't really a colonel's job, either, but it really wasn't a general's. He took a deep breath. "Can you track him?"

"Negative," Salawi said. "He's cloaked. The jumper's off our sensors entirely."

And that was that. Jack took a breath, put Sheppard and his suicide mission firmly out of his mind. "All right," he said aloud. "Dr. Beckett, I'm going to take the chair. We're going after Queen Death's fleet."

Ronon made his way down to the detention cells, wanting to look in on Rodney. He'd been trying not to think of the man as his friend while he was considering using Hyperion's weapon, trying to think of him as already dead. But he wasn't dead, and it must have been driving him crazy to be locked up with the city in flight and a battle about to begin.

John and Carter would find some way to destroy the weapon, he was sure, and then Todd's Wraith would jump in on their side. They'd beat Queen Death, and then... they'd go on fighting the Wraith. He wasn't sure whether he hated himself for letting the weapon that would have ended that fight out of his hands, or whether he felt a deep sense of relief. Maybe both, as little sense as that made.

If he told Rodney that he'd been planning to use the weapon, Rodney would tell him he was crazy. He could already hear him yelling: *What were you thinking? You would have killed me! There are enough things in this galaxy that want to kill me without having to worry about you!*

But Rodney would forgive him. He wasn't sure if Teyla ever would, if he ever told her. Not when Torren's life had hung in the same balance. But Rodney would, in his own strange way, understand. Maybe he should tell him, and give him a chance to shout about something and wave his hands around. It would only be fair, and it might make Rodney feel better.

He palmed open the door, and stopped stock-still. The force-field that should have surrounded the cell was down, and the cell was empty.

"McKay," he snarled, and reached up to turn his radio on. "Sheppard, this is Ronon. McKay's loose." There was no answer. "Sheppard. Do you read me?"

Still no answer. Maybe he was heading out to the *Hammond* with the weapon. "Woolsey, this is Ronon. You read me?"

"Yes, Ronon," Woolsey said, sounding distracted.

"McKay's gone," Ronon said. "I just checked his cell. There's no one here."

"Damn," Woolsey said shortly. "All right. We'll send out security teams looking for him. Hopefully we can find him before he does too much damage."

"Where's Sheppard?"

"On his way to drop the weapon into the sun," Woolsey said. His voice was strained. "Which is probably a one-way mission."

"Understood," Ronon said after a momentary pause. "I'll look for McKay."

"Please don't hesitate to stun him when you find him."

"Believe me, I won't," Ronon said grimly.

He wasn't going to think about one-way missions yet. There would be time to start thinking of John as dead later, and time to mourn. For now, all he could think about was that he had been right about McKay, right all along: Queen Death had broken him, and now if they weren't lucky, Rodney was on his way to gut the city from the inside so that Queen Death could kill them all.

Atlantis's chair looked exactly like the one in Antarctica. Jack eyed it with disfavor as Carson Beckett detached himself from its embrace, wondering if it felt the same. But that wasn't something he could ask — wasn't something anyone else could answer, except Sheppard. The last time he'd sat in a chair like this, tried to take full control of its systems, he'd nearly died. Of course, he'd also had his head stuffed full of the Ancient database, which had probably been the real problem, not the chair itself.

"— much better for you to fly the city under battle conditions," Beckett was saying. "Not only is it not exactly something for which I was trained, but I seem to have bad luck with the whole thing. I set off drones by mistake, the hyperdrive blows on my watch — I'm just much happier when someone else is driving."

Jack forced a smile. "And I expect you're going to be needed in the infirmary anyway, Doctor."

"Aye." Beckett gave him a shrewd look. "And I expect you wish I weren't, but, believe me, this is better." He was gone before Jack could decide how to answer.

"Is it just me," Jack asked, "or are things weirder than usual?"

There was no answer, and he'd expected none. The chair stared back at him, empty and waiting. He took a deep breath, and settled himself gingerly against the curved metal. It was warm beneath him, not as though it had been warmed by someone sitting there, but as though it was waiting for him, and he made himself lean back as though he were relaxed. He flexed both hands and laid them palm down against the connective gel. He winced as the familiar stabbing pains shot through his fingers and up his wrist, the city grabbing for control the way Ancient things always did, overloading nerves and synapses. He breathed through it, struggling to keep himself distinct, felt the first wave recede into something manageable.

*Come on*, he thought. *Give me a tac display.*

There was a perceptible lag, and then lines faded into view, a pale overlay on the walls of the chair room, hard to see against the dark walls. It wanted him to close his eyes, to see the patterns without distraction, but he refused.

*A 302's heads-up display's better than that.*

Grudgingly, the lines brightened, became legible, readouts floating in the air around him, closing him inside a sphere of data. There was the tactical display, *Hammond* and *Pride of the Genii* now fully engaged, Darts and 302s weaving deadly magic around them, and now the rest of Death's fleet was moving to close the gap. He stiffened, wondering if they were going to try the microjump, and the city whispered in his ear.

*Data suggests they are not drawing power for such a tactic.*

*Well, that's something.* Jack started to swing the chair, then remembered that, unlike a normal commander's chair, the thing was fixed in place. The city anticipated him, however, and the sphere of data revolved, the city's status display settling in front of his eyes. Everything looked good, drones ready — *but not yet in range*, the city murmured — the shield solid, maneuver and subspace and hyperdrive engines all on line, and Jack cleared his throat.

"Woolsey."

"Yes, General."

"We're ready to go."

"All personnel are standing by," Woolsey answered.

"Right, then." Jack took a breath, imagined swinging the chair again, and the city spun the data, bringing the navigational display to the front. The tactical screen appeared beside it, *Hammond* and her 302s tangled with the Darts, *Pride of the Genii* exchanging fire with a cruiser, but he made himself concentrate on the city. *We need to go*, he thought, imagining the maneuver. *We need to support our people.*

There was the briefest of hesitations, as though the city's heart skipped a beat, and then he felt the shift of vectors, the tug and rumble of maneuver engines firing. Atlantis shifted in her orbit, heading reluctantly into the fight.

*I know*, Jack thought. *You don't want me here, you want*

*Sheppard. Well, I don't want to be here, so we're even. But I'm what you've got. Let's make this work.*

He could feel the power building, thrust released to send the city along the plane of the ecliptic, angle converging to a meeting point not too far distant, but still further than he would like. This was all the power there was, the city told him, firm resistance when he tried to push beyond that limit, and he made himself relax again. Surely it would be enough.

Lorne's fingers tightened in the connective gel as he watched the ships wheel in the tactical display. The *Hammond* was trying to recover her 302s, but the big cruiser was pushing her hard. He felt a flicker of reaction, almost a wince, from the ship, and consciously relaxed his grip. *Hammond* needed a distraction, and he brought the *Pride of the Genii* up and around, trying to get a better shot at either of the cruisers pushing the *Hammond*.

"Port batteries, fire if you get a shot," he said, and vaguely heard the acknowledgement. His world narrowed to lines of force, patterns in the deadly dance; he rolled the *Pride* as though she were a 302, stars spinning in the main screen, and came up behind and beneath one of the smaller cruiser.

"Hit her with everything you have," Radim said, his voice tight and controlled, and every gun that would bear fired, a ragged rolling volley.

"Cruiser behind us," someone shouted, but the *Pride* had already felt its presence, and Lorne rolled again, flinching as the new cruiser's shots slammed into the aft shields like a kick to the kidneys. He jinked left, then right, cutting the turns tighter than the cruiser could follow, and came out above and on its tail.

"Forward guns," Radim said, before Lorne could speak, and he felt them fire, lines of blue stitching across the cruiser's stern. "Bring her around again, Major, we're hitting it hard!"

Lorne could see the damage, too, could feel the *Pride*'s shields still all at eighty percent or better, and for a moment he ignored the other cruiser to bring the *Pride* around for another pass.

"Now!" Radim said, and the guns fired, less raggedly this time, shots converging on what was surely part of the engine. Something exploded on the surface, ripping a long hole in the tough hide, and that was followed by an internal explosion that split the hull, releasing a cloud of debris.

"Again, Major!" Radim said, but Lorne shook his head.

"She's out of it, sir. Power's dead, she's leaking atmosphere — looks like they're abandoning her."

The *Pride* shrieked a warning, and he snatched his attention back to the ship just in time to roll away from the worst of the incoming fire. The third cruiser flashed past them — shields holding, the ship whispered, but dorsal shields are down 15 percent. Lorne could feel it, like a soft spot in a melon, and rolled again to put the good shields between them and the remaining cruisers.

"Sir!" That was the Genii navigator, his voice echoing the *Pride*'s sudden alarm. "The hives are moving in."

"How far?" Lorne asked, and man and ship answered together, words and pictures flowing into a seamless whole.

"Five minutes to firing range."

Sometimes you just had to slug it out. Sam gripped the arms of her chair as the *Hammond* jerked, inertial dampeners compensating for the volume of fire from the cruiser. "Get us in closer," she said, and Chandler responded.

It was counterintuitive, but correct. The cruiser's dorsal and ventral weapons emplacements couldn't depress or rise far enough to track them because of the shape of the hull, while the *Hammond*'s rail guns were laterally mounted. Close enough, and the fire volume would go their way.

A 302 slipped between, narrowly missing friendly fire, but the Dart pursuing didn't. It incandesced for a moment and was gone, caught in the point blank fire from the rail gun.

The cruiser began pulling back, turning to present undamaged hull and the dorsal array.

"Stay with them," Sam said. "Stay close. But not too close," she amended. If they were overloading the cruiser's power plant...

A flight of Darts skimmed in, and for a moment the viewscreen flashed blue, the forward shield darkening with the energy absorbed. The cruiser was dropping back, trying to dive between two of Death's hives, and the Darts provided a screen. The rail guns would destroy a Dart instantly of course, but their tracking was far too slow to provide an effective cover.

Mel pulled wide, trying to get a good look at the bigger picture for a moment. That was the squadron commander's job. The second cruiser was venting atmosphere, pulling back at an uneven pace, obviously damaged, but the hives still packed a full punch, and the Darts still outnumbered them. More importantly, the *Hammond* was in too tight to retrieve 302s.

It had been six minutes.

In the rest of the world that was barely time to get through a fast food line, but in space combat that was forever.

Mitchell's voice, calm on the line. "I've got one on my tail. Assist."

"Coming," Mel said, and banked hard right to follow.

## CHAPTER NINETEEN
# Fatal Choices

"WHAT can I do?" Vala asked, stepping back out of the way of the pandemonium in the gate room. She didn't really have an excuse to be there, but no one had told her to leave yet.

Woolsey looked at her as if aware for the first time that she was there. "Find McKay," he said. He didn't sound as if he really expected her to, but she nodded brightly and then gave the matter her most serious consideration.

Everyone was busily looking for McKay all over the city, assuming that he was planning to sabotage some essential system. But he'd had every opportunity to do that for days, and the only thing he'd shown a seemingly unnatural interest in was stealing Hyperion's weapon.

All right, then. Assume what Daniel swore was a maxim of Earth philosophy, that the simplest explanation was most likely to be correct. Vala could think of a lot of complicated explanations that had turned out to be correct, but it seemed worth a try. McKay had stolen Hyperion's weapon because he was under Queen Death's control, and he wanted to make sure the weapon wasn't destroyed.

If she'd stolen something vitally important, the first thing she'd have been looking for was a means of escape. There was really only one means of escape from Atlantis while it was in orbit, and that was a puddlejumper. One puddlejumper had launched without authorization, contents assumed to be John Sheppard plus Ancient device, but in reality unknown.

"I'm just going to go look in the jumper bay," Vala said. She didn't think Woolsey heard her, or at least he affected not to hear her. She slipped out and made her way down to the puddlejumper bay.

She tried to work her way backwards through what might have happened as she went. If McKay had stolen the weapon and left Atlantis with it, he'd stolen it from Sheppard. Sheppard had left the control room, probably on his way to the jumper bay to make a brave and suicidal gesture. But if he'd run into McKay there...

She nearly stepped on Sheppard, and had to flail to keep from tripping over him where he lay sprawled on the deck of the jumper bay, unmoving. "What do you know, philosophy works," she said, and bent down to see if he was still breathing.

One cruiser disabled — abandoned, according to the *Pride*: it was a start, but there was no time to enjoy the victory. The Darts and 302s still wove a glittering net, flashing into Lorne's awareness as they came in range, vanishing as soon as their danger was past. Radim was handling fire control, and they were his problem, if and when he thought he had a chance to hit them. The remaining cruisers were the problem, the cruisers and the hives.

*Comm*, he thought at the ship, and a light flicked on, followed by a hollow emptiness in his ear. "Colonel Carter. We can cover if you want to try to get the 302s back in —"

"Thanks, Major." Carter's voice was calm, but the *Pride* was sensing weak spots in the *Hammond*'s shields, the remaining cruisers moving to catch her in crossfire. "That would be a help."

The *Hammond* dived out of the trap, shields flaring, and Lorne heeled the *Pride* to come up beneath the larger of the two cruisers. He heard Radim give the order, and saw blue fire blaze across the cruiser's belly. No real damage, though, and the second cruiser was on him at once, spinning to catch him broadside. He caught his breath as the shots hit home, heavy blows along the starboard shield. There was a distant bang somewhere, and Radim swore.

"We've lost a gun emplacement."

"Get a technical crew down there," Lorne said, to Radim, to the ship, not caring who obeyed, and spun the *Pride*, trying to take advantage of the tighter turning radius to come up behind the cruiser again. Its commander wasn't fooled this time, and peeled off at an angle, trying to draw the *Pride* into its sister's fire.

*Shields at 60 percent*, the ship murmured. Lorne could feel them softening like cardboard in the rain, pulled up and around to present a narrow target. The first cruiser swept after him, but the other turned its attention back to the *Hammond*. Lorne's eyes narrowed as he judged relative positions, lines of force relative to the ships' twisting courses. Yes, just there — he brought the *Pride* up in a sweeping loop, freeing himself from the cruiser. There was time for one good shot — he heard Radim talking, urging his people on — and then they were past, bearing down on the cruiser attacking the *Hammond*. Lorne saw a handful of their shots strike home, and then they were wheeling away again, but the cruiser didn't follow. He shook his head, lining up for another pass, but Carter spoke in his ear.

"Negative, Major, it's not going to work. They're not being distracted."

"Copy that," Lorne said. The *Pride* rocked as the first cruiser swung past, firing, and he turned to chase it.

John Sheppard struggled up from unconsciousness to the sound of footsteps. Hands seized him roughly, flipping him over onto his back in the perfect feeding position, his head lolling, a black leather boot against his face. Any moment now the Wraith would bend to open his tac vest.

John flailed out uncoordinatedly, rewarded by a very human sounding "Ow!" He opened his eyes.

Vala Mal Doran looked down at him rubbing her chin. "That wasn't nice," she said. "And what happened to you?"

He was lying on the jumper bay floor, and it came back to him in a rush.

"Rodney stole the weapon back," he said. "He stunned me and he stole a jumper." He sat up, reeling. "How long have I been out?"

Vala steadied him. "How should I know?"

"He's still working for Queen Death." John hated to say it out loud, but it was true and now they were all screwed. If only he hadn't trusted Rodney so much! He grabbed Vala's arm, scrambling to his feet. "I've got to get down to the chair."

The civilians had been ordered to a set of windowless rooms on the lowest level of the central tower. The lights were on, there were chairs and couches and cots, and there was even a coffee urn and hot water and baskets of cold sandwiches. It all seemed incongruous, William thought, but he made himself a mug of tea all the same. A number of people had their laptops going, monitoring the battle, but William didn't really know how to tap into the city systems, and wasn't sure he wanted to know. Winning or losing, there wasn't anything he could do about it; the best he could manage was to keep out of people's way.

With that in mind, he edged toward a quiet corner, but stopped short as he saw that one of the three chairs was occupied. "Oh. I'm sorry, Dr. Robinson."

"Eva," she said. "I won't be offended if you want to be alone, but I'm not averse to company."

William considered the idea, and gave a fleeting smile. "Actually, neither am I." He seated himself carefully in the chair opposite her, the Ancient padding adjusting itself instantly to his body, and took a careful sip of his tea. "I rather thought you'd have been gone by now."

"I could say the same for you," Eva answered, with a smile of her own. "But I have the ATA gene, and Mr. Woolsey asked for those of us who had it to stay if we could, so…"

William nodded. "I wish I had it. I'd feel more useful." He hadn't meant to say that, and winced, but Eva seemed to take the words at face value.

"If I understand correctly, you're here to be useful if we have to abandon the city. So I kind of hope you're not going to be useful."

"Thanks," William said, and looked up as a shadow fell across his chair.

"Oh." Daniel Jackson stood there, cup of coffee in one hand. "Mind if I join you?"

"Be my guest," Eva said, and Daniel took the third chair.

"I'm surprised you're not in the control room," William said.

"No, uh — actually, Jack, General O'Neill, kicked me out," Daniel said. "And then I was getting the impression that I was in the way in the infirmary."

"There's not much call for archeology right now, I suppose," Eva said. "Or psychology."

There wasn't anything to say to that. William wrapped both hands around his travel mug, wishing it was over. It was the waiting that was hard — they'd be safe here through anything short of the city's destruction, safe and comfortable and even well-fed, but it was impossible to believe it entirely. He looked past Daniel's shoulder to see the rest of the group, maybe two dozen people, one group clustered around a laptop, others with iPod headphones jammed in their ears, books and tablets raised like barricades. He was reminded sharply of his grandfather's stories of the Blitz, of trying to behave normally—properly—jammed down a Tube tunnel with a thousand strangers. This was entirely different, and yet somehow the same. He only hoped he'd make the old man proud.

John Sheppard swam through space. At least that was how it seemed, as though it were he who moved through vacuum easily, skin accustomed to the cold. His skin was the forcefield, and his eyes were the city's, ten thousand sensors feeding a pattern to his brain. To know anything the city knew was easy. It was nothing so complex as examining instruments or reading screens, or even glancing at a heads up display. It was like using his own eyes and ears, like seeing what was right in front of him.

The battle was a tangled mess, the *Hammond* and the *Pride of the Genii* tangled with Queen Death's hive ships, while vertical to the elliptic Todd's fleet waited, stationary and uncommitted. Darts and 302s dove and fought, now and then one winking out, a life extinguished.

*We are in range of the Darts*, the city said. Trajectories and speeds slid past, each piece of data rendering a possibility.

But that wasn't what was happening. Two of the hives were accelerating, leaving the others to mix it up with the *Hammond* and the *Pride*, bearing for the city with all thrusters. One cruiser followed them, a half dozen 302s breaking off to stay on the cruiser's tail. Blue leader, the display provided. Mel. They were seriously burning fuel out there.

The city showed him drones ready to launch, targeting enabled. *Wait*, John said. There were so few drones left. Every one had to count. None of them could be wasted on the Darts. They had to be for the hives, and the hives were not in optimal range. *Wait*.

Somewhere, a headset spoke in his ear, General O'Neill in the control room. *"Hammond, you need to break off and get back here."*

"Negative, we can't do that." Sam's voice, distant and tinny.

"Repeat, disengage," O'Neill said. "Carter, it's time to get out of there."

"Our 302s are not aboard."

"We're hanging in there, sir." Lorne's voice.

Come on, Lorne, John thought. Don't be a hero. Not today. But he wouldn't leave Carter, and she wasn't about to leave her 302s. Some of them must be getting close to the end of their fuel from so much close combat, and if they couldn't set down they'd be sitting ducks for the hives to pick off.

"Crap, Carter," O'Neill said quietly, as though he didn't realize the channel was still open.

John urged the city forward, massive thrusters firing. It was time to get in the action.

"Atlantis is engaging," Franklin said. Unnecessarily, as Sam could see the city moving.

"Stay with the cruiser," Sam said. "Keep us close and keep hitting it." The cruiser was trying to run, but it was too late. She could almost hear her father say, "Ride your kill, baby. Ride it right to the ground. You don't know it's out until you see it hit." He'd been talking about the F-102 Delta Dagger, not anything like the *Hammond*, but the principle was the same. Keep hitting it until it blows or you see a chute.

Forward rail guns spoke again, driving heated metal across the vacuum, and the cruiser twisted. For a moment it seemed that it would fire again, but then thrusters flamed irregularly, twisting to get away, accelerating sideways to starboard, surely not a move the crew intended. It collided with the next cruiser, side crumpling as the other cruiser veered away.

"That's it," Sam said. "Distance now."

Chandler hit the retro thrusters as fast as possible, but the shock wave still tossed the *Hammond* as the cruiser blew, a cable blowing overhead as Sam held on to her chair. The other cruiser's skin held, but it was pelted with a shockwave of debris, pitting the surface and sending it spinning out of control.

"One down, one damaged," Sam said. "Good work, people." She really wished Jacob had seen that.

The cruiser blew in a silent fireball, the *Hammond* streaking past unscathed while the second cruiser fell off to the side, hull

bleeding air and volatiles. Lorne saw it out of the corner of his
eye even as he locked onto the tail of the remaining cruiser. That
commander must have seen it too, and was distracted for a fatal
second. Lorne bore in on it, lining up perfectly on the port side,
all guns ready.

"Now," Radim said, and the guns spoke, tearing through the
cruiser's hull to release a burst of flame. A single gun spoke in
answer, a kick beneath the *Pride*'s belly, but the cruiser's pilot
was diving away, trailing a plume of vapor. The cruiser heeled
over further, too far, spinning toward the planet; lights flared
irregularly along its sides, and the *Pride* assessed damage to the
maneuver drives. It would spiral down to the planet unless its
commander was very lucky or very good, and there were plenty
of other things to do.

"Bogey four is down," Lorne said, on the all-ships channel, and
brought the *Pride* back to the fight.

The city's sensors showed heavy damage to the second cruiser,
external thrusters on one side crushed, adrift for all practical purposes. Okay, John thought. That evens it up a bit. The first hive was
in range, the city eager to fire. Hang on, John thought. Wait for the
shot. No need to hurry. Just take the best angle.

*The drones would do that*, the city replied. *The drones will correct.*

Which was true. All on that one hive, he said, and felt the drones
stir in their cradles. Eight. Eight was optimal, all at once from four
platforms, four and four 0.97 seconds behind.

Fire.

The drones streaked up, passing through Atlantis's shield and
out, bright against the darkness, through the 302s without touching, their internal guidance systems golden.

Eight solid hits.

John felt the flare in the dark, the city's sensors registering up
and down the electromagnetic spectrum. Critical hits, a plume of
atmosphere, a plume of vapor. The hive dived vertical to the elliptic, falling out of the fight. Aboard, crew would be rushing to sta-
bilize life support, the commander in ship trance overcome by a
flood of pain.

"Bogey number four is down," someone said in a distant place. Lorne. That was Lorne's voice on the comm, he realized. He was so deep in the city that it seemed strange to even remember that someone named John Sheppard sat in the chair, a headset against his ear.

Jack paced from console to console, dividing his attention between the main tactical display and the individual systems, glaring at the screen as though he could move the numbers by sheer will. Light flared against the shield, a flash like a camera's across the control room, but the city barely shuddered: the Darts couldn't do a lot of damage on their own, but enough of them would eventually weaken even Atlantis's shields. One hive was falling back, still venting atmosphere and the occasional spurt of flame as something gave way inside the hull. The other hive was still coming, though, nosing left to curve around the base of the city, and the largest of the cruisers followed the Darts up and over the city. Sheppard launched drones, two for the cruiser, three for the hive; Jack counted three hits, but the others were decoyed away, confused by the swarming Darts. We need 302s, Jack thought, but they were back with *Hammond* and the *Pride of the Genii*, locked in close combat with Death's own hive. Carter was holding her own, but they needed to get out of there.

And she would if she could, but if she couldn't recover the 302s, it wouldn't do Atlantis any good anyway. Jack glanced at the shield readings again, reassuringly steady around ninety percent. It would take time and numbers for the Darts to make a difference, but the Wraith definitely had the numbers. In the screen, the hive rolled into a turn, surprisingly nimble for something of its bulk, evading a drone that crashed instead into a Dart. More Darts formed up ahead of the hive, diving under the city's base, weapons blazing. The hive followed, its bigger guns targeting the same points, and he heard Zelenka swear under his breath.

Atlantis shuddered, a heavy sustained rumble like an earthquake beneath his feet, and something exploded in the distance. Lights flared red on half a dozen consoles, and there was a sudden burst of chatter.

"Crap," Jack said, but he knew better than to interrupt.

"East Pier maneuver engine is off-line," someone said.

"Yes, yes, I see that," Zelenka said. "Cross-circuit, please, see if you can route around—"

"Not working, Doc."

"Shields?" someone else called, and it was Airman Salawi who answered, her voice high but steady.

"No breach. We were down to sixty percent, but the number's back up, eighty-nine and rising."

"Copy that."

"Patch into the secondaries," Zelenka said. "Yes, I know it won't take the full load, but it's better than nothing."

There was a voice missing, Jack realized, and his heart skipped a beat. He touched his radio. "Sheppard?"

"I'm here." Sheppard's answer was a hair slow, but otherwise he sounded all right. "Looks like we've lost a thruster."

"I am working on that," Zelenka said. "We will get it back on line."

"Sooner would be better," Sheppard said, his voice fading again.

Jack glanced back at the tac display. "Looks like they're trying again, Sheppard."

"I see it."

In the weapons display, half a dozen drones rotated toward their silos, flaring to life at Sheppard's order. He launched them in pairs, not at the Darts but directly at the hive, two pairs slamming home against its nose before its pilot wheeled away, running for room as the third pair pursued, to hit at last harmlessly on the left flank. Jack nodded.

"That ought to discourage them."

"One would hope so." That was Woolsey, standing bolt upright behind the environmental station. He'd been paler when he faced the IOA, Jack thought, and had to admit the man had more guts than he'd expected. "Dr. Zelenka, what's our status?"

Zelenka didn't answer for a moment, his head cocked to one side as he listened to something in his earpiece, but then he nodded. "Okay, keep trying. See if you can find a clear path from here." He swung in his chair so that he was facing Woolsey. "That last run overrode the shield or caused a superheated patch to form, we're not entirely sure which, but the result was an explosion in the East

Pier maneuver drive. It's offline right now, and we are trying to reroute power to the system to see if we can restart it."

"And if you can't?" Woolsey asked.

Zelenka shrugged. "It's not good, but it's not terrible? We can compensate to some extent with the other engines, but we will not be making any fast course changes now. Not that we were that fast to begin with."

"What about the hyperdrive?"

"That is fine," Zelenka said. "We can still open a window, the city can still stand the stress, it's just — we're pretty much stuck on our current course." He put his hand to his ear again. "Ah. Okay, don't waste any more time, just get me the best diagnostic you can manage." He looked back at Woolsey. "It looks as though there is actual damage to the engine controller, not just to power conduits. It can be fixed, but we'll need to send a team down there to do it. Dr. Sommer has volunteered."

Jack pursed his lips. That was risky as hell, even with the transport chambers to get them there and back in a hurry — always assuming the transport chambers kept working, which he wouldn't like to bet on. The East Pier was well outside the area that would be covered if Sheppard had to collapse the shield to save power: Dr. Sommer, whoever he was, had to be thinking about that, too. From the look on his face, Woolsey was making the same calculations.

"All right," he said. "But —" He reached for his own radio. "Dr. Sommer, this is Woolsey. You have permission to attempt the East Pier repair, but if there is any problem here, we are going to pull you out. Is that clear?"

Jack couldn't hear the answer, but Woolsey nodded. "Good luck, Dr. Sommer."

## CHAPTER TWENTY
# Fire Ship

THE CRUISERS were beaten back, at least for now, but the hives were still coming, their fleet splitting to divide the city from its covering ships. Lorne spun the *Pride* through 360 degrees, twisting as he went, but the hive's fire still clipped the weakened port shields. He rolled left, presenting the ventral shield instead, and winced as another shot slammed home. This was not the flagship, the *Pride* whispered; *Hammond* was engaged with Death's ship, the two orbiting each other, struggling for position. *Hammond* was faster, but her guns were doing little damage so far, and her own shields were suffering. Maybe two of us, Lorne thought. If I can break *Pride* loose, hit Death's hive, it'll give Carter a break, and maybe two of us can do some real damage.

The other hive swept in again, and he turned to meet it, presenting the strongest shields while Radim called the fire points. Blue light flamed across the hive's mottled skin, leaving scorch marks, but the damage was minimal. Lorne heeled away, and the *Pride* clamored alarm: too close to the damaged cruiser. Lorne winced as the shots struck home against his shields.

That was enough to give the hive another shot, and Lorne arrowed under it, presenting dorsal shields. Radim called for massed fire as they passed, but to no avail. The hive heeled up and over, fighting for advantage, and the *Pride* shuddered again as more shots struck home. *Sorry, Colonel*, Lorne thought. He wasn't going to be able to help — he had his hands full with this hive already.

The loss of the East Pier was like a stutter, the loss of a cylinder, a missed beat in the steady rhythm of the city's systems. John shifted in the chair, searching for a workaround, and felt the city interpret his movements, adjusting the other engines to compensate. Distantly, he could hear Zelenka explaining that the actual engine was damaged, and felt its absence like a missing tooth. They could maneuver, but it was clumsy, on the verge of overbalancing one way or another; better to stay on the present line, he thought, and try to get rid of the current attackers.

The city agreed, offering trajectories, fire points; he dismissed the ones that targeted the Darts, lobbed another pair of drones at the hive. It, at least, was standing further off, apparently chastened, but the cruiser was still closing, following the Darts down. The city offered firing solutions, the changing vectors flicking through his fingers. Not yet, not yet, he thought. Three drones, ready in their silos... They clicked into place, stones ready to throw, fireballs to launch like some comic book hero —

*Now,* he thought, and the silos opened, the equations elegant on his skin, flicking the drones out into the night to meet the cruiser. Its pilot saw, swerved wildly, scattering Darts as they wheeled out of its path, but the drones kept coming, homing in on the weakness the city saw in the cruiser's frame. They hit, three strikes in quick succession, and the cruiser's hull gave way, fire eclipsing the stars. The shock wave rolled across the shield, shaking the city, but leaving no damage in its wake. John grinned, and felt the city's satisfaction echo his own.

Atlantis was fully engaged now, maneuver engines glowing beneath the curve of the lower hull, shields protecting the fragile towers, sealing in the air. A swarm of Darts surrounded it, one of Death's hives following in their wake, and trails of light rose lazily from the central spire, swooped out to dot the hive with blooms of fire. Guide watched, outwardly impassive, but cold fear crawled along his spine. That was what he remembered from his youth, the Darts swarming even though they knew all but the luckiest would die: it was never skill that overwhelmed the Ancients' defenses, merely weight of numbers. Guide had been lucky then, and it was a lesson he would not forget.

Hasten turned away from his console, and came to stand beside him, off hand brushing Guide's shoulder in private communication. He was almost as old as Guide, old enough to remember at least the blades' stories, cautionary tales whispered in the crèche, and he kept his eyes resolutely from the battle on the screen.

*All our systems are at full readiness. If we were to attack now, we could overwhelm the Ancient city.*

*And then what?* Guide glanced sideways, one corner of his mouth curling up in something like a smile, but he could tell Hasten was not deceived. "We cannot defeat Queen Death, not with what we have.*

Hasten dipped his head. *No. But — it goes against my grain to see that city destroying our kin.*

*She is not our kin,* Guide said, but the words lacked force. He shook his head, denying his own fears. The Lanteans were not the Ancients — John Sheppard was no Ancient, though he might carry their genetic marker. And why had he not acted by now? Surely he knew how desperate his situation was.

*So she has said.* Hasten's tone was muted. *We should act, Commander.*

*We wait,* Guide answered, and turned away from his touch.

*Commander.* That was Precision, the other conversation unsensed, perhaps unnoticed. *Commander, if we were to send Darts in support of the Lanteans — surely that would not be too much.*

Out of the corner of his eye, Guide saw Alabaster cock her head, and answered before she could respond. *No. We had a bargain, which they have not fulfilled. They are counting on us to be desperate, but we must play a longer game.*

*If we don't back one side or the other,* Bonewhite said, *there will no longer be a game.*

*And why should we back the Lanteans?* Ease demanded.

*There can be no truce with Queen Death!* That was Ember, sharp and out of turn, and Alabaster bared teeth in a smile.

*The cleverman speaks truth,* she said. *The bridge is burnt.*

One of them was a traitor, Guide thought. Ember had warned him of the sabotage, shared his certainty that it was one of the council, and he believed Ember. Trusted Ember, though he had been betrayed by clevermen before. Bonewhite and Alabaster were waiting for him to speak, to make all right again, but he said nothing. Let the traitor act now, and Guide could deal with him — assuming always he did not have too many allies.

Hasten hissed softly. *To join with the Lanteans —*

*Is our only choice,* Alabaster said sharply. *And your queen's will!*

*But only the queen's will,* Ease said.

*And mine,* Guide said. He was almost sure now, Ease or Hasten or both together, and he shifted his weight, balancing on the balls of his feet.

*You are not queen here,* Ease said. *Nor is your daughter.*

Guide almost moved then, but he held his hand, knowing he would need full proof to keep the council on his side in Steelflower's absence. *Steelflower is queen,* he said, and saw Bonewhite shift uneasily. The Hivemaster knew the truth, of course — would he betray the fiction?

*This is a fool's game,* Ease said. *I put it to you all, lords of the council. Guide has overreached — again! — and we are trussed to pay the price for his folly. Our queen is vanished, who knows where, and whatever plan was made with the Lanteans has fallen to pieces. We must join Queen Death — we have no choice but to join her — and if we join her now, while the outcome of this battle is in doubt, we may win her favor.*

*This is Steelflower's hive,* Ember snapped. *And you do not speak for me.*

*I speak for Steelflower,* Alabaster began, and Bonewhite lifted his head.

*It is so, Snow's Daughter, but you cannot speak for her in this, any more than her Consort can.*

*Madness!* Ember said. *And I remind you all that someone has already tried to sabotage our ships, to achieve this same goal by less honorable means.*

*If it's for the council to decide, let it decide.* Guide's tone was silken, but he glanced quickly from one man to the next, trying to guess how they would jump. Ember and Alabaster were on his side — for an instant, he regretted bringing his daughter so soon into his intrigues — and Precision, and he thought Bonewhite, but the others…

*I am Steelflower's man,* Bonewhite said, with a sigh. *And Queen Death will not deal fairly with us, not if we brought her the

Lanteans' queen and all her court to feed upon.*

*And I,* Precision said.

Hasten bowed his head unspeaking.

*Fools,* Ease snapped, and reached beneath his coat. Both Ember and Precision lunged from their places, putting their bodies between the weapon and the young queen, but Guide had been ready for that move. He leaped across the open platform, off hand rising to bat aside the weapon. He heard the beam shriek past him, felt its kiss along his ribs, and then he had Ease by the throat, sinking claws into the soft skin. He forced Ease's head back, forced his body back against the console, feeling a depth of hatred he had not suspected as they met skin to skin.

*Traitor indeed,* Guide said, as much for the others as for his own satisfaction. *What did she promise you that you would betray your queen?*

*Victory and her favor,* Ease gasped, defiant, *and the feeding grounds of Earth.*

*Which are not hers to give.* Guide set his claws, snarling, hand-mouth fastening hard, and Ease screamed in fury and despair. He drank deep, life flowing into him as Ease withered beneath his touch, let the husk fall at last to the deck. *Is there anyone else who questions our tactics?*

Silence was the only answer.

Radek bent over his displays, frowning as though concentration would keep the fear at bay. It didn't entirely, of course — he was dry-mouthed, sweating — but his hands were sure on the controls, and his brain was clear. The city was holding up well under the attack, except for the damage to the East Pier, and Dr. Sommer was taking a team down there; with any luck he'd have it back on line shortly. The shield was only down about ten percent, and Sheppard was spending the drones with uncanny effectiveness. Well, canny enough, that was the way they were supposed to be used, and that was the one thing that was going to save them if Todd didn't join the fight —

A light flashed on his board, and he touched keys to see the warning. One of the Wraith cruisers disabled in the first passes of the battle was drifting closer to the city, its course converging with theirs. He had seen the cruiser abandoned, shedding Darts and men, but he scanned it anyway, found no sign of life on board. Or was there? His frown deepened, and he grabbed control of a single sensor suite, ignoring the flare of protest. The deeper probe was ambiguous: was that the cruiser's own quasi-living structure that he was reading, or was it a skeleton crew.

"Zelenka," Sheppard said in his ear. "I need those scanners."

"Yes, yes," Radek answered, but touched keys to return control to the city. "Colonel, we are on a collision course with that drifting cruiser—"

"Yeah, I saw that," Sheppard answered. "I've corrected for it."

"But—" If Radek hadn't been watching, they might have missed it, or taken it for one more release of gases from a damaged ship. But he was watching, and he saw the vent open, the vapor plume sparkling as gases froze instantly to snow in the vacuum. Even then, he might have dismissed it as automatic response, systems still struggling to function, nothing of significance. In his screen, the numbers shifted again, the line of the projected course curving back to cross Atlantis's shields in less than thirty minutes. He swore in Czech.

"Problem?" General O'Neill asked, looming over his shoulder.

"Yes, and a bad one." Radek pushed his glasses up on his nose. "Sheppard, do you see?"

"Yeah. Was that deliberate?"

"Was what deliberate?" O'Neill asked.

"That damaged ship." Radek pointed with his chin, his hands busy on the sensor controls. Scan the cruiser properly this time, he thought, see what's really in there—full spectrum, not just lifesigns and power usage. "It was on a collision course, and we moved to avoid it. But it—maybe it's coincidence, but it vented atmosphere in the just the right place to nudge it back into our path again."

"Crap," O'Neill said.

"I can take it out," Sheppard said. "I don't like wasting the drones, though…"

Radek ignored them both, analyzing the readings as they came in. Power usage was way down, main power plants disabled; the lifesigns remained ambiguous. Atmosphere — well, there still was some, though it wouldn't be very nice to breathe, and there was a weird chemical trace that he didn't recognize. He adjusted the scanners, trying to home in on it, and his eyes widened at the results. "Jesus, Mary, and Joseph."

"What?" O'Neill bent closer.

"The cruiser is stuffed full of explosives," Radek said. The readings kept coming, weight and chemical composition — Death's people must have filled every unused storage space in the center of the ship. The spaces closer to the hull were empty, presumably so that the cruiser wouldn't blow before it accomplished its mission, but the rest... The explosion would be strong enough to breach Atlantis's shields.

"Avoiding," Sheppard said, his voice distant again as he communed with the city.

On Radek's board, lights flickered as the remaining maneuver engines fired, and in the tactical display, Atlantis's course shifted, pulling away from the drifting cruiser. It hung motionless, the line of its projected course falling further and further from the city. Radek allowed himself a breath of relief, but then lights flared, a secondary engine firing from the cruiser's trailing edge. The lines began to converge again.

"Goddamnit."

"Maybe it's time to waste some drones," O'Neill said, his tone tighter than his words.

"I don't have that many," Sheppard said, but the city monitors showed a drone settling into the silo. "It's got to be one good shot."

"Wait!" Radek stared at the numbers forming on his screen, answers to a question he really wished he'd never had to ask. "For God's sake, don't fire!"

"What?" Sheppard said, but in the monitor the drone eased back toward dormancy.

"We're already too close," Radek said. "If you destroy the ship here, it will severely damage the shields."

"What if Sheppard just takes out the engines?" O'Neill asked.

"I think the cruiser will blow anyway," Radek answered. "They'd be stupid to rig the ship any other way, and besides, the lifesigns — there may still be a skeleton crew on board, and they will detonate it."

"What's stopping them from blowing it up right now?" O'Neill glared at the screen as though he could stop the cruiser with mental force.

"I think — I assume they are waiting for a better shot." Radek punched keys, tracing the shape of the explosion, the pattern of damage. "If they fire it here, they will damage us, yes, but the city will not be entirely destroyed. There is a remote chance we could still get away."

"Crap," O'Neill said, not quite under his breath. "We can't keep playing dodge'em —"

"Sheppard is trying," Radek said. The city's course shifted, but there wasn't much more they could do, not with the East Pier engine off line. He touched his radio. "Dr. Sommer! Report your progress, please."

"We're not to the engine yet," Sommer answered, his voice distorted by hissing static. "There is a hull breach, it's going to take some time to get around."

"We have a situation," Radek said. "Take suits if it will be faster."

There was a little silence, and then Sommer said, "Okay, Dr. Zelenka, we're on it."

"They're not going to be fast enough," O'Neill said.

Radek shook his head. They weren't, and there was no other way down to that part of the city — Sommer had already gone through the closest transport chamber.

"Call them back," O'Neill said.

"But —"

"You said it yourself, they're not going to be able to fix it fast enough, and they're too exposed. Get them back, we'll deal with the engine after we solve this problem."

"All right," Radek said, and turned back to the radio to give the order.

"General O'Neill," Teyla said. She had been silent for so long that Radek had almost forgotten her presence. "I have a proposition."

Teyla moved to stand beside General O'Neill, the tactical display now laid out before them in Radek's central screen. "We cannot evade effectively—we are under fire, and the East Pier engine is damaged. But I can fly a Wraith cruiser. Radek says there is only a skeleton crew, or perhaps none at all. Let me go across and fly it to safety."

"Death will pull the trigger as soon as you board," O'Neill said.

"I think not." The pattern unfolded itself before her, clear and simple, what had been a tangle resolved by the cutting of a single string. "They will not waste their best weapon, not for a small party, and if we go by jumper, they may not know we are coming until we are aboard. And then we can create enough confusion that they will not know whether or not to detonate until it is too late."

"But once they know you have control, they'll blow it," O'Neill pointed out.

"If detonation is controlled remotely," Teyla answered, her voice steady. That was, of course, the great risk, but if it was the only way to save the city—she saw no other, and thought her odds were better than even.

"She'd be stupid to play it any other way." O'Neill gave her a mulish stare.

"But." Radek swung away from his console, lifting a finger. "We can jam the signal, that is not hard. We know their communications frequencies, and we can block them. And—if I go with you, I can probably defuse the bombs. Or help you send the ship on another course. I have worked on a cruiser before."

O'Neill's face stilled. Teyla could almost read the calculations, the balance of risk and reward, the city's need against the possible loss of his people. "How sure are you that you can jam the signal, Doc?" he asked.

Radek smiled. "I will bet my life on it."

"You're betting more lives than that," O'Neill said. "Woolsey! Who've we got who can fly a puddlejumper that we don't need somewhere else?"

Woolsey frowned, but answered directly. "There are ten civilians currently in the city who have the ATA gene, and all of them are checked out on the jumpers. Why?"

"See that cruiser?" O'Neill nodded to the screen. "It's full of explosives. We need to get somebody over there and defuse it before it hits us. Teyla has volunteered to lead a team to do just that, but I don't have anybody with the ATA gene that I can spare."

Woolsey's thin mouth compressed, lips almost vanishing, before he spoke. "I'm sure there will be someone. Teyla?"

She followed him into his office, the door sliding softly closed behind them as though this were just another meeting. He reached for his laptop, tying into the city's communications system, and looked at her over its lid.

"You don't have to do this, you know."

"But indeed I must." Teyla smiled to show him she accepted the risks. "I am the only one who can." This is what it meant to say it was a Gift, she thought suddenly. This was the thing she could do that no one else could manage, that could very possibly save the city and everyone in it, and that was indeed a gift she had not anticipated.

"Yes. I suppose so." *But I don't have to like it.* Woolsey's expression said that as clearly as if he'd spoken aloud, but he turned his attention to the screen. "All personnel." He ran through the situation quickly and clearly, laying out the problem and the proposed solution and the need for a volunteer who was checked out in the jumpers.

There was an instant babble of response, at least four voices clamoring to be chosen, and Teyla's heart swelled. That was the thing she had grown to love about the people of Earth, or at least these Earth people, the ones who had walked through a gate knowing they would not return unless they found their own power source on the far side. They were a people for risks, for gambles, in a way that the people of Pegasus could not afford to be, Culled as they had been for millennia. She sorted out the voices — Coleman, one of the line cooks, on duty now with the other airmen protecting the lower floors of the central tower; Dr. Majeski, who blushed and stammered and knew more about the city's use of gamma radiation than any man alive; Eva Robinson, her voice cutting through the babble. Woolsey's eyes flicked closed for an instant.

"Dr. Robinson," he said. "If you'd join the party in the jumper bay. And thank you."

Teyla nodded. Eva was the one who could best be spared. She fastened her tac vest, and started for the bay herself.

## CHAPTER TWENTY-ONE
# Boarding Party

EMBER stared at the image. If he had not been shaking already in the aftermath of Ease's death, he would have shuddered: those were the Ancient weapons, the ones legend said had nearly broken the Wraith in the first war, before the queens had overcome them by sheer weight of numbers. For the first time, he thought he understood what it might have been like to have been born in those days.

He glanced back at his boards, the data trickling monotonously down the screens, repeating that *Just Fortune* was as ready for battle as it would ever be. And still they waited. He risked a glance over his shoulder, but Guide's face was impassive, impossible to read. Alabaster was easier, frowning in more than mere concentration as she watched the cruisers twist in the central screen. She wanted to join the battle, Ember thought, but deferred to her father's judgment. Though surely Steelflower would want to see Death defeated first, and whatever agreements must be made with the Lanteans could be resolved later…

Precision hissed softly, and Guide said, *Not yet.*

*We cannot wait forever,* Alabaster said.

*We must,* Guide answered, and there was that in his tone that silenced any protest.

Ember looked back at his boards as a sudden knot in the data caught his eye, and touched his controls to disentangle the problem. It was the status transmission from Farseer's hive, power spiking suddenly in the secondary systems, and he snarled in spite of himself. The readouts wavered, warnings blooming and dropping, only to vanish as Farseer's clevermen fought the problems. The hive had been badly damaged when Farseer fled Queen Death's fleet, and the repairs had been hastily made.

"Commander!" The voice came from the communications console, Farseer's face and shaved head snarling from the screen.

"Commander, we have a problem with our maneuver engines —"

"Sabotage?" Guide's tone was controlled, but Ember saw his feeding hand open and flex.

"No, damage from our last fight — some of the repairs have come adrift."

Ember looked back at his console. The stream of warnings had slowed, but now the off-line indicators pulsed ominously, an all-too-familiar pattern. He had warned Whirlwind that the patches would not hold.

"We've lost lateral thrusters," Farseer went on. "My men are working on it, but — your cleverman, Ember, he did the first repairs. It would speed our work if we could borrow him again."

Guide glanced toward him, and Ember met his gaze. *I will go, Commander.*

*Very well,* Guide answered. *Take a shuttle, and be quick about it.*

Ember glanced back the screen as he left the control room, seeing the Lanteans still locked in battle with Death's fleet. Surely Guide would act, and soon.

John watched the puddlejumper go, trying not to change course too much until Eva cleared the shield. Cloaked, it was invisible to the Wraith, but he still held his breath until it was out of the fire zone, zipping for the crippled cruiser.

The city took another strong barrage from the hive ships, the shield holding firm. How much power was there?

The answer was there immediately, the city answering his thought — the ZPM is at 83 per cent and dropping slowly. Well, it would have to be, considering the power required to maintain the shield. Which was getting increasingly harder. The city showed him, information flowing in.

John surfaced, his eyes opening though he remained in the chair. "We're going to have to withdraw the shields from the edges of the city," he said.

"Why?" Woolsey replied on the headset. "We have power."

"We've got plenty of power. That's not the problem," John said. "But the repairs we made to the city's systems while we were on

Earth are way not up to spec. Our stuff isn't nearly as good as the
Ancient stuff, and it's not handling the load right when we're taking this kind of fire and holding the shield against hard vacuum.
It's using too much at one time. We've got to cut power to something. And I'd rather it wasn't the hyperdrive, or we won't be able
to bug out if we need to."

There was a long silence.

"Okay," Woolsey said at last. "We'll give the warning and then
pull the shield back from up here."

"Sounds good." John closed his eyes again, tilting back into the
chair's embrace.

One of the hives had gotten free of the *Hammond* and the *Pride*,
coming on strong.

Drones, John thought. There were still more than twenty left.
Another flight of eight, two and two and two and two, all set for
the same coordinates, firing in pairs so that the power required for
launch and for the shield breach would be spread out. Two and two,
launching and passing through, as, in some separate world, John
heard the evacuation order for the outer areas of the city ringing
through human ears.

Three on target, a fourth decoyed away…

Four more launches, straight and true through the dark.

The hive reeled, alarms flaring, the main engines offline and
systems shutting down, falling away from the plane of engagement.
Darts scrambled to get away from it, fleeing the expected shockwave.

Another one down, John thought. Nineteen drones left.

The infirmary was quiet, the calm before the storm. So far the
most serious injury was one of the computer technicians who had
been caught under a falling rack of equipment as the city rocked
under fire. She had a concussion, and Marie was monitoring her
closely, although Jennifer thought she'd pull through without too
much permanent harm done.

Their only other patient so far was Patterson, who had missed
his footing on the stairs and twisted his ankle as he landed. It
wasn't broken, only a bad sprain, but it was already swelling as she
wrapped a compression bandage around it.

"I should get back to my post," Patterson said, swinging his legs down from the bed, although he winced as his toes touched the ground.

"You should elevate your foot," Jennifer said. "And I'll get you an icepack."

The infirmary shuddered, and she could hear the rattle of boxes shifting in the drug cabinets.

"We're under attack by the Wraith," Patterson said. "I've got to get back out there."

"You are not putting weight on your torn ligaments right now, I'm sorry."

"Look at it this way, son," Carson said, patting the Marine on the shoulder. "If the Wraith make it into the city, we'll all be glad you're in here protecting us."

"I guess so," Patterson said, looking mollified.

It wasn't exactly a lie, but Jennifer and Carson both knew there was little chance of a fight in the city. If the shield held, the Wraith couldn't penetrate it with their transport beams, and if the shield failed, they'd all be dead in the vacuum of space. The Wraith would only come then to salvage what was left.

Still, it seemed to make Patterson feel better to think about what he could do for them.

"I'll go ahead and put a walking cast on it," Jennifer said. "That way if you absolutely have to put your weight on it, you can. But promise me you won't unless you have to."

"Okay, deal," Patterson said.

She opened one of the cabinets carefully in search of the plastic boot, rearranging the boxes so that they wouldn't spill out the next time the city shuddered under fire.

"Attention all personnel," Woolsey said. "We are withdrawing shields from outlying areas of the city. If you are in the areas currently marked red on all city maps, move *now*. You have ninety seconds to reach the city core."

"Ninety seconds," Jennifer said, shaking her head. That was how they'd lost an entire team the first time they'd flown the city, dead in vacuum as the shield collapsed inward without warning. This time everyone knew not to leave the city core.

Everyone but one small, insatiably curious Siamese kitten. She told herself firmly that Newton had never been outside the central tower, and that he wouldn't choose this moment to start exploring. He was probably hiding under a couch or curled up in a crawl space, as safe as any of the rest of them.

"I'm sure nobody's out there," Patterson said.

"I'm sure everybody's fine," Jennifer said, and started strapping on his plastic cast.

The puddlejumper crept through the battle, cloak and shields at full power, Eva Robinson at the controls. She looked less nervous than Radek felt, but then, he thought, she was a psychiatrist. She'd had a lot of practice hiding unacceptable feelings from her patients. It was reassuring anyway to see her there, frowning slightly in concentration, her hands spread on the controls. Teyla sat beside her, her head moving steadily as she looked from console to windscreen and back again. Radek could see the cruiser in the distance, drifting and apparently dead, and checked his gear again. He had the tools he'd improvised to work on the cruiser they'd salvaged, and his P90 and as much extra ammunition as he could cram into his pockets — when had he become that man, as prepared to fight as he was to do his real job? It didn't matter; what mattered was getting on board the cruiser and either defusing the explosives, or directing it away from the city.

"Hey, Doc." That was Sheffield, the young lieutenant in charge of the Marine detail, scalp and chin shaved bare. "Let me see that schematic again, will you?"

"Yes," Radek said, and turned his tablet so that the other could see the plans on the screen. "We will be coming aboard here, in the shuttle bay, and then these are the corridors that lead to the control room."

Sergeant Ramirez was looking over the lieutenant's shoulder, studying the map for the dozenth time, and Teyla turned in her seat, hearing their voices.

"I think we will take the central corridor if we can. It is the most direct route."

"Yeah," Sheffield said, still swiping at the tablet to get a better view, and Ramirez looked up.

"Any idea yet how many hostiles on board, Ms. Emmagan?"

"Not yet," Teyla answered, her tone utterly tranquil. "Not many, I do not believe."

That would be good, Radek thought. 'Not many' was a number he could live with.

"Teyla," Dr. Robinson said. "We're coming up on the shuttle bay."

The mottled hull loomed in the windscreen, the bay left gaping when the ship was abandoned. A few telltales flickered within, weak power in the conduits, and Teyla closed her eyes for a moment. "There are no Wraith in the bay," she said at last. "And their force-field is still holding atmosphere. Go ahead and bring her in, Eva."

"All right."

"Sergeant," Sheffield said, and Ramirez nodded.

"Sir!" He waved his hand, forming the Marines up on either side of the tailgate, weapons ready, and Radek stuffed the tablet into his pack. He pulled out the jamming device he'd hastily cobbled together, set it to cover the full spectrum of Wraith transmissions. Eva brought the jumper carefully into the bay, rotating it as she landed so that it was facing out again, ready for a quick getaway.

"Grazyk, Hatton, Ling, stay with the jumper," Sheffield said, and looked at Teyla, who looked at Radek in turn.

"Is the device ready?"

Radek nodded. "Ready to go."

"Go ahead."

Radek flipped the switch and twisted the dial all the way to maximum. That should kill internal transmissions as well as any signal from the hive intended to detonate the bombs, and he watched as the power built. "Ok. We are at maximum power. They should not be able to set off the bombs remotely."

"Excellent," Teyla said. "Lower the tailgate, Lieutenant."

"Yes, ma'am."

Radek braced himself, clutching his P90, but the bay was empty, the lights dimmer even than usual on a Wraith ship. Teyla paused for a moment, considering — communing with the ship? — and then waved them toward the open hatch. "I can sense no Wraith nearby. There are four in the control room, I sense no others."

Sheffield nodded, gesturing to his men, and Radek followed Teyla across the bay. "If no one is watching the explosives, perhaps I should try to defuse them now," he said, breaking into a trot to stay at her heels. "It may still be possible to override the jamming."

"Let us take the control room first," Teyla answered. "If we can first secure the ship, then everything else will be much easier."

Well, yes, Radek thought, but that presupposed they could take the control room without too much trouble. He hurried after Teyla and the Marines, hoping she was right.

The cruiser looked old and dirty, even taking battle damage into account, but that made sense, Radek thought. Of course the Wraith wouldn't use a new, strong ship for this mission. The colors of the bulkheads were faded, the decks faintly uneven underfoot, as though worn by many years of use, and he wondered just how long one of these ships could last. How long it could live. Teyla said they were indeed somewhat alive —

"Lieutenant!" Teyla's voice was precisely pitched to carry to all their party and no farther. "Wraith — three of them, coming to us along this corridor."

Sheffield waved his men back against the bulkheads, and Radek copied them, flattening himself against the rough skin. Ahead, the corridor curved slightly, turning toward the bow, and a shadow moved, black coat and flowing white hair. The Marines opened fire, kept firing; the first Wraith fell, but the others dodged back into the limited protection of the curve. A moment later, a Wraith grenade bounced around the corner, flashing blue. Radek froze, but the boy next to him moved without thought, grabbed it and threw it away behind them. It exploded in a flat crack of light, the shock wave knocking Radek's glasses askew, and the remaining Wraith whirled roaring from cover, energy weapons blazing. A Marine fell, and another, but the rest concentrated their fire on the Wraith, knocked them back, staggering, until finally they fell.

"Thank you," Radek said, to the Marine, and the boy held up his hand with a rueful smile to show it trembling.

"They are dead," Teyla said. "But the other — he has locked himself in the control room. We must take it, quickly. I do not know what he can do from there."

"Yes, ma'am," Sheffield said. "Ramirez! Let's go!"

Radek hurried after them, fetching up at the closed hatch that led to the control room.

"Locked," Ramirez said. "C4!"

"Wait," Teyla said. She rested her hand on the bulkhead beside the locking mechanism, and closed her eyes for a moment. "I can open this."

"How many hostiles inside?" Sheffield asked.

"Just one. But he believes himself well armed."

"Right. Can we risk a grenade?"

"A stun grenade, perhaps," Teyla said. "But we must damage as little as possible."

"Right," Sheffield said again. "Ok, Stone, Jenks, Alavarez, when the door opens, throw a flashbang and go in after it. Take out the pilot — and you heard Ms. Emmagan, don't shoot up the consoles if you can help it."

There was a ragged chorus of affirmation, and Teyla laid her hand on the lock again. Radek saw her draw a deep breath, and then another, and then she opened her eyes. "Now."

The hatch slid open as she spoke, and a bolt of blue light blasted through after it. One of the Marines threw a stun grenade, and then the team barreled in after it, P90s firing. The Wraith fired again, and then there was silence. Teyla shed her weapon as the nearest Marines dragged the Wraith's body away from the commander's station, and settled herself at the controls. Radek turned in a circle, finally found the main environmental controls and began setting up his tablet.

He swore as the readings began to come through. The Wraith had used every kind of explosive they could find, their own and bombs taken from human settlements, so that things like dynamite lay wired to iron spheres filled with raw gunpowder and blocks of an unfamiliar compound that had to be the Wraith equivalent of C4. It ran in a long chain along the cruiser's spine, more than a ton of it, enough to vaporize most of the cruiser and overload Atlantis's shields. The wiring was complex and redundant, and there were pressure sensors on the outer hull —

"I am attempting to take control of the ship," Teyla said. "Radek, can you disconnect the pressure sensors?"

He looked at the schematics, spinning the images to find the access points. "Yes. Yes, I think so —"

"Ramirez, Kelly, go with Dr. Zelenka," Sheffield ordered. "Everybody else, we're with Ms. Emmagan."

Radek nodded, grabbing his pack. "This way," he said, and started down the long corridor.

"Atlantis is dropping her shield!" Franklin's voice was incredulous, and Sam quickly came around to look over his shoulder at his screen.

Not dropping, no, not quite. "They're reconfiguring," Sam said. "They're pulling the shield back to just the central area." She'd seen that before, two years ago and more, when they had been adrift and badly damaged. It conserved power. But now, with a cruiser on a collision course... Well, maybe it was the best option, all things considered, to save the power for the critical moment.

"*Hammond* and *Pride of the Genii*, pull back to cover Atlantis." That was Jack's voice on the comm, Woolsey behind him saying something else into another microphone. Definitely a problem of some kind.

Another problem.

"Chandler, see if you can get us in to cover for the *Pride*," Sam said. "They're in tight and won't be able to disengage."

A swarm of Darts rotated around the *Pride*, twenty or so taking potshots. Each one did minimal damage, but the constant pinpricks to the *Pride*'s shields cost power, and while surrounded by this screaming whirl of Darts it was impossible to disengage.

"Yes, ma'am."

The *Hammond* waded in like a whale through a school of fish, and was about equally as effective. The rail guns couldn't target the Darts — too fast, and too maneuverable, but her size at least screened the *Pride* somewhat.

And then the Darts were on them instead. It was like being surrounded by a cloud of biting flies, each one firing at a different spot, each prick drawing a drop of blood.

"Forward shield at 25 per cent," Davies said. "Ventral at 40 per cent. Ma'am?"

"Give it a minute," Sam said, watching the *Pride* twist trying to get free, the cruiser sticking to it, dogging it with shots, still tight on its course.

"Ventral at 35 per cent."

Crap, Sam thought. They were overloading the *Hammond's* shields with sheer volume. "Where are my 302s? Hocken?"

There was no reply.

Mel spun her 302, diving beneath *Pride of the Genii* on the tail of a Dart. The fuel warning light flashed yellow on her screen, three quarters of her fuel gone — 302s carried a light load, and they weren't meant for sustained combat. Fast and maneuverable, yes, but the cost of that was operational range. Her flight was fast coming to the end of it. They'd have to land and refuel before long, or simply become expensive paperweights with guns, continuing along their last course until they hit something or more optimistically were dragged in by the *Pride of the Genii's* tractor beam.

Two Darts dashed over the horizon of the *Pride's* stern, head on at incredible speed, like the fastest game of chicken ever invented. She fired, fingers tightening convulsively, and then pulled up.

So did one of the Darts. They hit wingtip to wingtip, a touch barely a few inches long, but with enough speed and force to send her 302 spinning out of control, rotating madly over and over.

Mel had half a second to swear, and then the other wingtip hit the *Pride's* shields at full force and the world went black.

## CHAPTER TWENTY-TWO
# Grace

LORNE felt the pressure ease, most of the cloud of Darts drawn now to the *Hammond*, and he let his awareness expand from its tight focus on flying the *Pride*. The shields were dropping, all around 40 percent, but there was no serious damage beyond the gun they'd lost earlier. In the back of his mind, he could hear Dahlia Radim and Dr. Campbell directing technicians to shore up systems here and there, but the *Pride* could manage without them. He could hear the 302s' line chatter, too, voices sharp and high with stress — they'd be running out of fuel soon, he told the ship, be ready to tractor them aboard —

Something struck the rear shield, a heavy blow but not an energy weapon. Dart? he wondered, and the *Pride* answered instantly: 302. A 302 spinning uncontrolled, pilot dead or unconscious —

*Tractor*, he said, and felt the ship respond, faster than the technician at the console could ever answer. The beam leaped out, caught the spinning ship; he felt the *Pride* shudder under the inertial stress, and then the technicians took over, reeling the 302 back from the brink. He took in the pattern of ships and Darts, the volume of fire directed at the *Hammond*, and thought she'd hold just a moment longer.

"Open the port bay door," he said aloud. "Get that 302 on board fast as you can. Don't worry about damaging the bay, just don't smash up the pilot."

He heard the acknowledgement, his attention already elsewhere. Any other 302s in trouble? Not obviously, but the fuel shortage —

"*Pride*, I am out of fuel." A man's voice, no one he knew. "Can you take me?"

*Yes*, the ship said. The bay was clear, the first 302 in and secured.

"Come on aboard," Lorne said. "Blue Flight, Gold Flight, this is the *Pride of the Genii*. I can take two more, repeat, two more."

"Blue Four coming in," a voice answered, thick with relief.

Lorne steadied the *Pride*, making himself an easy target. The

Darts were distracted for the moment, swarming on the *Hammond*; in the tactical display, he could see a 302 wobbling as it tried to line up on the bay.

"Teal'c, how's your fuel?" That was Mitchell, cool as ever.

"Adequate for now, Colonel."

"Ok, Linney, you're next."

"Negative. Negative, I am out of fuel. I'm not going to make it."

"Major Lorne," Mitchell said. "I've got a man down, can you grab him?"

The third 302 was on its line, engine stuttering. As long as the *Pride* held her course, he'd be Ok. Lorne turned his attention outward, looking for the other 302, Linney. Yes, there it was, engines dead, on a flat course to nowhere, except that a Dart was bound to see it first and finish it off. *Tractors?* he asked and the *Pride* answered instantly.

*Too far. Just out of range.*

But not for long. Lorne checked the bay — there was the third 302, too high, scraping through the opening to come in hard against the inner barriers — and the calculations presented themselves. Yes, there, just a touch of acceleration to close the gap, roll left to put the *Pride* between the mess of Darts and the drifting ship, and tractor on, to catch her, slow her down...

*Tractor is secure. Bringing the craft on board.*

"Darts," Radim said, and in the same moment the *Pride*'s sensors screamed the alert. The *Pride* had been on the same course too long, the Wraith flight commander had been bound to notice.

"Take them if you can," Lorne answered. He could see the Darts shrieking toward them, heard Radim calling his shots. A Dart exploded, another sheered clear, nearly wrecking its neighbor, but the *Pride* shuddered under the force of the attack. The tractor beam dimmed, the *Pride* shunting power to the shields; the 302 wobbled, and then slid neatly into the bay.

"Close up!" Lorne said, and didn't care whether it was the ship or a technician who obeyed. "We're going back for the *Hammond*."

Rodney could hear the line chatter from the 302s, the pilots speaking their own gibberish as they spun and dodged, engaged with the darts and the cruisers. Occasionally Sam's voice cut across, warning of some threat. Was that Cameron Mitchell, he wondered, distracted a moment from the jumper's systems by surprise. What was he doing here?

The cloaked jumper sounded a warning — they were directly on course, too close to the system's sun.

"Acknowledged," Rodney said, turning it off. He knew precisely where they were — threading a course around the edges of the battle, staying between the tangle of ships and the sun. The jumper warned that the *Hammond*'s shields were almost down, one of her thrusters responding awkwardly.

"Not looking good," Rodney said grimly. Sam couldn't see him. Nobody could. And it had to stay that way until the very end.

Collision alarms sounded and Rodney jerked the jumper around, a powered dive beneath a hive ship that had come out of hyperspace almost on top of him. It couldn't see him, of course, but he almost squeezed his eyes shut as he slid beneath it, point blank range for its guns.

Nothing happened. He was out the other side, the hive ship behind him, streaking unseen through the dark.

"Ma'am, we have another hive ship coming out of hyperspace."

Sam clutched the back of the helmsman's chair as the *Hammond* shook with another blow, Chandler trying to turn on a dime to present the ventral shield to the fire.

"Forward shield at 10 per cent," Franklin said. Beads of sweat stood out on his brow. "Ma'am?"

The new hive rotated, positioning guns to bear. It was smaller than most of the others, and even from here Sam could see that some of its guns weren't operative, but another hive ship was the last thing she needed right now.

"Try to put the cruiser between us," Sam said. Firefighting foam made the deck slippery beneath her feet. "We can't take a full forward barrage." The hive ship's guns were powering up, four of them at least.

*Oh, not good*, she thought. Their luck had run out.

The forward guns of *Promised Return* were charging, nearly ready to fire. Thorn stood at Waterlight's elbow, disapproving but silent, always at her back whether he disagreed or not, ready to guard her.

Bronze looked back from the weapons console, his face all keen elation.

Waterlight lifted her chin, visuals from her ship playing before her eyes with the touch of her fingers on the interfaces — the faltering vessel of She Who Carries Many Things locked in a fatal dance with Queen Death's ship and one of her cruisers, the swarm of Darts and other ships around.

"You may fire as you wish," Waterlight said.

Sam caught her breath, a sound stopped in her throat. The hive ship's main batteries discharged, graceful arcs of blue fire streaking toward Queen Death's ship.

"They're firing on the other hive!" Franklin said. "Oh, God!"

Sensors registered hits, the hive lurching under the unexpected fire. It spun slowly, retargeting.

"Who is it?" Franklin said.

"Teyla's work," Sam said. Whether Teyla was actually aboard that ship or not, it was her work. "Consider them an ally."

Queen Death's ship came about, returning fire from the other hive, momentarily distracted from the *Hammond*.

"Look for a gap," Sam said, scooting over behind the gunner's chair. "Look for a gap for the rail guns." She put her hand on the bulkhead steadyingly. *Come on, baby*, she thought, *one good shot*, and hoped the *Hammond* heard her.

The jumper shook, lights darkening, inertial dampeners blinking for a moment, and Rodney was thrown from his chair, plastered against the ceiling for one long moment as the gravity failed. Seven or eight g-forces pressed against him, and then the Ancient systems righted themselves. Down became down again, and he fell forward, knees against the back of the pilot's chair and his head plunging toward the floor. He had the presence of mind to throw his arms up, catching his full weight on his left wrist.

And then for a moment he blanked out too, the world a screaming dark pain as bones snapped audibly.

The lights flickered, stabilized, and Rodney rolled over, his eyes watering and his heart racing. "Oh no oh no oh no." The nerves in his arm screeched when he tried to move the fingers of his left hand, but he could move them. It was the wrist. It had to be.

Okay, Rodney thought as the jumper rocked again, white carpet beneath him pristine and perfect, though his hand was on fire. I broke my wrist. Okay. That's all. I broke my wrist and it hurts like hell but it's not going to kill me. And Carson or Jennifer will fix it up. The worst thing will be that I have to have surgery on it and a couple of months in a cast, which will be very inconvenient because I have to use the keyboard, but it's a broken wrist. I can live with that. It just hurts. A lot. But if this jumper gets blown up, it will be a lot worse.

Slowly, Rodney hauled himself to his feet. The board was blinking yellow, systems shouting for his attention. "What happened?" he muttered. Surely the hive ship hadn't hit him. He'd been sure he was clear of its shot. And he couldn't have collided... And yet sensors were showing external physical damage, the shield generator damaged, the drone launching systems destroyed, as though...

Rodney swore. The *Hammond* had clipped the cloaked jumper with its rail guns. Rail guns fired a solid projectile. The jumper's shields had absorbed most of the kinetic energy, or his molecules would be spread across the solar system, but it couldn't make the solid projectile disappear into thin air.

Did he still have the cloak? Rodney's hands flew over the board. Yes, at least temporarily. The cloak was holding. None of the hive ships had seen him. The jumper's shields were at 40 per cent and steady, but one of the two generators was out of commission. And the launching systems were completely destroyed...

Rodney went cold.

The launching systems that were supposed to deploy the weapon, to launch it into the sun. Without them he had no way to complete his mission. Decloak, broadcast what he was trying to do so that Todd could see it, and launch the weapon into the sun. Without the launching systems, he had no way to destroy the weapon, to get it from the jumper into the sun. If he just opened the back tailgate and let it float out, it might take days before the sun's gravitational field drew it in enough to destroy it. It needed propulsion. It needed to be sent into the sun at speed.

Rodney's hands stilled, looking ahead at the bright glow of the sun filling half the front window.

Of course there was one way left, one means of propulsion — the jumper's systems. He could send the jumper into the sun with the weapon aboard.

The *Hammond* was behind, closely engaged. The *Pride of the Genii* was halfway across the system, protecting Atlantis and engaged too. No one was in range to beam someone out.

He could fly the jumper into the sun with the weapon aboard.

Rodney's wrist throbbed as he moved his hand. There was no one else. There was no alternative, no more than there had been for Peter Grodin when the first Wraith fleet bore down on Atlantis, stuck on the weapons satellite to fire one critical shot.

Okay, Rodney thought. That's how it goes. He pushed the jumper's engines as far as they would go, course set for the sun.

"One good shot," Sam said. And then they had it, the right angle, the right instant.

The rail guns fired, superheated metal streaking through the vacuum, cooling to black in absolute zero, and then plunging through the hiveship's hull at full speed.

"Yes!" Franklin said, punching his fist in the air.

The hiveship reeled, turning to present its intact side to the *Hammond*, guns bearing full against the new interloper. Blue energy fire streaked out. It was a long way from finished.

"We're losing the forward shield," Franklin said. "Ma'am?"

"Pull back," Sam said. "Reroute power to get a patch on it." They couldn't keep punching that way, and the new ship had at least bought them time to regroup. "Hocken, what's your status?"

"Colonel Hocken's ship has been destroyed," Teal'c said solemnly. "We have ten 302s in service."

Ten out of twenty. Crap. But at least two of those had landed to refuel, and one had skated in badly damaged. Another was trying to line up on the bay now, signaling an emergency landing, one thruster flamed out from fuel starvation. As she watched the other flamed out, an unpowered landing without even the dregs of fuel for maneuvering thrusters. Mitchell.

"Hold us as steady as you can," Sam said, leaning over Chandler's shoulder. At the moment they could actually stop bobbing and weaving, probably the reason he'd waited so long.

The 302 lined up on the bay, sliding in with several feet to spare below, hitting the emergency webbing at bone-jarring speed. That had to hurt, but there were worse landings. Any one you can walk away from...

*Pride of the Genii* was still after the hive ship, following up with energy weapons. Lorne must be out of drones, Sam thought.

"How's that shield?" she asked.

"Forward shield back at 12 per cent," Franklin said. "It's not much."

"Well, let's get in there," Sam said. The *Pride* couldn't do it alone, and neither could their new ally.

This is how it ends, Rodney thought, just like it had in that alternate world Elizabeth had avoided so long ago, in which he'd drowned at his post, staying to the last to save the city. That was what Rodney McKay's fate always had been. It was just that in this world it had taken five years longer. This was the story of how Rodney did what needed to be done and in the end he died for it, the jumper on course for the sun and the battle behind him. He was going to die to save Atlantis, and that had been the name of the game from the moment he'd stunned John in the jumper bay. It wasn't John's turn, not this time. He had way too much to live for.

Time to decloak. The radiation monitors were climbing, but not yet at critical levels. With the shields damaged he didn't know how much time he had. Rodney turned the cloak off and the transmitter on.

"This is Rodney McKay," he said clearly, and his voice found strength as he went on, the hard, decisive voice of a hero. They might play this back as his memorial, a hundred times better than those recordings he'd made during the siege, the real deal. "I have Hyperion's weapon. And I'm going to destroy it. It's on board this jumper and it's going into the sun."

He could hear the replies, distinct and indistinct, Lorne saying something far away on his ship, hold on or something else irrelevant, as if he could wait that long!

Sam was closer. "Rodney, you don't have to do this."

"Yes, I do." The *Hammond* was way behind, still snarled with the hive ship, one thruster entirely offline. "It has to go in the sun or Todd won't engage and we're out of time." He cut the comm. There was no point listening, not now.

The sun filled the entire forward screen, radiation warnings creeping into scarlet. How many minutes of this could he stand before they breached the jumper's shields for the last time?

The others... He could see their endings now with painful clarity. Sheppard would turn into the old guy who knows it all, the Pegasus expert who went native a long time ago, our man in Pegasus with his kids and his wife and his friends, the opinionated go-to guy who could get it done. Teyla would be the diplomat, the one who knit people together, human and Wraith alike. And Ronon would be a leader despite himself, part of a new Sateda rising from the ashes, an ally and a friend. Jennifer would go home and maybe she'd remember him sometimes. Yeah, that would be how it was. He'd be the tragic thing that happened in her past, the thing that changed her.

For him, there were no choices left to make.

The jumper was on course to its ultimate rendezvous.

It was curiously peaceful. He, Rodney McKay, was going to die and he really didn't mind at all.

Somebody had to, and it was his turn.

"Rodney?"

He jumped at the voice behind him, knowing that the jumper was empty, knowing that it had to be. There was no way anyone else could be here. No way.

And yet he twisted around in his chair.

She stood between the two rear seats, her hand on the backrest of one, in her old red Atlantis shirt, her hair pulled back from her face, and his mouth opened and closed. "You can't be here," Rodney said.

"I'm not supposed to be," Elizabeth Weir said. With quick, sharp movements she came forward and sat down in the seat beside him.

"You're dead." It wasn't the most brilliant line ever, but it did spring to mind.

"Ascended," Elizabeth said, glancing over the tactical controls.

"Aren't Ascended people not supposed to mingle with mere mortals?"

That did win a smile from her, a little sideways smile like the ones he remembered and had always liked and never said so. "Yes," she said briskly. "And if I get in trouble I'll pay the price. But you need me to do this if you're going to get through it in one piece. So I'm here." Elizabeth raised her head. "Let's do this, Rodney."

"Dr. McKay, if you'll hang on for a minute…" Sam heard Lorne's voice over the line chatter from the 302s, and she knew whatever he had to say was pointless. The *Pride of the Genii* was too far away, much further than the *Hammond*. Even if they'd managed to get beaming technology operational, Lorne could never get in range.

Nor could she. Chandler weaved and bobbed, shots telling home against the hive ship, but their batteries were still working. The *Hammond* was taking heavy fire. To turn tail and run would doom the ship, and even if they made for the jumper at maximum speed, the *Hammond*'s Asgard beams were short range. Rodney was at eight to ten times the *Hammond*'s maximum reach.

"Rodney, you don't have to do this," Sam said, but there was no answer. And of course there wouldn't be. He was right. It had to be done and nobody else could do it. But it was worth a try. "Ikram, can you get a lock on Dr. McKay?"

"No, ma'am," Ikram said quickly. "It's too far."

Franklin looked around, asking with his eyes whether they were breaking off. Three Darts screamed toward the *Hammond*, concentrating fire on the weakened forward shield, and Chandler dived, presenting the dorsal shield instead. A pair of 302s rose straight up the *Hammond*'s bow, guns flaring as they skimmed over the surface just shy of a shield collision. One Dart incandesced, and the others streaked by, the 302s passing just short of the aft rail gun.

"Nice job, guys," Sam said.

"It is a pleasure, Colonel Carter," Teal'c replied with his customary aplomb.

The jumper was too far, the friendly hive ship closing on Death's ship.

"Ma'am?" Franklin asked.

Sam glanced at the screen. Already the radiation was spiking above what any human being could bear, the jumper beginning to glow. Its comm was silent. *Goodbye, Rodney*, she whispered to herself. *Goodbye.*

*You can't*, John started to say. On the city's sensors the jumper was so close and so distant at once, but he already had. The jumper didn't explode. It simply dissolved. The heat and radiation melted through the skin. One moment it was there and the next it was a dispersing cloud of complex atoms.

"Was someone aboard that jumper?" Woolsey asked over the comm.

"Rodney," John said. His voice sounded odd and even, not his own. "I guess he wasn't working for Queen Death, huh?" And then anger overtook him, anger at himself and Woolsey and Todd and the entire rest of the universe.

"We couldn't know," Woolsey began.

"He took my mission," John said. "My mission," and Woolsey fell silent before the fury in his voice. He opened the comm. "Todd? You see that? Todd! That was Rodney destroying your precious weapon and getting killed doing it. Now get your skinny Wraith ass into the battle! You hear me? Get your ass into the battle!"

Woolsey broke in. "We've fulfilled our part of the deal. Now fulfill yours."

The city's sensors reported movement, the ships of Todd's alliance powering weapons, the flagship beginning to move.

"We are engaging," Alabaster said over the comm, her voice tranquil. "All ships, fire as you have targets. Your cleverman's sacrifice shall not be in vain. All ahead full, please."

With a distant surge of energy, Guide's alliance opened fire.

GRAHAM · SCOTT · GRISWOLD

## CHAPTER TWENTY-THREE
# Falling

ON THE computer screen in front of Jennifer, the spot of light that
had been Rodney's jumper was gone. The audio feed from the control room continued — Sheppard was yelling at Guide to get into the
battle, hot rage in his voice — but she felt like a blanket of silence
had descended around her, a sudden fall of snow.

Marie was saying something, probably all the right words of
sympathy, but Jennifer brushed away a comforting hand.

"I knew this would happen," she said.

It felt less like a sudden death was supposed to than like the end
of a terminal illness, the feeling that something she'd been struggling to hold onto for so long had been torn from her, and now she
was lighter whether she wanted to be or not. She wouldn't wonder
any longer how many more times she could fight to bring Rodney
back from the brink of death before she lost him. That was over.

The floor rocked as another heavy barrage of fire hit the city's
shields, and she steadied herself until the tremor passed. When
she looked up, Carson had come in from the next room, his face
showing that he knew.

"Did you see…?" he began.

"I know. I saw."

"Oh, Rodney." His voice was choked. "He was doing a very brave
thing."

"That was Rodney," Jennifer said, and then the tears were wet
on her cheeks, although she held her voice steady. "I should have
married him, you know? I mean, given the way things turned out.
It… it would have meant a lot to him, I think."

"You can't think that way. You couldn't have known —"

"I knew," Jennifer said. It was the price of living in this beautiful crystal city, so deceptively beautiful and so incredibly deadly.
Rodney had wanted to spend the rest of his life in Atlantis, and

that meant dying young.

For a moment anger and grief knotted together in her throat. There were so many things she had hoped they could have together, work and laughter and a baby for Rodney to insist on bundling in clothes too warm for the weather, a baby to wear tiny T-shirts with mathematical jokes on them. There were so many places she had wanted to see, so many things worth doing, and she would see them and do them, she knew, but not with him.

"I am so terribly sorry," Carson said softly.

"So am I," Jennifer said. She swallowed hard and brushed away tears she couldn't afford yet. "But we still have work to do."

"That we do," Carson said, and turned to check on their patients. They'd have more than enough work soon.

*Just Fortune* leaped willingly into battle, all systems perfect, glad in its way to finally do its part. Guide rested his hands on the controls, half in and half out of the ship-trance, a skill he had perfected over the years. The ship responded eagerly to his familiar touch, arcing up and over the dome of Atlantis's shields to bear down on the other hive. Mist's hive, he thought, or perhaps Noontide's; the two ships had been very nearly indistinguishable, grown from similar Seeds in the same year. It didn't matter. He could see the marks of damage on their mottled hide, could hear the blades at the guns marking those wounds and setting their targets. The hive could flee, or it could die.

A part of him wondered distantly why Sheppard had waited so long, why they had sacrificed McKay in the end, for sacrifice it had been, there had been no mistaking the true grief in Sheppard's voice. Was it possible that Death had retained some hold over him, broken only at the last moment, in time to make that final choice? Or had Sheppard and McKay had to act alone, overruling Woolsey and Carter's Consort? Most likely he would never know, and a part of him regretted that, even as he regretted McKay's death. But the main thing, the vital thing, was that Hyperion's weapon was destroyed, and he would fulfill his part of the bargain.

A second hive was drifting damaged at the edge of the battle, but he could see thrusters firing, struggling to bring the ship back into the battle. Better to stop that before it started, he thought, and opened a channel to the rest of his fleet.

"Copper, Thunder, take the damaged hive."

The two smaller cruisers peeled away, heading for the struggling hive. Guide saw its thrusters flare again, ragged and uneven, unable to turn in time to meet the attack. Energy weapons sliced across heavy hide, scoring deep into the hive's systems. The hive rolled, trailing vapor, main engines firing. It dropped out of the plane of the ecliptic, the cruisers in pursuit, but the hive opened a hyperspace window and was gone.

"Leave them," Guide said, and the cruisers turned, obedient. In his own screens, the less damaged hive swung to meet him, weapons blazing. He saw them strike home, felt the ship's pain and anger and steadied it on its course. His gunners had their targets, he could hear the chatter confirming it, but discipline held. A little longer, he thought, just a little more—

"Fire," he said, mind and voice alike, and *Just Fortune* staggered with the weight of its own attack. Lines of light cut across the darkness, spearing the other hive, each weak point targeted and hit. The other hive shuddered, bucking, and then a hole opened in its hull just aft of the central gap. Atmosphere boiled free, and then the explosion followed.

"Atlantis," he said, switching to the familiar channel. "Sheppard."

"He's busy." That was Carter's Consort, O'Neill. Of course Sheppard would be in ship-trance.

Guide said, "Farseer and Copper will remain to cover you. If I share our Dart code, can you get it to your ships? I do not wish my people destroyed by their allies."

"Send it over," O'Neill said. "We'll pass it on."

Guide touched his controls, releasing the identifying code. "Can you read that?"

There was a moment's pause, and then O'Neill said, "We have it. I'm transmitting it to our ships and the 302s."

"Then we will take the fight to Queen Death," Guide said. He looked across the control room. *Bonewhite. Can you give me another short jump?*

Bonewhite bared teeth in a fighting smile. *Already calculated,

Commander.*

*Excellent. Whenever you're ready, then.*

*Just Fortune* gathered itself beneath him, and leaped into the night.

Jack frowned at the tac display again. Yeah, Guide finally getting himself into the fight was making a difference. Atlantis had some breathing room, and Guide's Darts were mixing it up with Queen Death's, but — the drifting cruiser was still on what looked like a collision course with the city. He looked to Zelenka's station — Dr. Kusanagi had taken over there, her hands busy and her expression intent — and he came to look over her shoulder.

"Not to bother you, Doc, but isn't that cruiser still coming toward us?"

"Yes, I'm afraid so, General." She gave him an apologetic look, as though it were somehow her fault. "But Teyla will take care of it."

"Yeah." Jack stepped away, studying the converging line, then looked at Woolsey. "Any word from Teyla?"

"Not yet." Woolsey's expression was grim.

Crap. Jack touched his radio. "Sheppard. We're still converging on that cruiser."

There was a pause before Sheppard answered. "I'm working on it, General."

*Work harder.* Jack swallowed the words, and looked back at the screen. A light was flashing at the bottom of the screen, Ancient characters glowing red, and for a moment he wished he hadn't sent Daniel down to keep an eye on the civilians. But you didn't have to read Ancient to be able to guess that it was a collision alert. "Come on, Sheppard," he said, under his breath, and clasped his hands behind his back.

John sank deeper into the chair's embrace, frowning as the damaged cruiser drifted slowly closer. The city was worried, alarms flashing somewhere distant; closer at hand, it presented a series of new courses, fanning away from the cruiser. That one, John thought, and felt the engines fire, the city shifting ponderously. And then the steady rumble faltered, an overloaded conduit crumpling, and he swore silently. *Shut it down!*

The city was there ahead of him, feathering controls, opening new routes and damping out the power surge. The outrush slowed, steadied: the North Pier engines were now at 40 percent of capacity. Any more, the city whispered, and the entire system would collapse. He let the power fade in the other engines, balancing the output and steadying the city against the system's gravity. In the back of his mind, he felt more power flowing to the shield, the city ready to re-expand its coverage, but he held it back. *Wait on that*, he said. *Let's see where we are first.*

The city displayed the new course. They'd pulled away from the cruiser, but not far enough; they'd still pass close enough for the cruiser's wing to brush against the very edge of the trailing pier. *Put on the brakes?* he thought, and the city showed the solution: still not enough. They didn't have enough power to do anything except re-extend the shield...

"Sheppard!"

O'Neill had said his name before, John realized, and he let himself rise out of the city's embrace. "General, we're going to restore the full shield."

"I thought you said we didn't have enough power for that," Woolsey said sharply.

"We didn't. But I told you, we've overloaded our repairs, so we can't put through as much power to the engines. We've got that to spare, plus we're not under direct attack —"

"And if that cruiser hits us, we want the shield," O'Neill said, his voice grim. "Do it, Colonel."

John felt the shield wash over him, expanding like long-held breath. Much better, more comfortable, a too-tight collar loosed at last.

"What about the cruiser?" O'Neill asked.

"It's up to Teyla now," John answered.

Teyla stood in the commander's place, her hands buried in the controls, eyes closed as she fought to bring the cruiser under her will. It was old and stubborn and afraid; it did not know her touch and did not trust it, fought to do what it had been told. Distantly, she could hear the Marines' chatter — Radek in the core of the ship, working to untangle the array of fuses; Eva in the shuttle bay; Sheffield close at hand, relaying readouts from the various consoles. It did not matter. All that mattered was the cruiser, her hands on its controls, her will bending it to obedience. The engines were damaged, the control circuits balky; half the dorsal thrusters were inoperable, and the cruiser wanted nothing more than to fulfill its mission.

*No,* she said gently. *That is cancelled. You will turn away, and I will take you home to be made whole.*

The cruiser had Atlantis in its sights, Ancient enemy, and would not respond, yearning toward destruction.

"Ms. Emmagan!"

She looked up sharply, eyes flying open. "I don't have time —"

"Ms. Emmagan, I'm sorry, but General O'Neill wants to know your progress." Sheffield peered worriedly at her from across the commander's station, and it was all she could do not to bare teeth at him.

"Tell him I am aware of the problem," she said, tightly. "I am working on it."

"Yes, ma'am."

Teyla closed her eyes again, focusing all her strength on the cruiser's controls. *I am queen,* she said, *and you will obey...*

O'Neill scowled at the tactical display, the warning flashing more urgently below the converging course lines. *Yeah, I know it's going to hit us,* he thought. *Give me some options here.* Behind the cruiser, the other hiveship hung between them and the rest of the battle, and he turned abruptly to the communications station.

"Banks. Can you get me the commander of that hive out there?"

"I'll try." She adjusted her microphone with one hand, and touched keys with the other. A moment later, a screen lit, a bald Wraith staring out at him with bared teeth.

"This is O'Neill," Jack said. "We've got a problem with that cruiser."

"I am aware of that," the Wraith commander answered, "but there is nothing we can do that you cannot." He stopped abruptly, glancing over his shoulder at a long-haired Wraith who stood just outside the camera's focus. "Wait. This one has volunteered to help your crew. He is a cleverman, and an expert at ships' systems. I will send him across at once."

"We'll take him," Jack said. "I'll inform my people to expect him."
And let's hope he's as good as you say.

*Just Fortune* and the cruisers *Adamant* and *Evermore* swept
down on Death's fleet, Guide still wavering between ship-trance
and full awareness. Death had not been expecting their move, or
had not believed in it; her second hive scrambled to interpose itself
between Death and the incoming ships. *Evermore* dived beneath
it, weapons blazing a path across the hive's belly. *Adamant* followed, but too slowly. Guide snarled, seeing the mistake, and the
first shot struck the engines, sending *Adamant* careening sideways,
its commander fighting for control. Death's hive swung to bring
its guns to bear, and *Evermore* interposed itself, taking fire for a
fleeting moment before Death's hive had to swing back to face the
Lantean ships. *Adamant* was tumbling slowly, Darts spilling from
its bays as non-essential crew abandoned the ship, and *Evermore*
came around again, applying a tractor to steady it while its crew
fought for control.

Guide snarled again, hearing *Evermore*'s commander organiz-
ing the evacuation, and brought *Just Fortune* around to strafe the
other hive before it could fire on the cruisers. *Just Fortune* shuddered, the maneuver stresses tugging at its bones, but held firm. The
other hive swung to engage, and he felt its first shots strike the hull.

*Fire as you will,* he said, and felt the blades respond, a seemingly ragged volley of fire as each gun took its best shot. He saw
the bolts strike home, leaving long marks, but the other hive was as
tough as his own, suffered no worse damage. He rolled left, accepting additional damage to protect the cruisers, twisting to try to give
at least the dorsal guns a decent shot.

*Adamant*'s commander reports that all his men are off the ship,*
Bonewhite said.

Guide nodded, the battle unfolding in the tactical screen. The
Lantean ships were still hard pressed along with the strange hive
that had joined them. If he could only get across, he could buy them
time — but Death's other hive still had him solidly engaged. *Tell
Thunder to engage Death's hive.*

*He can't hold them,* Bonewhite said.

*No.* Guide glared at the screens, seeing the strange hive falter, bleeding atmosphere for an instant before its clevermen sealed the wound. *But our ally needs help.*

Bonewhite spoke into his communicator, and in the screen Thunder's hive rolled away from the tangle of Darts. It dove on Death's hive, Thunder cutting between the stranger and Death, shooting for the gap that opened as both pilots pulled away. A beautiful maneuver, Guide thought, except his timing was imperfect. Death's gunners caught him as he tried to turn, and flame blossomed from the hive's stem.

*Thunder has lost engines,* Bonewhite said. *Shall we assist?"

*No.* Thunder could hold out a little longer; there were more important targets. *Take out this hive,* Guide said, teeth bared, and his gunners answered, each firing as they found their target. The hive staggered under the volume of fire, and the first serious damage showed black on its hull. *Evermore* swept up and under, harrying, and Guide turned again, accepting hits to bring the greatest number of guns to bear on the target.

The other hive hung for an instant in the center of the attack, then blew apart, the fireball washing over *Just Fortune*. Guide steadied his ship, the litany of damage pulsing against his skin. Nothing serious, nothing they couldn't handle, and in the communications screen *Evermore* reported similar status. The stranger hive was still fighting, the Lantean ship and the Genii's Ancient warship struggling to stay with it, but not enough of their shots were striking home. The Lanteans and Genii he could excuse, they didn't know the stress points, the best targets — but the stranger's commander seemed no more experienced. He put *Just Fortune* into a turn, but Queen Death saw and turned to meet him.

Ember brought the borrowed Dart into the shuttle bay, the doors sealing behind him, and settled it with its weapons carefully pointing away from the Lantean shuttle. Its door opened as he clambered from the cockpit revealing three humans with lowered weapons; the Dart's system clamored at him, warning him of a readied drone as well. He lifted his hands, showing them empty, and hoped the humans had been warned of his arrival.

"I have been sent to help."

There was a silence, and his muscles tensed. He could survive the first shots, but the Lantean weapons were more than capable of overwhelming his ability to regenerate.

"Yeah." That was their leader, short and stocky, and the noise of the Dart faded away as the drone disarmed itself. "Ling, Grazyk, take him to the control room."

*I know the way.* Ember swallowed the words, knowing they were pointless—nor would he have allowed a strange human to roam a hive without escort. Instead, he let them surround him, one before, one behind, hurrying down the main corridor toward the control room. They passed bodies, Death's blades crumpled where they fell, and he heard the man behind him cock his weapon nervously. Ember ignored him, though every knob of his spine felt tingly and exposed, and at last they came to the control room.

"Lieutenant! It's Ling. We've brought the Wraith."

The door slid open, revealing a handful of humans at the consoles, and a human woman standing in the commander's place, her hands steady on the controls. Surely that could not be right, Ember thought; a commander controlled the ship through force of will, just as a queen controlled her hive, but no human could speak mind to mind—except that manifestly she was doing so. Her eyes opened and she fixed him with a startled look.

*Ember.*

The mind was Steelflower's, enough to send him to his knees before he thought, but he looked up, frowning, knowing his confusion was plain to read. *Lady?*

The human's mind was closed to him, tight as fingers protecting the handmouth, and yet even the stance, everything about her said she was his queen. *How—?*

*There is no time for explanations.*

The mental touch was unmistakably Steelflower's, complex and beautiful and sharp as the metal that made her name. And the body was human, impossible, brown eyes and brown skin and nothing Wraith about her except the touch of her mind on his.

*We must turn the cruiser,* she said. *It will obey, but it is slow.

Something holds it back. Find it, Ember, find it and fix it for me.*

Ember rose to obey, checked for an instant still in disbelief. This could not be his queen, and yet it was — and there was no time for that. In the main screen, Atlantis loomed, too near, too large. She had spoken truth there, whoever, whatever, she was: there was no time left. He turned on his heel, surveying the consoles. Yes, there, the engineering display looked off, and he moved quickly to call up its details. Someone had installed a governor, restricting power, restricting the use of the maneuver engines. He ran his hands across the boards, and was not surprised when they did not respond.

"Ms. Emmagan," one of the humans said. "Atlantis says it can't evade —"

"I'm trying," Steelflower answered, her frustration almost palpable. "Ember!"

He did not answer, but whirled to the next console. It would be easier to override the blockages from the Hivemaster's station, and he remembered codes from his time on Death's hive. He entered them, holding his breath, and a window lit, data cascading down the screen. There — there was the block, and there the codes that would release it; he punched in the numbers, reached for levers to control the shifting power. *Try now, Lady.*

"Yes." The word reached ears and mind alike, and he felt the old ship respond at last to her touch, grateful for the sure hand that steered it. In the main screen, Atlantis's image seemed to fall away, though it was they who moved, tilting ponderously out of its path.

*Well done,* Steelflower said, generous and proud, and in the same moment the human woman spoke. "Radek! What about the fuses?"

"The proximity fuses are disabled," a voice answered. "But the bombs are still live."

*How?* Ember asked again. *How can you be my queen?*

The woman turned to look at him, her mind brushing his with gentle regret. *I am Teyla Emmagan, Teyla of Athos, Teyla Who Walks Through Gates, and I am Steelflower, Osprey's many-times-great granddaughter. Long ago, a cleverman mingled his blood with that of humans, and the end result is me.*

The Old One had spoken truth. Ember shuddered, remembering the story shared with him when he was briefly the Old One's prisoner: the Wraith were the Ancients' mistake, their terrible creation, their doom. And Guide had known, he realized. Had known all along, and seized the weapon that came to hand, this woman with the mind of a queen, because without a queen, they could never have stood against Queen Death. He bowed his head, cleverman to queen, but spoke aloud, so that the other humans could hear his submission. "What should I do, Lady?"

Her gratitude washed over him, as much balm as it would have been had she in truth been the young queen she had seemed. "Help Radek defuse the bombs. We are still too much a danger, drifting like this. Corporal Ling, go with him, please."

"Yes, ma'am," one of the males said, and Ember turned to follow.

Rodney was surrounded by white light. *What do you know,* he thought. *I guess there is something after death.* It shone brightly in his face, blinding and pure, and his left wrist throbbed with pain. But shouldn't that be okay? If he was dead, how come his wrist still hurt? Rodney tried to sit up.

There was a shriek and the sound of something heavy hitting the floor. And then he fell off whatever he'd been lying on, landing solidly on scuffed linoleum smelling like disinfectant.

Not an afterlife, Rodney thought, as his wrist hit the floor and he screamed.

"He just appeared there," someone said. "I didn't see the beam shimmer."

Another voice, also male, distracted. "Well, he must have been beamed aboard from one of the 302s." A shoulder under his right arm, an arm in scrubs. "Easy, there. You're okay. Just take deep breaths." The arm shifted. "McNair, help me get him up on the table. Probably hypoxia. That's what the 302 pilots usually have."

"He's not in a flight suit."

"I broke my wrist," Rodney said through gritted teeth. The pain was blinding, the overhead lights right in his eyes.

"I see." Even, medical voice. "Okay, just take deep breaths. Let's get an oxygen mask on you. McNair?"

"Where am I?" Rodney managed before the mask came over his face.

"You're safe aboard the *George Hammond.*"

## CHAPTER TWENTY-FOUR
# Last Hopes

LORNE brought *Pride of the Genii* in on the tail of Death's hive, forward guns blazing. There were no more drones, hadn't been for what seemed like forever, but Radim's gunners couldn't miss at this range. The shots struck home, blasting metal and fittings from the hive's engines. The hive swerved, and Lorne let it go, putting his ship between it and Todd's other hive. It was drifting, damaged, but even as he watched a new light flared in the central engine bell. Powering up again, the *Pride* whispered, minimal maneuver engines and full power to the guns. The strange hive, though, the one that had jumped out of hyperspace at the last possible minute — it hadn't been in good shape to start with — was starting to show real damage, atmosphere leaking from a hull breach forward. The *Hammond* had her hands full, the last of her 302s on board but now surrounded by a swarm of Darts. Some of them were Todd's, Lorne thought, but there was nothing he could do about them, any more than there had been anything he could do for Rodney.

No, he thought, and felt the *Pride* gather herself before he'd even been able to articulate his commands. There was nothing anyone could have done for Rodney, not at that distance, and if there'd been any other way, McKay of all people would have found it. So that was the only option, and the only thing he could do now was make it count. Todd's hive was turning, driving Death's hive toward the *Pride*. Lorne calculated the angles in a glance, and dove on Death's hive.

Radek worked his way deeper into the crawlspace, pushing his flashlight ahead of him. Even he could barely fit between the heavy bundles that were the explosives, but he could see the fuse just ahead of him, a lumpy oval with half a dozen knotty cords reaching out along the crawlspace. It showed inert, unpowered, but he paused long enough to direct a scanner at it. There was still no sign of power, and he hauled himself another meter further, until he could reach the box.

It was a remote trigger, he thought, intended to take a signal from the pressure sensors on the hull or from a following hive. But the pressure sensors were disabled, he had destroyed the proximity fuses, and the jamming device should override any signal, so all he should have to do was disconnect the cables. Unfortunately, they seemed to grow organically from the box, not plug into a socket; he squirmed around to see how it connected to the nearest explosive, but the connection vanished behind the webbing that held the bomb in place, utterly inaccessible.

Fine, then, he thought, and wriggled himself back so that he could reach the box again. He had brought clippers — they were in fact modified garden shears, acquired from Botany when he was working on Teyla's cruiser — and now he worked them out of his pocket and positioned himself to cut the first cable. The blades bit through, releasing a spurt of unidentifiable liquid, and the cut end thrashed free of his grasp, twisting back as though it was trying to rejoin its other half. Radek caught it, flattened it against the floorplates with all his strength, and at last the flailing died away. He released it carefully, but it seemed to be inert.

And he would have to do that five more times just to defuse this section, and a dozen more just like it, and they were running out of time. He shook his head, and reached for the next cable, clamping down hard to hold it still. It fought back, but now that he knew what to expect, he could hold it. It seemed to die more quickly, or perhaps it was just that he understood the process now, and he moved on to the next.

He was damp and faintly sticky when he had finished, but at least these bombs were defused. A dozen more to go, if he'd scanned them correctly. There had to be a better way, but he didn't know one, hadn't seen it in his hasty scan. Maybe if he looked again, if he had time… He touched his radio.

"Sergeant. Have we cleared the city?"

"Yes, sir," Ramirez answered.

Okay, that was good. Radek hauled himself up and over the

now-disconnected fuse, dragging himself toward the next junction. That would give a little more time, maybe enough to figure out something better than brute force.

"Doc. We've got a Wraith. Ms. Emmagan says he's here to help."

A Wraith. One of Todd's people, presumably, and, yes, someone who really understood how these systems worked would be extremely useful. And if Teyla said he could be trusted, well, Radek would rely on that. "I am on my way."

He worked his way back out of the crawlspace, dropped down to the corridor in front of the waiting Marines. And the Wraith. He was one of the long-haired ones, with two thin wisps of beard trailing from the points of his chin and a tattoo like stylized wings between them. It was hard to read his expression, but Radek thought he might be frowning.

"You are the human clever — engineer?"

"Yes, that is me," Radek answered. "You're here to help?"

The Wraith nodded. "The bombs still need to be defused?"

"Yes." Radek stretched for the tablet he had left at the entrance to the crawlspace, turned it so that the other could see the schematic he had built from the Wraith data. The Wraith leaned closer, his hair whispering across the leather of his coat, and in spite of himself Ling raised his P90. Radek gave him an admonishing look, and pushed his glasses up on his nose. "This is what I've been able to trace. The explosives are here, all along the spine of the ship, and they are wired to a series of fuses within this central access space. I have cut the connection to the proximity fuses and the pressure sensors on the hull, but the bombs are still armed."

"Presumably they are intended to be detonated remotely," the Wraith said. "But?"

"We have jammed any transmissions," Radek answered. "Or at least any likely frequencies. But —"

"There are still too many fuses," the Wraith said. "There was no central control?"

"I have not found one," Radek answered. "You'd know better than I would where it might be hidden."

The Wraith hissed softly, and reached to turn the tablet for a better view. Radek made himself stand motionless as the feeding hand with its heavy vein slid along the metal next to his own fingers.

"I—this is not a tactic I would recommend," the Wraith said, after a moment.

"Effective, however," Radek said dryly, and thought the Wraith smiled.

"Yes." He looked back at the tablet. "To pull the fuses one by one will take too long."

"I am open to alternatives," Radek said. "If you were doing this, where would you put a master fuse?"

"I wouldn't," the Wraith said. "A kill switch, I think, some way to render the ship inert if it were not used as intended—"

Radek reached for the tablet, a new idea taking shape. "When I ran a power trace, there was an odd end. I thought it was part of the ship's systems, but—"

"Yes." The Wraith fumbled with the tablet's controls, claws clicking on glass and metal. Radek took it from him, touched the screen to expand the image. "Yes, there, in the engine room—"

"That's where that system goes," Radek said, nodding. "But how does it connect—?"

"There." A green-black claw tapped the tablet's screen. "There will be other connections within the engine room, but there—that's where the fuses will come together."

Radek studied the schematic. The point the Wraith indicated was not quite all the way to the engineering spaces at the stern but at the end of the ship's spine, where several of the access conduits came together. There was a power node there, but he'd assumed it was just part of the ship's normal systems. "Yes, I see. All right, we'll take it out there." He touched his radio. "Teyla. We are heading aft to disarm the kill switch."

"Copy that." It was the Marine lieutenant who answered, not Teyla, and Radek lifted his eyebrows. That could not be a good sign.

"Come. We must hurry."

The access hatch was the same as all the others he had found, a narrow oval that yielded reluctantly to the pulse of his probe. He turned to beckon to Ling—the hatches were too heavy for one man to move—but the Wraith put his shoulder to it, rolling it aside.

"Thank you," Radek said, and shone his light into the opening. Yes, there was the usual set of handholds, not quite a ladder, and then the maw of the access tube. For a moment, he wondered if it would be better to send the Wraith ahead of him, but that would mean giving him first access to the device. He took a breath, and pulled himself up into the tunnel.

It was larger than the ones he had been in before, large enough for a man to go on all fours and two abreast, though the Wraith stayed at his heels, claws loud on the hardened surfaces. More probably it was his boots, Radek told himself, not claws, and anyway he was here under orders to help. And beyond that, he himself had taken Dr. Keller's retrovirus, so probably he wasn't going to die even if the Wraith decided to eat him — He stopped abruptly, the tunnel widening ahead of him into a hemispherical chamber. A device like a stunted tree stood in its center, dozens of vine-like cables winding their way into its branches.

"I would guess this is it," he said, and pulled himself aside so that the Wraith could see.

The Wraith hissed in answer, teeth sharp and white in the dim light. "Death's men were taking no chances."

"What do you mean?"

"See there?" The Wraith pointed to a knob that protruded from the device near the junction of the upper limbs. "That is intended to receive a detonation signal. Apparently your jamming device works."

"Apparently." Radek cleared his throat. "So. Do we cut these cables, or is there a central switch, as you said?"

The Wraith tipped his head to one side. "Both would be safest, I think. But where to start…"

Radek let the beam of his flashlight play over the device, picking out what looked like a primary control node. "Is that it?"

"Yes." The Wraith crawled closer, reaching beneath his coat for a tool of his own. "I do not see any particular protection."

And how the hell am I supposed to tell if there's some sort of booby trap? Radek swallowed the words as unhelpful, and leaned close himself. "There are — wires — coming off in four, no, five places. Are they part of the mechanism, or a trap?"

The Wraith showed teeth again. "An excellent question." He probed carefully, then sat back on his heels. "I believe they all belong to the mechanism. And that means we should cut the head wire first."

"Head wire?" Even as he said it, Radek realized what the Wraith meant. The wires were laid out in a star pattern, or like a human figure spread-eagled. "This one?"

"Yes."

"All right." Radek was closer, and he reached for his cutters. "You're sure?"

"As sure as I can be."

And if he was wrong, there would be no second chances. Radek touched his radio again. "Teyla. Are we clear of the city? We are ready to cut wires, but if we are wrong..."

"We are far enough away from the city," Teyla answered, her voice serene. "Go ahead."

Radek braced himself and worked the clipper's blade under the head wire. He took a deep breath and squeezed hard. The blades sheared through the organic cable with a dull click, and that was all. Radek heaved a sigh of relief, and looked at the Wraith. "All right. Which one next?"

"I don't think it matters," the Wraith said. He looked deeply relieved himself. "I will start cutting the connectors, just to be sure."

"Yes," Radek said, already snipping wires.

*We are losing life support,* Bronze said.

Waterlight pursed her lips. The ship was shrieking in her mind, bleeding air from twenty wounds, precious fluids leaking into vacuum. Queen Death's hive ship rotated nearby, almost on top of them, point blank range for their weapons. *Promised Return* was dying.

*We have no choice,* Thorn said in her mind.

*I will not surrender!* Waterlight replied. *What mercy do you think we will find if I do?*

*Not surrender,* Thorn said, the shade of his mind grim. *Grapple and board. It is our only hope.*

Waterlight blinked. Yes, they were within range. And there was a docking port. The umbilicals still responded to her mind. *Grapple and board,* she said. She looked at Bronze, his wild elation tempered with fear held in check. *And give me your knife. We must make this queen to queen.*

The cruiser was responding at last, slower than *Eternal* had been, but finally willing. Teyla circled back around Atlantis's bulk, surveying viewscreen and tactical displays. Atlantis was surrounded by a swarm of Darts, Death's men and Guide's locked in combat above the shield; beyond the city, Death's hive heeled over, exposing its underside as a second, smaller hive battened onto it. The smaller ship looked familiar — *Promised Return*, Teyla thought, the young queen Waterlight's hive. It was in no shape to attack, and surely Waterlight didn't have enough men to board — and if she was making the attempt, she must feel she had no choice. Teyla toggled her radio.

"Major Lorne."

"Teyla?" Lorne's voice was tight, but the *Pride of the Genii* did not seem particularly hard-pressed at the moment.

"I am going to board Death's hive in support of *Promised Return*," Teyla said, the plan taking shape almost as she spoke. "Can you get a team on board as well?"

"Hold on," General O'Neill said. "Teyla, you don't have enough men to try that."

"Queen Death must be defeated face to face," Teyla said. "This is the best chance, now that *Promised Return* has begun the attack."

"I have a boarding party ready," a new voice said — Ladon Radim, cool as ever. "Major Lorne says he can deliver us."

"All right," O'Neill said. "We'll keep the other ships off you. Guide! Did you hear that?"

Teyla closed her mind to the acknowledgement, to the rest of the conversation, focused her will to bring the cruiser around again. She could see where the other access port lay, how she would have to turn to come alongside, and the cruiser took the course from her mind, rolling over in response. Teyla touched her radio again. "Dr. Robinson. I want you to take Dr. Zelenka and Ember back to Atlantis."

"No, no," Radek interrupted. "I will stay. The engines —"

"Your cleverman and I are needed here," Ember said, in almost the same moment.

Teyla glanced at the engineering console. They were both right, the engine controls were unstable, and she nodded. "Very well."

"I'd rather stay here myself," Eva Robinson said. She sounded surprisingly calm, under the circumstances. "I'm not really comfortable flying into that mess."

"Very well," Teyla said again. "Lieutenant Sheffield, take your men to the airlock, here. I'll join you as soon as we're alongside."

The cruiser knew its business. It followed her commands almost before she could form them, dodging a drifting ship and a tangle of Darts to come smoothly alongside Death's hive. The grapples fired, pulling the ships together, and Teyla felt the hulls touch, the ports matching smoothly.

"We've got green lights on the airlock," Sheffield reported. "We're through and the corridor is clear."

"Wait for me there," Teyla ordered. She seized her P90 and ran to join them.

Cadman flattened herself against the uneven wall of the hiveship, looked across the corridor to Johnson on point. He lifted his hand to signal all clear, and she swept forward, weapon ready, stopped at the next cross corridor to consult her tablet. The Genii filled in behind her, and Ladon Radim leaned over her shoulder.

"Well?"

"We're here," she said, pointing. They were about at the mid-point of the hive, just astern of the point where it divided around the central opening. "Teyla's further up the right side, I think — she came aboard here. Heading for the control room. I guess the other Wraith are headed that way, too."

Radim nodded. "Join up with her, or take out the engines?"

*You're asking me?* Cadman swallowed the words, and touched her radio. "Teyla, this is Cadman. Can you hear me?"

There was a moment's silence, and then the familiar voice sounded in her ear. "I hear you, Captain."

"I'm on the hive with Chief Radim and forty men. Do you need support?"

"If you can spare any, yes. But it's crucial that you disable the hyperdrive."

"Copy that," Cadman said. She glanced over her shoulder. "Johnson, Peebles. Chief Radim, can you spare some of your men?"

"Yes." Radim began pointing, sorting out a group, and Cadman took a deep breath.

"Johnson, take these men to join Ms. Emmagan. You're under her command. The rest of you — with me." She touched the radio. "Teyla, I have ten men coming to you."

"Thank you, Captain," Teyla answered.

Cadman looked back at her tablet. It looked as though there was one quick and obvious way to the hive's engineering spaces, and even if the Wraith were waiting for them, she couldn't see a better way. Radim nodded as though he'd read her thought, and pointed to the same corridor.

"This way," he said, and gave her a wry smile. "Sometimes you just have to attack head-on."

"That's what Marines are for, sir," Cadman said. "Johnson! Move out!"

Radek glanced around the cruiser's engine room, squinting in the dim light. About half the consoles were dead, and the others shimmered with caution lights, warning of hull damage and crushed maneuvering vents and dropping power levels throughout the ship. The Wraith — Ember, Teyla had called him — was busy at a secondary console, and a moment later a larger overhead screen lit, showing a series of images from what Radek guessed were the main sensors. Atlantis was still moving toward them, but there were fewer Darts surrounding it, and it looked as though the rest of Death's ships were finally on the defensive.

"What else can we do?" he asked, and Ember glanced at him.

"You see the power drain."

"Yes."

"That is Death's hive, fighting us. We must block it, if we can, or attack in kind."

That made a weird sort of sense, considering that the Wraith ships were in some sense alive, and Radek nodded. "Show me what to do."

There were Wraith ahead of them, Teyla knew, nearly a dozen drones and a pair of blades, but she couldn't pin down the location. Somewhere beyond the next bulkhead, she thought, and waved for Sheffield to slow down. Before she could warn him, however, the bulkhead to her left burst open, and the first pair of drones emerged.

Sheffield swung, firing, caught them in the chest; Ramirez, an Atlantis veteran, aimed for the legs, and brought the second pair down kicking, for the next man to finish off. Teyla fired past them, hoping to catch the controlling blades, but they were staying back behind the drones. One of the Marines went down, screaming as a drone fed; the woman behind him leaped to try to rescue him, but another drone batted her aside. She went flying across the corridor and collapsed against the opposite wall. One of the Genii interposed himself, firing his repeating rifle, and then someone hit a blade, and the drones staggered, momentarily uncontrolled. Teyla swung her P90, raking the first rank, and the Marines took out the rest, leaving only bodies. There were still Wraith ahead, Teyla thought, but none alive here.

But she had lost men. Two of the Genii lay withered, and a Marine, and the Marine woman was staggering to her feet, blood covering one side of her face. Another Marine pressed a field dressing to the cut, and she settled her helmet over it, wincing. Lieutenant Sheffield was looking at her, and she forced herself to meet his eyes.

"Which way, ma'am?"

"The control room," Teyla answered. "I sense some Wraith ahead —" She stopped abruptly. "There are more Wraith behind us, too. We must find a way to cut them off. Through here."

They piled through the next hatchway, and she closed the door behind them. The ship would not respond to her, and there was no time to enforce her will; she turned her head away and fired into the controls. They exploded in a burst of spark and flame and she turned away to see Sheffield grinning.

"Ma'am, it looks like the next cross corridor's a strong point. A couple of us could hold off those guys behind us, keep them off your back."

And die doing it, Teyla thought. But there was no other way. "Yes," she said, and hurried on.

Ember bent over the controls, biting back a cold fury. This ship was old, too old for battle; it should be safe in orbit somewhere, where blades could learn to pilot and budding clevermen could learn their trade easing its death. To bring it here, stitched full of explosives — to demand that it fight — that was abomination indeed. He spread both hands flat on the console, heedless of his handmouth, seeking the cruiser's will. For a moment, there was nothing, and he caught his breath, afraid that it was too far gone, but then he felt it, the slow pulse that was not intelligent but not unliving, either. *Feed*, he whispered, *you are starving. Feed*. He felt it respond, fumbling toward the hive's greater life, and looked over his shoulder at the human cleverman.

"The umbilicals. Extend them."

"Yes, yes." The human hit the correct sequence, then reached for the levers, guiding the heavy cable across the few meters that separated the ships. "Okay, it says they are touching — they have set."

"Yes," Ember said aloud, and nudged the cruiser again. *Feed, there is life for the taking…* He felt it fumble and then latch on, drawing power with more assurance. "That will cause them trouble."

"What exactly are we doing?" the human asked.

"I have enabled our ship to feed off Death's hive — to do what they were trying to do to us," Ember answered. "That will drain their power plant, and make it much harder for them to escape."

"I think you have annoyed someone," the human said, and pointed to the main display.

Ember snarled at the sight. Another cruiser was heading toward them, visibly damaged, but with forward weapons charged and ready. "They will try to knock us loose."

The human touched his ear. "Eva! We are coming under attack —"

The cruiser fired, the volley ragged, and Ember ducked in spite of himself. "Quickly —"

The decking rattled, the entire ship shuddering. Alarms blared — atmosphere leak, power loss, life support failure — and Ember grabbed the human by the shoulder. "We must get to your jumper —"

Another shot hit, and more alarms blared, gravity wavering for an instant before it was restored.

"If we can," the human said, grimly, but scrambled ahead of him up the narrow corridor.

## CHAPTER TWENTY-FIVE
# Queen to Queen

SMOKE swirled around Waterlight like a living thing, twisting through the corridors of Queen Death's hive ship. Only Bronze was with her now. The last drone was dead, and Waterlight had watched Thorn twist before her, shielding her with his shredded body. The air was acrid and stank.

Ahead the bulkhead door was closed. *We must open it,* Waterlight said.

Bronze nodded. His hair had fallen from its clasp and fell over his shoulders, matted with blood and other things. *I will go first,* he said, his hand on the door override.

*I will let no more men die for me,* Waterlight said. *Because I am queen.*

Her hand was on his wrist, and so she knew what he did not need to say. Not because she was queen, but because she was Waterlight. Not a distant hope, a privilege and an ambition, but the friend of all his years since he had come aboard as a thin and half-grown foster-ling, his Waterlight, his playmate turned princess, his only family.

*We will go together,* she said, with no word for this strange ten-derness that stirred in her. *Whatever there is, we will face it together.*

He nodded and opened the door.

Less smoke but more bodies. A half dozen drones lay dead, and there were two humans as well, one withered to a husk while another bent over him. All dead, Waterlight thought, and then the bending one straightened.

It was a human woman, slight and dark, the muzzle of her weapon rising to track them in an instant.

And then her eyes widened with recognition, the point of the weapon dropping again, her relief shuddering through the air like a palpable thing. A worshipper? But would Death arm her worshippers thus? Yet her relief was almost audible, as though she had said their names aloud. As though she had spoken mind to mind.

"Who are you?" Waterlight said, but even as she spoke, she knew. The feel of the woman's mind was unmistakable, though her face was unfamiliar. Her stance was the same, her height, her way of moving. And her mind. *Steelflower.*

*I am Teyla Emmagan of Atlantis,* the woman said, and her weapon pointed to the floor, standing before them as though she feared nothing. And why should she? She did not see what humans saw, Blade and Queen, bloodthirsty revenants, but frightened younglings barely out of childhood, adult estate thrust upon them by war, stained by the blood of their kin shed to protect them.

*What are you?* Waterlight said. Steelflower and not...

*I am human,* she said. "And I am not. I am Teyla Emmagan of the line of Osprey. A cleverman in days past mingled his blood with that of my human ancestors. And I am Steelflower. I took the name and appearance of a young queen who was lost.*

Bronze frowned. *Why would you do that?* The stunner in his hand did not rise.

She held her hands out to the side. *What man would follow me otherwise?*

Steelflower. And not. A human woman, given the blood of Osprey by a renegade cleverman... And in that moment the paths of the future and the past stretched out before Waterlight, clear as the path of sun on water, all the twists and turns made straight

*And my kinswoman still,* she said, *Steelflower or not. That cleverman was my mother's brother. Brother and sister there were, and you are of him and I of her, your grandmother and mine the same .*

Teyla blinked. That did indeed surprise her.

*You did not lie to me,* Waterlight said. *Though you meant to.*

*I did not lie when I offered you alliance with Guide,* she said.

Waterlight reached out her off hand, touching it to her wrist, queen to queen. *You are Guide's queen.* And how not? He could not rally men against Death without a queen at his side, no matter how she appeared or what she truly was.

*I am of Atlantis.*

*Who are Guide's allies,* Waterlight said. *But we are united in one thing.*

*We must end this,* Bronze said, his voice surprisingly steady.

Teyla smiled, and her eyes closed for a moment, watering at the corners. *We must,* she said. *Will you face Queen Death with me?*

*We will,* Waterlight said.

There was only one way it could ever end — queen to queen.

The Wraith tried to stop them twice on the way to the engine room, and each time Cadman blasted through, leaving bodies behind them in the dim corridors. Not so many of Radim's, and none of hers, for which she was unabashedly grateful, and plenty of dead drones, which was even better. The hatch that gave access to the engineering spaces was locked, and one of the Genii fiddled for a moment with the controls before he stepped away, shaking his head.

"C4," Cadman said, and reached into her pocket.

"They'll be expecting you to blow the door," Radim said.

She nodded, molding the soft explosive around the central node. "Yes, sir. But I don't see any alternative. I figure we follow up with flashbangs and then rush them."

Radim nodded sharply. "Good idea, Captain," he said, and turned to give the orders.

She set the fuses and waved her people back into shelter, pulling out the remote detonator. She gave them all a final look, her Marines ready with stun grenades, the Genii with their repeating rifles ready, and raised her hand. "Fire in the hole!"

The door blew in with a satisfying whump, and her people followed with the stun grenades, rushing the smoking opening on the heels of the first flat crack. She charged after them, planted her back against the nearest bulkhead to give covering fire. The cavernous space echoed with the sound of gunfire and the roars of the angry Wraith, and then, abruptly, there was silence. She straightened, automatically checking her people. Hernandez was down, and her breath caught, but his face was unchanged and even as she realized that, he began to stir. Just stunned, then, she thought, and kept counting. Four, five more Genii down, and Radim was bleeding from a cut along his forehead, but they were still in business.

"Okay," she said, swinging her P90 so that its light played across the tangle of cords and weird organic stuff in the center of the room. "What next, sir?"

Radim swabbed impatiently at the blood on his face, and pointed to one of the objects protruding from the ceiling. It was wrapped in what looked like vines, or maybe tendons, and a web of more fleshy cording connected it to consoles below it and to the bulkheads to either side. Within that sheath, a bulbous cylindrical core glowed softly orange. "That's the hyperdrive. If we can disable that, Queen Death won't be able to escape."

Cadman reached into her pocket, pulled out another packet of C4. "Can do, sir."

*The control room is this way,* Teyla said mind to mind, sheltering behind the corner of a wall. The corridors of the hive ship were filled with smoke, the air thin. Somewhere there had been a hull breach now sealed, but the damaged systems had not fully managed to restore life support. Waterlight and Bronze stood behind her, Bronze with a pike taken from a drone, Waterlight with a stunner. They were not what she would choose for a boarding party, but with her radio smashed she could not know where any of the others were.

*How many?* Bronze asked, as Waterlight put her hand to the wall.

Her eyes closed. *Seven, maybe eight.*

*Too many,* Teyla said. She could not rush the control room with three on seven or eight, certainly not with two who were practically children. They must wait for her team. John would be in the chair in Atlantis, but surely Ronon would come soon. Or Cadman. Cadman and a Marine team would be welcome. Surely they were aboard.

Waterlight reared away from the wall, her eyes opening. *She knows I'm here!* she said. *She felt me. She knows we are here.*

*Retreat,* Teyla said. *This way.*

They scrambled back down the corridor, Teyla dropping back to cover them. Behind, the door of the control room opened, and she felt as clearly as if she'd seen — Queen Death and four of her blades. She would handle this personally. The arrival of another queen on her hive was a challenge old as the Wraith themselves. A more prudent queen might have waited or sent only her men, but Queen Death was hotheaded and angry. She did not stop to think. Or perhaps she was only too used to having her own way.

*This way!* Waterlight had retreated into the first room, the outer hall of the zenana, deserted now during the battle, a little table on its side, the game pieces scattered across the floor. Bronze looked around the door, the pike in his hands. Their fear was almost palpable.

That would not work, Teyla thought. They would retreat until they reached a door that would not open. Fortunately, Death was so focused on the young queen that she would not expect —

Teyla lunged out, P90 rising with a spray of bullets across the corridor. The two foremost blades pitched under the hail of fire, one dropping to his knees and the other reeling against the wall as Teyla slid into cover on the other side of the hall.

And still they came on, Death and the other two men. They would simply overwhelm her.

Teyla dove across again, firing as she went, a knee-high raking fire. She heard a bellow of pain and stunner bolts streaked just over her head, coalescing against the wall behind her. She landed hard on her right hip, the old bone bruise shrieking in pain, slowing her down. A blade stood over her, stunner in hand.

And then it was knocked away by a pike, flying from the Wraith's hand. Bronze brought it around backhanded, slashing the blade across the forearms. *Run!* he yelled as Teyla got to her feet.

Stunner fire followed them as they dived through the doorway, Waterlight closing it just behind them, as Bronze pitched into Teyla.

*Bronze!* Waterlight shrieked, catching at him.

Teyla leapt for the door control. *Do not open,* she told it. *Seal.*

Three stunner blasts had caught him at once. Bronze lay unmoving on the floor. Waterlight put her hand against his face. *Please be well!*

*He is stunned,* Teyla said. She felt a heavy thud against the door. *He will live if we do. But I cannot hold this door. This is Death's zenana. She will simply order it open and the ship will obey*.

The door shuddered open. Teyla brought up the P90. Bullets flew, and the remaining blade fell back under withering fire. Two shots caught Queen Death in the chest, but she stepped through it calmly, her hand closing about Teyla's neck. She lifted her off her feet like a rag doll and threw her across the room. Teyla's head struck the wall, and she knew no more.

They were almost at the shuttle bay. Radek forced himself onward, his leg burning from the old injury, the Wraith — Ember — panting at his heels. The deck felt unsteady underfoot: either the gravity was going, or the inertial dampeners, or maybe both. Something exploded down a side corridor, a flash of light and heat, and he heard Ember snarl behind him. Only a little further — yes, there was the beacon they had left behind when they first came on board. He made himself stop, check the door controls to be sure there was atmosphere in the bay, and touched his radio again.

"Eva! We are at the door."

"You'd better hurry," she answered. "I don't know how much longer this is going to hold together."

"We are hurrying," Radek answered, and the door slid back. The puddle jumper was waiting, tailgate down and ready, but Ember turned back to do something to the console beside the entrance. "Come on!"

"I must seal this hatch, or we will not be able to open the bay door," Ember answered. As he spoke the door began to move, but there was a snapping sound overhead. Radek looked up to see the central conduit splitting open, raining sparks and debris, knew in an instant that he would not be able to avoid it. And then Ember lunged at him, faster than a human could move, shoving them both toward the jumper's open stern. Radek fell, sliding to a stop at the end of the tailgate, the deck wavering unpleasantly beneath him, looked back to see the Wraith half buried by a pile of smoking debris.

"Eva! Get ready to leave!" Radek dragged himself upright, the floor wobbling again, and turned back to Ember's body. He stripped off his jacket, wrapped it around his hands to drag at the smoking conduit — thick cable, heavy but not impossible to move. The heat seared his palms, and he swore loudly, but the cable moved.

"They've knocked us loose from the hive," Eva called. "We have to go now."

Radek swore again. Ember's coat was shredded, the skin beneath it green with blood, and there were half a dozen finger-sized pieces of metal embedded in his back around the knobs of his spine. But he wasn't dead. A hand moved, and then his head, and Radek grabbed him by the arms and heaved, dragging him up the tailgate and into the jumper. He slapped the door controls, saw the tailgate begin to lift. "Ok, go!"

The puddlejumper lifted, hovering a meter or so above the deck. "I can't get the door to open," Eva said.

"Try a drone!"

"Oh. Yes, of course."

Radek saw her shoulders hunch, and a moment later a drone flashed into view, exploding against the cruiser's inner hull. The bay door blew out, debris pelting the jumper's hull, and outside the stars pinwheeled past. There was no sign of any other Wraith ships, but... "We're tumbling," he said.

"Yeah." Eva's voice was tight. "There's a gravity field holding us steady relative to the cruiser, right?"

"Yes."

"What happens when we leave it?"

"The jumper should compensate," Radek said. "Go!"

"I really hope you're right."

The jumper lurched into motion, arrowing for the center of the bay door. Radek braced himself against the rear seats, one arm across Ember's body in what he suspected would be a futile attempt to keep him still, and abruptly the cruiser seemed to spin around them.

"The gravity field's down!"

Eva didn't answer, all her attention on the controls as she fought to keep the jumper steady. They were falling sideways, heading for the edge of the bay door. Radek ducked his head, closing his eyes, and felt rather than saw the jumper scrape hard along the jagged metal where the drone had hit. It staggered, metal keening, and then they were free.

"We're all right!" Eva said. "We're okay..."

Her voice trailed off, and Radek looked up quickly. "Except for?"

"One of the engines is out, and the jumper — either I can't fly it without it or it won't fly without it, but we're out of power."

Radek pulled himself up to the copilot's seat, scanning the navigation console. "We're okay," he said. "We're not going to run into anything immediately, and we're not going to hit atmosphere any time soon. We're okay." He suspected his voice was shakier than his words.

"Yeah." Eva nodded slowly. "Yeah, I guess we are. So we just wait?"

"We wait till they stop fighting," Radek said. "And then we ask nicely for someone to come pick us up."

There were voices that echoed through Teyla's head, not through her ringing ears but through her mind itself.

*I am Waterlight of the line of Osprey.*

*You are nothing but a child!*

Waterlight. And Queen Death. Teyla opened her eyes, blinking as her vision swam. She had only been unconscious for a few moments. She lay half behind one of the seats in Death's zenana. Before her Waterlight stood with her back to Teyla, facing the other queen.

Death stood just inside the doorway, alone, but no less menacing for that, her long black hair caught up in combs of bone, her voice filled with fury and triumph. She had no eyes for anyone but Waterlight, and Teyla understood. Death had not seen Steelflower either. She had seen only a worshipper, a grunt at Waterlight's back, no more to be regarded than Bronze, stunned and forgotten on the floor.

*I am not a child,* Waterlight said. *And you will not kill me like one, craven and begging for my life.*

*So be it,* Death said. *Queen to queen.* She took a step forward, and though her hands did not rise, Teyla felt it like a physical blow, the force of her mind pressing, just as Coldamber's had in the drilling station beneath the sea. Inexorable. Heavy as weight, strong as gravity, pressing her down. Teyla had fallen beneath Coldamber's first onslaught, unexpected and relentless. She had only won later because Coldamber was befuddled with drugs. She knew she could not have stood against her.

But that was three years ago. That was before Guide's tutelage, before she had used her mind as she could, back when she still feared what she was. These things went through Teyla's mind in the moment that she saw Waterlight sway, the moment before Waterlight crumpled to the ground, a small, sad pale heap on the floor.

And Teyla Emmagan stood up. Her hip was bruised again and her leg shook beneath her, but there was the back of the seat to hand. "Look at me, Death," she said aloud.

Death raised her head from where Waterlight lay, no doubt seeing a human guard prepared to die to give her queen one more chance.

*Look at me again,* Teyla said softly, her mind like polished iron, like flowers wrought of steel.

*You will die as surely as your overlady,* Death said, but there was a flicker of uncertainty.

*I will not,* Teyla said. *This is not my day to die. It is yours. Unless you surrender and leave off this war.* An odd serenity gripped her. This was no different from a knife fight, no different from the bantos sticks, mind to mind, though anyone watching would have seen nothing of the maneuver and block, of the clash of one stick against the other.

*You...*

*I am Steelflower,* Teyla said. *And I will give you one more chance. Surrender and we shall make terms, you and I. Otherwise, I will kill you.*

*You cannot be!* Death said. *You aren't.*

*I am.* Block and parry and advance, though they stood still as statues. *The world is not what you think. I exist, part human and part Wraith. We are not so different. Now come. Let us put aside the past and look to the future together. Lay aside the burden of old wrongs.*

Pushing, so very strong, but with no discipline, no sorrow beneath it. For all her bravado, Death was very young. She was not so much older than Waterlight, and filled with anger untempered, ancient pains turned outward, every desire fanned as something that she deserved.

Teyla held, as a fighter holds her opponent at bay with both hands on the stick, holding off the pressure at arms' length, elbows locked. *Put it aside,* she said. *Whatever you have been told, whatever of the First Mothers you remember, whatever injustice you are heir to. Put it aside. You will destroy your people and all others too. What shall your blades and clevermen eat when you have made the galaxy a wasteland, killing that which you cannot consume? How shall the

Returned survive when you have narrowed all bloodlines to your own? Do you not understand that you will doom your own people as well as all the other children of the Ancients?*

And there in Death's mind was the Old One — Ashes, Teyla realized with a shiver of recognition. His was the voice that whispered in Death's ear, his the promises of sweet revenge.

*Put him aside,* Teyla said, and still she held, defending but not striking. *Let it go, my sister.*

*I am not your sister!* Death said, and shoved with all her mental strength, crushing and dark as a wave, consuming all within its depths.

The surface of the water broke, and from it rose the white bird. Spray flew from its wings as they extended.

*You cannot defeat me,* Teyla said, and in that moment she knew it was true. The greater strength was hers, born of experience and life, of compassion and love, of all she had overcome to stand there. *But I can defeat you. And I shall if you will not yield.*

*I will never yield to you.* Attack again, all strength extended, a fire that rose to consume —

Quenched by mist. It cut off all light. It cut off breath, shutting down those parts of the brain that made her lungs work, holding synapses inactive though Death's body screamed to take a breath.

*Yield,* Teyla said, and she held. She held until the end, until Death died in the prison of her orthodoxy, until her eyes dimmed and she fell to the floor.

Teyla staggered, leaning forward over the seat and lowering herself shaking beside it. Her hands shook against the soft floor covering, and she sat amid the bodies. In a moment she would get up and see if Waterlight lived. In a moment.

There was a rattle of P90 fire somewhere far away, the sounds of footsteps, of minds, human and Wraith alike. A Wraith boarding party was there, nine strong, and with them three Marines and Captain Cadman. It was Guide's man Swiftripen who led them, the one who had so wanted to impress Steelflower. Teyla felt them check at the door, heard one blade go to one knee beside Bronze.

"This one lives," he said aloud.

Laura Cadman looked in, P90 at the ready, and Teyla moved.

Swiftripen came behind her, and then he saw Waterlight and Death. "What has happened here?"

Teyla did not pull herself to her feet. She was not certain she could yet, but her voice was strong. "Queen Waterlight met Queen Death," she said. "And Waterlight prevailed. Though I do not know if she has survived her victory."

Cadman's eyes widened, and Teyla shook her head a fraction. No. It must be as she had said.

Swiftripen hurried in, flinging himself to the floor beside Waterlight and turning her over gently. "She lives!" he said, his hand to her neck. "The young queen lives!"

"The other is dead," Teyla said. "Death is dead."

Cadman helped her to her feet, one arm about her waist. She smelled of cordite and improbably of oranges. "Are you okay?"

"I shall be," Teyla said. "I am only stunned."

"Okay," Cadman said. "Hang on." Her eyes went to Death where she lay on the floor. "What happened?"

"It is over," Teyla said. Her hip twinged as she put her weight on it, and so she leaned on Laura. "It is over."

*Queen Waterlight did it!* one of Guide's blades said wonderingly. *So young and so brave.*

*And so beautiful.* Swiftripen's thought followed.

They lifted Waterlight up and tenderly laid her on a couch, while another bent over Bronze. Yes, Teyla thought. This is how the legend begins. The brave young queen in her white dress met Death face to face, and hope killed death and the world began again. That is what happened once above the City of the Ancestors, long ago and far away.

She closed her eyes and leaned on Laura Cadman's shoulder.

## CHAPTER TWENTY-SIX
# The End of the Beginning

RADEK crouched on the jumper floor, staring at the injured Wraith. He wasn't dead, but that was about all Radek could say for him. Wraith were supposed to be able to regenerate almost anything, but this wasn't looking particularly good. If he were a human — Radek had had the usual first aid training, but nothing he could remember seemed likely to help, and opening the kit carried in every jumper didn't reveal anything that looked particularly useful. Ember opened his eyes then, the pupils contracted to narrow slits; he grimaced, hands scrabbling for a moment along the padding, but then relaxed.

"We are on the jumper," Radek said. "We will be able to call for help soon."

"Not soon enough…" The words were barely a whisper.

"Tell me what to do."

"Must feed…" Ember's eyes closed again, his feeding hand lax on the padding. Was he unable to attack, Radek wondered, or was he choosing not to?

"I heard that," Eva said. "Radek, you might want to step away."

Radek ignored her, his own heart racing. He'd taken the retrovirus, he could, in theory, survive a feeding, and if Ember hadn't saved his life back in the shuttle bay, he'd certainly saved him from serious injury. "It's all right," he said, and heard his own voice thin and strained. He opened the neck of his jacket, and the shirt beneath it, aware that his hands were trembling. "I took Dr. Keller's retrovirus. He — I can let him —"

"We don't know for sure that that works," Eva said. She turned backward in her chair to stare at him. "Radek, it's too much of a risk."

"Yes, well." Radek spread his hands. "I can't just let him die." *And what is the world coming to, that I am thinking this about* a Wraith? What is it coming to, that a Wraith saved my life? I'm not Sheppard, these things don't happen to me... He took a deep breath. "Ember."

The green-gold eyes flickered open. "I heard. We also... worked on such a thing."

"Do it before I change my mind," Radek said.

Impossibly, something like a smile crossed Ember's face. His feeding hand moved as though of its own volition, faster than Radek had expected, fastening onto the bared skin of his chest. Pain lanced through him, worse than he would have believed possible, a hundred heart attacks, a thousand knives. It had all gone wrong, he thought, hazily, Keller was wrong, and I'm going to die. Except... his hands were unchanged, unwithered, remained ordinary and unmarked even as the pain pulled him down into the dark.

Eva swore under her breath, scrambling out of the pilot's chair, grabbing for the heavy wrench someone had left tucked into the jumper's wall straps. She had no idea what she was going to do, how she was going to stop the Wraith, but she had to try. She stopped abruptly, seeing his hand flex and release, Radek sprawling back against the base of the jumper seats, apparently unconscious but not visibly changed. Ember rolled over, his back healed beneath the drying blood and ripped leather, moved away from her, out of reach of both of them.

"I think — he is all right?"

Eva lifted the wrench, fumbled for a carotid pulse with her other hand. Yes, there it was, strong and regular, and she relaxed just a little. "I think so. Don't try it again, though."

"No." Ember shook his head. "This... I am in his debt."

"Yeah, you are," Eva said. "You better believe it." She hauled herself back into the pilot's chair, checking the navigation screen. All the ships were green, friendlies, and she let the cloak slide away. "*Hammond*, this is Dr. Robinson. I'm on a puddlejumper —"

"We see you, Doctor." The voice on the radio was reassuringly steady. "Can you bring the jumper back to the city?"

"I can't. I've lost an engine pod."

"Don't worry, Dr. Robinson." That was Colonel Carter, calm

as ever. "We'll tractor you aboard."

"Thank you," Eva said, and braced herself for the jolt of the beam attaching.

Five pilots lost, six injured. Four other crewmen injured. As usual the 302s had taken the brunt of the casualties. Sam nodded, listening to Franklin give the report. The *Hammond*'s systems were stable, though the port thrusters had taken external physical damage and the shields were extremely low. But it could have been worse. Much worse. They hadn't lost a life aboard the *Hammond*. They'd lost five pilots.

And Rodney.

"Franklin, you have the bridge," Sam said, getting up. Everything was on course for the moment.

As soon as Atlantis landed they would follow suit, resting beneath Atlantis's shield to repair, but for now they'd maintain orbit while their allies cleaned up. The damaged Wraith ships were surrendering to Alabaster, who was granting their parole or something with oaths of allegiance to her and to Waterlight, the young queen who seemed to have finally killed Queen Death. What exactly had happened aboard the hive was a mystery to Sam, though she knew she'd have Cadman's report when she got back. Cadman had sounded like there were things she thought it best not to say on an open channel, and she respected Cadman's judgment there. Cadman was coming along nicely. Sam was very proud of how she'd handled the last few weeks, and it was time to tell her so.

But first, the infirmary. As soon as the shooting stopped and the ship was in no immediate danger, it was time to check on her people, at least the ones who were here. Hocken was on *Pride of the Genii* with a concussion, but she seemed to be in one piece. She hoped Mitchell hadn't managed to do too bad a number on himself with that crazy landing. He'd hit the barrier pretty hard. With any luck he hadn't broken bones.

An airman hit the wall outside the infirmary as she approached, and Sam acknowledged the courtesy with a smile. They'd all done well. Her team was coming together.

"No, I am not going to let you set it! Dr. Beckett is going to do it. He's a real doctor!"

Sam stopped dead in the doorway. That couldn't be. That complaint, that voice… "Rodney?"

Rodney McKay was sitting on the edge of the examining table wearing a hospital gown while McNair, one of the two physician's assistants, tried to immobilize his left wrist.

"I thought you were dead!" Sam managed.

"Well, I'm not, unless your inept military pseudo-doctor kills me!" Rodney said indignantly. "I told him to just bandage it up and transfer me over to Carson, but he won't do it. Do you realize how important it is for me to have full use of my left hand?"

"I thought you were dead," Sam said again. "We couldn't beam you aboard."

"Obviously you did," Rodney said. He looked at her with a frown.

"Obviously I didn't," Sam said. "You were at eight times the range of our Asgard beams." Something was strange here.

"Colonel Carter?" her radio beeped. "Major Lorne needs to talk to you on the bridge."

"On my way," Sam said. She looked at Rodney again. It was clearly Rodney. And just as clearly there was no way the *Hammond* had picked him up. A thought struck her. "Did you arrive here in your clothes?"

"Of course I did!" Rodney replied. "What? You normally beam people without their clothes and just have them appear places stark naked?"

"*I* don't," Sam said.

"Ma'am, Major Lorne says it's urgent."

"Coming," Sam said. It would wait.

"There is much to discuss," Alabaster said, her eyes on Waterlight. "And many things that must be decided between us before we treat with others."

"Yes," Waterlight said. To Teyla she felt awkward, unused to adult counsels without her father at her side, a place that he would never fill again.

There was a soft chime at the door, and Bronze's voice came in filled with elation. "My queens, we have the Old One!"

Alabaster let out a soft hiss. "Bring him in," she said, and Teyla moved to stand beside her, Waterlight to her other side.

He was dignified as ever, flanked as he was by Bronze's blades. They seemed like boys beside him, too sharp and unfinished.

"You have done well, my blade," Waterlight said, and her voice was even.

"Thank you, my queen."

"Leave us," Alabaster said.

Bronze hesitated. "He is dangerous," he began.

"We know that," Waterlight said. "But not to three queens."

Bronze blushed, backing out with his men before him.

"I do not see three queens," the Old One said contemptuously. "I see two, and those hardly more than fruit-fed little girls."

"Do you not?" Alabaster said, spreading her hands from her sides, one toward Waterlight and one toward Teyla. "Perhaps you should look again."

His regard shifted to Waterlight and then to Teyla.

*Do you not?* she said softly, mind to mind. *Do you not see me?*

The Old One stopped, his eyes narrowing, and in that moment she saw what he saw, a young woman, dark skinned and fine boned, her black clothes stained from battle and her weapon at her side, the tenor of her mind sharp as bone. She was Osprey and not Osprey, fresh from the mayhem of a boarding party as Osprey had been in those first days, and yet not. Her face, her eyes, were human and like Osprey's own, like Osprey grown up on Athos and never transformed, Osprey left whole, her memories intact and her body unchanged.

*Yes,* Teyla said. *I am Osprey's human daughter, and I stand with my sisters.*

His eyes searched her face. *You cannot exist,* he said.

*But I do.* Her words were as heavy as her implacable truth.

*You are Abomination,* he said.

*I?* Teyla took a step toward him, and anger sang through her, sweet and true. *You dare say that, who were Kairos? You, who killed your own wife and drank her life? Who have murdered again and again, from one end of the galaxy to the other? You, who incited Death to war against her own kind and who slaughtered the peoples of many worlds not for your hunger but for your sport? You call me Abomination? You dare do such when the blood of the Manarians and the Tricti and all the rest cry out in anguish for justice?* She raised her hand without thinking, as though there were a feeding slit there that could take his life.

Alabaster and Waterlight did not move. *When you killed my Father,* Waterlight said. *The last of your murders.*

He stood still. Even his eyes did not waver from Teyla's face. *I have done what must be done,* he said. *The Ancients must die for their crimes.*

Alabaster laughed. She shook her head, long red hair falling over her shoulders. *Old fool,* she said. *The Ancients are dead. They are gone thousands of years, every single one who harmed you. Yes, they were guilty. And they are dead. Their bones are dust and their names are gone. You are telling fables of a time that is no more, fighting shadows instead of living in the world that is.* She stepped forward, shaking her head. *Look at me. I am not Osprey. I do not live in Osprey's world. That past is done and gone. I am concerned with the world to come.*

His mental voice was stern. *We must never forget.*

*Yes,* Alabaster said. *We must.*

Teyla's hand was shaking. If she could feed, oh if she could, in that moment she would drink his life and it would be right. Every last broken body left amid the ruins of their homes on Manaria, every one of their people fallen in the attack on Atlantis...

*He is yours,* Alabaster said to her. *Your people have suffered most recently. His life is yours to take.*

*You give me to the Abomination?* the Old One snapped.

Waterlight's voice sounded choked, her face pale. *Will you not repent of your wrongs even now?*

*I am not wrong,* he said. *And you doom your people, little fool!* He raised his head, standing unflinching before Teyla. *Go on then, Abomination! Do what you wish.*

And like a tide it seeped out of her, all the vast anger that had risen, leaving only sorrow. *No,* Teyla said. *I will not. I will not have blood for blood. I will not take revenge. Let your hate end here, and may your anger become nothing but a sad relic of days that are past.* She took a deep breath, tears starting behind her eyes, but there was Waterlight at her side, a choking lump in her throat for her father, but clean and clear.

Waterlight's fingers brushed hers, a quiet comment aside. *I think you are right,* she said. *Let it end.*

*If I had a daughter,* Teyla Emmagan thought, *I would wish she were just like you.*

Waterlight smiled, quick and fleeting. *Perhaps you will,* she said.

*I remand you to the custody of my sisters,* Teyla said to the Old One. *May you face Queen's judgment. Do with him as you wish, sisters. I am done.*

*I am done*, she thought, *and I will go home to Atlantis.*


John opened his eyes, letting himself ride up and out of the city's embrace. It let him go willingly enough, the data pooled and ready for any possible question, and he focused on the displays, the conversations surrounding him. Death's hives were either destroyed or drifting, and somewhere in the background he thought he heard Alabaster's calm voice accepting someone's surrender, the transmission relayed to Atlantis for their benefit. O'Neill was talking to Lorne, the *Pride of the Genii* reporting its damage and its losses. Death was dead, and Teyla was safe and unharmed and Cadman with her; two Marines were dead and more injured, but that was better than he'd dared hope. The 302 losses were worse, a voice John didn't recognize reciting the dead and injured. Guide's voice, asking permission to remain in orbit while his people sorted out their ships. And now Carter, brisk and confident.

"— Picked up Dr. Zelenka and Dr. Robinson and the missing Wraith Guide was worried about. And we have Dr. McKay, though we're not entirely sure how he got here —"

McKay? John sat up sharply. "McKay's alive?"

The city found video feeds, presented him with a picture of Carter frowning through hazy air, the hair at her forehead damp with sweat. "That's right, Colonel," she said, with that familiar grin that said they'd gotten away with something. "He's in my sickbay with a broken wrist, but otherwise he's none the worse for wear."

McKay wasn't dead. John felt a grin of his own spreading across his face. He didn't care how — didn't really care about anything except the simple indisputable fact. Neither of them had paid the price this time. "That's good," he said, knowing the words were hopelessly inadequate. "That's great."

"Yeah." Carter's grin widened.

"What's Atlantis's status?" Woolsey asked, and John shook himself back to the business at hand, the readings jumping to present themselves.

"Shields are at about seventy percent. The East Pier maneuver engine is still out, but we have better control now that nobody's shooting at us."

"Can we land the city?" O'Neill asked.

John considered, the answer coming not from the displays but directly through the chair, as though he could feel the damage like bruises on his own skin. There would be work to be done, but the repulsors were all still intact, and there was plenty of power left in the ZPMs. The repaired conduit was fragile, but holding, and the city projected that it would not need to use more than those repairs could stand. In fact, the sooner they were down and could lower the shield, the sooner they could reroute power around the damaged areas. "Yes, sir," he said. "Whenever you're ready."

"Take her home," O'Neill said.

John relaxed into the chair's embrace, easing the city down through the layers of the atmosphere, bleeding speed against the night sky, the aurora leaping around them. If there had been anyone to see, Atlantis would have blazed like a comet, friction flaming bright against the shields, more massive than any meteor, trailing dark smoke across the stars. Now the aurora flashed cold around him, the shields trailing streamers of blue and green and scarlet. He held the city steady, balanced against gravity, the lines of force holding them safe, the fragile towers cradled at the still center where all the forces intersected.

And then they had slowed enough, dropped below the level of the aurora, and ahead the horizon glowed white as they rushed toward the dawn. This time, there was plenty of power, plenty of time to choose his line, to find his perfect landing spot, the city laying out the pattern as though he had all the time in the world.

The sun was rising, the city sailing to meet it around the curve of the world, the ocean stretching clear and empty as he brought the city gently down to meet the waves. Atlantis struck, slowed and settled, the water heaving away from her blue and foam-streaked in the new light. Satisfaction filled him, his own, the city's, mingled and indistinguishable, the job well done at last..

"Atlantis has landed," he said, and let the city wash over him.

Jennifer leaned forward in her chair in Woolsey's office. It was still early morning, but with blessedly few casualties for the infirmary to treat, she wanted to seize the moment. "I've been talking to Guide," she said. "He and Alabaster plan to conduct a large-scale test of the retrovirus on Alabaster's people."

Woolsey raised his eyebrows. "Do we think this is a good thing?"

"I really don't know. For these particular people, yes, I think it is. It means that when they go to Alabaster for healing, they won't be giving up years of their lives, or even risking death to save the patients."

"I wasn't certain she'd be going back."

"I don't think she plans to stay there permanently. I understand she's settling in on *Just Fortune*. But the test is going to take some time, and once it's done, I expect the hive will return to the planet at intervals to feed."

"As long as that's a voluntary choice for the local residents."

"I hope it will be. If Alabaster heals their sick when she visits, I think there will be enough people who feel that undergoing the discomfort of being fed on is a fair exchange. But I'd like us to be able to monitor that. Plus I'd like to actually see the results of the test, and find out if there are long-term side effects or improvements we can make."

"What are you suggesting, Dr. Keller?"

Jennifer took a deep breath. "I'd like to go with Alabaster and Guide. Not just for the initial administration of the retrovirus, but to monitor its effects over the next few months. And then after that to work with them as they administer the retrovirus to other human worlds. Hopefully, they'll pick worlds they already control, rather than just showing up on a random planet and forcing the locals to take the retrovirus. But I understand we're still negotiating about that."

"We are," Woolsey said. "I expect those negotiations will be ongoing for some time. The Wraith would like us to cede control over half the Pegasus Galaxy to them in exchange for leaving the other half entirely alone. I have no idea what the IOA is going to say about that."

"What do you hope they say?"

Woolsey met her eyes frankly. "Dr. Keller, I wish I knew."

"You and me both."

"I understand that you want to monitor the administration of the retrovirus, but we will need you here in Atlantis."

"You need a chief medical officer," Jennifer said. "I'm — I guess I'm proposing resigning from that position. This retrovirus — I know we can't control what the Wraith do with it at this point, but surely we'd like to know what they are doing with it."

"We certainly would like to know," Woolsey said. "And you're proposing actually living with the Wraith for a period of months?"

"Or more," Jennifer said. "If nothing else, it's an opportunity we've never had to study the Wraith. There's so much we don't know about their biology, and even more we don't know about their culture."

"And you think they'll be willing to share this information?"

"Probably not at first. If they take me with them, it'll be because they think I'm a useful animal, like some kind of service dog. I don't have any illusions that I'll be much more than a pet. But I'll get to see parts of Wraith life we've never seen, and working on the retrovirus together is going to teach me a lot about their biotechnology."

"You will also probably see them killing people," Woolsey said.

"I know," Jennifer said. "Believe me, that's the part I've been thinking hard about. But... they're going to do that whether I'm there or not. If anything, I hope that having human pets around — me, and Alabaster's humans — will encourage the Wraith on *Just Fortune* to limit their diet to humans who've had the retrovirus. I'm not a vegetarian, but if I could have a perfect substitute for meat that wouldn't require killing animals, that would sound pretty good to me."

"I also expect that some people would find it unnatural."

"I expect there to be some resistance. Yes. And there's the question of the humans in the feeding cells, which is… frankly disturbing. My hope would be that they'll be willing to maintain a population of humans aboard ship who are willing to be fed on instead, and give them reasonable living quarters while they're there."

"That's just your hope."

"I can't promise anything," Jennifer said. "It's like doing humanitarian relief work in a war zone. You may not like the war, but you also can't stop it. You can only help the people you can."

"Believe me, I appreciate the potential benefits," Woolsey said. "I'm just concerned about placing you in such a risky situation. You'll be entirely isolated, and any contact with Atlantis will be entirely on Guide and Alabaster's terms. We may not be in a position to retrieve you if they decide to break off ongoing relations with us."

"I understand that," Jennifer said. "But this retrovirus — this was my idea, and I feel a responsibility. More than that — I want to do this. It feels a lot more important than being here in the infirmary taping sprained ankles and trying to figure out whether stomach pains are indigestion or an ulcer."

"Those things are important, too," Woolsey said.

"I do know that. But I don't think I'm the best person to do them."

"Very well, Dr. Keller. I'll put your proposal to Guide and Alabaster," Woolsey said. "If they agree, I'm afraid you'll need to be ready to leave in a matter of hours."

"Of course," Jennifer said, but she felt a bit flustered. "I can do that, but… you're saying yes, just like that? I just thought you'd want some time to think about it."

"I expect that as soon as the IOA has time to think about the events of the last few days, they're going to recall me and start looking for my replacement," Woolsey said. "So I'm authorizing this mission now, and accepting your resignation as chief medical officer effective immediately. Unless you're having second thoughts?"

There was some reflexive part of her that wanted to say *Yes, this is crazy*, but underneath she could feel the same calm certainty that came to her in surgery when someone's life was in her hands. "No," she said. "This is the right thing to do."

"Then I wish you the best of luck," Woolsey said. "And I'm sure the next head of the Atlantis expedition will appreciate whatever information you can pass along."

"Thank you," Jennifer said. She stood, and hesitated. "If they do replace you — I'm really sorry."

"Thank you," Woolsey said. He sounded more surprised than she thought he should.

"For what it's worth, I've been glad to have a civilian in this position. Not that I'm criticizing Colonel Carter, but — I just think it helps everybody remember that the point of being here is not just to be a military base. And I think you've done a really good job."

"So have you, Dr. Keller," Woolsey said, and shook her hand like they were already saying goodbye.

John found Ronon out on the balcony, elbows on the rail, staring out at the water.

"Ronon."

Ronon turned, looking unsurprised to see him. "I'm sorry."

"Are you?" When he didn't answer for a moment, John went on anyway. "I'm not actually pissed off that you nearly got me killed," he said. "I talked you out of using the weapon, and I was ready to take the consequences. If you'd gotten Rodney killed, I would have been pissed off. And if I were Sam, I expect I'd be pretty pissed off right now."

"I wasn't trying to get her people hurt," Ronon said. "I was going to use the weapon before the Wraith engaged her ship. Only when it came down to killing McKay and Teyla and Torren —"

"You couldn't do it. I know. I also know I ordered you to bring me the weapon as soon as you found it. And don't say you didn't really think it was an order."

"It was an order," Ronon said.

"If you were in the Air Force, they'd court-martial you. And they'd be right."

"You want me to leave?"

"I want me to say you won't do it again." John looked Ronon straight in the eye. "I have to be able to trust you not to take off on your own like that. If you have a problem with what we're doing, you come to me."

"And if I think what you're doing is wrong?"

"Then walk away if you have to. If you can't stay on the team, we'll still be friends. You said that yourself. But as long as you are on the team, you have to trust me."

"I joined the team to fight the Wraith," Ronon said. "If we're not doing that, I don't know how long I can stay."

"Maybe not forever. I get that. But while you're here, should I be watching my back, or are you on my team?"

"I thought you were going to court-martial me."

"I can't actually do that when you're not in the Air Force."

"I can't join your Air Force."

"So I don't have to court-martial you."

"You don't have to watch your back," Ronon said. "As long as I'm here, I'm on your team."

"Good," John said. "I'm glad to hear it."

"You really think McKay's going to be the same as he was before the Wraith took him?"

"No," John said after a moment. "But I think he's going to be okay. And so are we."

## CHAPTER TWENTY-SEVEN
# The Heirs of the Ancients

THE MORNING sun shone brightly through the gateroom windows as Jack O'Neill came into the control room above. The wormhole was bright, three figures disappearing into the blue glare. Dick Woolsey watched as the gate deactivated. He'd been grateful for SG-1's help, but he had to admit he was also grateful to see them go.

"So everyone off?" O'Neill said.

Woolsey nodded. "All of the seriously wounded have been sent through to the SGC. That was SG-1 going home."

O'Neill frowned. "That was only three of them."

"Dr. Jackson asked if he could stay several more days. Apparently there's some work in the Ancient database he wants to do, and he's excited about Dr. Lynn's work over on the island. I don't see any reason he can't stay a while if he wants to," Woolsey said, shrugging. "After all, he is…"

"…the foremost authority on the Ancients, yeah, yeah." O'Neill shook his head. "Your problem, not mine."

Behind O'Neill, McKay was leaning over one of the airman's shoulders, one arm in a sling, grumbling about something on the screen in front of him.

Dr. Parrish came up the steps with a box in his arms. "Dr. McKay?"

"What now?" McKay said.

The box let out a yowl. A Siamese cat poked his head out the top where the flaps didn't quite meet, expressing Siamese disapproval at full volume.

"I found him in the botany lab," Dr. Parrish said. "Sitting in a pot of *nepeta cataria*. I think he belongs to you?"

"He does," McKay said, hurrying over to the box. Newton oozed out the top, climbing up his shoulder with all claws and butting McKay's chin with his head, purring wildly. "Hey, Newton. Did you get lost? Was it scary down there?" Newton butted him again, rubbing his chin against McKay's as McKay clutched him awkwardly one-handed to his chest.

"Newton?" said Dr. Parrish.

"After Sir Isaac Newton," McKay said.

Dr. Parrish sniffed. "That's not very original. I think you should have named him Tesla."

"At least I didn't name him Edison," McKay said.

"I don't see any cat here," Woolsey said, and O'Neill snorted a laugh.

Once back in his office, Woolsey gazed at the trio in front of him with something like benevolence. McKay had stowed Newton safely out of sight in his quarters, and he took the visitor chair, nursing his injured wrist, while Zelenka and Beckett hovered in the background.

"And therefore it seems to me that all systems are stable," Zelenka finished. "We are somewhat closer to the equator now, and while this is not as warm a world as Atlantis' previous homes, the weather is somewhat better. We can expect moderate temperatures today and above freezing tonight. As we are near the equator, it may be that we can expect this kind of weather year round."

"Every day is a beautiful spring day," Beckett said with satisfaction. "For the Outer Hebrides."

"It's not that cold!" Zelenka said. "For the thousandth time!"

"It's not snowing," Rodney said. "That's an improvement. Now, when can I get back to work?"

"Today," Woolsey said. He held up one finger. "But! Dr. Zelenka is still Chief of Sciences. The IOA still has doubts."

"What would it take to prove to the IOA that I'm fine?" Rodney expostulated. "Me being dead?"

"Possibly," Woolsey said. "But let's not try it, shall we? They do take a dim view of having been previously dead."

"Of all the…"

Zelenka shook his head. "And if we are all done here except for Rodney flailing, I am going to bed. I have not seen my own room in two days, and I am finished."

"Yes, of course," Woolsey said. He should have noticed that

Zelenka had been going nonstop since before the city took off. It was his job to notice. "Go on, Doctor. I think we're through."

"I'm going to get some work done," Rodney said with satisfaction, following Zelenka out.

"Be careful of your arm!" Beckett called after him. "I said to be gentle with it!" The door closed behind Rodney. Beckett shook his head, turning around. "Are you all right?"

"Of course," Woolsey said.

"The IOA," Beckett replied. "They can't be happy, can they?"

Woolsey sighed. "No. They never are. But if they do relieve me, I will know I've done the best I possibly could. And it's worth the price."

"Aye," Beckett said, glancing around at the control room bathed in morning sunshine through the great windows. "Atlantis is worth the price." He picked up his laptop. "And now it's back to the infirmary. Good day, Mr. Woolsey."

"Thank you, Dr. Beckett."

The door closed, and Woolsey looked around his quiet office. Nice and quiet. With no crisis at the moment. He had a pile of paperwork to catch up on. He was certainly going to enjoy that. Dick Woolsey looked around once more, taking in the busy duty crew outside, the gate waiting quiet and watchful, the stained glass patterns across the floor. Yes indeed. He was certainly going to enjoy catching up on his paperwork.

Radek made his way up from the transport chamber in the golden morning light. Food. Shower. Bed. The day could not possibly improve. The labs had suffered no major damage in the battle, though some of the experiments had been disrupted and would have to be restarted; Rodney's cat had apparently eaten more than the pot of catnip someone had collected on M5W-2842, but suffered no more ill effects than producing a massive hairball overnight, deposited conveniently on a stack of pending paperwork. In the background, he could hear Rodney retelling the story, complete with sound effects, and quickened his step, not wanting to have to hear it again.

"Radek!"

He turned, to see William Lynn beckoning from one of the smaller conference rooms. "Yes?"

It wasn't just William, he saw; Dr. Jackson was there, and Ember, looking sleek and entirely recovered. The Wraith bowed in greeting, and Radek nodded, not sure what to say. They hadn't really spoken since the jumper, and Radek doubted there was any point of etiquette that would smooth the awkwardness. Jackson, however, seemed oblivious to the possibilities.

"What is McKay on about?"

"His cat," William said, before Radek could answer. "Sorry, I already heard the story twice."

"What about his cat?" Jackson looked from one to the other. "Why is there a cat on Atlantis?"

"That is a question better not asked," Radek said, and to his surprise Jackson grinned.

"Right. McKay's involved. Never mind." Jackson stuck his head out the door. "All clear. Dr. Lynn, thanks for your help — and yours, Ember — and I'll definitely take that up with General O'Neill when I see him."

The door slid shut behind him, and Ember tilted his head to one side. "Quicksilver — Dr. McKay — seems to produce that reaction."

"He is a difficult man," Radek said, and stopped. "And also brilliant, though you need not say I said so."

"Believe me, I would not," Ember answered. "That one knows his worth all too well."

"But he backs it up," Radek said.

Ember nodded. "Otherwise — you are his second, yes? As I was on Death's hive. Otherwise someone would have murdered him long ago."

"He was like that when he was a Wraith?" Radek waved the words away. "No, no, why should he be different?"

"I wondered how he had lived so long," Ember said, baring teeth. "Even being that good. You have my sympathy."

"As do you." Radek smiled back.

William cleared his throat. "Look, I don't want to interrupt, but Guide asked me to be sure to get you back to Alabaster's ship before she leaves —"

"Yes," Ember said, but made no move to follow. "There is, however, a thing I have to say before I go. This — what you did, to give me of your life, that is the mark of brothers, and I hold it no less so between us. I name you brother, if you will have me, and my life is yours to claim."

Radek saw William's eyebrows rise, and didn't know what to say himself. He'd never expected, never wanted, and yet — "I'm honored," he said, and realized that he meant it. He held out his hand, and Ember clasped it, awkwardly, the heavy claws scraping across Radek's skin. "Besides, you already saved my life."

"Well," William said, after Ember walked away. "Brother to Wraith."

Radek spread his hands. "And I was to say no to that?"

"One more reason to stay on Atlantis. My good friend Radek is 'brother' to a Wraith cleverman." William smiled. "It's wonderful for research."

"I didn't think you were planning to stay," Radek said, and William shrugged.

"One may change one's mind."

"Yes," Radek answered. "Yes, indeed."

The wormhole to Sateda had just opened, late that afternoon, when Mel Hocken came hurrying into the gate room, coming up to join Ronon.

"I thought you were in the infirmary," he said.

"I was," she said. "But it was just a little concussion. I hit my head on the canopy, but my head is pretty hard. Besides, what's a little concussion?" Mel gave him an impish grin, turning to face the wormhole. "I wanted to come along," she said. "Mr. Woolsey said it was fine."

They stepped through into warm sun and the smell of food cooking, smoke rising from chimneys and cooking fires around the square. More of the rubble had been cleared away since the last time he'd been there, and above the broad doors of what had once been a train depot hung the banners of the Satedan Band. Cai must have been able to persuade them to post at least a token force here, to discourage any more raiding.

"They've been busy," Hocken said.

"Looks like it," Ronon said. He made his way across the square to the old hotel that Ushan Cai had made the headquarters of his provisional government. "I've got to talk to Cai about some things," he said.

"So do I, actually," Hocken said. "I'll come in and wait."

He shrugged and pushed open the doors. The lobby of the old hotel was still dimly lit by lamplight, but through the doors into what had been the bar, he could see that the glass was back in two of the windows that opened onto the square, a patchwork of irregular pieces heavily leaded to fit where once there had been perfect squares.

Cai was talking to two women, a map spread out between them, but he raised a hand to Ronon in greeting, and Ronon nodded. He waited until they were done, Hocken turning to look out the window with the easy stance of someone used to waiting at attention.

"Ronon," Cai said finally, as the women went out. "And Colonel Hocken. It's good to see you. We've been hoping for news from Atlantis."

"Queen Death is dead," Ronon said. "Her alliance has fallen apart. I wanted you to know."

"I'll drink to that." He poured drinks for them, not the strong liquor that had survived Sateda's fall but a dark beer. "Courtesy of the Genii," Cai said, tapping his own mug. "We're brewing our own, but the first new ale won't be ready for another week yet. Or so I'm told."

"You can't rush beer," Hocken said, although he noted that she didn't touch her drink, only sensible after a head injury.

"It won't be long."

"There's more," Ronon said, taking a drink and trying to decide how to put the words together. "Our scientists have created a medicine, what they call a retrovirus, that makes people immune to being killed by the Wraith. The Wraith can still feed on you, but you won't die."

Cai looked up from his mug sharply. "You're certain of this?"

"It works on the people who've tried it. Our doctors are still testing it."

"People have tried before. We've heard about the disaster that was the Hoffan drug."

"This one works. And it doesn't kill Wraith who try to feed on you. It just means that you survive."

"If so, I would think that's a great piece of good fortune."

"That's just what people are going to think," Ronon said. "But it's a mistake. The Wraith are going to use this for their advantage. They'll still fill up their feeding cells, but they'll be able to keep those people alive forever. And instead of culling and leaving, they'll come to stay and raise us like farm animals."

"What do they say about that in Atlantis?"

"They want a peace treaty with the Wraith," Ronon said, putting all his skepticism into the words. "To divide up the galaxy so that Sateda and Athos and a bunch of other planets are left alone, and abandon half of the galaxy to the Wraith. They'll make them slaves and cattle."

"The treaty isn't a done deal by any means," Hocken said, glancing sideways at Ronon. "We'll have to talk to our allies — Sateda, Athos, the Genii, the Travelers — and it's not our decision to make. It's the IOA back home that would have to be on board."

"But it's what the Wraith are offering."

Cai gave him a searching look. "Why are you telling me now?"

"They're going to offer the retrovirus to Sateda," Ronon said. "I don't think we should take it. If the Wraith attack Sateda, and we know they won't kill us, it would make it just too tempting to surrender. People would be calling for the government to agree to slavery rather than death."

"And you think I should buy them death rather than slavery?"

"I think we should fight," Ronon said. "If it comes to that, I'd rather fight."

"But having your retrovirus might make us better fighters," Cai said. "Better able to infiltrate Wraith hives and Wraith-controlled worlds."

"Maybe. But I don't think it's worth it."

"I think it might be worth it," Cai said. "But it won't be up to me alone. We're trying to put together a real government, and have elections — it's hard right now with the population changing so much day to day. It won't be this year. Maybe next year, but I wouldn't swear to that either. A decision like that will be theirs to make."

"I'd rather trust someone I know," Ronon said. "Rather than politicians."

"So stay and help us make sure they're good politicians," Cai said. "Better yet, stay and be one of them. You're probably our single greatest hero right now. They'd elect you anything in a heartbeat."

"That's not me," Ronon said.

"Think about it. When you retire, at least. Come out to Sateda and have your own house and a seat in the legislature. You may have to put in glass windows for yourself." He nodded toward the patchwork windows. "But I can't imagine you're afraid of hard work."

"I have a job in Atlantis," Ronon said. "And good friends there. But, maybe. One of these days."

"You'll be welcome," Cai said. "And I appreciate you telling me about this. Especially if your Mr. Woolsey didn't exactly give you permission to tell me yet." There was a question at the end of that remark.

"I'm still Satedan," Ronon said, and Cai nodded and held out his hand. Ronon clasped it firmly, Cai's grip firm even if he wasn't a soldier.

"Colonel Hocken, I'm glad you came along," Cai said. "I have a proposition to make to you."

"I hoped you might," she said, her face lighting.

"We used to have a very good army. We will again, once we have enough of a population to support one. But what we've never had is an air force, and from what I've heard about your air force on Earth, I want one."

"A whole air force is going to take a while," Hocken said. "You're not in a position yet to build fighter planes, and I don't think ours would do you much good — you'll want something that can go through a Stargate. Plus I can't actually buy you a fighter plane. But I can buy you an ultralight." She laid her tablet on the table and pulled up pictures of a tiny, light aircraft, sailing above green hills in a very blue sky. "We'll have to figure out fuel — the Genii probably have something that'll work, if you can trade with them. And you'll want to build more, and modify the design for your own purposes. But right away you'll be able to scout a lot further than you can on foot, and look for people who may still be out there, cut off from big cities and the gate."

"That would be worth a great deal to us," Cai said. "Say, a commission as the chief of the new Satedan Air Force? I can't actually pay you right now, mind you. But I'm certain that the new government will as soon as it can."

"That's not really what matters most to me," Hocken said. "It's the chance to do it, with nothing holding me back." She shook her head. "I've been waiting too long for that to happen in our air force. I'm tired of waiting to start my life."

"There's one waiting for you here," Cai said.

"I'll be out at the end of the year," Hocken said. "And I'll bring you all the equipment I can. If I pull out all my savings —" Her expression was speculative as she scrolled rapidly through lists of airplane parts.

"I don't know if Woolsey's going to approve you supplying all this tech to the Satedans," Ronon said.

"That's just too bad, isn't it?" Hocken said, raising her chin. "I'll be a private citizen, and none of this is classified military technology. If I want to move out to Sateda, and accept Satedan citizenship —" She looked questioningly at Cai, who nodded. "Then all I need is for someone to give me a ride out to Pegasus, and I imagine I can talk somebody into it."

"We'll be glad to have you," Cai said. He offered her his hand, and she clasped his arm firmly in the Satedan fashion, her smile delighted. "You're sure we can't lure you away from Atlantis as well?" he said, glancing over at Ronon.

"Not yet," Ronon said.

Cai nodded. "Whenever you're ready, we'll be here."

"I'm glad," Ronon said. Outside the patchwork windows, people were crossing the square, and one woman lifted a toddler on her shoulder; the little boy reached up toward the sky, where a flock of birds arrowed across the brilliant blue.

Above the waves that broke white against the piers there was an ocean of stars. It was hours yet until dawn, but the wind which whispered around the towers was soft with the promise of coming spring. The Wraith cruiser *Eternal* occupied the south pier, a dark shape against sky and sea. At the bottom of the ramp two figures stood, an arm's length between them. Only their hands touched, her hand about his wrist, Teyla and Todd.

"What do you suppose they're talking about?" Sam asked. Her voice sounded curious and just a little bit wistful.

"Who knows," Rodney said. He had some idea, but he didn't want to think about that. Even if he healed, especially if he healed and the telepathy went away, he'd be forever sealed off from that communion. He'd never know that kind of intimacy again, mind to mind, quick as thought.

"Rodney?"

"Yes?"

"What happened?" He looked around at her. Sam's face was still. "On the puddle jumper. I don't see how you got out before impact. I don't see how you could have done that."

"You wouldn't believe me if I told you," Rodney said.

"Try me."

Rodney shook his head. The stars were very bright. The auroras that had concealed them were gone with the tilting of the world on its axis, gone to come again next year. "It was Elizabeth," he said finally. "Elizabeth Weir. She was there with me on the jumper. I know it can't really have been her. I know that. But it was. Elizabeth was there." Rodney put his hands in his pockets. "She said she'd be there until the end, that she wouldn't leave no matter what. I remember..." He took a deep breath. "I remember the radiation alarms going off and the shield failing and then... I woke up in the Hammond's infirmary. That's all I know." He shrugged. "You don't believe me."

"Actually I do." Sam's eyes glittered in the dim light. "When Daniel was Ascended, something a lot like that happened. But he got in a lot of trouble. The other Ascended beings kicked him out. They dropped him off on some random planet not even remembering who he was. Because he helped us. Because he interfered."

Rodney took a long, cool breath of sea air and something in his chest loosened, something he didn't know he'd held for far too long. "You think it was Elizabeth?"

"I do."

"And you think she could be out there somewhere?"

"She could be," Sam said. "Or maybe she didn't get caught. But if she did, yeah. She's out there somewhere."

Rodney took another breath, longer and deeper. "We could find her," he said.

"We could. We never leave a man behind." Sam put her arm awkwardly around his shoulder and Rodney twisted to look at her skeptically.

"You did not just hug me."

"No." Sam stepped back. "I didn't."

"Because if you did, I'm never going to let you forget it."

"It was a friendly hug!"

"Now I know how you really feel about me."

"I feel like I want to squash you like a bug!" Sam said, but she was laughing.

"Come on now. You know it's always been me!" Rodney was grinning.

"In a pig's eye. If it had been up to me, the Wraith could have kept you!"

"Yeah, sure," Rodney laughed, and then his stomach sank. Jennifer had come out of the nearest building and was walking toward them, her hair in a ponytail and the dark leathers of her field clothes making her look already far away.

If Sam could have dematerialized she would have. "I've got some stuff to do," she said quickly, stepping away as Teyla also turned, her hand falling from Todd's arm. "Teyla? All set?"

"I believe that I am," Teyla said serenely, coming to join them.

"Jennifer," Rodney said.

"Rodney."

"Then let's go check out that thing we were talking about earlier," Sam said to Teyla. "You know, the thing I wanted you to look at."

"I believe I do," Teyla said, and shook her head at Rodney as she followed Sam toward the door.

Todd still stood on the ramp, turned toward them, impassive beneath the faint bluish running lights of the cruiser.

And now there weren't any words, not any good enough. "Jennifer," he said again, and then fell silent. He wanted to tell her that she was crazy for doing this. He wanted to promise her that if she would just stay he wouldn't ask her to marry him again, that he would take things as slowly as she wanted. But there weren't any words.

She looked up at him, her eyes searching his face as though she were looking for something, or maybe she wanted to remember it. "I'll be fine," she said.

"Sure," he said. "You'll do great."

"I need to do this, Rodney."

"I can see that. If the retrovirus works, if people will accept it — well, people and Wraith, I suppose I should say…"

"I think you mean people. Humans and Wraith."

"People," Rodney said. "If they do, you'll be saving a lot of lives."

"Well, I'm going to try," Jennifer said. She looked ridiculously young and slight in her black leathers, not like Teyla, not scary. But not like a girl either. Just a lot like Alabaster.

"It's just…" He couldn't quite finish the thought. "I thought you wanted to go back to Earth," he said. "I thought you wanted to get married and live in a suburb or maybe in the country somewhere and practice medicine and… I thought you were the one who didn't want to come back to Pegasus. I thought you wanted…" He waved his hands at all the things he couldn't name. "Strawberries. You keep saying you miss strawberries and there aren't any in Pegasus. And daylilies. You know. Those yellow flowers. Or the red ones."

"Poppies," Jennifer said. "They have those here. I've seen them."

"I haven't," Rodney said.

"When do you ever look at the plants?"

"When they're trying to eat me," Rodney said. "But that's beside the point. You don't even like it here. And there are leeches. You hate leeches. And it's a long way from your dad, and you don't even have email, and…"

She put her hand on his arm. "Rodney."

"Yes?"

"I want to do this." Her eyes were very clear. "When I get back… maybe then I'll want to go home and have all those things. In their time. But right now it's time for me to do this."

"I can't wait forever," he said quietly. "Don't get me wrong, I'm not *old*, but I'm not getting any younger. I was hoping we could get married here in Atlantis, maybe even — well, after all, Teyla has Torren, and how much more trouble would having one more child in the city be? Woolsey let me keep the cat." He couldn't ask the question, but he hoped she heard it anyway.

"You take care of Newton, all right?" It wasn't an answer, or maybe it was. They had never been very good at finding words. "I'm doing what I need to do. You should do what you need to do."

"I will," he said.

"You always do."

There wasn't any answer to that. And so he smiled at her like a sturdy adventurer ought to. "Take care of yourself," he said, and gave her a sketchy salute. "And if you need anything, just whistle."

"I'll remember that," Jennifer said. She pulled herself up, shoulders squared, and gave him a little smile.

And then she turned and walked across the tarmac toward the cruiser, toward the dark figure at the foot of the ramp. He loomed over her, bending to speak, and then she went past him up the ramp, her head high and her back straight, Todd following after. Jennifer didn't look back. The ramp retracted and the docking port irised closed, blue lights winking out. Wind gusted as the cruiser's thrusters came online.

Sam and Teyla were still standing in the doorway to the building, whatever pretend errand of Sam's forgotten, and Rodney hurried out of the landing zone as the cruiser's engines rose in a rising whine, the wind swirling around him.

Teyla put her hand on his arm, steel presence comforting as sunlight. "She will be all right," Teyla said.

"I know." He'd thought this was the story of how he turned himself into a hero and got the girl and they lived happily ever after. And maybe that story hadn't really been about the girl at all, but only about becoming a person he could be proud of when he looked in the mirror. He had done that, and sometimes it took him by surprise to realize it.

Teyla looked up at him. "Do you wish you were going with her?

"On a Wraith ship?" But there was some part of him that ached for that still, and wondered if walking aboard the cruiser would have felt like coming home. *I'm already home*, he told himself, and knew that for him that was true. "Don't be silly," he said briskly. "Besides, do you have any idea how much work I have to do?"

There was only a little lump in his throat as he watched the cruiser *Eternal* lift into the darkness and vanish over the storm tossed sea, a darkness against the stars which swiftly disappeared.

It was a day of rest, and the captain of the *Hammond* was going fishing.

"How's that?" Sam said.

"Not too bad," Jack said. "If I reposition a little…"

"Move around all you like," Sam said. She unfolded her chair and sat down, propping her feet up on the low stonework of the edge of the pier.

Jack moved his chair around a little more, fussing with it, then sat down and adjusted his baseball cap, looking out at the calm sea.

Sam sighed happily. "Look at that! Almost worth coming all the way out here for, isn't it?"

"Almost," Jack said.

Sam shrugged as he baited his line neatly and cast. "Yeah, but not many guys can say they've dipped their pole where you have."

He stopped, the rod dangling in his fingers. "I can't believe you just said that, Carter."

"Fishing, Jack." She cast her line with a smug look, watching it plop satisfactorily into the water next to his.

"I think I've got a bite already," he said, leaning forward.

The end of his pole bobbed, then a tentacle rose from the surface of the water, exactly the same shade as the fishing line. It waggled back and forth, then purposefully wrapped around the end of the pole and jerked it out of Jack's hand, disappearing into the depths.

"I'll be damned," Jack said as Sam started laughing.

"I guess we'll just have to enjoy the view," she said.

Supposedly, it was a day of rest, and the morning stretched before Teyla invitingly empty. She cradled her coffee mug in her hands, her elbows resting on the railing of the balcony, looking out at sea and clear skies. It was warm enough that she was comfortable in a light jacket. This passed for a beautiful spring day here, on their new world, and she could not say it was otherwise.

The doors slid open and John came out, his sweatshirt sleeves pushed up to his elbows, a mug in his hands. "I thought I'd find you out here," he said.

"I am enjoying the sunshine," she said, tilting her face up to the light, feeling it warm on her own skin.

"This planet is starting to grow on me," he said, taking a sip. "There might be some interesting stuff here. We've only just started going through that Ancient installation Ronon found on the island. Now that we've got some time, maybe we can actually do some exploring."

"It would be a nice change," Teyla said.

"There's an awful lot we could do," John said. "Next year or the year after. And when that Indian research vessel launches I expect they're going to want to leave a team here. And Jackson was saying that there needed to be a bigger social sciences presence."

"I expect Alabaster will want a permanent envoy," Teyla said. "And Jinto is annoying Halling, begging that Dr. Zelenka would like him to be his apprentice, if Mr. Woolsey will allow it."

"That could work," John said, leaning on the rail beside her, looking out over the light-touched towers. "There's plenty of room in Atlantis."

"For all the children of the Ancestors," Teyla said. And that was right and good. They were all heirs to the Ancients, all heirs to their pain and their hubris and their beauty and their insatiable curiosity.

"Yeah," John said. He looked contented.

"And you," Teyla said. "You are talking about the future as though you mean to see it."

He lifted his head, his eyes on the distance. "I guess so," he said slowly. "When I was getting ready to go on this last mission to get rid of the weapon, I didn't want to."

He said it as though it were a painful admission, and Teyla looked at him sideways. "Of course you didn't want to."

"I didn't want to die. I had to do it, but I didn't want it. I don't want..." He trailed off, and Teyla waited in silence, waiting for him to find the words. "I didn't want life to be over. And now that it's not, it feels like a reprieve. Like some guy waiting on death row and then finding out he's been pardoned. If that makes any sense."

"It does," she said. Teyla blinked into the sun, because of course it was that the glare hurt her eyes. "You were willing to be the sacrifice, and then you did not have to be. You have broken the geas. You have left it behind. And now there is your life before you."

"Maybe so," he said, and took a drink of coffee. "Maybe so." The wind tugged at his hair, and he smiled into the eye of the wind.

"And in us the Ancients have secured their future also; you, Ronon, even Rodney, might father a child one day."

"Pretty scary," John said. "Rodney being a father, I mean..."

Teyla smiled. "I would not be sorry to have another child someday myself."

"It probably wouldn't have the Gift, not like you and Torren..."

"Nor would Rodney's, I think. Nor would any child of yours likely have a naturally expressed ATA gene," she said, leaning against the rail beside him. "They would all be... only human."

And yet both legacies would live on in their blood, recessives carried forward down the centuries, the inheritance of the Ancients.

The doors slid open again and Ronon came out, checking when he saw them. "Sorry. Didn't mean to interrupt."

"Come on out, Ronon," John said. "It's a beautiful day."

"Please," Teyla said.

Ronon came over and stood against the rail beside John, taking a deep breath and seeming to straighten up from somewhere deep inside, looking out at sky and sea. "It is," he said.

"I was thinking that we needed to finish checking out that Ancient outpost you found," John said. "How about taking an archaeological team over there tomorrow?"

"Sure," Ronon said, and smiled.

John returned Ronon's smile, and then turned to gaze out at the white-capped sea that stretched out to meet the bright sky arching overhead. It was a good place for Atlantis, John thought, and good flying weather. He was itching to take a jumper up into it, to explore without the constant worry he'd felt since Rodney had first been captured by the Wraith.

The balcony door slid open as if in answer to his thought, and Rodney came out onto the balcony, pulling his jacket around him in the brisk breeze. He hesitated, and John beckoned him over to the balcony. Rodney leaned on the railing, his elbows next to Teyla's, his white hair catching the light. It was still weird, but John figured if it didn't grow back in brown, they'd all get used to it.

He glanced over at Ronon, who'd been visibly tense about dealing with Rodney ever since they'd gotten him back from the Wraith. Ronon seemed at ease, looking out over the railing at the horizon, his hair stirring in the breeze.

"So I've been thinking that we should investigate the Ancient outpost over on the island," Rodney said. "I'm not convinced there's nothing interesting left over there."

"Way ahead of you," John said. "But not today. We're taking today off."

"What, you don't think searching for Ancient technology is fun?"

Ronon looked at Rodney sideways down the rail. "Remember the man-eating bears?"

"We don't know that they're man-eating."

"They looked like they wanted to eat us."

"The cave-in probably took care of all the bears, right?"

Ronon shook his head, but he looked amused. "We should check it out when it's not our day off. I won't let the bears eat you."

"Thank you," Rodney said. "Thank you very much." His tone was a little too serious.

Ronon shrugged. "You're my team. All three of you."

"No one is letting bears eat anyone," John said. "And today is a nice day, and we do not have to deal with any bears today."

"Sometimes I wonder how we wound up having a life where that's a normal thing for someone to say," Rodney said.

John looked up at the clear blue sky, remembering with sharp clarity the moment when he'd flipped a coin high into another sunny sky, trusting his future to its fall.

"We walked through the Stargate," he said. He'd chosen then without knowing what he was getting into, or even what he wanted. He knew now, and he'd make the same choice now, open-eyed, every time. "I think that was a pretty good choice."

"I believe it was, too," Teyla said, and she leaned into the circle of his arm.

Beyond the balcony, the sea stretched out sparkling until it met the blue arch of the sky, as blue as the rising towers of Atlantis, bright and wide and waiting for them.

Stay in touch...
Follow us on Twitter
@StargateNovels

Find us on Facebook at
facebook.com/StargateNovels

Sign up for our newsletter
at StargateNovels.com

**THANKS!**

# STARGATE SG·1.    STARGATE ATLANTIS™

**Original novels based on the hit
TV shows STARGATE SG-1 and
STARGATE ATLANTIS**

**Available as e-books from leading online
retailers**

**Paperback editions available from
Amazon and IngramSpark**

**If you liked this book, please tell your
friends and leave a review on a
bookstore website. Thanks!**